KILLER HEELS

Rebecca
CHANCE

SIMON & SCHUSTER

London · New York · Sydney · Toronto · New Delhi

A CBS COMPANY

First published in Great Britain by Simon and Schuster, 2012
A CBS Company

1 3 5 7 9 10 8 6 4 2

Simon & Schuster UK Ltd
1st Floor
222 Gray's Inn Road
London
WC1X 8HB

www.simonandschuster.co.uk

Simon & Schuster Australia
Sydney
Simon & Schuster India
New Delhi

A CIP catalogue record for this book is available from the British Library

ISBN 978-0-85720-486-8

Typeset by Hewer Text UK Ltd, Edinburgh
Printed and bound in Great Britain by CPI Group (UK) Ltd,
Croydon, CRO 4YY

For everyone who can work the hell
out of a pair of six-inch heels.

Acknowledgements

Huge thanks to:

At Simon and Schuster: Maxine Hitchcock, who edited this book wonderfully, and improved it tremendously to the very last line! I am really lucky to have her on my side. And to Georgina Bouzova, Libby Yevtushenko, Clare Hey and Emma Lowth on the editorial side, plus Sara-Jade Virtue and the amazing Marketing team – Malinda Zerefos, Dawn Burnett, Ally Glynn and Alice Murphy - who have done the most brilliant job of promoting and marketing my books. I couldn't be more grateful for all their hard work and creativity. Plus, in London, the sales team of James Horobin, Gill Richardson, Dominic Brendon and Rumana Haider and in Sydney in Sales, Kate Cubitt, Sharon Bryant, Lucy Barrett, Lou Johnson, Anabel Pandiella, Rose Harvey and Melanie Barton who have all been absolutely amazing

At my agents: Anthony Goff, my wonderful agent, is, as always, a rock and a star, which technically is impossible – and yet he manages it. Marigold Atkey has been hugely helpful and Ania Corless, Tine Nielsen, Chiara Natalucci and Stella Giatrakou in foreign rights are always brilliant.

My darling webmistress, Beth Tindall, for whom nothing is ever too much trouble.

The beautiful, blonde and bubbly Katharine Walsh, PR extraordinaire, probably the hardest-working and most glamorous woman in London, and the team at Brooklands, who treated us so wonderfully when we stayed there.

The dapper Mr Kandee for letting us use his amazing shoes for the covers and competitions – aren't they gorgeous?

My New York party crew, Jamie Ranieri, the Fruit Fli supreme, Marco de los Rios and Travis Pagel. They're even prettier and naughtier in person, believe it or not. And look up the Fruit Fli parties if you want a gay old time of it the next time you visit Manhattan. Thanks to Caroline and Craig Raeburn and Xavier Fan for lending me their names – even if Caroline's was deemed too posh! And to Hans de Bruijn, physiotherapist and masseur extraordinaire, who has double-handedly made sure that I don't get RSI from tearing out my books at lightning speed.

All the really hardcore Rebecca Chance fans on Facebook for making me laugh and keeping me sane: Angela Collings, Dawn Hamblett, Tim Hughes, Jason Ellis, Tony Wood, Melanie Hearse, Jen Sheehan, Helen Smith, Julian Corkle, Helen Smith, Diane Jolly, Adam Pietrowski, John Soper, Gary Jordan, Travis Pagel, Lisa Respers France, Stella Duffy, Shelley Silas, Serena Mackesy, Alice Taylor, Marjorie Tucker, Teresa Wilson, Margery Flax, Valerie Laws, Simon-Peter Trimarco, and Bryan Quertermous, my lone straight male reader (bless). Plus Paul Burston, the Brandon Flowers of Polari, and his loyal crew – Alex Hopkins, Ange Chan, Sian Pepper, Enda Guinan, Belinda Davies, John Southgate, Ian Sinclair Romanis and Jon Clarke. If I've left anyone out, please, please, send me a furious message and I will correct it in the next book!

Thanks for their lovely reviews to Nicola Atkinson, Zarina de Ruiter, Georgina Scott, Laura Ford, Rose McClelland and Rosemary Millburn van Eeden.

And to McKenna Jordan and John Kwiatkowski at Murder by the Book, bringing Rebecca Chance filth to Texas readers one book at a time!

And as always – thanks to the Board. They move in mysterious ways their wonders to perform.

Prologue
Manhattan: Now

Coco

Coco Raeburn stared down at the display on her bathroom scales, excitement rising in her as she scanned the figures on the screen. Actually, the chrome and glass device on which she was standing was much more than a set of scales; it was a body composition analyser, informing her not only of her weight but also her body fat percentage, her total water content, and her BMI. By now, Coco was so used to seeing her fat percentage displayed that she didn't bat an eyelid at the brutal truth; and today it was a mere 8 per cent. Under 10 per cent body fat! That was wonderful enough in itself, but the real prize was the main display, the large figures in the centre of the screen.

There were only two of them. Two figures. She had done it; she'd reached her goal, cracked the hundred.

Ninety-eight pounds. She could hardly believe it. In fact, she stepped off the scales, let the screen clear, and then tapped the base of the scales to restart them. Cautiously, almost tentatively, she set one bare foot, then the other, on the rubber indents, watching, breath held in anticipation, as the monitor scanned her once more and then spat out the figures that by now – as far as she was concerned – defined Coco more completely than anything else.

Ninety-eight pounds, again. Not only had she cracked the hundred, but she had an extra pound to spare in case of any slipbacks.

Well, there won't be any of those, she told herself, determined. I'm staying at ninety-eight if it kills me.

Coco shivered in the air-conditioned bathroom; the trouble with only having 8 per cent body fat was that you felt the cold much more acutely. But she didn't go into the hallway to adjust the temperature on the built-in thermostat: she couldn't drag herself away from the sight of her thin, thin body in the full-length mirror set into the wall. With approval, she noted how much bone and muscle she could see. Her tummy had sunk in below her ribcage, a tight concave band of muscle, firm from all her Pilates classes and training sessions with Brad. She pummelled it lightly with her fists: hard as a rock. She could count every one of her ribs, the top ones slatted like a set of Venetian blinds. People commented on those, and the protruding collarbones. *I need high-cut necklines to cover them,* she thought. *Diane von Furstenberg's doing some great blouses for spring/summer. I'll get someone to call them in.*

Blouses with high necklines and long sleeves: those would be ideal. Coco was dressing very differently than when she'd been what she now considered *huge* – an English size 12–14. Gigantic! She shuddered at the thought of how fat she'd been. Then, she'd shown off her rounded shoulders, the boobs that she'd now completely lost. Now, folds of fabric hung on her skinny frame as if from a hanger, concealing not only the too-visible bones, but the bruises and chafe-marks that patterned her pale skin.

At each hip, perfectly parallel, were five livid purple imprints where a man's hands had dug into her, held her down. Big hands, which spanned half her body with ease, now that she was so thin; the bruises were so clear that a police pathologist could almost have taken fingerprints from them. On her stomach, a pattern of small red smudges bore witness to hot wax that had been dripped on her, her abdomen so hollow now it was like a shallow bowl he had taken pleasure in filling. As for her wrists and ankles . . . well, Coco took it for granted these days that she needed to cover them whenever she was out in public. She worked out in leggings and slim, long-sleeved tops, careful not to let the cuffs slide back and show the reddened indentations on her skin. If they were planning a trip to St Barts, to a beach where she would be on display, if there were any chance that someone might see Coco's body, he switched to velvet-lined restraints well in advance, so that there would be no telltale rope-marks on her.

Anyone entering the bathroom at that moment would have gasped aloud in shock at the sight of Coco's white, almost skeletal body, the visible vertebrae like a fragile tower of stones reaching from nape to coccyx, the contusions on her almost-flat buttocks, the welts around the wrists and ankles. They would have rushed forward, reached for a towel or dressing-gown to cover her vulnerable, bruised nakedness, asked what had happened to her, if she had gone to the police.

But then they would have noticed the faraway, otherworldly look in her eyes as she stared at herself, raising one hand to her neck, where two thumbprints could just be made out, one above each collarbone point. And they would have realised that this was not a woman who had been subjected against her will to a series of attacks which had left their livid evidence on her body. Coco's expression was dreamy, hypnotised; her gaze passed right over all the marks, not even noticing them apart from the faint, daily registering of what she needed to cover up, protect from the critical attention of the outside world.

She was looking, instead, at her extreme weight-loss, and feeling dizzyingly proud of herself.

Her elbow joints were almost wider than her forearms, her kneecaps dwarfed her skinny legs. Her inner thighs didn't touch at all as she crossed the bathroom floor and almost reluctantly drew on her Leigh Bantivoglio silk robe, wrapping it around her waist, tying it with the matching sash that could have gone round her twice. Briefly, Coco remembered the days, back in London, when she wouldn't ever belt a robe or a coat, convinced it made her look like a potato on legs. She'd never been able to tuck in a shirt, or wear a pair of jeans without making sure that her top fell below the first few inches of the waistband, concealing the area where the jeans dug in, the button fastening them pulling at the buttonhole, stretching it with tension, her soft flesh bulging gently over the top.

Well, those days were long gone. She was what everyone in fashion dreamed of being: size zero. The awareness was as heady as a drug running through her veins. Coco reached down and, through the silk of her robe, tried to pinch that place above the hipbones, below the waist, where the last ounces of fat always clung.

Nothing. Her fingers couldn't get any purchase. Not a lump or a bump. Nothing at all.

Heart beating fast with anticipation, she crossed the bathroom, passing the floor-to-ceiling glass window set into the brushed-concrete wall, into the bedroom, which also had floor-to-ceiling glass windows. This apartment building had been thrown up just last year, and the developers knew exactly what their hyper-rich, hyper-trendy customers wanted: cutting-edge design that was as stripped-down and sleek as themselves, a dazzling array of built-in gadgets and devices, and huge walls of glass windows that were perfect for exhibitionists who worked out every day of their lives, watched their weight like hawks, and were more than happy to show off their slim, toned bodies for the benefit of their neighbours across the narrow street – who, of course, were doing exactly the same.

The Halston was in the hippest area of what insiders called 'the city' and outsiders called Manhattan. On the Bowery, once a slum best-known for its drunks and dive bars, it was a forty-storey glass and steel palace, towering over the wide avenue, signalling clearly that the Bowery and the Lower East Side were the latest destination for the torrent of gentrification dollars that were flooding through the city, sweeping out the crumbling buildings, filling up disused lots, throwing up fabulous edifices into which the next generation of Manhattanites were ready to move. The starving artists, the performers, the drag queens, had colonised this section of the city which once had been full of sweatshops and cheap brothels: now they were moving on, priced out of the city, crossing the bridges to Brooklyn and Hoboken, washed away by the green river of new money.

Coco's bedroom floor was dark walnut, underfloor-heated in winter, smooth and cool in summer. She dropped the robe onto her wide, low bed and padded naked to the far wall, which was entirely filled with fitted cupboards, discreet lighting snapping on as soon as she slid open the frosted glass doors. Flicking through the carefully-curated racks of clothes, knowing how lucky she was to have this apartment, she still couldn't help a twinge of envy when she thought of her boss, Victoria, who had an Upper East Side townhouse. It was large enough for Victoria to have a whole room dedicated to her wardrobe, the corridor which connected it to her bedroom lined with shoe racks on one side and handbag shelves on the other, all velvet-padded to protect her priceless accessories collection.

Very soon, Coco thought, ambition fizzing in her like bubbles in carbonated water, very soon I'll have everything Victoria has – the job, the house, the no-limits expense account, the status right at the top of the New York society pecking order. Just as soon as I get married, I'll have everything she has – and more.

Coco reached for a padded hanger at the very end of the cupboard, a black silk dress, fragile as a whisper of cloud, draping from it. *No hanger appeal,* said her razor-sharp fashion editor's brain, slicing through categories of clothes. *Has to be seen in movement*. It was trimmed in charcoal lace, elaborate, exquisite hand-made lace that was marginally heavier than the silk to which it was appliquéd, a slip of a dress that billowed around the shoulders and narrowed to a tiny, clinging skirt.

It was Chanel, of course. A present from her fiancé. Coco had never been able to do up the zip before; now she stepped into it, easing it up over her protruding hip-bones, slowly and with great care to avoid snagging the delicate silk, slipping her hands into the wide draped armholes, shrugging the dress over her shoulders, settling it into place before she dared to reach around behind her back – a gesture that made her collarbones jut out as if they were about to break through the paper-thin layer of skin that was their only covering – and start to raise the tag of the concealed zip.

It kept sliding up. Past her almost non-existent buttocks, past her waist, up each visible knob of her spine, right up to her shoulderblades. One hand was pulling up the zip, the other holding the dress up at the nape of her neck, almost unable to breathe, sucking in everything she could as she went. Until the zipper tag found no more teeth to slide up, until it snicked to a halt at the very top . . .

Coco spun to look at herself in the mirror, letting out her breath, her heart pounding. The dress was perfect, a sexy, flimsy wisp of silk that ended high up on her slender thighs, managing to be both seductive and elegant, its sleeves double-lined chiffon, gathered at the wrists to hide the reddened skin there.

Perfect with my new Balenciaga shoes, she thought instantly. The shoes were high-cut, fastening around her ankles, concealing the restraint marks. She raised her hands to the nape of her neck, lifting her beautifully-streaked light brown hair, hand-painted by her colourist in artful shades of butterscotch, ash and honey. *Definitely hair up and back to show off the neckline. And those huge Lara Bohinc earrings I got in London, with the crazy faux-pearls in rose gold.*

Oh God, he's going to love me in this.

She turned slowly, appreciating with a professional eye the

way the skirt clung to her bottom, making it seem positively minuscule, the superbly cut float and drape of the silk over her shoulders. You could always, instantly, spot couture. This dress had been made specifically to her dimensions, but she had never been able to wear it before, never been able to draw up the zip with such effortless ease – because it had been tailored to the measurements she would have when she was a perfect size zero.

After all this effort, all the extreme dieting and the exercise and the ironclad self-denial, here she was, standing in her perfect designer apartment, in her perfect designer dress, the perfect designer size. This was it.

Coco Raeburn was finally perfect.

And as she looked at her image in the mirror, she had to press her left hand against her bony chest to calm herself down, reassure herself. On her fourth finger was her engagement ring, an enormous, two and a half-carat princess-cut diamond in a simple platinum setting, so big it made her hand look impossibly fragile, so big it looked as if it weighed almost as much as she did. In America, the rule was that the fiancé should spend two, possibly three months' salary on an engagement ring. But Coco's fiancé was so rich that, as her friend Emily had commented in awe, she could never have, for daily use, a ring that had cost him that much money; she'd have to be shadowed by a pair of bodyguards wherever she went.

Size zero. She had reached her goal. Their goal. She was beyond excited, into some realm of high altitude that made her head spin with exhilaration and terror. Coco recognised the sensation: it was the same light-headed dizziness she experienced when he fucked her, when he held her down, tied her up, slid the ball gag between her lips, fastened the eye mask over her face. Deprived her, utterly and completely, of any freedom, any ability to move, to speak, to protest anything he might choose to do to her.

Coco had given herself over to him completely. The gigantic ring was a symbol of her dependency, just as much as the bruises on her body and the chafe-marks on her limbs. She was too tiny now, and the ring was too huge. Everything in her life was out of proportion. She was caught now, carefully and skilfully brain-washed by him, pinned down in his net, starved to skin and bone. Bucking under him as he dripped hot wax on her, her pain and pleasure sensors so blurred together by everything he had done to her in the last months that she could no longer have said whether she would have screamed in ecstasy or distress, would have pleaded for him to stop or go on, if she could have made anything beyond a flicker of sound around the firm rubber sphere of the ball gag fastened between her lips.

With him, she was wordless, sightless, but never deaf. He wanted her to hear the sounds he was making, his grunts and moans of pleasure, the snap of the match as it lit the candle whose melting wax she was about to feel, the flick of the rubber whip as he tested it against the post of the bed before bringing it down on the backs of her thighs. He wanted to hear her try to gasp in anticipation, to guess where she would feel him next. To see if she would recoil at the unmistakable sound of him returning from the bar in the living room, ice cubes clinking in their metal container, knowing that he would be merciless with them, would slide them over her body and trail them, slowly, tantalisingly between her legs, making her jerk and try, futilely, to escape their burning cold on the most sensitive areas of her body. Hoping that his hot mouth would follow them, licking and biting her, sending her into spasms of orgasm that seemed even more intense because she couldn't see, couldn't speak, could do nothing but buck against her bonds, coming over and over again, feeling him drive her beyond anything she had thought she could take, over a dark precipice where she nearly fainted with the intensity of one orgasm thudding after another, all the while knowing that his teeth and lips would leave her wincing and sore.

Or nipple clamps, a tiny little snip of sound as he flicked them open and closed before attaching them to her, pulling the soft pink flesh, hearing her whimper. Bending over her, listening to the tiny sounds she was struggling to make, before he pulled out the ball gag, tossing it aside, and straddled her, giving her barely any time to gasp a breath before his weight settled heavy on her chest, his cock hot and wide in her mouth as it drove into her, her lips eagerly closing around it, sucking and pulling hard, hearing his groans of encouragement above her. Knowing how much she was pleasing him, trying to make him come as hard as he had just made her writhe with orgasm, drinking his come down with fast, practised gulps as he flooded her mouth with hot, salty, almond-scented liquid. She had learned to suck it down swiftly, a series of short, frantic swallows so that she didn't choke, her mouth distended with his stubby thrust of cock, her throat full of come.

Eighteen months ago, Coco had been a girl who had a well-developed sense of humour, a quick wit. But she was too tense now, too skinny, her nerves too on edge for her to be able to relax enough to see the funny side of anything, to think ironically: *This is the only time he doesn't worry about the calorie content of what I'm eating. The only time he rewards me for swallowing something – instead of gently pushing my plate away when I'm halfway through, and telling me I've had enough, that I still have more weight to lose . . .*

He'll be happy now. Surely he will. Now that I'm perfect.

But beneath her pride in her achievement was a creeping fear. Not so much of him, but of herself.

Because she had been starving herself for so long that she was frightened that she wouldn't know how to stop.

Part One
London: Then

Jodie

The waiting room was full of clones. Slim, elegant girls with their hair pulled back into chignons, wearing crisp white shirts tucked into tailored trousers or skirts in shades of grey or beige, their wrists loaded with wide bangles, their make-up simple and discreet. They sat in the moulded white chairs that lined the walls, their legs crossed to show off their high stiletto-heeled cage shoes, heavy with straps that reached up to the start of their calves. On their laps were the latest It bags, or very good imitations, decorated with buckles and tassels and zips. They were all staring straight ahead, not deigning to notice each other's existence, as if they were the originator of their style and all the other girls were inferior copies.

Jodie stood in the doorway, her portfolio under one arm, looking at the clones with disbelief that gradually morphed into panic. No one had bothered to look up at her: it would be beneath their dignity to show interest in the new arrival. And the assistant, sitting behind her glass desk, tapping away at her computer, didn't look up either. Why should she? Jodie was simply the sixth girl to be interviewed this morning for the coveted job of Victoria Glossop's assistant, one in a long line of Identikit young women who had done their best to dress like their idol's poorer, younger sister. It was for Jodie to go over to the desk, to give her name in a hushed voice, to sit down next to one of the other Victoria Glossop replicas and wait for her turn, her chance to show Victoria that she was different from the rest of them, the stand-out applicant whom Victoria really had to hire . . .

Sod this. Jodie's hand clenched tightly around her portfolio, sinking into the leather. It was real, and even though she'd bought it on sale from Bilberry it had cost an absolute fortune. She was proud of it: dark green, patent, embossed, with a heavy brass clasp, she'd been planning to lay it on Victoria Glossop's famously immaculate desk and pull out her layouts. At least it's not beige, she thought savagely, glancing from one clone to the next. But it was the only thing in Jodie's possession that wasn't. The clones were so upsetting because Jodie had, exactly like them, dressed to replicate Victoria Glossop's famous style, her hair pulled back, her clothing colourless and perfectly tailored. Victoria's hair was always in her signature chignon. She wore white, beige and grey, with touches of black-and-white fur: snow leopard, zebra, sable. Victoria loved heavy bangles. Victoria *loathed* hoop earrings. Victoria—

Jodie took a deep breath. She'd never win if she took these girls on at their own game. Most of them were thinner than she was: Jodie was a size 12 – on a good day, and in a label that had a more generous definition of that size than one that sold to skinny teens or model wannabes. A Marks & Spencers 12, rather than a Lipsy or Stella McCartney. And at five foot six, that was a perfectly happy weight for her – or it was, till I came to London to work on fashion mags, she couldn't help thinking. Because none of these girls was over a size 10, and she'd bet that several of them, at least, had independent incomes, rich boyfriends, or much better PR contacts for freebies than she did. She'd already spotted a Marc Jacobs bag, a Miu Miu skirt, and some amazing Zanotti heels, minimum £450 retail.

I can't compete at this level, Jodie knew, without a hint of self-pity. Her family hadn't got a penny to spare; all she lived on was her minimal salary as fashion editor of *Wow* magazine, and the freebies she could scrounge up using *Wow* as a lever were distinctly low-status. Her white shirt was Jil Sander, but Jil Sander for Uniqlo, her pencil skirt Karen Millen – it fitted her beautifully, but it was high street, not high end.

The girl sitting closest to Jodie glanced up, probably because she'd become aware that Jodie was standing in the doorway, hovering nervously. She zipped her eyes up and down Jodie, taking in every detail of her appearance, pricing her hair, her clothes, her shoes: in thirty seconds, a tiny smile lifted the corners of her mouth and she turned away again, visibly relaxing with an attitude that said all too clearly that Jodie was no competition for her.

She's probably called Chloe, or Caroline, or Natasha, Jodie thought viciously. Something posh or foreign, something much classier than Jodie.

The open contempt that Chloe or Caroline or Natasha had just demonstrated was exactly the spur that Jodie needed. It had been hard enough to even get this interview, and she wasn't going to buckle under pressure now. She might not have the advantages of money and class that the Chloes, Carolines and Natashas did, but she came from a stable, loving, supportive family, she'd been brought up to be confident with who she was, and so what if she was a bit bigger than the other girls? She was healthy and happy, and she had great instincts for what women – real women – wanted to see in fashion magazines. Clothes they could actually wear, models they could identify with. Jodie knew she had real talent.

I need to stand out from the crowd – show Victoria that I'm not just a clone.

There were five girls in the room: that would give Jodie at least an hour before her interview. No time to go home – unable to afford a place of her own on her tiny salary, Jodie still lived at home with her mum and dad in Luton. There was no way she could ever make it back there to change her clothes.

No, I'm going to have to think on my feet.

And there Jodie had a real advantage, because she did that all day long. Jodie was a grafter; she'd been climbing the greasy pole so far by working harder, thinking faster and being more creative than anyone else around her. Fashion editor at *Wow* wasn't much, and her budgets were small, but she'd managed miracles with the little she had, and her layouts had been good enough to secure her an interview with her idol Victoria Glossop, editor of *Style*.

Nipping over to the desk, Jodie gave the receptionist her name, and offered to bring her back a coffee of her choice if she ensured that Jodie was called last. Agreement secured, and an order taken for a skinny grande latte with extra chocolate, Jodie shot out of the Dupleix building on Brewer Street, turned right and hurtled up to Oxford Street as fast as her shoes (Zara, loose interpretations of 3.1 Phillip Lim) would take her.

Sixty minutes later, she was back, breathing fast, but the skinny latte was unspilled. As Jodie set it down, the receptionist did a double-take, her eyes widening as she realised that this was the same person who had spoken to her an hour earlier.

'You're next,' she said in hushed tones; everyone at the *Style* reception spoke in an artificially-lowered voice, as if they were in church.

It is a sort of church, Jodie thought as she took a seat in one of the uncomfortable, but highly fashionable white chairs. *We're all worshippers, with Victoria Glossop as a cross between the High Priestess and God.*

The atrium of the Dupleix magazine building, which housed many other publications as well as *Style*, was extremely smart, but the fifth-floor reception that led to the hallowed ground of *Style* was decorated entirely in Victoria Glossop's signature palette; it might have been her own entrance hall. Huge white vases held black orchids, the only flower that was ever allowed to grace the receptionist's desk. The walls were greige – that perfect blend of grey and beige where neither one had predominance – and the huge Chinese six-fold screen that hung on the wall behind the desk was of a snarling white tiger, black brushstrokes on cream paper in a black lacquered frame. It was the screen, the seventeenth-century painting as vivid as if it had been executed only days ago, that really showed how excellent Victoria's eye was: the rest of the room would have been in perfect taste, but bland without the huge, magnificent animal sprawling across its folds, bringing the décor to life.

Jodie's phone beeped: a message coming in. Pulling it out of her bag, she checked it quickly.

All right darling? Get the job? Making your fave dinner – shepherd's pie! Can't wait to hear how it went. And turn your phone off!!! X x

Her mum, checking in. Jodie couldn't help smiling as she put the phone back in her bag, making sure it was set to silent.

Thanks, Mum. I'd've forgotten that.

The thought of her mum's shepherd's pie, rich, fragrant meat under the whipped potato topping, made her stomach rumble in happy anticipation. Briefly, she allowed herself to imagine returning to Luton in triumph: sitting down for dinner with her parents and sister, tucking into a delicious plate of home-cooked food, announcing that she'd pulled off a miracle, actually succeeding in getting a job on *Style*—

One of the opaque glass double doors swung open: an impossibly thin girl in skinny grey jeans and five-inch heels emerged, followed by the interview candidate who had sneered at Jodie in the waiting room an hour ago. She wasn't sneering now. Her head was held high, but her eyes were suspiciously red and she was biting her bottom lip, hard, trying not to cry.

'Jodie?' the girl in skinny jeans said, looking at a list in her hand. 'You're next. God, it's taking *forever*.'

Jodie jumped up, smoothing down her skirt.

'I hope you've had a stiff drink,' Skinny Jeans said without an ounce of compassion in her voice, holding open the door for Jodie. 'She's in full bitch mode. I could hear her through the wall ripping that one's throat out, and once she gets the taste of blood . . .'

'That one', visible through the glass doors, waiting for the lift, had wrapped her arms around herself and was giving vent to a series of whimpering sobs that she probably thought were inaudible to the people in reception. Crossing the office, Jodie glanced up to the snarling white tiger on the Chinese screen: its pink tongue, the sneering curl of its nose, the sharp, dagger-like white fangs. It occurred to her that the tiger screen wasn't just the perfect final decorative touch, but that Victoria Glossop had hung it there to symbolise herself. A warning that anyone who crossed her was liable to get their head bitten off.

And when Skinny Jeans ushered Jodie through the assistant's antechamber into Victoria's office, snapping the door shut promptly behind the latest victim to avoid any last-minute attempts to flee the ordeal awaiting them, Jodie almost raised her hand to her throat in self-protection under the laser stare of Victoria's cold grey eyes.

'Well!' Victoria said in a voice as crisp as her perfectly-starched white shirt. 'At least you're original. Five points.' She scribbled something on her Bilberry notepad with a slender silver Tiffany pen. 'Though I'm deducting two for cheapness. Those shoes. Always spend money on shoes. People notice. Sit.'

Jodie was so shocked by this stream of words that she didn't immediately obey the last one.

'Sit!' Victoria repeated impatiently, pointing with the Tiffany pen to the beige leather chair in front of her desk. 'You should be grateful – I didn't even ask the last girl to sit down.'

Victoria shuddered at the recollection, as elegantly as she did everything else. Her nose was long, narrow and patrician. Generations of Glossops had looked down that nose at peasants, intimidating them very effectively even before they'd said a word.

'I gave her a minus ten for appearance,' she informed Jodie, who was sinking into the chair, grateful for its support; her legs were feeling distinctly weak. 'And *no one* recovers from a minus ten.'

There hadn't been one girl in that waiting room who could conceivably have been described as a minus ten – not, at least, by Jodie. Heart in her mouth, she stared at Victoria, who had swivelled her chair and was crossing her legs, tapping on the notepad with her pen. It was true, what Jodie had heard: the back of Victoria's chair was bolt upright to ensure perfect posture, beige leather made to her own specifications. Her blonde hair was swept back perfectly, literally not a single hair out of place, the side parting over her ear as straight as if it had been executed with a ruler. The collar of her 3.1 Phillip Lim shirt was flicked up, emphasising Victoria's long, slender white neck, heavily twisted-around by strands of huge black pearls, gleaming purplish against the pale background. Victoria's desk was a shiny sheet of glass, uncluttered by anything but a silver Apple Mac, the notepad, the pen, and a silver-rimmed glass of bubbly water in which a slice of lime floated. Through the clear glass, Jodie could see Victoria's waist, impossibly small, and her legs, most of which were on display in her tiny beige mini-skirt.

'So,' Victoria said, snapping Jodie out of the trance into which she had fallen while taking in the exquisite perfection of Victoria's appearance. 'Am I to assume this was deliberate?'

She flicked the pen up and down in the air, indicating Jodie's hastily-assembled outfit. Jodie opened her mouth to give one answer, made a series of lighting-fast calculations, and told the truth instead.

'I came in for the interview,' she said, 'and everyone was dressed exactly the same.'

Victoria's blonde brows drew together. 'Including you?'

Jodie nodded. 'And they were all doing it better than me. So I ran out and got some new stuff as fast as I could.'

'And your hair?' Victoria asked. 'Because frankly, it's a dog's dinner. It actually gets worse the more I look at it. Minus two.' She made another note.

Jodie hadn't had time to get her hair restyled. All she'd been able to do was to pull it out of the chignon she'd spent so much time on that morning, brush it out and leave it loose. She was growing out the layers, and it looked shaggy, she knew; but she'd given it a quick spray with styling lotion in Boots just now, and at least it was smooth.

She reached a hand up to it, embarrassed, as Victoria said, 'So, tell me about this outfit that you cobbled together.'

At least she hasn't deducted points for my outfit yet, Jodie thought frantically. It was hard to breathe: Victoria's narrow grey eyes were fixed on her face, noticing, Jodie was sure, every spot and blemish that she'd done her best to cover up that morning.

'Well, the T-shirt's from Benetton,' Jodie started nervously. 'I know it's not trendy, but they're really good quality and the cut is timeless. I picked navy because that suits me better than white, and it's a classic colour. And long sleeves, because I wanted to keep the bangles and I really like them piled up over a sleeve. It looks sort of medieval, which is coming back in. I think it'll be huge next year.'

She lifted one arm to show off the effect; the hem of the sleeve was pulled down to the base of her thumb. Victoria nodded.

'Plus four,' she said. 'Go on.'

Emboldened, Jodie continued, 'The jeans are Karen Millen. She cuts really well for my shape and they're classics too—'

'Minus two for describing them as classics,' Victoria snapped. 'The grey will date fast and there's too much branding. I can see the name on those hem zips from here. I *loathe* visible branding. But,' she paused, 'they do work with those cheap shoes of yours. The length is right, and they fit you well. Plus two. We'll call it even.'

Jodie gulped.

'My hair was in a chignon,' she said feebly. 'But I pulled it down and brushed it out. I thought anything was better than looking like all those other girls. And to be honest, it looked better on most of them than it did on me.'

Victoria huffed: it took Jodie long painful seconds to realise that this was a laugh.

'Yes, you won't do well copying my style.' Victoria set down her pen, recrossed her slim legs under the glass table, and swung the one on top as if to show off her beige crocodile-skin Prada shoe. 'You're not thin enough, frankly. You don't have the bone structure to pull your hair back fully. And there's too much pink in your skin for you to wear white.'

She looked down complacently at her legs, tanned to a delicate gold. Though naturally pale, Victoria was known to have weekly spray-tanning sessions in order to achieve her perfect, even colour.

'Remind me where you're working now?' Victoria asked.

She huffed another little laugh when Jodie muttered, '*Wow* magazine.' Jodie felt ashamed even mentioning something so lowbrow in front of Victoria Glossop. 'It's a weekly. I don't have much of a budget, but I've done some good layouts. I can show you . . .'

She leaned down to pick up her portfolio, which she'd placed by the side of her chair when she sat down, sensing that it would be a huge no-no to put it on Victoria's immaculate desk. Even now she hesitated, not wanting to set it on the smooth sheet of glass in front of her unless she was specifically invited to do so.

'Don't bother,' Victoria said, waving it away with an imperious gesture. 'It'll all be cheap, cheap, cheap.' She shivered. 'I *despise* cheap. You know this job isn't an editorial one? You'd be working as my assistant. As far as status goes, you're below the junior shoe editor and the handbag girl whose name I can never remember. You're at my beck and call. I'll put you through hell. I assume you know all this already – I'm well aware of my reputation.'

She smiled, briefly flashing even white teeth, each one polished to an opalescent gleam. Somehow, Victoria's smile was even more frightening than her words; it was anticipatory, looking forward to the appalling treatment to which she would be subjecting her next assistant.

'So tell me why you want this hellish job,' she continued.

Jodie leaned forward eagerly, her eyes bright, only to be stopped by Victoria holding up a hand to stop her. Her huge grey diamond engagement ring blazed on the fourth finger, precisely the colour of her eyes. Jodie, who had read up everything that had ever been written on Victoria, knew that although it had been bought by her husband, Victoria had seen it in a Sotheby's auction catalogue in a sale of jewels owned by the Bavarian royal family: she had had her assistant send it on to her then boyfriend with a note that this would be the only ring Victoria would consider accepting when he proposed – as she assumed he was bound to do. He had instantly fallen into line, as everyone seemed to do around Victoria. Once duly presented with it, she had promptly had it reset more fashionably than the Bavarian royal family's jeweller could achieve, and insisted that Alexander McQueen, who had designed her wedding dress, match the exact shade of grey for the embroidery on the bodice.

'I don't want to hear that this is the opportunity of a lifetime,' Victoria said briskly, ticking off no-go areas on her fingers. 'Or that you'll work harder than anyone else I've ever employed, or that I'm your idol and you'd do anything to sit at my feet and learn from me. Or any variations on those themes. Surprise me. Tell me something that no one else has today. And make it quick,' she added. 'I've wasted far too much time on these interviews already.'

Jodie forced herself to sit back in her chair, to try to look as cool as the woman sitting opposite her, who held the key to her future in her manicured hands.

'I just completely restyled myself in less than an hour,' she said. 'And I bought your receptionist a coffee to make sure I got to see you last. If I can think that quickly on my feet, I can do anything you need me to do, and faster than anyone's ever done it before.'

Victoria stared down her nose at Jodie, tapping the toe of her shoe against her silky-smooth golden calf.

'Plus ten. Fine. You start in three weeks,' she said. 'Davinia goes off to run the fashion cupboard in a month, and she'll have to spend a whole week training you up first. But there are two conditions. First, go out now, buy some decent shoes and throw out those ghastly ones. I can practically smell the cheap leather from here, and it's making me nauseous. Second, lose seven pounds, minimum. No one who works for *Style* is more than a size ten, and you're clearly at least a twelve. If you step over the threshold in a month's time and haven't lost the weight, I'll spin you on your heels and send you packing. Are we clear?'

'As crystal,' Jodie said valiantly.

No shepherd's pie for me, she thought. Mum'll be so disappointed, but she'll have to understand. The diet starts now – I'll live on Ryvita, apples and zero fat cottage cheese. I can do this, she told herself determinedly. It's totally worth it.

Victoria was flapping her hands at Jodie as if she were shooing geese, the grey diamond flashing; it was the signal for Jodie to jump out of her chair, grab her bag and make for the door.

'Oh, one last thing,' Victoria said, head turned towards her computer monitor. 'Your name. That's a minus ten. I can't possibly have an assistant called Jodie.'

Utter panic spiked through Jodie's veins, a surge of adrenalin so sharp she flinched from the shock. She froze as if she were playing a game of Musical Statues, portfolio under one arm, the bag dangling from her other hand the only thing that moved as Victoria continued:

'We'll have to call you something else. Believe me, I'm doing you a favour. Hmm . . .' she glanced down at her skirt '. . . I'm *loving* Chanel at the moment. Coco! There you go. From now on, you're Coco. Don't bother to thank me. Tell Davinia on your way out.'

Mouth open, fingers sweaty on the handle of her bag, Jodie staggered out of Victoria's office. Skinny Jeans, aka Davinia, was sitting at the desk that would be Jodie's in a month's time.

She looked up at Jodie and drawled, 'Do tell me you got the bloody job, won't you? She'll be even more of a bitch if I have to line up six more girls for her to rip to pieces.'

Jodie nodded, wordless with shock.

'Oh, thank *God,*' Davinia sighed in relief.

'Only now I'm called Coco,' Jodie managed to get out.

Davinia didn't even blink at the news. Looking at her – slim, confident and off to the dizzy heights of the fashion cupboard – Jodie wondered whether Davinia, a year or so ago, had also been a size 12 girl with a bad haircut, called Nadine or Cheryl or Kimberley, with a much less posh accent than she had now . . .

'Well, good luck, Coco,' Davinia said dryly to her replacement. 'You're going to need it.'

Victoria

Victoria Glossop had never spared a thought for other people's sensibilities. Not her parents', not her three brothers', not a single person with whom she had ever come into contact. Feelings were messy and unpredictable, a swamp in which you waded around, not knowing what you'd step on next or what would wind itself around your legs and try to pull you down into the fetid depths. Victoria had always had her own feelings very firmly under control, the more vulnerable and sensitive ones shoved down so far that she would have had great difficulty accessing them. Not that she had any wish to do so. Even when she got angry, threw a tantrum, rampaged around the office shouting at her terrified staff, she knew exactly what she was doing, was able to measure the precise level of fear and trembling she wanted to induce in her victims.

An indifference to other people's feelings was one of the principal reasons Victoria had been so successful. The other was her world-class ability to charm and flirt with powerful men, honed by years of practice on her father and brothers. A brilliant lawyer who had climbed the career ladder smoothly from QC to judge, Victoria's father was the incarnation of an authoritarian paterfamilias who bullied his sweet fluffball of a wife and ruled his sons with a rod of iron. He had never realised how much he wanted a daughter until Victoria was born, the last child and by far the most indulged one. From the moment she could walk and talk, Victoria's sharp little brain had identified her father as the one with all the power. She had quickly been able to wrap him round her little finger. Judge Glossop had chosen a pretty, feminine woman to marry; if Victoria had been a different kind of girl, she might have considered it very unfair of her father to pick an adorably ditsy, scatty wife and then spend the marriage criticising her for precisely the qualities for which he had proposed to her in the first place.

But Victoria had always been on her father's side. The side with the money, the control, the intelligence. Having worked out how to manipulate her father, she used the same techniques on her brothers: charming, beautiful Victoria, always dressed, by her mother, in the kind of pretty clothes that her father considered appropriate, cut a swathe through her entire family from an early age. Her mother was dazzled by her, openly admiring Victoria's ability to do what poor downtrodden Mrs Glossop couldn't – get exactly what she wanted from the judge.

Victoria could easily have been a politician or a lawyer, if her father hadn't emphasised how important he considered femininity in a woman – and if she hadn't hugely enjoyed the process of choosing clothes, dressing up and then twirling in her new finery in front of her besotted father. The only items in poor Mrs Glossop's household budget which her controlling husband never questioned were the huge sums spent on Victoria's outfits. Her brothers, all competing constantly to please their father, were now, respectively, a QC, a decorated naval officer, and something in MI5 that he wasn't allowed to talk about, but the child Judge Glossop boasted about constantly, the one whose photograph had pride of place on his desk, was Victoria, editor-in-chief of *Style*, a fashion icon in her own right.

Still, despite Victoria's meteoric rise to success, all she had achieved in her thirty-four years of life, she had one more crucial goal to achieve. And – she checked her slender gold watch bangle, a Vacheron Constantin antique which had cost her husband nearly ten thousand pounds as her birthday present last year – it was almost time for the dinner appointment which might bring the ultimate prize within her grasp.

Victoria's heart pounded with excitement. This meeting had been a long time coming. She'd schemed and planned and manoeuvred for years to get here, worked every single contact she had, charmed her way inexorably towards the ultimate goal: the crucial conversation she was going to have over dinner with Jacob Dupleix, head of the Dupleix media empire, the man whose name was on the building, who made the ultimate decisions about who edited his flagship magazines. Jacob's range of investments was enviably extensive. He had been an early adopter of the internet, and his tentacles stretched far and wide throughout the media. But no matter how much money Jacob coined from all the pies in which he had fingers, his real love was print. His magazines were his babies, his editors carefully chosen for their artistic skill and business sense, but also for their ability to incarnate the magazines they represented.

Thin, elegant, hyper-chic Victoria was the living, breathing embodiment of *UK Style*; however, this coveted, prestigious job, was, to her, simply a stepping-stone to the definitive job in fashion. The peak of the pinnacle. The biggest prize of all.

Picking up her Bottega Veneta bag, Victoria pushed her chair back and stood up from the desk. She looked around her office with a critical eye, at its polished teak floor, silk rugs and custom-made cherrywood bookcases housing back issues of *Style*, and her own huge collection of photography and fashion tomes. She strode towards the door in her high-heeled United Nude pumps, designed by the famous architect Rem Koolhaas – white leather ballet-style shoes set at a stratospheric angle to the blocky black heel. They were very hard to wear, very hard to build an outfit around, which was precisely why Victoria had chosen them. Thousands of women would try to copy her by buying the Block Pump Hi and fail abysmally to look as good in them as Victoria did.

By the time she had opened the door, Coco was already on her feet and moving towards her boss with a loop of wide brown sticky tape already wrapped around her hands, as if she were winding wool. Victoria opened her arms as if she were being crucified. She stood there motionless, the huge white handbag dangling from one wrist, as Coco meticulously went over her with the tape, lifting every single tiny piece of lint from Victoria's clothing. Coco unwound the tape, dropped it into the wastebasket, produced a lint roller and repeated the process, now including Victoria's wide suede belt, which she had avoided with the tape, the delicate surface of the suede being too fragile to be touched by anything sticky.

'Your car's waiting, Victoria,' Coco said as she finished the linting. This was a procedure she executed at least four times a day – when Victoria came into work, before and after her lunch, and when she left for the evening. Plus, of course, after Victoria had been looking at angora or cashmere samples, or whenever she capriciously deemed it necessary. 'It'll be pulled up outside when you leave the building. The Fiji water in the car is chilled to twelve degrees this time. I've instructed the driver to take it out of the fridge three minutes before he picks you up.'

Victoria merely nodded, but that was more than enough praise for Coco, who continued, 'Your table at the Wolseley is waiting and Mr Dupleix's assistant has confirmed he's on his way there. He's due to arrive at least five minutes before you.'

Victoria refused to enter a restaurant unless she was sure that at least one of the people meeting her was already present. She had been known, on being informed by a greeter that she was the first member of her party to arrive, to turn on her heel and return to her car, making the driver circle round the block until her assistant had rung to assure her that the person she was meeting had checked in at the restaurant in question.

'And when I leave?' Victoria asked, holding out her hand imperiously for her shaved-mink jacket, silver-blue, soft and luxurious. 'Last time—'

'You'll ring me when you're getting up from the table, and by the time you walk out, the car will be on Piccadilly waiting for you,' Coco said quickly. 'I have the driver's number, and I'll liaise with him the second after I hear that you're finished with dinner.'

Coco was perfectly well aware that the demands of her job meant that she couldn't make evening plans which entailed switching off her phone. No theatre, no concerts, no clubbing, because she couldn't guarantee during those activities to be able to grab a ringing mobile and answer it within two rings in an environment quiet enough for Victoria to hear her with perfect clarity. She had tried the cinema, sitting right at the back, by the exit doors, keeping one hand on her phone at all times so she could feel it vibrating and dash out into the corridor, but ever since she'd been so absorbed by a thriller that she'd overlooked the tell-tale pulsating of the phone on her lap, and been subjected to a fierce tongue-lashing by Victoria the next morning, she'd given that up too.

Everything in Coco's life came a dim second to her job. And she wouldn't have dreamed of complaining about it for a moment.

Victoria smoothed down the jacket, enjoying the silky texture of the fur, burned-out in a subtle devoré velvet pattern. She was used to criticising her assistants, finding the flaw in their arrangements, driving a stiletto knife into it and twisting, exposing their incompetence, leaving them in a state of heightened nerves that motivated them better than any other lever she had ever found. However, Coco was different. Her organisational abilities were extraordinary. She'd made a few mistakes settling in, but not only had she never repeated them, she'd improved so fast that in a mere three months she was unequivocally the best assistant Victoria had ever had.

Which left Victoria in something of a quandary. Because Coco would clearly soon deserve a promotion. But Victoria had no desire to promote Coco; ideally, she would have kept Coco as her gatekeeper forever.

'All right,' Victoria said curtly, walking out of the office. 'See that it all goes smoothly.'

From her, this was a huge compliment: not a single negative word. Briefly, Victoria considered throwing in something snippy, to keep Coco on her toes – but Coco was always on her toes, alert and ready.

Like the best kind of dog, Victoria thought, amused. Always anticipating what you're going to ask it to do, but not slobbering over you or licking your shoes.

The car was waiting outside the glass doors of the Dupleix building, the driver running to open the door as soon as he saw Victoria exit, resplendent in her mink jacket and impossibly short white grosgrain Cavalli mini-skirt. Sinking into the leather seat, crossing her endless legs, Victoria debated briefly with herself on how to make sure Coco stayed in her current job for as long as possible. How could Victoria bear to lose the only assistant she had ever had who never, ever, bothered her boss with a single piece of information about her private life?

God, how I loathe women and their endless compulsion to tell each other everything! Victoria thought crossly. I've already looked at enough bloody family photos and pretended to care about my bosses' fiancés and weddings and babies to last me the rest of my life. Why don't people realise that you don't actually give a shit about their stupid boyfriends? Anyone who listens to you drivel on is either sucking up, or biding their time till it's their turn to witter on about their own love life . . .

Years ago, as a feature writer on *Vogue*, Victoria had been sent to interview a female producer at the BBC who had worked on a sitcom parodying the sacred monsters and over-the-top characters in fashion PR. Written by a woman, with an almost entirely female cast, it had been a template for all the girls-behaving-badly comedies that had followed it, a huge and enduring success, a flag-planting moment for women who wanted power in the media.

She would never forget what the producer had answered when Victoria had asked her about working with other women. Leaning forward, digging both her hands into the roots of her curly hair, dragging the skin of her forehead tight, the producer had said bitterly, 'I never want to have to start another bloody meeting at the BBC sitting down at the table and having to do the round of: "Ooh, you look good, have you lost weight? I *love* your jacket! No, I love *your* suit! Your hair really suits you like that. How are Jack and the kids? Lily's just starting school, isn't she – how's she settling in? And is your cat better after it got that infection last year?" God!'

She stared at Victoria, eyes dragged outwards by the fingers in her hairline, face distorted.

'You know what it's like,' she said cynically. 'You work in magazines, it's all women there too. Shit, the time I waste on that rubbish! And they get really offended if you don't remember the name of their cat or their kid or their husband! You know who doesn't do this? Men. They don't give a shit about each other's families and they don't bloody pretend they do. Women are such hypocrites.'

She caught herself.

'That's all off the record, of course.'

Victoria's article hadn't been much good – she was no writer, and was quickly moved back to the fashion desk ladder by the editor who was mentoring her. But that producer's words had echoed in her mind ever since. It was a bare five-minute ride from Brewer Street across Regent Street to Piccadilly, and by the time the car pulled up outside 160 Piccadilly, the stunning Grade II listed building with its three grand arches, decorated with elaborate and delicate wrought-iron struts and curlicues that had housed Wolseley cars in the 1920s and was now one of the most fashionable restaurants in London, Victoria had determined to keep Coco in her assistant job as long as possible. Coco would kick and scream and plead for a promotion, she was sure, but Victoria would hold her off. She was simply too valuable where she was right now.

And she wants what I can give her enough to stick it out for at least a year longer, Victoria thought with satisfaction as she strode up the marble steps and into the Wolseley, past the liveried doorman who was holding open one of the enormously heavy glass-and-iron doors. *I've got her over a barrel.*

Victoria didn't give her name to the greeter at the front desk; she expected to be recognised instantly, and she was.

'Ms Glossop!' the greeter said quickly. 'How nice to see you again. Mr Dupleix is at his usual table.'

A waiter led Victoria past the black-lacquered bar, over the black and white zigzag marble floor to the table for four where Jacob was waiting, placed strategically near the entrance, so that Victoria could see everyone and be seen in her turn. The Wolseley hosted the most famous actors, TV presenters, writers and business tycoons in London, a clientele which was used to instantly recognisable faces passing their tables every few minutes, and which was far too sophisticated to gawk openly.

But Victoria Glossop's arrival turned every head. Though as stunning as an actress or a model, Victoria had infinitely more power. She could make careers by declaring a woman a fashion icon or putting her on the coveted front cover of *Style*. She had the looks of a professional beauty and the authority of a tyrant, a combination rare enough that everyone in the Wolseley had to sneak a quick look at her, to see her for themselves. Many raised a hand in greeting, and Victoria cast brief smiles in their direction, though without slowing her catwalk stride. Jacob Dupleix rose from his seat to greet her, arms outstretched, and the sight of him drew even more attention. The actors and presenters and writers were supplicants, famous as they were. Jacob and Victoria were the fame-makers, the powers behind the scenes who pulled the strings and made the puppets dance. They were the ones who needed to be courted, flattered, fawned to. And they knew it.

'Darling!' Jacob said, enfolding Victoria in a warm embrace, then pulling back to look at her, holding her shoulders, before planting a kiss on each cheek. Though Jacob had been born and brought up in New York, his family's origins were a complex mixture of European and Middle Eastern wealth and influence, and his manners were elaborate and courtly.

'You look as beautiful as ever,' he said fondly. 'Please.' He gestured to the leather banquette beside him, waiting until Victoria had smoothed her minuscule skirt underneath her tiny bottom and sat down before he took his place beside her. This was how Jacob always preferred to be seated when he dined tête-à-tête with an attractive woman, on a banquette they shared; and he had the status, even at the best restaurants, to reserve a table for four if necessary to ensure his preference.

'An apéritif, Ms Glossop?' a waiter enquired, gliding up to the table.

'VLT,' Victoria ordered. 'Plenty of ice.' Vodka, lime and slimline tonic was the carb-free drink of choice for fashionistas watching their weight.

'So,' Jacob said, as she shrugged her arms out of the mink jacket, draping it over her shoulders. 'How are you, my darling?' He smiled happily. 'I've been taking meetings with my editors all day, but this is the moment I've been looking forward to. My fervent congratulations. You've done the most amazing job.'

Victoria smiled complacently. She knew she had, but it was pleasant to hear her boss say it, rather than having to make the point herself.

'*Style*'s brighter,' Jacob continued. 'Livelier, hipper, peppier. Younger. And the advertisers love it. The circulation is rising and we've just managed to raise ad rates, even in these terrible economic times.'

Victoria's smile deepened, but she didn't say a word. When people were praising you, you let them keep going. Most women would have felt obliged to murmur a self-deprecating comment at this stage, but the reason Victoria was so successful was that she wasn't most women. And she certainly didn't do self-deprecating.

'Your cocktail, madam,' the waiter murmured, sliding it in front of Victoria. 'Are you ready to order your dinner yet?'

'Tomato soup and steak tartare, no frites,' Victoria said without even looking at the menu.

'Half a dozen fines de claire oysters and the sea bass,' Jacob said cheerfully. 'Give me her frites on the side, why don't you? I love the way you guys do them here. Even better than Balthazar,' he added, naming the famous SoHo bistro that was the Wolseley's New York counterpart. 'And bring me some mayo too, why don't you.'

The waiter gathered the menus and slipped away. Jacob raised his glass of champagne to Victoria in a toast.

'To my star editor,' he said fondly. 'Jesus, Vicky, how long's it been?'

'Oh God. *Decades!*' Victoria said jokingly, clinking her glass with his.

It had, in fact, been twelve years or so since Victoria, an achingly-ambitious, twenty-two-year-old, very junior editor at *US Style*, had targeted, focused on and succeeded in dating an influential, much older art dealer simply because he was a good friend of Jacob Dupleix. Twelve years since she'd been taken by the art dealer to Jacob's mansion in the Hamptons, the stretch of Long Island where the truly rich New Yorkers maintained beachfront houses that cost in the tens of millions, for Jacob's renowned Fourth of July party, and, between the firework displays and private concert by Mariah Carey, had wangled an introduction to the great man himself. Exquisitely turned-out in a white poplin Armani mini-dress and stratospheric heels, looking as cool as a cucumber, her cut-glass English accent enchanting even the most jaded of Americans, Victoria had been an instant hit with Jacob even before she casually dropped into the conversation that she was one of his employees.

'You know what I tell people about you?' Jacob asked rhetorically, drinking some champagne. 'I could tell from the moment I met you that you had more ambition in your little finger than most people have in their whole goddamn bodies. I can smell it on people. It's my special talent.' He grinned. 'Baby, if you could bottle that and sell it, we'd be billionaires.'

Jacob Dupleix made being in your fifties look like the prime of life. It helped that his complex ethnic origins had given him a smooth, Mediterranean skin colour that looked as if he had a perpetual tan, and that his lightly-silvered mane of hair was still so thick that it made his balding, hair-plugged contemporaries grind their teeth with jealousy. His dark eyes gleamed with seductive warmth; everything about his demeanour spoke of worldly wisdom and the kind of sexual experience that made women melt with anticipation. In his time, he had been compared to Jeff Goldblum, Antonio Banderas, Imran Khan, even King Juan Carlos of Spain.

Although Jacob was definitely not running to seed, decades of five-star living had put a little excess weight on him; he had a personal trainer and nutritionist, but he ignored their instructions as much as he followed them. His dark Hugo Boss suit was expertly cut to flatter his silhouette, and his big frame could carry the extra pounds that fine dining and finer wines had packed on.

He's as charismatic as ever, Victoria thought, sipping her VLT and looking Jacob up and down with open appreciation.

'I know, I know,' Jacob said, his dark eyes glinting. 'I could stand to lose a few pounds, and you look as skinny as always. I should take diet tips from you, Vicky. You look amazing. Jeremy's a lucky guy.'

'He certainly is,' Victoria said briskly. 'And he knows it, too.'

Jacob's grin deepened. 'Yeah, I bet you remind him morning and evening just how lucky he is,' he said. 'I shouldn't, but I will,' he added over his shoulder to the waiter extending a wooden tray of freshly-baked rolls. 'Give me that one, the tomato bread. And don't even bother showing the lady anything with carbs in it – am I right, Vicky?' He ripped open a roll, bringing it to his nose, nostrils flaring with pleasure as he inhaled the delicious, yeasty smell of the bread studded with sundried tomatoes. 'Mmn, that smells good.'

Victoria, never one to be distracted from her goal, completely ignored the pleasure Jacob was taking in his roll.

'Jeremy may be lucky,' she said, taking another measured sip of her cocktail, 'but I'm not. Because I work like a Trojan for everything I've achieved. I push everyone around me hard, but I push myself hardest of all. You know that, Jacob.'

'I do,' he agreed through a mouthful of fluffy bread.

'And I'm ready for my next challenge,' she continued firmly.

'Now, Vicky—' he started.

'I've done everything you asked me to do.' In a characteristic gesture, Victoria raised her slim hand and ticked off the points on her fingers. 'Raised circulation, increased advertising, raised ad rates, practically doubled the subscriptions, made the magazine the most fashionable periodical in the UK. It flies off the shelves, and the website's won a whole string of awards. You know how shitty that website was before. Practically non-existent. I sacked everyone on it and brought in my own people. Have you looked at it recently?'

'I look at everything,' Jacob assured her, dusting the crumbs off his hands. 'Believe me, I do.'

'So you know what a transformation I've created!' She smoothed back her already perfect chignon. 'It's just what you wanted, much more vibrant and alive. I instructed all my editors that everything had to be shot in motion. The girls jump and run and smile much more than they used to.' Victoria pulled a face. 'God, the fuss everyone made at first. "It's not the British way to smile in fashion shots," they told me,' she said sarcastically. 'Everything was so dour and serious. Well, not any more! And it's what women want to see,' she added passionately. 'American energy and drive. It's so much more fun.'

The waiter brought their first courses, but Victoria completely ignored her tomato soup; she was turned away from her place setting, towards Jacob, making her pitch with fervency.

'And that brings me to exactly what I want to talk about,' she continued unstoppably.

'Oh, Vicky baby, I know exactly what you want to talk about,' Jacob said, hugely entertained. He selected an oyster, carefully squeezed a single drop of lemon juice into the bivalve, then picked it up, tilting it to his mouth, pursing his full lips as the oyster slid through them. With great relish, he swallowed it slowly and dabbed his mouth with a starched white napkin.

'I might as well get straight to it then,' Victoria said, quite unabashed. 'I want to be the editor of *US Style*.'

'You will be.' Jacob picked up another oyster and dispatched it, using the time it took to dress and swallow it to make Victoria wait for his next words. 'In two years' time,' he went on, reaching for the napkin again. 'Just as we agreed in New York.'

'But I'm ready *now*,' Victoria pleaded. 'I've done everything you wanted at *UK Style*, and in half the time you thought it would take. I've cleared out all the dead wood and brought in a really strong team. I have a new editor lined up to replace me, so I could take over in New York tomorrow, and *UK Style* would run perfectly well along the lines I've laid down.'

'It's not that simple, Vicky,' Jacob said, his smile even more charming. 'We discussed all this in New York, two years ago. You were going to do four years in London, turning round *Style* for me. Then – and not before – I was going to move you back to the States. I know perfectly well that's why you agreed to leave *Harper's*. You wouldn't have settled for *UK Style* alone, and I respect that.'

'I want to be in Manhattan,' Victoria said intently. 'It's the centre of the media world. I should be there. I should be there *now*.'

She steepled her fingers together under her chin, her grey diamond flashing, but her eyes shining even brighter.

'You know I should,' she insisted. 'My whole career's been leading up to this – it's the job I was born to have! And this is the right time for me to have it.'

Jacob was finishing his oysters; he didn't speak, and Victoria, though inwardly seething with frustration, knew that she had to wait for his response. She'd pushed hard enough.

As he picked up the last fluted shell, she found herself running through the entire trajectory of her career since meeting and impressing Jacob that Fourth of July. She'd spoken no less than the truth just now: her entire career had been leading up to this moment.

With Jacob's influence, Victoria had risen quickly up the masthead of *US Style*, propelled by his interest and her own undoubted talent. Jacob was well-known for talent-spotting, finding protégés and expediting their rise: it was known in the US as 'Jacob's ladder'. But Victoria's meteoric ascent to power was faster, more jet-propelled, than anyone else's. By twenty-five she was in charge of a magazine start-up which was a raving success from its first issue; by twenty-eight, she was back at *Style* as executive fashion editor, a prestigious position which she manoeuvred to give her almost as much authority as the editor herself. An increasingly vicious power struggle between Victoria and Jennifer Lane Davis, the editor, sent both of them complaining to Jacob, telling him that they were unable to work together. Victoria had wanted Jennifer's job; Jacob had told her she wasn't ready. In pique, Victoria had flounced off to *Harper's Bazaar* as editor – Hearst had been courting her for years.

Her run at *Harper's* had been Victoria's one stint as editor that wasn't an unqualified success. Hearst and Victoria Glossop weren't a perfect fit; their ethos was more classic, more timeless, and Victoria was always impatiently onto the next thing, the most cutting-edge fashion, finding new ways to push the envelope. *Harper's* had never been her ultimate goal. She had known it, and so had Jacob.

'Do you remember what you said when I asked you where you saw yourself in ten years' time?' Jacob replied eventually, pushing away the china platter loaded with empty shells, their interiors gleaming with a pale mother-of-pearl sheen, dappled with drops of juice from the bivalves. 'When I first got talking to you in Montauk, you said you wanted to be editor of *US Style*.' He grinned, his teeth perfect and white, showcasing American dentistry. 'At twenty-two! You see, I even remember how old you were. It was quite something.'

'I could have done it,' Victoria told him.

The waiter was hovering, waiting to clear their plates, concerned that Victoria hadn't touched her soup; she waved him away with a quick, brisk gesture, and took a couple of spoonfuls, her eyes fixed on Jacob's face.

'Nah, I thought I'd let you cut your teeth at *Harper's* first,' he said casually.

'You let me stew there for years!' Victoria's spoon clattered back into the bowl; she pushed it away impatiently, signalling that the waiter could take it.

'Oh, you did good at *Harper's*,' Jacob said. 'Hey, can I get a new napkin?' He smiled charmingly at the waiter.

Victoria fumed with impatience, but she had to play Jacob's game now, go at the pace he was setting.

It's all a big game to him, she thought. He loves to put his hand out and play with us, moving us back and forth like pawns. She remembered the superbly detailed, nineteeth-century Venetian chess set in Jacob's New York office, Murano glass, burnt orange versus viridian green, each piece flecked with gold, the board edged richly in 18-carat gold; Jacob amused himself by working through classic chess problems, his spatulate fingers looking even bigger as he moved the pieces from square to square.

Well, I'm the Queen, she thought with a flash of humour. I can go up and down, from side to side and diagonally too. But I still can't bloody move unless Jacob lets me . . .

'Here's the thing, Vicky,' Jacob said, and she perked up: finally, they were getting down to business. 'Jennifer still has two years of her contract to run. You know that. We talked this over when I came after you at *Harper's*. You'd do four years here in London – nice little stay back in the motherland for you, and it was a good move for me. The Brits at *UK Style* weren't pulling their weight, and tactically it was great for me to send in a Brit to get 'em to shape up. After four years, Jennifer's contract would be over and I'd move you back to helm *US Style* instead. You agreed to that, honey. You know I told you Jennifer's contract is cast-iron – I'd have to give her a huge payoff if I sack her now.'

Jacob spread his hands wide. 'You can't just try to change the rules of the game halfway through,' he finished. 'And don't tell me you'll take a pay cut to make up what I have to give Jennifer, because I won't believe you.' He grinned. 'I know how much you love your perks.'

'I'll make back every penny of what you have to give her in increased ad revenue alone in the first six months,' Victoria said sharply. 'You know I will. Jennifer's wasting money over there. She's playing it too safe, spending tons of money on big names. I can slash her budgets, get actresses who'll model for free instead of the expensive girls she's using, up-and-coming photographers instead of the Top Ten she's been relying on . . .'

Their main courses arrived, delivered by a waitress who could tell they were deep in conversation; she slid the plates in front of them and disappeared without a word.

'Plus,' Victoria added, her voice rising, 'what kind of stupid name is that – "Jennifer Lane Davis"? I despise women who stick their husband's name onto their own when they get married. Either bloody well take his name or don't! It's a ridiculous American habit, and it never ends well. The husband never double-barrels her name with his, and they always get divorced in the end, and then she looks like a total idiot.'

Jacob was laughing now. 'You're always entertaining, Vicky,' he said appreciatively. 'I love your rants.'

'Just sack her, Jacob,' Victoria pressed on. 'Do it.' She finished her cocktail, needing Dutch courage for what she was about to say. 'Because if you don't – well, I've just had an amazing offer from Bilberry. They've been taken over by LVMH – you know, after all the scandal – and they want me to be their creative director.'

Bilberry was a high-end English leather company, which was now diversifying into stationery and other luxury goods. Its takeover by Moët Hennessy/Louis Vuitton had come after the sensational arrest of its CEO on an unrelated charge, and provided a huge influx of investment funds which allowed Bilberry to court a fashion editor as high-profile and prestigious as Victoria Glossop.

'They say they'll double my salary,' Victoria said smugly. 'And give me an unlimited expense account.'

'Right,' Jacob said, taking a frite, dipping it into the ramekin of mayonnaise and eating it with relish. 'But they won't let you live in New York, will they? Which is what you're dying to do.'

Victoria's grey eyes narrowed: she started to speak, but Jacob held up a hand, cutting her off.

'I know you have a whole spiel ready to convince me you're ready to up sticks and head for Bilberry, Vicky,' he said gently. 'And I know it'll be really convincing. But I'm not going to believe it.'

Her heart sank. She looked at the mound of glistening dark-pink steak tartare on her plate, surrounded by smaller piles of chopped red onion, capers, anchovies and lemon slices, topped by the miniature yolk of a quail's egg, presented in its half-shell. It was her favourite dish, but she had no appetite for it at all.

'I don't have to,' Jacob continued. 'You've made your case.'

It took a few moments for his words to sink in; when they did, Victoria froze, barely able to believe it.

'Give me a month,' Jacob said, forking up some sea bass and chewing it with gusto. 'I'll go back to New York and set the wheels in motion. I don't need to tell you not to breathe a word in the meantime. We'll bring you over in two months, max. You and Jeremy can have the Columbus Circle penthouse. Happy now?'

He glanced over at her affectionately. 'Oh come on, Vicky, say something. You got it. You got what you want!' He raised a hand, and a waiter shot over to answer Jacob's summons.

'Two glasses of the Pol Roger,' he ordered. 'We've got a celebration on our hands here.'

The champagne arrived almost instantly. Jacob touched his glass to Victoria's; she had recovered enough by now to lift her own and clink back.

'To the new editor of *US Style*,' Jacob toasted.

Victoria barely ever allowed champagne to touch her lips. The first taste was deliciously intoxicating, forbidden fruit, sweet and golden, peaches and almonds in a glass. She set the glass down before she was tempted to finish it in one go.

'Was that a test?' she asked. 'One of the games you play with yourself, Jacob – like those chess problems you love?'

'Why, Vicky, whatever could you mean?' Jacob asked, smiling, one arm thrown along the leather back of the banquette.

'I know you,' she said. 'You and your tests. I think you meant to give me the job all along, as long as I fought hard enough tonight.'

Jacob's smile deepened, but he didn't say a word.

'I learned that from you,' Victoria said, taking a delicate mouthful of steak tartare; it was delicious. 'How to test people. I remember every single one of the tests you put me through.'

'And you passed every one,' Jacob said with great satisfaction, taking a handful of frites. 'From the very start, when you were a little slip of a thing barely out of your teens.' He looked at her fondly. 'You had no hips at all, honey.'

'Just the way you like them, Jacob,' Victoria said dryly.

She was overwhelmed with excitement at having achieved her goal, adrenalin flooding through her veins like liquid silver. But she knew she had to act cool; Jacob didn't like women who gushed or sobbed or displayed any emotional excesses.

'Uh-huh,' Jacob said, quite unfazed. 'Just the way I like them.'

He reached out and squeezed Victoria's leg briefly, high up, his large hand sliding under the hem of her mini-skirt, almost wrapping entirely round her narrow upper thigh. It reminded her of a trainer she knew assessing a new piece of horseflesh, squeezing the horse's flanks, checking them for strength and alignment. Victoria smiled, proud of how well she'd kept her figure; she'd been an American size zero ever since she'd moved to the States and promptly slimmed down to what Manhattan considered an ideal weight.

'You haven't put on a pound,' he said appreciatively. 'Not a single pound. Good girl.'

His hand lingered for a moment, his index finger reaching

up just a little further, tracing slow seductive circles under her skirt, an intimate caress completely concealed from any passing waiter, anyone at the facing tables. The circles widened, deepened, his hand radiating heat, his finger just grazing the lace trim of her silk Myla French knickers; he flicked his fingertip against the lace, once, twice, a little tease, but also a gesture of control.

I know what underwear you have on, his gesture said. *I can touch it if I want.*

And Victoria's body responded. Her thighs relaxed on the banquette, easing apart just fractionally, her groin dipping down, demonstrating to Jacob that his clever, caressing fingers were having the effect he wanted. It was as if he had stroked a cat just enough to coax it into rich, heavy, satisfied purring before he removed his hand. Giving her leg a pat of approval, he returned to eating his main course with a complacent expression on his full lips.

How very Jacob, Victoria thought, raising her own fork to stir capers and onions into her finely-minced steak, tilting the quail's egg yolk into the mixture and placing the empty shell on the side of her plate. Her hand was perfectly steady, she was pleased to notice. *He's given me a hugely powerful position, and in return, he's had his little dominant moment, made the point that he has the ultimate power.*

Well, that's fine with me. I've always been happy to play Jacob's games; I've always come out of them exactly where I wanted to be.

Victoria heaved a long sigh of release. She was finally free to relish her dinner. For a moment, her fork toyed with the chopped anchovies, tempted to mix them into the tartare, but then she pushed them aside, her self-control as acute as ever; she loved anchovies, but the high salt content would cause her to retain water.

'So who are you seeing now, Jacob?' she asked, deftly directing the sexual tension that lingered at the table into safe waters.

'Jools,' Jacob said, and Victoria nodded at the name. Jools

Gosling was the latest hot British model, a runway sensation with her high-stepping walk, boyishly-cropped hair and flat-chested, long-waisted figure. 'Lovely girl. She's on a shoot in Morocco for a few days.'

'Aww, what a shame, Jacob,' Victoria teased. 'I bet you still want it every night, don't you?'

'Hey, take me to Annabel's after dinner and I'll pick up a slim young thing,' Jacob said easily. 'One of your upper-class girls. I like 'em, you know that. Some Camilla or Vanessa or Florence. See, I even know all the names. It's not like Jools and I are exclusive.'

'You know, Jacob, you should get married,' Victoria observed. 'To a nice Camilla or Vanessa or Florence. It's about time, don't you think? When the models you're dating are less than half your age . . . Jools is barely twenty.'

Jacob's thick eyebrows shot up. 'Marriage? Honey, I did that once, in a galaxy far, far away, a loooong time ago,' he said, drawing out the vowel for comic effect. 'And that was enough. I've learned my lesson. Besides,' he added, reaching out to lay a hand on hers, 'I like my serious women really smart. You know that. Your English aristocrats, they're not so bright. No hips, big brain: that's my ideal woman.'

'Well, I'll happily come with you into Annabel's,' Victoria said, finishing her steak tartare with satisfaction. 'And you can pick up some skinny Sloane, spin her on her axis, and show her the time of her life.'

Dinner at the Wolseley, a celebration toast in full view of all the tables that count, and then off to Annabel's, Victoria thought, anticipating the visit to London's most exclusive nightclub, its membership list packed with hereditary titles, where Lady Gaga, no less, had played a private set just last year. *And we'll have another celebration toast there. Jacob told me not to breathe a word about my new job, but I won't need to. London gossip will do it for me.*

Jennifer Lane Davis is going to feel a cold wind blowing over the Atlantic and down her neck very, very soon. Better start packing up your desk now, Jennifer.

In her mind, Victoria blew her rival a little goodbye kiss.

Bye bye, Jen. Don't let the door of the editor's office hit you on the way out.

Coco

'Absolutely. Yes, Victoria. I will. Okay then, good . . .' Coco's voice tailed off as she realised that her boss had already hung up on her. Victoria saw no point in staying on the line after she'd conveyed what she needed to. Coco set the phone back on the bar table.

'All okay?' her sister Tiff asked, slurring her words a little, her eyes bright with alcohol. 'Whasshe want now?'

'To make sure her driver's waiting outside the restaurant for her and Jacob Dupleix,' Coco said, a thrill running through her at merely saying his name; he'd been in the building today but hadn't come into *Style*, which had been a huge disappointment. Ambitious as ever, Coco had been dying to impress the head of the company with her efficiency and organisational skills. 'They're going on to Annabel's. That's a really posh club in Berkeley Square,' she added for her sister's benefit.

'So d'you need to stay up all night and sort out her sodding car to take her home 'cos she's too bloody lazy to do it herself?' Tiff persisted.

'No, that's the great thing about Annabel's,' Coco said with a sigh of relief. 'The doorman takes care of that. And parking in Berkeley Square at ten-thirty in the evening is a lot easier than

Piccadilly or St James's at dinnertime – the driver can wait close by till she's ready to go.'

'Poor bastard,' Tiff muttered.

'Oh, he's paid well, don't worry,' Coco said, rolling her eyes. 'I should know, I process all the bills. Besides, she won't be that late. Victoria never is. She'll make a big entrance, have a VLT and a mineral water, be sure everyone important sees her with Jacob, and then go.'

'She sounds like a total fucking nightmare,' Tiff said, throwing herself back in her seat and crossing her legs sloppily, nearly flashing her knickers.

'She's the best editor I'll ever work with,' Coco said with utter seriousness. 'It's like a crash course in magazine editing. I'm learning so much.'

She took a small sip of her own VLT. Before Victoria, Coco had drunk margaritas, cosmos, daiquiris; sweet, girlie drinks. Now, after months of studying and committing to memory every detail of Victoria's behaviour, she wouldn't have dreamed of it. Victoria's horror at a model's confession that she had been knocking back mango daiquiris the night before a shoot had been legendary. Victoria had stormed up and down the photographer's studio, moving faster in her Gina heels than most people did in trainers, screaming that she could see the sugar and alcohol bloat on the girl's body, that the girl was an idiot – had no one told her how many calories there were in fruit and rum, and sugar? She, Victoria, was ringing the model's booker immediately to rip her to pieces for not keeping her girls under stricter control.

The model had burst into hysterics, the booker had apologised profusely and sent Victoria a bouquet so big that Coco had staggered under its weight when it arrived, the shoot had been re-booked at considerable expense, and the model had turned up with forty-eight hours of clean living under her belt. Coco had taken some of the Polaroids from the first, aborted shoot and the one that had gone ahead, to compare: Victoria, she realised, had been entirely correct. The model's jawline, cheeks, hips were all more distinct, more photogenic in the second set; in the first, there was a minimal puffiness on her face that had entirely disappeared by the time of the rescheduled shoot.

Other staffers on *Style* had rolled their eyes and complained about their editor's insane perfectionism. Coco had not.

'So d'you like it here?' asked Emily, the assistant beauty editor, returning from her cigarette break on the outside terrace. Coming to the bar high up in the Oxo Tower, on the south bank of the Thames, had been her idea. Night had fallen, and the light spilling from the high glass Embankment interchange made a breathtaking spectacle, especially if you had grabbed a window table and were sitting in front of the sheer cantilevered glass sheets that offered uninterrupted views of one of London's most beautiful panoramas. The Oxo bar was a destination in itself, a place to see and be seen, and its sweep of white bar, its pale chairs and black tables, were a deliberately neutral backdrop against which the pretty, shiny clientele could peacock.

'I always say it's better to sit on this side of the river, so you can look at the other,' Emily drawled, sliding her cigarette packet into her baguette bag. 'It's so much prettier. That's the one downer about going to the Savoy – you have to look at the South Bank Centre – all that ghastly 1960s concrete.'

She eased herself down carefully into the leather bucket chair next to Tiff – carefully, because her skinny jeans were tight enough to cut off her circulation. Like many of the aristocratic girls at *Style*, Emily had the smooth pale skin of a delicately-painted wax doll, and a long tangle of blonde hair with which she fiddled incessantly, tossing it from shoulder to shoulder. Her jaw was too square, her lips too thin; without the cascading mane of hair, she would not have been considered a beauty, and she knew it. All the *Style* girls were acutely aware of their physical strengths and weaknesses.

But Emily was not a typical posh girl in other respects. Unlike most of the other Jacquettas and Savannahs and Katies, who could smell a girl from the lower classes at fifty paces, Emily had been nice to Coco from the moment Coco had started work. Emily had stopped to chat every time she passed Coco's desk, dropped off samples from the beauty desk's extensive collection, even passed on an appointment for a facial that she couldn't make herself. Coco was aware that there was some self-interest in Emily's friendship, a hope that Coco would put in a good word for her with the boss, but Coco had been so grateful to have someone actually hang out at her desk and chat to her as if she were a fellow human that she didn't care.

Besides, Coco thought cynically, we're all out for ourselves in fashion. It's totally cut-throat. So what if Emily thinks there'll be an advantage in befriending me? She's got me some really great Estée Lauder face cream that would have cost a hundred pounds if I'd had to pay for it. And that Dermalogica facial at Comptons in Covent Garden made my skin glow for days afterwards.

Coco had never had a proper, Eastern European-style facial before: as well as a massage, gentle peel and moisturising, it included steaming her face and then squeezing out sebum from blocked pores, most of which seemed to be on and around her nose. It had been excruciating, but utterly worth it, leaving her skin delicately pink and exquisitely smooth. Now, like many of London's beauty and fashion editors, she went religiously to Compton's every month, and got her blowdries and hair colour there too.

Emily's always given really good advice about where to go, Coco thought. She's taken me out to a lot of amazing launch parties – and she's come out with me and my sister tonight, which can't be much fun for her.

Tiff had come into London from Luton for the evening, making it clear that she wanted a grand tour of her younger sister's new life now that Coco had snagged her dream job. Not only that, Tiff had been tasked by their worried mother to check out what Coco was getting up to in the evenings, and meet at least one person she worked with. Ever since Coco had started at *Style*, she'd been absolutely exhausted. She didn't go out at the weekends any more, conserving all her energy for the brutal weekday grind. She was expected to be at work by eight-thirty and rarely left the office before seven; even then, an imperious Victoria might call out of hours with an idea she had had for the next day's work, needing Coco to make a note of it, demand a last-minute restaurant booking, or tell Coco to organise a car, or ring a photographer in New York, LA, Rio di Janeiro – quite indifferent to the fact that Coco might have to stay up late or get up before dawn to compensate for the time difference.

And of course, for all this hard work, she was paid practically nothing – certainly not enough to afford to leave home and live closer to work. She was lucky even to be paid at all – the way the job market was at the moment, Victoria could have got an unpaid intern as her assistant if she hadn't been so picky about who she wanted in the position.

'Yeah, it's okay here, I s'pose,' Tiff answered Emily, shrugging and reaching for her Singapore Sling.

Coco was embarrassed by her sister's dismissive tone. She knew it was because Tiff was overwhelmed by both the chicness of the Oxo bar and the confidence that Emily projected, the gift of an expensive upbringing in the Home Counties and an equally expensive private education.

'It's *so* much nicer here since Harvey Nicks took it over and did a revamp,' Emily said, reaching for her white-wine spritzer. 'It was a bit of a hole before, frankly. Do you remember, Coco?'

'Oh, um, yeah, of course,' Coco said quickly, though this was the first time she'd ever been to the Oxo bar.

'Crappy service and dodgy drinks,' Emily said. 'I honestly thought they watered them down!' She laughed, a bell-like peal, tossing her hair back. 'But now it's *so* much nicer. And of course, I know Raffy—' she waved at one of the handsome young Sloane boys behind the bar – 'so he's taking good care of us.'

'Coco!' Tiff echoed, shaking her head. 'I still can't get my head round it. Mum did her nut when she found out you'd changed your name, Jodie.'

'You changed your *name*?' Emily said, eyes widening.

Coco wanted the floor to open up and swallow her. She'd assumed that Davinia had told everyone at *Style* that Victoria had made her change her name – it was a tasty piece of gossip, and she couldn't expect Davinia to keep her secret. The *Style* girls might have giggled behind her back, but no one had been nasty enough to taunt her with it directly. Now the humiliation was direct and immediate, and made even worse by the fact that she knew how very posh Emily was.

'I didn't actually change it myself,' Coco said, unable to meet Emily's eyes. 'It was Victoria. She didn't think "Jodie" was – well, fashion-magazine enough.'

'Bloody snob, if you ask me,' Tiff said bluntly. 'Do you know what Mum said when she heard? She said Gran's aunt was a housemaid – you know, like in the TV series, cleaning out fires and everything. And when she got hired, the lady she was working for asked her name – which was Mary – and said she couldn't be called Mary, 'cos she had a friend called Mary and it would be too confusing. She told Gran's aunt that she'd have to change her name to Jane. She said that was a better name for a housemaid anyway.'

Emily's forehead squinched up in tiny lines. 'It's not *quite* the same though, is it?' She said, sounding distressed. 'I mean, really, Victoria's *helping* Coco.'

Tiff snorted inelegantly.

But then, nothing about Tiff was elegant, Coco thought disloyally, seeing her sister with a fresh eye. She felt awful and guilty, judging her sister like this. It was very wrong to look down on your family, to reject where you came from just because you'd found a lifestyle you thought was better. The Raeburns were an enviably close family; Coco and Tiff still lived at home with their mum, a kindergarten teacher, and their dad, a baggage supervisor at Luton airport. Their brother Craig worked at the airport too, and though he had moved out with his fiancée, they lived only four streets away from the Raeburn family home. The children had wanted for nothing growing up, and their parents, apart from the normal squabbles, were a happy couple. It had been an enviably safe and secure upbringing, and Coco knew how lucky she was.

I'm the only one born with the ambitious gene, she thought ruefully. *The only one who wanted to get out of Luton and head for the big city*. None of the others understood her drive and restlessness. Craig and Tiff would be in Luton all their lives, Craig at the airport, Tiff at Boots as a sales assistant. She was supposed to be saving, too, for a deposit on a flat, but most of her spare cash was spent on going out and having a good time; her indulgent parents didn't seem to mind.

'I don't see how it's helping her,' Tiff snapped. 'Changing her name, working her like a fricking slave all day and all night.' She realised that the skirt of her bright red jersey dress had risen up again, and pulled it down.

Top Shop, Coco thought, looking at Tiff's outfit. Not even that cheap, but not well-made. That jersey fabric's so thin it's almost see-through, and that elastic belt's digging into her.

'And she's starving herself,' Tiff went on, looking at her younger sister. 'Mum's going mental about you not eating dinner with us any more. Not even the Sunday roast. She says you're living on bird food.'

'I'm a size ten now, Tiff,' Coco protested. 'That's not starving myself.'

Tiff rolled her eyes. The Raeburns weren't a skinny family, and both Tiff and her mother were built along substantial lines. The weight suited them, and Tiff was never short of admirers; she had a personality as big as her generous curves.

'Mum cares about you,' Tiff said firmly. 'We all do. She just doesn't want to see you all stressed out and bony.' She glanced at Emily's exiguous frame. 'No offence,' she added, looking down complacently at her own plump legs.

'Oh, not at all! Do you come up to London a lot, Tiff?' Emily asked politely.

Coco was hugely relieved at the change of subject. Emily has really good manners, she observed. Victoria wasn't the only one Coco was learning from; Emily's upper-middle-class, head-prefect, well-bred social etiquette was something she wanted to emulate. Tiffany was a typical Raeburn; they were all blunt to a fault, never beat around the bush. That might be how Victoria Glossop operated, but Coco was at the bottom of the pile, not the top, and she couldn't afford to be as curt as her boss. I need to be able to talk like Emily, Coco thought. Be diplomatic and tactful and handle people like she does.

'I should come up more,' Tiff answered, finishing her Singapore Sling with gusto and letting out a small burp. 'Keep an eye on this one. Sometimes she doesn't get home till well late. I wouldn't mind if you were out pulling, Jodie – *Coco*,' she corrected herself, grimacing, 'but I know lots of times you're sitting on your bum in that office, having no fun at all. Like last week! You didn't get back till past midnight, and you missed Gran's birthday party. Mum's still moaning about it to me.'

'Tiff, my job's really important,' Coco said defensively. 'That time I was organising logistics for a shoot in Havana that went arse-up. You remember, Emily?'

She turned to her work colleague and saw Emily flinch at the words 'arse-up', a flinch she quickly converted into a nod of agreement. It was the tiniest of involuntary movements, and no one but Coco, who was hyper-alert, would have noticed. Fuck, Coco thought, swiftly consigning that word to the dustbin as well. It's my accent. Posh girls can swear as much as they want – 'shit' and 'fuck' and 'bugger' sound brilliant in their accent. But in my bog-standard one . . . not so much.

'The fashion director had food poisoning,' Coco told her sister, 'the photographer went AWOL with two local rentboys, and the model was freaking because her medication got confiscated by Cuban customs.'

'What kind of medication?' Tiff's eyes were wide. 'Oi!' she shouted at a nearby waiter. 'I'll have another one of these Singapore thingies. I need to get bevvied up.' She looked at Coco and Emily. 'You two want another? My shout.'

'No, thanks,' they said in unison.

'Bor-*ring*!'

Tiff was well on her way to being drunk now. Coco knew the pattern. Tif would get louder and more friendly, try to dance on tables, start molesting waiters, and then, with little warning, crash like a giant oak. Coco would have to make sure that was her last cocktail, then pour Tiff into a frighteningly expensive cab. They'd have missed a direct Luton train from London Bridge, and no way could Coco manage to manoeuvre Tiff, in her drunken state, on and off the two tube trains it would take to get them from Waterloo to King's Cross, then haul her over to the St Pancras platform for the late-evening Luton train.

God, I'd love to be able to afford to live in London, or at least on a tube line, Coco thought wistfully. But low-level fashion magazine jobs paid practically nothing. That was why the magazines were mostly staffed by girls like Emily – ones with private incomes and parents who bought them flats or subsidised their rent.

'Let's get some food into you, Tiff,' Coco said, reaching for the bar menu. 'Oh, look, spicy chips. Shall I order you some of those?'

'Mmn, chips,' Tiff said, grabbing the menu. 'Yum! We all getting some, then?' Even in her tipsy state, she couldn't fail to see the recoil of both Emily and Coco at this suggestion.

'Oh, no thanks,' Emily said swiftly. 'I'm actually really full from lunch.'

'Yes, me too,' Coco chimed in. 'I had a big plate of brown

rice salad.'

'You had a plateful of *brown rice*?' Emily said unguardedly.

Oh bollocks, Coco thought gloomily. I thought that was a healthy choice – it's full of fibre, isn't it? And there were peppers and spring onions in it – and some feta. Well, quite a lot of feta, I suppose.

She put her hand defensively over her tummy, which bulged out more than it had done this morning. Getting down to a size 10 hadn't been that difficult, driven as she was; she'd eaten more sensibly, cut out Danish pastries and sausage rolls, banned herself from picking up breakfast from her local Greggs bakery, chosen fruit salad for dessert and stopped drinking full-fat milk in her coffee. In addition, she'd found a studio called Pilates HQ in Islington that offered a free starter class, and it had been such hard work that she'd known straight away it was doing her good.

Coco had never been sporty, and so she had no idea about how to exercise properly; the few Pilates classes that she'd done so far had left her sore, activating muscles she'd never felt before. The teacher said that Pilates gave you a corset of muscles, tightened up everything, as if you were wearing an invisible pair of Spanx. She could already feel the difference; her waist was nipping in, her love handles were harder to pinch. By the time she'd started at *Style*, she was wearing size 10 skirts – and not size 10 from one of those shops that did vanity sizing to make you feel better, but proper size 10s from French Connection and Karen Millen.

Until the Pilates corset was fully formed, Coco was wearing Spanx constantly – okay, not *actual* Spanx, because they were very expensive and she couldn't afford them, but the M&S version. That wasn't a hardship; they were very comfortable, and she liked the feeling of having her tummy sucked in. Dressing up tonight, she'd managed to get into a size 10 dress, silk, tightly-fitted, in a pale grey that was very on trend, and accessorised it with a heavy tumble of carefully-chosen and layered necklaces that had drawn an approving nod from Victoria as she left for the evening. She'd practically bankrupted herself on the faux-snakeskin silver Stella McCartney shoes, but they were an investment, she'd told herself, wincing as she handed over the credit card; they'd go with everything. Her hair was straightened and pulled back into a smooth ponytail, and her green Urban Decay mascara brought out the matching green flecks in her hazel eyes. After a few months at *Style*, watching everyone else's dress sense, learning from them how to evolve her own way of interpreting the latest trends, she was already infinitely more sophisticated than she had been three months ago.

Well, of course I bloody am, she thought ironically. I'm called Coco now, aren't I?

She knew, however, that she was expected to lose some more weight. She couldn't, for instance, have borrowed anything from the fashion cupboard; its stock was much smaller than a size 10. She still had a tummy, while Emily's, under her clinging Comptoir des Cotonniers silk top, was practically concave.

And Tiff's – well, it wasn't fair to sit Tiff next to a skinny *Style* girl and make comparisons. More importantly, Tiff wasn't making those kinds of comparisons herself; she was perfectly happy as she was, with her plump bosoms, round tummy, and the generous thighs which the thin red jersey of her dress was straining to contain. Tiff had got herself up by her definition of smart tonight, heavy eyeliner all around her eyes, hair pulled back into a high ponytail, a big chunky Swarovski necklace sitting high on her collarbones, and though she looked very out of place in the Oxo bar, she had a confidence about her that came from knowing the men she fancied all fancied her right back.

Tiff knows who she is, and she's happy with herself, Coco thought, looking at her sister, who was now flirting with the waiter who'd brought her Singapore Sling in a manner that bordered perilously on sexual harassment. Coco's glance moved sideways to her new friend, so different from her sister in every way, belonging to a completely different tribe. Tiff was like a sturdy carthorse to Emily's glossy show pony.

Emily knows who she is as well. Where she comes from, the kind of man she's going to end up with, what she's going to call her kids.

So where do I fit in? Coco found herself asking. And the answer was almost immediate.

Stuck in the middle, in no-man's land. You don't know who you are or where you fit in. Luton's behind you, but you're not a Style girl yet; they're all so immaculate, so self-assured.

Tiff and Emily might be secure in the knowledge of who they were, but that wasn't enough for Coco. Her drive, her aspiration to make something more of herself, to push herself as hard as she could to achieve goals that would be out of reach for almost anyone else, singled her out, set her apart. Coco's dream was to have Victoria's job: one day, she told herself. One day I'll be editor of *UK Style*. But being set apart, even if it was her own choice, could feel horribly lonely sometimes.

Everything took a back seat to her ambition. Friendships, family, relationships. Tiff was giggling with the waiter now, pointing over at Coco.

'That's my lil' sister!' she was slurring happily. 'Pretty, isn't she? You single, mate? 'Cos she is. You should ask her out – she's got it all. Looks, brains and a fuck-off posh job.'

Coco squirmed uncomfortably, but the waiter, a handsome, smooth-skinned twenty-something with dark-chocolate eyes, followed Tiff's indicating finger and smiled at Coco appreciatively. Tiff knew Coco's type perfectly: dark hair, liquid brown eyes, skin a few shades darker than her own pink-and-white colouring.

'You got a girlfriend?' Tiff was asking the waiter. 'Or a boyfriend?'

He could easily have said he did and walked away; instead he stayed, still smiling at Coco, as he said, 'No, I'm young, free and single.'

'Whee!' Tiff clapped as he went on, directing his attention to Coco: 'So what's this posh job you do, then?'

'I work at *Style*,' Coco said. 'We both do.' She glanced at Emily.

Flatteringly, the waiter barely looked at Emily; he was concentrating solely on her.

'Cool! Maybe we can go out sometime,' he said. 'D'you have a card?'

Coco produced one from her bag and handed it to him; he put it in his pocket with a flourish.

'I'll be right back with your chips,' he said to Tiff, giving Coco a last smile over his shoulder as he turned away.

Tiff was grinning like a madwoman. 'Am I a good sister or what?'

'He is awfully sexy,' Emily said enthusiastically. 'You lucky thing, Coco.'

Coco shrugged. 'I hope he's not looking for anything serious,' she said. 'I've barely even got time for a one-night stand.'

'Aww!' Tiff slurped up a big gulp of Singapore Sling. 'Tell you what, if I had to choose between my job and getting my end away, there'd be no fricking contest! Right?' She elbowed Emily, who giggled nervously. 'Right? What kind of bloody job is *that*?'

The only one I want, Coco thought intensely. *The one I'd sacrifice everything for.*

Tiff was cross-examining Emily about her love life, and Emily was loosening up, giggling more genuinely, spilling the details with more and more enthusiasm. They've got more in common with each other than they do with me, Coco realised in shock. Tiff and Emily believed in a work-life balance: for Coco, her work was her entire life. The waiter, returning with Tiff's spicy chips, winked sexily at Coco. He was gorgeous. And she knew that if he rang her, she was going to turn him down. She couldn't afford a single distraction right now. To win the prize, she had to keep her eyes fixed straight on it, not deviate for a moment. She couldn't afford to look away.

Tears pricked unexpectedly at Coco's eyelids. It couldn't be the alcohol; she was only on her second VLT. Once she'd have been almost as tipsy as her sister; now she was measuring and dosing everything, learning self-control in a series of small, solitary life lessons. She was changing, breaking out of her chrysalis, and it hurt. *Fake it till you make it*, she'd read in an article years ago. Well, she was faking it successfully enough, but she was constantly afraid of being laughed at, mocked for thinking she could truly be a part of *Style*. Could she really manage to blend in with girls whose background was so much smarter, whose education was so much more privileged than her own?

All she had to hang onto was her knowledge that she was really, really good at her job, the hardest worker at the entire magazine. And sometimes, that didn't quite feel as if it was enough to keep her going.

Coco swallowed back the tears.

I'll be editor of UK Style in ten years' time, she promised herself. *All this work, all this struggle's going to be worth it in the end. So what if I have to skip one of Gran's birthday parties? So what if I can't date for a while? So what if I can't eat Mum's shepherd's pie or Greggs sausage rolls? I'd give up more than that to have Victoria's job. And nothing's going to stand in my way.*

Mireille

Already the temperature in the Moroccan desert was 40 degrees Centigrade, though it was only a couple of hours after dawn. Everyone on the *Style* shoot was sweating profusely; the make-up artists and fashion team were huddling in the tents that had been pitched to give them shade, fanning themselves and complaining in low voices about the heat, the stink of diesel from the jeeps and the big noisy generator, the smell of camel and horse dung, and how all their products were starting to melt in the heat. Jools, the tall, skinny, incredibly long-waisted English model booked for the shoot, white as a magnolia, with a shock of red curly hair that had been teased into a foot-high Afro, had to be followed by a Berber with a parasol at all times, keeping her white skin protected from the scorching sun; however, she was much taller than the parasol-carrier, and the poor man was wrenching his back with the effort of holding it up high enough to cover her head.

Even with the shadow from the sunshade, the glaring rays of the sun bounced off the glittering grains of sand and reflected up onto Jools's face. She blinked, hard; she was trying not to cry and spoil the elaborate metallic make-up she was wearing. Already she was sweating, but she didn't want to go into one of the tents, knowing that she'd be met with stony, hostile gazes. The shoot had barely started, and already it had run into a huge problem, which everyone seemed to be thinking was her fault . . .

'Did the stupid bitch actually say she could ride?' she heard the photographer's assistant ask. He was standing quite a way from her, across the other side of the wadi, so he must have pitched his voice deliberately high for it to carry over to her.

'Apparently. Silly twat,' snapped the photographer, feeling in the pockets of his safari jacket for a cigarette. 'Bloody models will say anything to get a job. Did I tell you about the one last year who said she could swim like a fish for an Italian *Vogue* spread? The little cow had some phobia about putting her head underwater! I said to Franca, "Let's throw her in the deep end and get some great shots of her drowning"!'

Jools's tears were perilously close now. She swallowed in a desperate attempt to ward them off. The man beside her adjusted the parasol, staring up curiously at the bizarre white girl, tall as a giraffe, looking like an alien who had just dropped to earth and wasn't getting a friendly reception from the locals.

I can ride – sort of, she thought miserably. I mean, I've done pictures on horseback before. I laid down on one for that Elizabeth Arden perfume campaign. I just didn't realise the horse would be so jittery – and then he got extra wound-up by the camels . . .

The foil trim of her linen T-shirt was itching, and the long-sleeved layered top the stylist had pulled over it was too hot for this blazing weather, beginning to dampen with her sweat. But that was fashion for you: you shot winter in summer, summer in winter, swimsuits in February and autumn layered dressing in what was going to be a 50-degree day in the Moroccan desert . . .

Hooves sounded in the distance. The camels stirred; decorated lavishly with bright harnesses trimmed with tiny golden bells, they jingled as they moved, their ponderous heads turning towards the approaching horse as it crested the far dune. It was a breathtaking sight. The huge dark stallion, its dark chocolate coat gleaming lightly with sweat, galloped effortlessly through the orange sand, its hooves moving majestically, its slim rider straight as a wand on its back. From a distance, it might have been a slight boy riding the stallion, a young Berber who had grown up on horseback, a *keffiyeh* wound around his head to protect his face from sun and blowing sand, its ends trailing picturesquely behind him in the desert breeze. It was only as the horse and rider drew nearer, slowing at the rider's command into an easy trot, that it became clear that it was a woman seated so elegantly in the saddle, her hands light on the reins, drawing the stallion to a halt in front of Jools with seemingly effortless control.

It was not a *keffiyeh* covering her head, but a vintage silk Hermès scarf, wrapped around her neck and knotted at the back. She wore a simple white cotton shirt, tucked into beige jodhpurs drawn tightly into her narrow waist with a wide woven leather belt. Her riding boots were black and highly polished, catching a flash of sunlight as she kicked one foot free of its stirrup, swung her leg over the horse and simultaneously freed the other foot, dropping to the ground in a single, smooth motion, one hand retaining a grip on the reins. She patted the horse's neck; he whinnied in appreciation of the exercise she had just given him.

Mireille Grenier, fashion director of *US Style,* one of the most influential women in the entire industry, looking like a 1940s film star, beckoned to Jools, who was staring at her with her mouth open. Although Mireille moved with the grace and ease of a much younger woman, close-up, the lines around her eyes and mouth, the fineness of her skin, indicated her true age, the early fifties. Her huge green eyes, glowing now with the excitement of the wild ride through the desert to calm down the stallion, rested their gaze on Jools, who was goggling at her in heroine-worship.

'Come and take the reins,' Mireille said, smiling at the young model. 'Make friends with him, now that I have tired him out for you. He'll be very good from now on, *n'est-ce pas, mon vieux?'*

She patted the stallion in valediction as she handed over the reins to Jools.

'Bring him some water,' she commanded no one in particular. 'We can start in five minutes. He will be quiet and good for her.'

'Mireille, you're a bloody miracle!' the photographer said in devout tones, chucking his cigarette on the sand and grinding the heel of his boot into it. 'Thank fuck for you. I thought we were buggered!'

With the same enigmatic smile, Mireille went towards the fashion tent; its occupants were gathered at the opening, gaping at her, a young assistant in the forefront holding out a chilled bottle of water.

'I didn't know you could ride!' the assistant gushed worshipfully, as everyone else chimed in with dramatic gasps of appreciation. 'That was like something out of a film – that horse so jumpy and shying away, not letting Jools get on its back or anything, and then you just walked up to it and vaulted on and rode off over the hill, and we were all freaking out a bit, but I mean, you obviously knew *exactly* what you were doing . . .'

She ran out of breath as Mireille finished the water and handed her back the empty bottle.

'All animals must be exercised well before a shoot,' Mireille said in her light French accent. 'It is an absolute rule. I gave precise instructions yesterday to the Berbers that the horse must be tired out before they brought him here.' She shrugged her narrow shoulders. '*Tant pis*. We will deduct 15 per cent of their fee.'

'Yes, Mireille,' the assistant said instantly.

'Tell Valerie to check Jools's make-up,' Mireille said, entering the tent, crossing to a table on which was resting the Birkin bag that travelled everywhere with her. 'Her eyes looked damp to me. And adjust her top. It is crooked, *un tout petit peu*.'

Two assistants shot out of the tent to obey her commands as Mireille pulled her BlackBerry from her bag and checked its screen. Even in the Moroccan desert, there was some signal, and Mireille was as aware as a professional spy of the need to be constantly informed of the latest developments in the fashion world; it was one of the reasons why, over decades, she had maintained her position as a key player in a viciously competitive environment. During that time, she had cultivated informants under the guise of gossip; gradually, as Mireille rose to the prominence of her current job, she had trained up a whole raft of assistants who had gone on to work on magazines all over the world – an entire network of fashionistas loyal to her who knew that Mireille would return in favours whatever snippets of information they could provide.

A text had come in. From London. Mireille's delicately plucked eyebrows rose as she perused its contents.

So Jacob is in London – well, I knew he was going there. And having dinner with Victoria. Again, not a surprise. But celebrating afterwards at Annabel's? Raising glasses in a toast?

Slowly, Mireille slid the BlackBerry into her bag. This could mean only one thing. Jennifer Lane Davis's days were numbered in single digits. Jennifer was out, and Victoria, two years early, was in.

Inwardly, Mireille sighed. Victoria is coming back to New York, thinking she can rule the roost. Well, it will be a battle royal, but I will win. I always do. Victoria may be a superb editor, but she has no grasp of subtlety. None at all.

Eh bien. I will make my preparations.

They were waiting for her outside. She walked to the opening of the tent, noticed all the faces turning to her with expressions of awe and devotion. Jools was being boosted onto the stallion by the Berber; she settled into the saddle, taking the reins with confidence now. It was an instant shot. The tall, white girl on the dark horse, the layers of her clothes blowing picturesquely in the breeze, the gold of her huge earrings and the foil trim of her top catching the sun, and behind them, the rising orange dune, the desert sands.

A new editor to battle. To vanquish. Yet another younger woman trying to make her mark, control my work. Suddenly, Mireille felt every year of her age; no, even more – as old as those sands, flowing gently in the wind.

And then a smile curved her lips.

But like the sands, I have seen so much. People have tried to ride roughshod over me, as they have tried to conquer the desert, and they have all failed, slipped away like the wind – while I am still here. Victoria may try to impose her will on me, but she'll fail like all the others.

And I will endure.

Victoria

On a wide, leafy street in Notting Hill lined with white stucco-fronted houses, the current editor of *UK Style – though not for much longer*, she thought triumphantly – was standing under her pillared porch. Extracting her door key from her bag, she unlocked the front door that was stylishly painted in Farrow & Ball's Castle Gray gloss. Lesser mortals who had worn five-inch high heels since eight o'clock that morning would have kicked their shoes off as soon as they closed their front door behind them. But Victoria was made of sterner stuff, and she tripped along the hall as easily as if she were wearing ballet pumps. It didn't hurt, of course, now that she regularly had Botox injections in the balls of her feet to amortise the pain caused by the near-constant wearing of vertiginous heels.

'Darling! How did it go?'

Her husband Jeremy was up, of course, as Victoria had known he would be, waiting to hear the news, sprawled on the big squashy sofa in his office. Jeremy had been playing poker online: his avatar was seated at a green baize table on the screen of his gigantic flat-screen television, a miniature version of Jeremy dressed in pyjamas, with the same wildly curling hair and small round glasses. The real Jeremy dropped his console and swivelled round to look at her as she stood in the doorway.

'I folded,' he said. 'What happened? Oh my God—'

He jumped up. Jeremy could read her expression immediately, even though Victoria seemed as cool and poised as ever, quirking an eyebrow as she watched her husband scrutinise her face.

'I know your tells,' he said with huge satisfaction.

'Oh please,' Victoria said, sounding bored. 'Spare me the poker vocabulary.'

But the gleam in her eyes, the slight curve of her mouth, were clear giveaways to someone who knew her as well as Jeremy did: he clapped his hands, his smile as wide as hers was restrained.

'You got it!' he yodelled. 'You got New York!'

Victoria dropped her bag onto the back of the sofa. 'Two months,' she said. 'And not a word to anyone till Jacob breaks it to Jennifer.'

'Oh my God! You're amazing.' Jeremy fumbled his bare feet into his fluffy slippers and skidded around the sofa, bumbling between it and the armchair, enfolding his wife in a warm, flannel-pyjamaed embrace. 'You did it! Two years early! That's just wonderful.'

Victoria was happy enough with her triumph to allow Jeremy to hug her for longer than the few seconds she usually permitted; when he pulled away and beamed at her, she even returned his smile with one of her own.

'Jacob says we can have the Columbus Circle penthouse,' she said, turning away and walking into the kitchen.

'Oh.' Jeremy looked briefly downcast. 'Just until I find us a house? I mean, this is it, right? We're going to be in New York for ages. I do want a house of our own, Vicky. A proper home for us.'

Victoria slipped off her mink jacket, and Jeremy took it, draping it over the back of one of the bar stools that were lined up on one side of the shiny, natural-oak kitchen island. She slid elegantly onto another bar stool, custom-built, the same natural oak, upholstered with a light yellow leather seat. Victoria preferred the bar stools to the chairs at the kitchen table; she liked to be as high up as possible.

'The penthouse has three bedrooms and a huge terrace,' she pointed out. 'It's probably got more square footage than most of the houses you'll look at in New York.'

'But a house is more – *family*,' Jeremy persisted, pushing his glasses up his nose with one finger. 'A house is a home. Come on, Vicky. Let me have this one. You'll never be there anyway.'

He said this without an ounce of reproach in his voice. Jeremy had no illusions about his wife, and never had. They had been together ever since university, where Jeremy had been a brilliant mathematician and Victoria the editor of a glossy magazine which she had founded, secured advertising and sponsorship for, and spent every waking moment working on. She had barely scraped a third, but that hadn't mattered; the magazine had been her springboard to her first job at *Vogue*. Even at university, Victoria had already been a legend, her name spoken in bated breath, dire warnings issued about getting out of her way if you didn't want to be mown down. Everyone was frightened of her; she was so polished, so ambitious, so obviously the star of their year, burning so brightly she would scorch you if you got too close.

But Jeremy had been undaunted. There was nothing he found more attractive than a powerful woman, and from the moment he had seen Victoria at a party he had pursued her with a singlemindedness that had been the talk of their entire year. Victoria wasn't looking for a relationship, didn't have time for one, wasn't even particularly interested in men; but Jeremy literally would not take no for an answer. He had applied the skills he was honing in his extremely advanced studies of higher maths and the philosophy of science, and used them to calculate how he could convince Victoria that she would be better off with him in her life.

Gradually, Victoria had realised that things ran more smoothly with Jeremy around. He ran errands for her, did her laundry, cooked her dinner and made sure her fridge was stocked with the few foods she would allow herself to eat. He escorted her to parties and waited patiently while she worked the room. After graduation, he took a job at a merchant bank as a research analyst and suggested she move into his South Kensington flat, as her salary as an assistant at *Vogue* would scarcely allow her to rent a shoebox in Acton Town. He made himself indispensable, and Victoria began to realise that she couldn't do better than Jeremy if she wanted a long-term partner. How rare was it to find a man who would always put her interests before his own, celebrate her achievements, be, in short, a traditional old-fashioned wife of the kind that barely existed any more – while still earning a good salary?

And clearly, she needed a partner, if only for social reasons. Single women weren't invited out half as much as girls who were tidily paired-up. Nor did she want to be the stereotypical ice queen, the awful sexist judgement on women that Meryl Streep's character embodied in the film of *The Devil Wears Prada*, which preached that career women couldn't keep a man because they worked too hard. Victoria would never let someone say that about her, never let herself be seen as vulnerable nor an object of pity. So when, after several years of co-habitation, Jeremy began to drop hints that it was time for them to get married, Victoria found herself shrugging, thinking, Why not? and researching an engagement ring that was the exact same shade of grey as her eyes.

It had been a surprise, however, that even her father had approved of Jeremy's proposal.

'Clever girl,' Judge Glossop had said, nodding benevolently. 'He'll give you your head in everything, run the house for you and pull in a good whack while he's about it. Frankly, he's a better wife than your brothers have managed to find.'

Her father had kissed her forehead.

'The best thing your mother ever did was to give me you– my precious daughter. You're a better man than any of my sons, my dear. I couldn't be more proud of you.'

Well, here I am, Daddy! Victoria thought now, looking around her at the glossy, open-plan, custom-made Smallbone Arts and Crafts-style kitchen which had cost a fortune, and in which she had barely even made a cup of tea. Jeremy had designed it, picked out the pale yellow tiles to blend smoothly with the light wood cupboards, a mix of chic town style – to please Victoria – and a rustic cosiness that appealed to Jeremy. It had cost a fortune, and she would leave it for good without a backward glance. *Forget London. New York has everything I ever wanted.*

She shrugged inwardly. What did she care whether they had a penthouse or a townhouse in New York? Jeremy was right, she'd barely be at home anyway.

'Whatever you want,' she said to her husband. 'We'll take the penthouse for the moment and you can start house-hunting straight away. Jacob says Dupleix will give us an interest-free loan for whatever mortgage we need.'

'Fantastic!' Jeremy's eyes shone behind the lenses of his glasses. 'London's all very well, but I really miss Manhattan. We had so much fun there.' He beamed. 'I told all our friends we'd be back soon – I didn't imagine it'd be only two years. Whoo-hoo! And this is it, isn't it, Vicky? We might never come back.'

'Not if I can help it,' Victoria said crisply. 'London's all very well, but there's so much more energy in New York. I simply can't wait.'

'Me neither.' He was beaming. 'I'll let Carpenter, de Vere know tomorrow, but I can't imagine they'll have any problems with me moving again. I mean, they didn't before. The time difference isn't that huge, and I'm in blue-sky research anyway.'

It hadn't even occurred to Victoria to wonder how Jeremy's

work would be affected by her new job. He worked for a hedge fund as what was picturesquely known as 'a quant', designing mathematical models for risk assessment and predicting market movements; 'blue-sky research' was the most arcane of all, but Jeremy, who had managed to study for a PhD while simultaneously working for a merchant bank, was capable of such intellectual flights that it was worth it for Carpenter, de Vere to let him doodle in speculative theory for months on end, trusting that eventually he would invent a new pricing approach for derivatives that would more than justify his salary and bonuses.

'*Now*, to celebrate your good news . . .' Jeremy shuffled behind his wife in his slippers and started to massage her shoulders. 'I checked your Persona fertility thingy this morning, and it's red. By my calculations, you're just about to ovulate. Shall we give it a go?' His voice slipped into a pleading tone. 'We really should get on with it, Vicky. We want two, and you're thirty-four, darling. No time to waste.'

A stab of panic shot through Victoria, as it did every single time Jeremy mentioned children. He was the one that wanted two so badly, not her; he was the one who wouldn't be content with a penthouse in one of the most sought-after addresses in Manhattan, who needed a proper house, with two small children running around, disrupting everything, making messes, and worst of all, ruining the figure that their mother had dieted and exercised so hard to achieve . . .

'I'm not sure it's the right time for me to get pregnant,' she said nervously. 'After all, there's the move now, and I'll be starting my new job—'

'Now, darling,' Jeremy said more firmly, 'you keep saying that it's never the right time, and you know that sometimes one just needs to get on with things. No time like the present! Besides,' he added cunningly, 'the younger you are, the quicker you'll snap back into shape. Remember the consultant telling us that?'

Jeremy knew just the argument that would convince his wife, the prospect of leaving babies so late that stretch-marks became a real issue. When Victoria had realised that Jeremy's heart was set on having children, she had toyed with the idea of adoption – so fashionable nowadays, everyone was doing it! First it had been China, but that was rather passé by now – Angelina Jolie had sourced hers from Vietnam and Ethiopia, Madonna from Malawi, Maxie Stangroom from Rwanda. The world really was your oyster. Victoria was so fair and blonde, a dark-skinned baby would look fabulous in her arms. She wasn't one of those fashion editors who eschewed black models – far from it, she'd always booked a whole range of ethnic types for shoots.

Reluctantly, however, she had had to concede defeat on the idea of adoption, at least until they had been trying for years and years to have a baby of their own. Jeremy would only agree to it under those conditions. She was desperately envious of bloody Jennifer Lane Davis, who had had not one, but two children made with her own eggs and her husband's sperm, implanted in a surrogate, who had then carried them to term. It cost, apparently, $100,000 a baby, with lawyer's fees and 'living expense' extras for the surrogate, but Jennifer hadn't had to go through morning sickness, swollen boobs, water retention, or any of the horrors associated with childbirth – let alone a schedule afterwards based round having to pump milk like a cow from breasts which, at that point, might as well have been udders.

Jennifer's story was that she was unable to carry children successfully herself, due to Irritable Bowel Syndrome; well, Victoria didn't believe a word of it. Jennifer just hadn't wanted to get fat, and Victoria couldn't blame her. It was increasingly common among actresses, singers, women whose bodies were forensically scrutinised by the media every time they stepped out of their doors or their limos, to go the surrogate route. Right now there was huge speculation that the leading, unquestionably A-list R&B diva of the moment had imported a poor Latin-American woman with a good track record of getting pregnant to New York, put her up in a lavish Manhattan apartment on the Upper West Side, and sent her to the best fertility doctors in town. The woman was apparently carrying a baby made from the diva's eggs and equally famous husband's sperm; once she had it, she would hand it over and slip back to her home country and her own children, with a fortune and a cast-iron confidentiality agreement. The diva, Victoria had heard, was perfectly capable of having children, as far as anyone knew. But neither she nor her husband had wanted to risk spoiling her famously curvy figure, or slow down the torrent of albums, live performances and, most lucrative of all, endorsement deals.

In the UK, however, it was much more difficult to pay a surrogate to grow and birth a baby for you. In the States, land of the free, the diva's arrangement – if not the secrecy surrounding it – was almost commonplace nowadays. Women who were too old to be fertile would even buy one woman's eggs, fertilise them with their husband's, or purchased donor sperm, and implant them in another woman, because that way the surrogate whose womb they were renting had no relation to the baby she was carrying, and therefore no right to keep it. One could even dictate what medical procedures the surrogate was to have at birth, induce the baby against her own preference, insist on a Caesarean if necessary . . .

A wash of hope flooded through Victoria as she realised that now she and Jeremy were moving to the US, now that she would be on a salary identical to the one that had permitted Jennifer to pay another woman to do all the hard work of carrying her children, that would become a real possibility. But then she looked up at her husband, who was standing over her, holding out a hand. He was absolutely set on their making their own children the old-fashioned way: his eyes were shining as if he were envisioning their babies, floating in front of him on twin puffy clouds, like cupids in a Renaissance painting, each with a little set of wings.

I'll have to go through with it for now, she thought gloomily, taking his hand and rising to her feet. But it's been a few months, and I haven't got knocked up yet – hopefully I won't. I know the consultant said we were fertile, but she also said there are plenty of women who simply can't get pregnant – 'unexplained infertility', she called it. How long will Jeremy take before I can start talking to him about surrogates? A year? He's so keen to start a family, maybe after we've been trying for a year with no success I can point out that maybe a nice woman with a fully-functioning womb in Vermont is the way to go . . .

Victoria had her own way in almost everything as far as her marriage went. Which meant that on the rare occasions when Jeremy put his foot down, he exerted a lot of power. Highly-sophisticated at picking her battles, she knew that right now, this was one she couldn't win.

Inwardly, she sighed again as they went out of the kitchen, Jeremy pausing, conscientiously, to turn off every light.

'I suppose you're right,' she said. 'But the usual rules apply.'

'Oh, of course,' Jeremy said eagerly. 'I wouldn't dream of changing anything.'

He padded after her like a loyal dog, up the stairs to the first floor, which was an entire, interlinked, suite of rooms; the master bedroom at the back, with a small bathroom for Jeremy and a large bathroom on the other side for Victoria, out of which a corridor with velvet-lined shelves for bags and shoes led to her equally large dressing room.

'I'm so excited,' he burbled. 'I can't *wait* for you to get pregnant! That's partly why I want a townhouse, with a garden. I know in Manhattan we won't have much of a garden, but still, somewhere for the baby to play as it gets bigger . . . Maybe we should get a puppy too – what do you think? Wouldn't that be lovely?'

'My God, Jeremy.' Victoria unfastened her earrings and dropped them into their silk-lined drawer in her dressing-table. 'You sound like my mother sometimes.'

But her husband was already in the bedroom, taking the decorative pillows off the bed and placing them on the chaise-longue. Whether he heard her or not, one of the secrets to their successful marriage was Jeremy's ability to ignore Victoria's snappishness.

'Hopefully we can manage two, one after the other,' he said happily. 'I'd love a boy and a girl, of course, but it won't matter really, as long as they're happy and healthy . . . Or twins! That would be wonderful!'

Victoria undressed, put away her clothes, set her shoes on their section of shelf, dropped her Myla bra and knickers into the handwash-only section of the pull-out laundry basket, slipped on a peach Jenny Packham silk nightdress, and walked back into the bedroom.

'I was thinking, when the baby's born, I might take paternity leave and look after it – what do you think?' Jeremy said. 'I know you'll be wanting to get straight back to work, and I don't like the idea of leaving our child with a nanny all day long.'

Victoria laughed. 'Why not just give up work completely and be its nanny full-time?' she suggested satirically. 'We won't need your income any more, not with what Jacob'll be paying me.'

Jeremy's eyes lit up even more. 'Do you know, I think I'd love that.'

His wife grimaced. 'I didn't actually mean it,' she said. 'Honestly, Jeremy, you should have known I was joking.'

'But many a true word is said in jest,' Jeremy said. He was sitting on his side of the bed, waiting for her, his pyjamas still on. 'Wouldn't it be a fantastic idea?'

Victoria started to snap at him, then caught herself just as she was about to bite his head off.

'You know,' she said slowly, 'that might not actually be the worst idea in the world. It would look awfully good in the press. I'm going to be in the public eye non-stop now, and image is so important these days. Working wife, house-husband raising the children . . . what a modern couple we'd be.'

She tapped her foot on the carpet. 'Remind me to give Katharine a ring about it,' she said, crossing the room. 'I'll go over it with her.'

Katharine Walsh was the PR dynamo who managed the Dupleix Corporation's British interests, a slim blonde with skirts as high as her heels and a business brain as sharp as the tailoring of her black Miu Miu mini-dresses. She was one of the very few women Victoria considered her equal.

'Katharine!' Jeremy said rather crossly. 'Sometimes I feel you listen to bloody Katharine more than you do to me.'

Of course I do, Victoria thought, as she sank onto the bed and opened the drawer of her bedside table. *You may be a maths genius, but Katharine's a publicity one. Far more useful.* Victoria was perfectly well aware that one of the reasons Jacob had been amenable to expediting her new job offer was that Katharine, a long-term ally, had been so effective at publicising the success Victoria had made of lifting *UK Style* out of its doldrums. Katharine had promoted Victoria as the reigning magazine queen of London, setting her up so effectively that it would seem only natural that Jacob would enthrone her as the Queen of Manhattan sooner rather than later.

But then Victoria pulled out from the drawer her favourite sex toy, the finger tickler, and as she slid it onto the middle finger of her right hand and pulled up the hem of her night-dress, Jeremy made a soft, contented sound and settled back against the headboard to watch, his brief grumpiness entirely forgotten. Victoria reached for the lube, squeezing sticky clear droplets onto the pink ribbed plastic on her finger. She lay back on the pillows, spreading her legs. She was entirely smooth, having lasered every single pubic hair away years ago. It had been painful, but by far the most efficient, time-saving method, and had been totally worth it; she never had to bother with a waxing appointment again.

And Jeremy loved it, too. Not that his wishes had formed part of her decision. But Jeremy was a born voyeur, and her smooth, hairless mound made it very easy for him to take in every detail of the spectacle as Victoria switched on the battery, spread her pink, swollen lower lips with her left hand, and slid the tickler between them, her hips starting to pump against it immediately in conditioned response.

Her eyes closed, her tongue moistened her mouth. The battery hummed away, and Jeremy was humming too, a steady, happy sound, as he undid the button on his pyjama bottoms and pulled out his cock. It was already hardening at the sight of Victoria's spread legs, pulled up at the knees, her pelvis tilting against the buzz of the deep pink toy, one hand between her legs, working on herself, while the other one gripped her breast, squeezing it convulsively through the thin silk of the nightgown.

'Fuck,' she moaned. 'Yes, fuck it, fuck it, yes, like that, shit, this is just what I fucking want . . . Yes, do it, fuck me, fuck me hard till I come like a bloody train – yeah, Jesus God, yeah, like that, fuck my cunt, fuck it and come so bloody hard, I'm going to come so bloody hard . . . aaah . . .'

She screamed as the first wave of orgasm hit her, her hips bucking frantically.

'Yes!' she yelled. 'Yes, fucking give it to me, you bloody bastard! Oh God, yes, I'm going to fucking come again!'

Her finger was still working frantically, tracing circles, stroking up and down, flicking herself expertly with the ridges of the tickler, sending her into one spasm of pleasure after another. The hand on her breast pulled away the silk of the nightdress, finding her bare skin, playing with her small pink nipple. Her head thrashed from side to side, her blonde hair falling over her face, her lips parted, a flush spreading over her neck and down to her breasts. She was utterly absorbed in what she was doing, a stream of swear words flooding out from her parted lips, giving herself completely to the sensations streaming through her, her pelvis pounding away against the hand between her legs.

Jeremy's cock was stiff, its head swollen and red, his hand sliding up and down its shaft, slippery with his own spit. His humming was louder now that Victoria was swearing noisily enough to cover any sounds he was making; he worked away at himself, scooting down the bed to get an even better view, knowing that Victoria was too lost in her own pleasure to notice what he was doing. Greedily, he stared at her spread legs, the dark pink plastic sex toy throbbing busily below the smooth pale skin of her mound of Venus.

'Shit, I'm coming so bloody fucking hard – yeah! God, there it fucking is, yeah!' she yelled.

Victoria bucked almost off the mattress, panting with her orgasm, her face and throat pink, long wails of pleasure pouring from her lips. Jeremy was at the foot of the bed now, his cock filling his hand as he took in the erotic spectacle of Victoria, legs splayed wide, utterly selfish in her complete abandonment to her own satisfaction. He could have watched her for hours, no matter what torture it was to him to wait until she was finished before he came himself; because he would never have dreamed of coming until she had finished, never allow himself release until Victoria had finally collapsed.

Finally, her hands fell limply from where they had been caressing her body, tumbling to her sides. She gasped a series of slow breaths, her heart beginning to slow back to normal, her mouth moist and soft, and her eyelids flickered open. Jeremy's heart pounded, his cock throbbing desperately in his hand, begging for the words of release.

'Right, you can do it now,' Victoria commanded. 'Make it quick.'

He needed no more encouragement; swiftly, he was kneeling over her, sliding between her legs, pulling them up around him, in her with one long stroke, groaning at how wet she was.

'You feel so good,' he mumbled. 'So tight, so wet . . .'

Oh, do shut up, Victoria thought, but she was too exhausted by her mammoth orgasm session to even manage to mumble the words. Jeremy was well-trained. In a few short pumps, he was coming himself, his hips jerking frantically as he moaned: 'Oh Vicky, it feels so good . . . Oh Vicky, darling, I'm coming inside you . . .'

He collapsed on top of his wife's smooth, slender body for the few blissful seconds she allowed him before she said into his curly hair, 'All right, you've had your fun. Get off now. And clean me up. God, the mess on the bedspread! We should have put a towel down.'

'Oh God! Right, sorry.' Jeremy levered himself off her, moving slowly, his penis still red and swollen. 'I'll just get some tissues—'

'And the wet wipes.'

'Oh, darling, really? I mean, if we're trying to get you pregnant, I don't think wet wipes are a good idea.'

'Shit!' Victoria said crossly. 'This whole getting-pregnant process is such a bore. All right, no wet wipes, but hurry up and clean me. I'm exhausted, and I have to be up in five hours.'

She stretched her arms out, luxuriating in the gesture, in the extreme content sweeping through her entire body. The release was exquisite. Every muscle felt deliciously loosened, every nerve in her body was soothed. Her husband bustled back with a handful of tissues, wiping her down with great care, and even as he tugged down the hem of her nightdress, she felt herself drifting off to sleep.

I can't wait to get to New York, she thought drowsily. *Back where I belong, at the centre of the universe. I'm going to rule that city with a rod of iron.*

And that's the biggest turn-on of all.

Mireille

Screams of denial and rage resounded down the stark white corridors of *US Style*'s New York office, screams so loud and piercing that if its occupants had been able to open the windows, anyone below, on Third Avenue, would have winced and looked up to the thirty-first floor of the Lipstick Building, asking themselves if someone high up there was torturing a cat. Every single employee shivered in fear and discreetly covered their ears.

Every employee, that is, but one. As all her fellow-*Stylites* cowered at the sound of the axe falling on their boss, the fashion director of the magazine continued flicking through the rack of embellished Michael Kors T-shirts that she had called in for a shoot, her hand perfectly steady as she clicked one hanger against another, discarding five, six, seven, eventually extracting a khaki silk top with elaborate beaded epaulettes and studying it with an expression of extreme seriousness before, finally, sliding it to one side for further consideration. It was as if the background of hysterical screaming simply did not exist. She had been back from Morocco for three days now – plenty of time to prepare herself for this latest upheaval.

Mireille Grenier had been *Style*'s fashion director for over twenty years, and she was still as beautiful as she had been when she first started at the magazine. Her bone structure was exquisite, her elegance timeless, even though the clear white light flooding through the windows of her corner office, high up above the city, illuminated the lines on her forehead, the crows' feet fanning out from her eyes, the half-moon creases bracketing her wide mouth which demonstrated that Mireille was a stranger to Botox. The hollows under her high cheekbones were slightly sunken; she hadn't chosen to inject fillers into them, plumping them up like so many actresses and models in their forties had done. She had once been a ballerina at the Paris Opéra, and ever since then, she had worn her hair in the same style, drawn back smoothly into a high bun which emphasised that marvellous bone structure. The hair, once black, was now threaded with silver, one thicker white streak at her hairline flowing back into the bun, wrapping through it dramatically.

'Mireille!'

Cinnamon, Mireille's assistant, scampered into her boss's office, eyes so large with panic that the whites were clearly visible all the way round the irises. She was gasping for breath, even though all she had done was run down the length of the corridor. Mireille, who had executed the famous thirty-two fouetté turns across the length of the stage as Odette/Odile in *Swan Lake* many times in her professional career, had ridden an over-excited stallion over the Moroccan desert for thirty minutes to calm him down and dismounted without betraying a sign of physical exertion, raised her finely plucked eyebrows at the lack of control exhibited by her assistant.

'Compose yourself, *s'il vous plâit,*' she said, selecting another silk T-shirt for inspection.

'But Mireille, it's Jennifer – she's in her office with Jacob.' A lock of Cinnamon's carefully pinned hair had come down, tumbling onto her shoulder. 'Can't you hear?' She flapped her arms like a deranged goose batting its wings. 'Zarina says Jacob's *firing* her!'

Jennifer was wailing now, banshee howls of misery. Something crashed, far down the corridor in the editor's office.

'I just went to listen at the door,' Cinnamon persisted, clearly frustrated that her boss seemed not to be grasping the gravity of the situation. 'She's totally freaking out – she isn't even screaming words. It's just, like, *No, No, No, No, No*.'

'Then,' Mireille said, placing the second T-shirt next to the first one she had chosen, 'one could fairly say that your interpretation of the situation is correct, *non*? Jacob is indeed terminating her employment here.'

Cinnamon sagged visibly against the jamb of Mireille's office door, like a marionette whose strings had been cut.

'But Mireille,' she whispered. 'Jennifer sounds like she's having a nervous breakdown – and Zarina says that Jennifer's got a four-year contract, and she's only been editor for two years – and Jacob's in there with her, and it sounds like she's *throwing* things.'

'*Et alors*?' Mireile shrugged. 'Jacob is much larger than Jennifer. He will call Security if he thinks he is in genuine danger. This is nothing to do with me or you. You must learn a sense of perspective.'

Cinnamon's lips parted, but no more words would come out; she gulped in air, trying to calm herself down.

'Go back to your desk and finish calling in those earrings I need from Boucheron,' Mireille instructed.

Cinnamon started to peel herself off the door jamb, the spindly heels of her D&G boots wobbling as they took her full weight.

'But—' she started.

'You have learned nothing,' Mireille sighed on a long outbreath. 'I am very disappointed in you. All the training I have tried to give you has been wasted. You are frightened for your job, correct?'

Cinnamon nodded mutely, eyes wide again.

'I have been here to see three editors come and go, if we

count Jennifer – which I think we safely can,' Mireille added wryly, listening to the howls coming from the woman's prized corner office. 'Jennifer and I were in accord, but scarcely friends. Why should her being fired impact on my job, *hein*?'

She regarded Cinnamon with a clear dark gaze. Cinnamon dropped her head, embarrassed.

'Now,' Mireille continued, 'you should know that Jacob was in London the day before yesterday, having dinner with Victoria Glossop. You are friends with Zarina, you should have ascertained that. You must always gather all the information you can. And you will not remember when Victoria was a fashion editor here, but you must surely have heard the stories about her. She is very ambitious, very confident. You know, of course, that *UK Style* has just posted its highest-ever ad sales and circulation figures?'

Cinnamon shook her head. Mireille clicked her tongue against the roof of her mouth, annoyed now.

'Oh, you girls! You think working here is all about your boots and your bracelets and whether you can meet a rich husband at the parties! I am so bored with you.'

'Mireille,' Cinnamon pleaded, panicking now. 'I'm sorry – I've been working so hard on getting those Balenciaga balldresses over from Paris—'

'The earrings, please,' Mireille said, cutting her off. 'By this afternoon. If Jennifer is leaving, that is all the more reason for us to work hard. And smooth your hair, *s'il vous plâit*. You are in a mess. It is not pretty.'

Mireille pivoted on her toe with the perfect posture of the prima ballerina she had once been, turning towards the windows, a third T-shirt in her hand, dismissing her assistant. Looking at her boss's slender shoulders, Cinnamon choked back a sob of discouragement as she obeyed Mireille's instructions.

A shame, Mireille thought as she examined the colour of the T-shirt, holding it up to see it in full daylight; no, it was taupe, and she wanted sand. She hung it back on the rail.

Cinnamon is proving to be a disappointment. No backbone, no nous. She will never be a serious player in this business.

When Cinnamon had befriended Zarina, Jennifer's assistant, Mireille had been very pleased. Cinnamon would learn all the gossip ahead of the rest of the *Style* staffers, be able to use that advance news to her advantage. Instead, it seemed that all Cinnamon had been concerned about was the freebies that were in Zarina's gift to hand out, presents and sweeteners sent to Jennifer by designers and publicists and model agencies.

A pair of D&G boots is all very well, but information is power, Mireille reflected. Cinnamon should have known that the writing was on the wall for Jennifer as soon as Victoria posted those spectacular figures for *UK Style*. Victoria had been using the UK magazine as a showcase for what she could do with the US version, and she had succeeded superbly. It was obvious that she was using *UK Style* as a springboard.

Mireille had trained up many girls in her time, girls who were clever and discreet enough to qualify as one of her elite protégées. As their mentor, she had ensured their loyalty and distributed them strategically through the New York media to Italy and Paris and London, in positions from which they could feed her snippets of crucial gossip and information that would allow her to maintain her position at the very apex of the publishing world. Dupleix, Condé Nast, Hearst: Mireille had tentacles stretching into them all, favours owed to her, allies to call upon. Not every one of her assistants, of course, met the criteria necessary for Mireille to bestow on them the benefits of her guidance and experience.

I'm not wasting any more time on that one, Mireille shrugged. She'll put in phone calls and make my tea, that's all. As they say in America, you win some, you lose some.

And as we say in France, tant pis.

She smiled, any thoughts of Cinnamon dismissed as she moved to the full-length mirror. Mireille checked her appearance multiple times a day, ensuring that her hair was as smooth, her make-up as perfect, her clothes as lint-free as they had been first thing that morning. In a brief glance she confirmed that her charcoal cotton Agnès B wrap dress was unwrinkled, the knot of her emerald and orange silk Hermès scarf was still in the correct position at the side of her neck, the wide patent-leather belt around her impossibly narrow waist was as shiny as ever and didn't require a quick buff-up with a tissue. Walking over to her desk, which was piled high with magazines, photography books and novels, many of them opened and layered on top of each other in a creative disorder that Mireille found inspiring, she removed her gold-cased YSL lipstick from the pen caddy and repainted her lips deep scarlet with two practised strokes. Her make-up style was extremely French; unlike American women, who spent a great deal of time applying make-up that was designed to look invisible, Frenchwomen generally disdained that kind of artifice. Mireille spent five minutes in the morning on her make-up: two expert black lines of liquid kohl on her eyelids, mattifying powder – she loathed shine – and her dramatic red lipstick.

She had just finished touching it up when there was a flurry in the outer office. Cinnamon was babbling something, jumping up, trying her best to give Mireille some sort of warning. She was brushed aside by Jacob, who strolled into Mireille's office, Cinnamon fluttering behind his wide shoulders like a particularly ineffective moth. She looked dazed, as women usually did around Jacob, dazzled by his aura of power and money, his sheer sexual charisma.

Lucky for her she's not Jacob's type, Mireille thought. Or she would certainly burn her wings.

'Well!' Jacob said, smiling at Mireille, who returned his smile with equal amusement. He held out his hands as he approached her; Mirelle came to meet him, the big emerald solitaire she always wore on the fourth finger of her right hand glinting as she set her fingers lightly in his palms. Jacob raised her hands to his mouth and kissed them in turn as Cinnamon, ignored by both of them, faded away.

'*Ma chère*,' Jacob said with deep fondness. 'You're always a sight for sore eyes. May I assume that, as always, you already know what I'm about to tell you?'

Mireille's smile broke into a laugh. '*Mon cher*,' she responded, '*everyone* knows what you're about to tell me. The men who drive the carriages in Central Park must have heard Jennifer screaming. Jennifer is out, and you're bringing Victoria over from London, I can only assume.'

Jacob opened his arms wide. He was wearing a dark navy silk suit, and the gesture made the sleeves of the jacket slide a little up his arms, showing off the heavy, yellow-gold ovals of his Asprey cufflinks, gleaming dully against the crisp white shirt cuffs.

'What could I do?' he asked rhetorically. 'Victoria wouldn't take no for an answer.'

Mireille quirked her head sideways a little. 'And of course, you knew when you scheduled dinner with her in London that she wouldn't take no for an answer,' she observed.

'Of course,' Jacob echoed. 'It's her time. Jennifer has done a good, but not an exceptional job.'

Mireille nodded in agreement.

'She's getting a huge pay-off,' he added. 'Her contract's watertight.'

'Nothing is watertight,' Mireille said, walking over to the window and gazing down at Third Avenue below. 'You could contest it.' Reflected in the big glass pane, she saw Jacob's heavy shoulders rise and fall.

'No point,' he said succinctly. 'We'd spend as much on the lawyers as we'd save. Besides, I can afford it.'

He regarded Mireille's narrow back, her perfectly erect spine, with great affection. If only all women were as poised as her, as self-controlled, he thought. But Mireille is truly unique.

'You're fine, naturally,' he said. 'I don't need to tell you that.

You and Victoria will make a killer team. I'm really psyched to see what you two cook up here together.'

Mireille's newly-scarlet lips pressed together in a brief, involuntary gesture that could have been satisfaction or something much less pleasurable. But although she could observe Jacob in the glass, read his face and body language, she was much too canny to let him see her own expression.

'I remember when Victoria worked here before,' she said, permitting herself a moment to regain full composure before she turned around to face Jacob again. 'It was not the most – shall we say, serene of experiences.'

Jacob grinned, his perfect white teeth flashing against his perfect tan. 'She didn't have what she wanted then,' he said by way of explanation. 'Now she's editor, she'll be a lot easier to handle. I know Victoria – she's just like me. When we don't have what we want, we're evil bastards. When we have it – well, we're pussycats.'

Mireille's eyebrows were raised so high that she didn't need to say a word: Jacob burst out laughing.

'Okay, she's not going to roll over and ask you to tickle her tummy,' he said, 'but you're the best in the business, and she's smart enough to know that. Plus, she can't touch your job, and you don't want hers. You two will rub along just fine.'

He glanced at his watch. 'Well, my work here is done,' he said, grimacing. 'I have a four o'clock with Bloomberg, so I'd better shoot.' He looked at Mireille with a hint of uncertainty, which was unusual for Jacob: he naturally exuded confidence and self-assurance. 'You'll pick up the pieces here, won't you?' he asked. 'Jennifer has to work out two months to get her settlement. I need as easy a transition as possible. Victoria'll have to get herself moved over, organise all of that as well as starting a new job – it has to be as smooth a handover as we can manage in the circumstances. I'll get her assistant to synch things with you so we only have a couple of days between Jennifer leaving and Victoria coming in.'

Mireille tapped her foot, long and narrow, clad in glove-soft leather whose dark forest green matched her patent belt exactly. She was obsessive about taking care of her feet, and had all her shoes made for her in Italy on her own personal wooden last. She had fittings twice a year, when she went to Milan for the collections.

'Don't worry,' she replied crisply. 'I'll make sure your mess is nicely tidied up.'

Jacob's face relaxed, his lips softening. 'What would I do without you, Mireille?' he said contentedly.

'What indeed?' Mireille smiled enigmatically. 'You should go, *mon cher*. Bloomberg will not be happy if you keep him waiting.'

Jacob nodded. 'We'll speak soon, okay? *Au 'voir.*'

'*Au 'voir.*' Mirelle raised a hand in farewell as Jacob left her office.

She stood there, perfectly poised, one foot in front of the other, watching his wide back shoulder through the doorway. He waved at Cinnamon as he passed, acknowledging the existence of a lowly assistant where many tycoons would not; Jacob always had such lovely manners, Mireille observed with approval. She had been fashion director of *Style* for fifteen years, but she had known him much longer, ever since she had been a ballerina, in fact. Their sexual relationship had long since faded: Jacob preferred his women to be no older than their early twenties, precisely the age Mireille had been when they first met. But Jacob had encouraged her ambition to work in fashion, helped her get her first job on *French Style*, and watched with satisfaction her meteoric rise, her move to New York and her dramatic success at his flagship publication.

Because the truth was that, as far as Mireille was concerned, she truly was at the top of her own pinnacle. She had absolutely no desire to occupy the editor's chair, to balance the competing demands of advertisers and designers, to play politics, do interviews, be in the public eye. Mireille shuddered at the mere thought. Discretion and privacy were crucial to her. She had no wish to be the figurehead of *Style*, to have the press assume that they could poke around in her personal life.

Her style was typically French, classic and elegant; she never wore the type of clothes that were in fashion that season and would date just as quickly, considering that kind of bandwagon-jumping utterly inappropriate for a woman in her early fifties. As a result, she was rarely photographed at the shows for fashion magazines, which limited themselves to a picture of her if they needed to represent French chic, with her Hermès scarves, fitted dresses and soft leather shoes. Her name was known by everyone inside the fashion industry, but very few outside.

Mireille's creativity was not expressed through her own clothes, but in the pages of the magazine that was as much her own as the editor's. Her imagination was seemingly limitless, her flights of fancy extraordinary, her relationship with the most talented and avant-garde photographers unparalleled. She had an eye for up-and-coming models, artists, designers, and her name was spoken in revered tones from Tokyo to Paris, Milan to London. Victoria Glossop could edit a magazine better than anyone currently in publishing, but Mireille Grenier's reputation as a stylist was just as high in the industry as Victoria's.

There will be clashes, Mireille thought, pursing her lips at the inevitable prospect. What a bore. I had just trained Jennifer up so nicely. But what can you do? Jacob decides, and we must all follow along.

There was a very good reason Jacob decided to focus on a publishing empire all those years ago, she reflected. Magazines are full of women. Publishing is full of women. And Jacob does so love to tell women what to do.

Time for her to deal with the Jennifer situation. She reached up a hand to touch her scarf, ensuring that it was correctly positioned, and left her office, not deigning to tell Cinnamon where she was headed. Halfway down the long, white-painted corridor, Zarina, Jennifer's assistant, came running to meet her.

'Mireille,' she said quickly. 'Could you please come? Jennifer's started to break things and I don't know what to do.'

Despite the gravity of the situation, Mireille was pleased to see that Zarina, unlike Cinnamon, was keeping her cool; her voice was still even, her demeanour urgent but not panicked. Nodding her head in approval, Mireille led the way to Jennifer's corner office, the mirror-twin of Mireille's own on the north side of the building. The sounds emanating from it had altered; Jennifer had stopped howling and was now, as Zarina had reported, smashing things. Mireille paused in the doorway, assessing the situation. Mugs, glasses, heavy silver photograph frames were strewn at Jennifer's feet, and she stood, panting heavily, in front of her desk, trying to wrestle the keyboard of her computer free from its attaching cable, presumably so she could smash that too.

'Jennifer!' Mireille said sharply, her voice low as always, but laden with such authority that Jennifer jumped, the keyboard dropping from her hands. It dangled from its cable, hanging off the desk at an extreme angle. Jennifer's expression was both guilty and furious as she turned to look at Mireille, Zarina hovering at her shoulders.

'He's *fired* me!' Jennifer said, gasping in shock as she said the words. 'Can you believe it? He's *fired* me!'

Mireille contemplated Jennifer. Tall and imposing, Jennifer cut an impressive figure, with a head of cascading dark curls and large blue eyes whose whites were now streaked with red that matched her flushed face. Jennifer had what Mireille considered an unfortunate predilection for wearing the latest trends, even if they didn't suit her, and today she was dressed in a pale green knee-length knit dress, belted at the waist with a silk obi, which flattered neither her size nor her shape. The dress was dolman-sleeved, and its arms flapped like bat wings as Jennifer, getting her second wind, grabbed the keyboard again and dragged it towards her, pulling it free from the monitor by brute force.

'I've given my *life* to this job!' she wailed, lifting one knee and trying to smash the keyboard over it. 'My entire *existence*! I've barely seen my kids in two years – I've put on weight because I don't have time to work out any more – I've done a fantastic job and I had two more years – *two more years* – on my contract. I told Jacob when he offered me the editorship that I wanted four years to make all the changes I had planned, and I made him put it in the damn contract because I *know* what he's like, I *know* he has his favourites, and I've never been one of them . . .'

Mireille's eyes narrowed. 'You are getting an excellent settlement,' she interrupted coldly. 'These things happen. Jacob is being extremely generous. He is not going to challenge the payoff terms in any way.'

'What do I care!' Jennifer screamed. 'I want my job. I *love* this job. Jacob's completely humiliated me – everyone will be laughing at me. Everyone!'

She whacked the keyboard so hard into her knee that she yelped in pain.

'Ow! Fuck!' she yelled, turning and throwing the keyboard like a discus across the room. It crashed into the glass of the window which, fortunately, was much too hardened to break. 'I'm a damn laughing-stock! I did a fantastic job here – and I'm being kicked out *despite* that, just for some stuck-up, snooty English bitch who used to suck Jacob's cock!'

Mireille stiffened. She had been prepared to allow Jennifer to let off some steam, but this was completely unacceptable. She shot a sharp glance at Zarina; following her unspoken instruction, Zarina turned to lift a large vase of flowers from a shelf beside her, handing it to Mireille. In one swift movement, Mireille removed the lily arrangement from the vase and dumped it into the dustbin that Zarina had grabbed from behind the door and was holding out to her. Mireille took two paces towards Jennifer, angled the vase and threw the water it contained directly into the contorted red face of the now ex-editor of *Style*.

'Aaah!' Jennifer screeched in shock.

She reeled back under the onslaught of water which, Mireille noticed with distaste, was greenish and a little smelly. Jennifer had not supervised her staff well enough to ensure that the water in her vases was changed every single day. Plus, the stems of the flowers should have been freshly trimmed; as Mireille had observed when handling them, this had not been done either. Zarina is good but not perfect, Mireille noted. I must have a word with her when all this has calmed down.

Jennifer had raised her hands to her face; she was trying frantically to flick the dirty water away from her eyes. She staggered on her feet, and Mireille caught her shoulders, pressing her back and down onto one of the upholstered chairs facing the desk.

'Pull yourself together,' she said briskly. 'Stop talking like this, it will do you no good at all. Calm yourself down, and go home when you are ready. But remember, you have two months to work here still. You must complete your notice. If you walk out now, you will forfeit everything – you will not get a penny of your settlement.'

She reached out a hand; Zarina laid a handful of tissues in it. Mireille dabbed Jennifer's face, wincing at the odour of the fetid water. Jennifer began to sob, long, gulping sobs which signalled that the anger had worked itself through her and the grieving process had begun. Mireille gave her another handful of tissues and stood back.

'There's nowhere for me to go now,' Jennifer wept. 'This was as good as it gets – the only way is down. Anna Wintour won't leave *Vogue* for decades, and I know who Hearst already wants for *Harper's*. What am I going to do? I don't even want to stay in New York! It's totally humiliating! Victoria's going to come here and lord it over everyone . . . I'll have to see her at every party, every gala. Oh God, what am I saying? I won't be invited to *anything* any more!' She doubled over in misery, her sobs becoming even gustier.

Mireille smoothed down her skirt. 'I advise you to talk to Bilberry,' she said calmly. 'They have just been bought by LVMH, and they are looking for a creative director. The job would be based in London, of course, but if you do not wish to stay in New York . . .'

Jennifer's sobbing stopped abruptly; she looked up at Mireille over the tissue she was holding, her mouth open.

'Just an idea,' Mireille said lightly. 'But it would suit you very well, I think. I will leave you alone now to recover.'

Zarina had been flitting round the office, pulling down the blackout blinds, darkening the room; Jennifer had had these fitted at great expense when she became editor, as she suffered from migraines. She had tried a whole range of medications, but the only one that worked had turned out to have the side-effect of causing her to put on a few pounds. Of course, she had immediately stopped using it, preferring to suffer horribly once or twice a month but remain a size four. To do her justice, practically every other person who worked in fashion would have made the same choice.

Mireille gave a small smile of approval at Zarina as she left Jennifer's office. Zarina, knowing where the power was located, followed Mireille out and closed the office door.

'I'll get Jennifer home when she's all calmed down, Mireille,' she said deferentially. 'I'm sorry I couldn't manage on my own.'

'Not at all.'

Mireille contemplated Zarina, who, on her father's side, was a de Ruiter, a scion of one of the oldest and best-connected New York families, dating back to the earliest Dutch settlers of Manhattan Island. Her mother was equally aristocratic, and her Persian origins had given Zarina her black eyes and enviably-thick mane of dark hair. Zarina's socialite background was typical for a *Style* staffer, but Mireille did not usually choose girls like her to mentor: in her experience, the richer and more privileged they were, the less able to think on their feet, act quickly and efficiently in a crisis.

Zarina, however, was clearly an exception to this rule.

'You did very well,' Mireille pronounced. 'I am very pleased with the way you handled that situation.'

Zarina flushed bright red with happiness.

'Look after Jennifer until she leaves,' Mireille instructed. 'Victoria will doubtless bring her own assistant over from London. When Jennifer goes, I will make sure you are re-assigned somewhere commensurate with your talents.'

Zarina's eyes brightened, and she said quickly, 'I'd really like to be your assistant, Mireille. I know I'd learn so much from you. If I could be your assistant, plus have some styling responsibilities, that would be my dream job.'

Mireille smiled, a slow smile of pure satisfaction. Cinnamon had signed her own death warrant that afternoon, and Mireille would need a replacement.

'Perfect,' she said. 'Consider it done.' She turned away, tossing over her shoulder: 'And the first thing I will teach you is the correct maintenance of flower arrangements. Remind me, please, the first day you start with me.'

Part Two
Manhattan: Now

Coco

Coco stepped out of the elevator and into the lobby of the Halston. It was a gorgeous December day in the city, sunny and crisp, and she had a huge pair of Dior sunglasses propped on the crown of her head. One of the delights of a New York winter was that although it could be bitterly cold, the norm was blue skies and sunshine, none of those low-skied, grey, miserably damp London winters.

The doorman of her building was outside on the sidewalk, clad in a bulky, loden-green overcoat with big gold buttons and military braiding, stamping his feet to keep warm on the icy pavement. He jumped to attention as Coco came through the revolving door, wrapped in an oversized, mink-trimmed Prada padded coat, beneath which her stick-thin legs looked impossibly fragile.

'Cab, Ms Raeburn?' he asked, and Coco nodded. He strode down to the edge of the sidewalk, lifting his whistle to his mouth; but he didn't need it. The Bowery was teeming with taxicabs, and one stopped almost immediately, the doorman popping open the door and holding it for Coco. It was one of the new SUV yellow cabs, big and comfortable, and Coco looked tiny in it as it rolled away. Six of her could easily have fitted into the high back seat.

'Five Fifth Avenue,' she said to the driver, and relaxed back as the cab threaded its way through the uptown traffic. The leaves on the linden trees bordering the Bowery had all fallen by now, the skeletons of the trees dramatic and stark, lightly loaded with the snow that had fallen overnight. Black and white, like the classic prints of the New York skyline.

Coco remembered the autumn foliage, beautiful and dramatic, like nothing she had ever seen in England. When the leaves changed colour here, it was an event heralded on the local news channel, New York 1, for weeks beforehand. As soon as the green started deepening at the tips to bright splashes of yellow and scarlet and amber, spectacular bursts of colour against the grey buildings, New Yorkers would get in their cars and head upstate for foliage viewing. She had thought they were crazy until her fiancé had driven her up to Pacific Palisades in late September to show her the woods there: she had been struck dumb at the sight. It looked as if cans of paint had been thrown onto the trees, a dramatic panorama of reds, oranges and yolk-yellows that signalled the arrival of fall.

A fantastic, all-American backdrop. Just what she'd needed for the shoot she was planning, just what Victoria would love. First thing Monday morning, she'd driven everyone crazy by re-jigging the entire shoot, a March-issue piece on neon-bright accessories, and bussing everyone up to the Palisades. The resultant shots had been phenomenal: long-limbed models stretching arms in elbow-length leather gloves, legs in micro-fibre tights, in fluorescent shades of lime and lemon and violet, sharp and spring-like against the blurred background of the autumn shades. *Fall into Spring*, Coco had called it.

She smiled, remembering how stunning the photos had been. Mireille had admired the artistry of the styling, Victoria the vivid colours and dynamic movement. Coco had managed to please them both.

And now I have a new job, where I don't have to please anyone but myself – and the advertisers, she thought triumphantly.

The cab crossed Houston Street and headed for Washington Square Park; its white marble arch, modelled after the Arc de Triomphe in Paris, loomed imposingly over the bright trees below and the elegant red-brick houses on the north side of the park. Coco wished, as she did every single time, that the cab could pass through the arch itself, like a gateway to one of the most beautiful stretches of Fifth Avenue – a wide, breath-taking panorama up to Madison Square Park. It was such a glamorous approach, she felt almost as if she should have been in a carriage, horses trotting in the shafts, like a princess on her way to a ball.

Well, we're going to a Christmas gala dinner and dance with Marc Jacobs and Roberto Cavalli at the New York Public Library, she thought. That's the equivalent of a modern-day ball! And I'm definitely marrying into New York royalty.

The cab pulled to a halt in front of Five Fifth, a beautiful, pre-war greystone monolith a block wide. It narrowed gradually after the twentieth storey, with fewer apartments on each floor, becoming larger and more expensive, their balconies and terraces just visible from the street, the greenery planted on them softening the imposing lines of the building. Five Fifth was too fashionable to have the traditional red carpet laid out from its main entrance to the sidewalk; instead, it had chosen a deep charcoal grey, bordered in cream, with linked '5's in its centre. The uniform worn by Franklin, the daytime doorman, was the same dark grey. He was already opening the cab door as Coco finished paying the driver, extending one gloved hand to help her out.

'Thank you,' she murmured, and Franklin looked at her admiringly as she stepped onto the grey carpet, at her elegant outfit, the sheen of money that buffed her to a high gloss. She's gotta be some kind of British aristocrat, he thought. A real nice way about her, always says please and thank you so politely. You can tell class as soon as you see it. No wonder he's marrying this one.

He followed her deferentially up the carpet to the door, executing the doorman shuffle, dodging in front of her to hold it open, commenting: 'Beautiful evening, Ms Raeburn.'

'Yes, it's gorgeous,' Coco agreed, smiling at Franklin.

He moved ahead, leading the way to the bank of elevators, extracting a big bunch of keys and sliding one into the lock beside the far elevator, then pressing the button to open the doors. Coco, of course, had her own key, but the more rich and privileged you were, the less you had to do for yourself, and part of Franklin's job was to ensure that she didn't have to do anything so vulgar as reach into her bag for an elevator key.

'All set,' he said, stepping back to let her enter. 'Enjoy the view up there. Great night for it, it's real clear.'

'I will, Franklin. Thanks,' she said as the doors shut and the elevator started its journey. There were no buttons inside apart from the alarm: the lift's sensors told it when it was occupied and sent it on one of the only two journeys it could make – down to the lobby, or up to the fortieth-floor penthouse. It was mirrored in the Art Deco style that echoed the period in which Five Fifth had been designed, and Coco instinctively checked her make-up and hair in the panel beside her as the lift ascended, pleased to see that even in the overhead light her skin looked smooth and poreless, her light-brown hair pinned and drawn to the side in a loose twist that was the latest style for twenty-something girls.

My eyes look huge, she noticed. They never looked like that when I was a size 12. She shivered at the memory of being that big. *What a heifer! God, I can't even bear to look at old photos of myself!* Proudly, she rested her hands on her hips, feeling the bones there, clearly defined even through the fluffy lace knit of the designer cardigan. *I'm perfect now. New York perfect. Sample size perfect.*

The doors slid open, a tiny, discreet peal ringing once to indicate to anyone in the penthouse that the elevator had arrived. Coco stepped out, directly into the living room of the apartment. She hadn't quite got used to the luxury of having no front door yet; it was still almost disconcerting, as if something were missing. The split-level living room was decorated in dark, masculine colours, the deep blood-red leather of the sofas gleaming against the dark oak flooring. Two richly-polished cherrywood humidors, one on either side of the bar, purred quietly away, and a priceless Isfahan carpet, wool woven on silk in an intricate pattern of red and indigo swirls on an ivory background, lay in the centre of the room, anchoring the colour scheme.

When she had first visited the apartment, Coco had gasped at the beauty of the carpet, reluctant to walk over it; now she stepped on it with her sharp Balenciaga heels without thinking twice. Familiarity bred, if not contempt, then at least casual indifference. She walked into the master bedroom, which was even more stunning than the living room, but one she had barely noticed on her first visit. She blushed, looking at the huge bed that dominated the room, with its elaborately-detailed mahogany headboard, its twisted, carved, wooden poles at each corner.

The bedroom, too, was split-level, and she descended the three steps that led to the open bathroom area, its bath on the same giant scale as the bed, chiselled from a single slab of black granite; it had fitted into the service elevator, but to bring it into the apartment, walls had had to be dismantled and rebuilt around it, the floor strengthened to hold it. The twin sinks were of the same granite, the bidet and toilet a matching black, made to order, and they, too, were all on view, not even a paper screen to block the sight of someone using one of the facilities from anyone else in the entire room. The mica-flecked tiles glittered subtly as Coco passed on her way to the French doors at the far side of the bathroom.

Unlatching them, she walked out onto the terrace. It wrapped around the entire apartment, an extraordinary luxury, big enough in its two main sections for dining tables seating sixteen, landscaped with planters containing tall trees, ornamental topiary, a herb garden off the kitchen and roses twining around the stone framework of the balcony. This was her favourite aspect, the south side. Here she could look down on the entire spread of Washington Square Park, see the arch from above, the fountain, tiny people moving on its pathways, kids on skateboards, the dog park, huge Rottweilers and Great Danes reduced to specks as they gambolled and played.

How far I've come in four years! she sighed, still not quite believing it. The wind was cold up here, sharp and piercing, and she held the fur-lined collar of her coat closely to her throat with her leather-gloved hands. What if someone came along, jerked the Isfahan rug from beneath her feet, told her that she was just Jodie Raeburn from Luton, a size 12 girl in a size 0 body? Would she accept it without question, agree that they'd found her out as an impostor?

Or would I tell them they're wrong, that I deserve to be here, high up in Manhattan, on top of the world? She raised her head, chin pegged high, no longer staring down at the people below, but the sky in front of her, the tip of Manhattan Island where it narrowed to the Battery, the grey waters of the Hudson and East Rivers merging into the Narrows, the choppy stretch between Manhattan and Staten Island.

Yes, I would. I'm good at my job, I deserve to have it. I'm loved, I'm valued. I've jumped through every single hoop that life's held out for me: worked harder, run faster, passed every test.

She heaved a deep breath. *And God knows, there have been lots of tests.*

Memories flooded into her mind, powerful, shaming memories. Words she had said, things she had done, commands she had followed. A velvet blindfold, tightly fastened over her eyes, the sensation of her eyelashes blinking frantically against the soft fabric, her wrists pulling against fur-lined handcuffs fastened to those carved wooden poles on the bed she had just passed. Dampness between her legs, soaking her silk knickers.

Fingers stroking every part of her, entering her, making her dance and pull against her bonds, teaching her exactly what he wanted, schooling responses from her. Ice cubes inside her, drops of wax on her skin, searing hot for just a fraction of a moment, tracing a line between her breasts, down her stomach, down further until she thought she could no longer bear it, and pleaded desperately for him to stop, and then realised that she could bear it, even wanted it . . .

Coco shivered, and told herself it was because of the chilly winter air. She was always cold these days, should really go inside: but she wanted to watch the sun set, shadows gradually falling across the stone flagstones of the terrace, the delicate burgundy leaves of the Japanese garnet maple tree casting a tracery across Coco's shoulders. She turned her face up to the sun, its rays on her face warming her skin gently despite the sharp breeze.

I'm finally thin. Really thin. I fit this dress precisely, she told herself, dragging her thoughts to a safer perspective, to something in her life that she could control. *At last I fit into it. Not just getting the zipper-up, squashed into it like a sardine. It hangs just right.*

And he'll know straight away. He'll see that. He sees everything. He'll see how perfectly it fits me, he'll know I'm at his target weight, and he'll be so pleased with me . . . He'll say that I'm finally perfect.

Slipping off the cashmere-lined glove on her left hand, Coco looked down at her engagement ring. She had had to buy winter gloves in a larger size to fit over it. Turning her hand back and forth, mesmerised by the huge, brilliant diamond, she heard nothing but the light whisper of the wind in the branches of the maple trees. Not the peal of the arriving elevator, or footsteps crossing the tiled bathroom floor, stepping out onto the terrace. Perhaps it was a deeper quality to the shadows that were slowly reaching across her body that triggered her sixth sense and told her that she was being watched.

She swung round to see a figure on the side of the terrace. The setting sun was in her eyes now, and she blinked, trying to make out who it was: a woman, and a very thin one, hair drawn back from her face, big sunglasses on her eyes.

'Who's that?' she asked, holding up a hand to shade her face. The huge diamond ring caught the sun and flashed out a million tiny shards of light, red and white and green and cyan, iridescent and glittering, sharp as daggers.

'Hello, Coco,' said the woman, stepping forward. She was holding something in each hand, a pair of small glass bowls on stems, their contents golden: champagne coupes. 'I thought we should toast your engagement,' she said. 'And your new job.'

'How did you—' Coco began, completely confused by this sudden appearance.

'How did I get in?' The woman was close enough now to hand Coco one of the glasses. Coco took it automatically, staring at her in disbelief as she continued, 'Oh, didn't you know?' She smiled. 'Jacob called me. He wanted us all to meet here. He has something he wants to say to both of us. What do you think it could possibly be?'

Part Three
Manhattan: Then

Coco

Coco had spent weeks planning for this moment. By which, of course, she meant planning what to wear. No wedding dress could have been more painstakingly chosen than the outfit she put together for her first day at work at *US Style*.

Her life had changed beyond recognition over the last eight months. It couldn't really be described as a Cinderella story, even though she felt as if a fairy godmother had swooped in and transformed her with the flick of a wand: because after the transformation, Cinderella didn't have to work harder than she ever had in her entire life. Coco wasn't just Victoria's assistant: she was her office cleaner, her de-linter, her personal waitress, her all-round skivvy. If there had been a working fireplace in Victoria's office, Coco would unquestionably, Cinderella-style, have been tasked with polishing the grate to Victoria's exacting specifications.

Still, to make the huge leap from *Wow* to *Style* was magical and unprecedented in itself; to be told, after barely six months on *Style*, that your boss was moving to New York to edit the US edition, and that she was taking you with her, really was a fairy-tale.

A very modern fairy-tale, Coco thought. One where you

have to struggle with the fairy godmother to make sure she doesn't keep you as her slave forever.

Because Coco had had to negotiate like a foreign office diplomat with Victoria to make sure that she didn't get stuck in the assistant position in New York.

'Normally, your assistants do a year and then they get promoted,' she'd pointed out to Victoria. 'But if I go to America as your assistant, I'll have to put in a whole year at least while everything gets settled in. And I've already done nearly six months here in London.'

Victoria's face had darkened – that was the only way to describe it. Coco had seen this phenomenon directed at others before, but never at herself; she'd sworn she wouldn't flinch, had braced herself in advance, holding onto the back of the chair in front of Victoria's desk. She wouldn't have dared sit down, not without specific instructions from Victoria.

With distinct trepidation, Coco watched as the tendons on Victoria's neck swelled against her necklace, which entirely filled the open neckline of her sharp white Alexander McQueen shirt with heavy twists of huge, semi-precious, rough-cut amethysts, peridots and citrines, set in 18-carat gold. It had been designed especially for her by Solange Azagury-Partridge. Victoria raised a hand, running a finger under the thickly-wound strands.

At least she can't break this one, Coco thought, thanking heaven for small mercies. A few weeks ago, Victoria had been pacing the conference room, screaming abuse at a cowering shoe editor and photographer who had, in her opinion, completely ruined a high-concept shoot at London Zoo featuring avant-garde stack heels, Chanel's latest hosiery designs, and lemurs, when she had become so incensed that she'd ripped at the choker she was wearing and sent black pearls flying all over the carpet. Which, since the carpet was charcoal-coloured, had entailed Coco crawling the length and breadth of it, squinting for the telltale opalescent gleam of pearls buried in carpet fibre. She'd counted them painstakingly, terrified that she'd miss one and have to search the whole carpet all over again. Of course, then she'd had to arrange a special courier to take them to be restrung, and Victoria, naturally, had not only failed to thank her, but had actually berated her for a few tiny slips in carrying out all her normal duties to her demanding specifications.

Definitely a modern Cinderella story, she thought. Or maybe a Grimm version. The really dark kind, with blood in shoes and ravens pecking out the Ugly Sisters' eyes.

'Please do tell me,' Victoria had said icily, 'why I shouldn't simply sack you on the spot? Any of the other assistants I've had in the past would be sobbing with gratitude at the idea of being taken to New York.'

'I *am* incredibly grateful,' Coco had replied. Her teeth were chattering in fear, and, quickly, she sank her thumbnails into the tips of her index fingers, hard enough for the pain to focus her. 'But I also know I'm the best assistant you've ever had.'

Victoria sniffed, but she didn't contradict Coco, which was acknowledgement enough in itself. Emboldened, Coco ploughed on.

'If you were in my situation, you'd say the same thing. You'd want some assurance that you'd be doing creative work as well.'

'As well?' Victoria jumped on this like a boa constrictor on a mouse. 'As well as *what*, exactly?'

Coco started to speak, but Victoria cut her off, one of her favourite power-plays.

'You have this all worked out, don't you?' she asked, curling her lip. 'I must say, you're fast. I gave you the news about New York a mere hour ago, you acted very excited, and now you're back in here, setting terms and conditions. Like one of those bouncy toys that pop right back again. What are they called?'

Coco was familiar with Victoria's techniques by now: distraction, confusion, throwing sand in the face of the enemy to disorient them. Because everyone was the enemy to Victoria, or at the least, an opponent. Every conversation was a battle to be won.

So Coco ignored the question, knowing that Victoria didn't seriously expect an answer. Her fingers, resting on the chairback, were sweaty; she pushed to the back of her mind the fear that the sweat would leave marks on its white leather, marks she'd have to clean away later, and continued with her prepared speech.

'I thought I could choose and train up an assistant for you instead,' she said, fixing her gaze on the perfectly smooth, perfectly empty surface of Victoria's glass desk, too intimidated to meet her boss's ice-cold eyes. 'I'd supervise her, make sure absolutely everything with the transition to New York runs smoothly, but I'd also have styling responsibilities. I'm dying to be able to show what I can do creatively.'

'God!' Victoria sighed theatrically. 'No one's ever happy in their job, are they? You get someone settled in and working well, and the next thing you know, they're whining about wanting a promotion! Ugh, it's *so* bloody exhausting.'

Coco bridled. She's such a hypocrite, she thought angrily. That's exactly what she's just done herself – gone running to Jacob and demanded a promotion! And now she's blaming me for doing the same thing . . .

She bit her lip to stop herself blurting out those very words. Victoria reached for the glass of water on her desk; it was nearly empty. Instantly, Coco rushed around the chair to grab the glass, dashing over to the built-in mini-fridge and removing a clean chilled, silver-rimmed tumbler into which she poured Victoria's Fiji water, dropping into it, with tongs, a slice of lime from a supply she had cut that morning. She shot back to the desk, placing the new glass exactly where the old one had been, keeping hold of the previous one, which she would hand-wash in the kitchenette off her office.

It was a display of complete submission, a demonstration of

how well-trained Coco was in Victoria's needs. And Victoria reacted to it in a way that made Coco's blood boil: she looked down her long nose at the new glass, not even deigning to touch it.

God, I hate her! Coco seethed. But at the same time she couldn't help but admire Victoria's air of utter entitlement. It was what kept her at the top of her profession, made everyone scuttle and run as she barked commands. Of course Victoria had the talent, but without her queenly, diva-like attitude, there was no way she would be on the verge of becoming the editor of *US Style*, two years above schedule.

Is this Stockholm Syndrome? Coco wondered. She'd heard that term before, and thought it meant identifying with someone who treated you appallingly. *I'll have to look that up*. She was, as always, hugely grateful for Google and mobile phones – they gave under-educated girls like her a more level playing field with the posh girls who had gone to private school and smart universities and seemed to know everything, effortlessly.

And God knows, no one helps you out here if you don't know a reference – they don't just laugh at you, they tell everyone else in their loud piercing posh voices that you didn't know Joan Miró was a man, for instance. I mean, he's called Joan! That's so confusing! Bloody posh cows.

'Women have to be bitches in this world,' Victoria observed, making Coco jump: it was uncanny how often her boss managed to read her thoughts.

Victoria sighed and pushed her chair back, crossing her legs, light glinting on the perfect pale-blonde twist of chignon at the crown of her head.

'I'm going to expect total loyalty from you, Coco,' she said, twisting the stones of her necklace between her fingers. 'The staffers at *Style* aren't exactly going to be jumping with joy at my arrival. They know I'll sack half of them and make the other half work harder than they ever have before. You're going to be my eyes and ears in the office. Even with people being careful around you, you'll see things and hear things that will be useful to me. I'll need to know where the alliances are, where the weaknesses are. Who's feuding, which ones never got on with each other before but are pretending to now that I've arrived, where are the chinks in the armour.'

She fixed Coco with a hard grey stare.

'They'll all try to turn you against me,' she predicted. 'They'll make promises and dangle favours. You'll be a fool if you let them. I'm the editor of *US Style* as of a month after next, and I'm not going anywhere for a long time. You screw me and you'll pay for it. I'll kick you straight back to London on the next plane. And you'll pay for your own ticket. What's more, I'll make sure no one in magazines in London will touch you with a bargepole. Even if you crawled back to *Wow*,' the sheer contempt she managed to get into that three-letter word was breathtaking, 'they wouldn't dare to rehire you.'

The threats were dire, but Coco was quick enough to realise that they were a positive sign: they were the payment Victoria was exacting for the concession she was about to make. And the single most important part of this tirade was that Victoria was still planning to take Coco to New York . . .

'I was *already*,' Victoria continued with froideur, 'planning to position you somewhere in the office that you could use to listen out to best advantage. And naturally, that wasn't going to be stuck at a desk in my outer office. Who's going to gossip there, or let their guard down so close to me?'

Victoria stared at Coco, tilting her head to one side as if the question had been genuine, but Coco didn't fall for it: she stood there silently, resisting the impulse to smooth down her dress, which had rucked up a little after her dash to get Victoria's glass of water. It's like facing down a vicious dog with its teeth bared, she thought with a flash of dark humour. *Don't move, don't show fear, and whatever you do, don't run.*

'So I had *already* decided to put you in the fashion cupboard,'

Victoria said. 'That's the hub of the entire magazine. You'll be in charge of running it. That's a full-time job in itself, plus you'll be interviewing, choosing and training up my new assistant. You won't have a free moment to yourself. You think you're working hard now?' Her eyes narrowed. 'In New York, you'll be begging for mercy. You'll be in the office all day and all night. I'm throwing you in at the deep end, and if you start to drown, no one's going to throw you a life belt. Understand?'

Coco knew she shouldn't smile; she should look grave, showing her consciousness of what a responsibility she was taking on. But she couldn't help it; she beamed with sheer happiness at the news, her grin huge and wide. Running the fashion cupboard! Seeing every piece of clothing, every shoe, every accessory, that came in and out of *Style*, meeting every single fashion editor and assistant as they rushed in and out, the fastest crash-course possible to bring her up to speed at a new job . . .

'Close your mouth,' Victoria said, swivelling back to the desk, signalling that the talk was over. 'I can practically see your back teeth. Which, by the way, you should get whitened. I'd recommend invisible braces, too. Oh.' She shot a swift, paralysing glance at Coco. 'And lose another seven pounds, at least. What are you now, a size ten? That's an American six. You need to get down to an American four if you don't want people in New York to call you a heifer. Believe me, the girls there don't have an ounce of fat on their entire bodies.'

That's Victoria, Coco thought ruefully now, ensconced in the Lipstick Building, watching the staff of *US Style* flap and buzz and tear up and down the corridors like bees who had just had the lid of their hive removed. *She'll give you something with one hand just to get you close enough so that she can slap you across the face with the other.*

At least Coco knew that her outfit was perfect. A pale grey Zero + Maria Cornejo stretch silk blouse, tucked into a zigzag Missoni skirt in muted shades of green, grey and orange;

Wolford tights, sheer as silk, and Tory Burch copper wedge pumps, the latest directional shade in metallics. Her Isabel Marant brass chain necklace had a coppery sheen too, echoing the shoes: her hair had grown out to one length and was cut into a smooth, fashionably long bob, parted at one side, tinted a pale golden-brown. She looked as good as any of the girls on *Style*.

If a few sizes bigger, she thought, wincing at the stick-thin figures dashing past her. Victoria's a mean bitch, but she wasn't joking about New York skinny minnies. Coco's clothes were an American size four, but they were cutting into her, and she was relying heavily on her slimming underwear, a one-piece bodysuit like a tight beige leotard which reached to mid-thigh. She pulled down her skirt hem, as she did every few minutes; she was paranoid about it riding up when she was sitting, exposing the nasty beige cycling-short legs of the suit.

'You *bitch*!' Caroline Chase Phillips, the senior fashion editor, screamed inside Victoria's office.

Coco didn't even flinch; Victoria had been conducting a long stream of interviews that day, and she'd started with the sackings. Victoria had no interest in ingratiating herself with anyone.

'I'll ruin you in this city!' Caroline howled. 'I know everyone. I'll get you blacklisted everywhere. I'll make it my personal mission to screw you to hell and back! I'll—'

Coco had been working through a stack of applications for the job of Victoria's assistant that had been sent to her by the Dupleix HR department, but now she stood up and went over to Victoria's office, opening the door. Caroline Chase Phillips had been a successful, second-tier model in the eighties; as her shelf life came to an end, she had sensibly decided to become a fashion editor and work her way through a series of increasingly rich property-developer husbands. Still very beautiful, if rather gaunt, she was pacing the office, waving her hands around and screeching like a bad soprano. Victoria was sitting behind her desk, cool and crisp and completely unaffected by Caroline's histrionics.

'Is everything all right, Victoria?' Coco asked.

It was the third time this morning she had had to intervene to speed up the firing process, and Victoria's answer was always the same: she heaved a beautifully-executed yawn of boredom, and said, from behind the hand covering her mouth, 'Another glass of water, Coco. All this firing makes terribly thirsty work.'

'You heartless *hag*!' Caroline Chase Phillips shrieked, and looked around her for something to throw at Victoria, Mercifully, Victoria had had the editor's office remodelled over the weekend in time for her arrival, and not only was it now painted the precise shade of greige with which Victoria was obsessed, but all the little shelves for ornamental knick-knacks, silver photo-frames and decorative vases which Jennifer Lane Davis had had installed had been ripped out, giving a much cleaner look. The office was large enough to accommodate Victoria's huge Japanese tiger screen, which had been hung behind her desk, so that anyone confronting her had to look not only at Victoria, but at the tiger's snarling muzzle, teeth bared, directly above her head.

Just as it had been in London, Victoria's desk was one smooth glass sheet, unencumbered by anything but her computer. There was almost nothing for Caroline Chase Phillips to grab.

'Let's hope she doesn't go for the keyboard,' said a voice behind Coco, modulated so that only Coco could hear her. 'Jennifer tried to smash hers when Jacob sacked her.'

Coco swung round and saw a very slim, very elegant girl standing there, her dark hair pulled back from her face into an enviably thick and glossy ponytail, wearing a beige suede dress that Coco instantly recognised as being from the Ralph Lauren pre-fall collection. It would have cost thousands of pounds retail, and if you got even one tiny stain on it, you might as well chuck it in the bin. Coco gawked at the girl, unable to help it. Suddenly her confidence in her outfit fell away; she felt like a fat lumpy peasant next to this exquisite creature.

'Tried to smash the *keyboard*?' she managed to ask, not quite believing what she'd heard.

The girl's wonderfully thick eyebrows lifted. 'Oh yes,' she said. 'It wasn't pretty.'

'Coco!' Victoria snapped. 'My water, *now*!'

Luckily for Coco, the fridge had not been installed in Victoria's office yet; it was a huge relief that she didn't need to step further into the room. Coco dashed into the kitchenette to fetch the water, dodging back into the office with it, putting the side of the glass desk between her and the furious Caroline Chase Phillips, keeping safely out of the line of fire.

'I think we're done here,' Victoria said, taking the glass and sipping from it, turning away from Caroline in her characteristically dismissive manoeuvre. 'HR will get in touch with you about your severance package, Caroline. Have a nice day, won't you?'

Left with nothing to say, Caroline Chase Phillips threw back her head, stuck her chin in the air and stalked from the office as if she were working a runway for a designer who had told the models to pretend they were stabbing their rivals to death with every thrust of their spiked heels. Coco couldn't help swivelling her head to watch her exit.

'Her catwalk was legendary, apparently,' Ponytail Girl observed. 'She's still got it.'

'Who are you?' Victoria snapped, looking past Coco. 'And why are you distracting my assistant?'

'I'm Zarina,' the girl said. 'Mireille's assistant. She'd like to schedule a time to formally meet and congratulate you on your appointment.'

Victoria sipped some more water, making Zarina wait for her answer.

Of course, Coco thought sourly. Of course she's called

Zarina. And I bet it's her real name, too. Nobody had to rechristen her because they didn't think her original name was smart enough for a top fashion magazine.

'Mireille can come in to see me now,' Victoria said eventually, setting down the glass. 'I've sacked everyone I need to.'

'Oh.' Zarina's heavy dark brows drew together. 'I'm afraid Mireille isn't available until the afternoon. She's got meetings back-to-back all morning, and then she's having lunch with Isaac and Tom.'

Oh, excellent one-upmanship, Coco thought admiringly, not daring to look at her boss. First she makes it clear that Mireille's busier than Victoria, and then she drops in Isaac Mizrahi and Tom Ford's names. Very nice.

No lowly assistant would dare to engage their newly-appointed editor in combat like this. There was no question that Zarina had been specifically instructed by Mireille Grenier in exactly what to say to Victoria Glossop, a ploy to make clear right from the beginning how high Mireille considered her status to be at *Style*.

Victoria took in this information, turning her left hand sideways, contemplating the fires dancing in her grey diamond engagement ring, sparked by the daylight streaming over her shoulder; she had had Jennifer Lane Davis's blackout blinds removed, and the view from the floor-to-ceiling windows was breathtaking. Coco, still unused to the height and spectacle of Manhattan's skyscrapers, couldn't help but be distracted by the panorama. She wondered if she'd ever get used to it, ever be blasé about the fact that she was working in midtown, in the heart of New York, commuting up from Brooklyn every day on the subway, sticking out her hand to hail yellow taxis, living like a character from one of the hundreds of films and TV series she'd watched for so long. She was like Rachel in *Friends*, Carrie in *Sex and the City*, Robin in *How I Met Your Mother*: smart single girls, walking confidently around the city, as if they owned it.

To think when I lay in bed back at Mum and Dad's and stared so wistfully at the TV, imagining myself inside it, living those girls' lives. And now I am! Rachel worked at Bloomingdales, Carrie wrote for Vogue, Robin's a news anchor – I'm in fashion and the media, just like them. No one in Luton can believe where I've ended up. It's like going to space, landing on the moon – not just being in New York, but working at Style as well.

Tiff, still aggrieved at having to call her sister Coco, had nicknamed her 'Andy', after Anne Hathaway's character in *The Devil Wears Prada,* who found herself working on a fashion magazine that closely resembled *Vogue*. But Andy didn't want to be in fashion, ended up rejecting it, while for Coco it was her dream – truly, at this stage, her life. Tiff, Craig, Mr and Mrs Raeburn, were all dying to visit New York, come and see her, but Coco kept putting them off, as she did the few friends she had left in Luton.

She had no place for them to stay, she emailed everyone. Which was true: the tiny flat she and Emily had managed to find in Fort Greene, Brooklyn, was really a one-bedroom, all they could afford. The people they were subletting from had put a bed in the living room, which at least wasn't open-plan with the tiny kitchen. After trekking round what felt like hundreds of places, they'd fallen on it with huge enthusiasm and signed a year-long lease then and there. One of the things sitcoms set in New York didn't show you was how people really lived, the cramped apartments with the only view out of the one window being the brick wall of the apartment building next door.

At least she was lucky to have Emily to share with; Victoria had wanted to bring over a few London staffers, to seed her own people through *US Style,* and Coco had casually suggested Emily, concealing from Victoria her own burning excitement at having a friend in New York with her. Victoria was quite capable of drawing a line through Emily's name just to show Coco who was boss. Coco was learning to handle Victoria just as she was learning her way around Manhattan. But it took all the time she had to spare.

Which meant she had no time for guests either, she'd gone on to tell everyone back home. Nights and weekends she was perpetually on call to Victoria, whose demands had intensified tremendously with the move back to New York, and when she wasn't rushing to meetings with realtors and interior designers on Victoria and Jeremy's behalf, Coco spent every waking moment in the fashion cupboard, determined to familiarise herself with every bracelet and pair of stockings it contained before she started her job there so she could hit the ground running.

I do have Stockholm Syndrome, she thought ironically, having Googled the term now: it came from a group of people in Stockholm who were taken hostage in a bank robbery, and not only resisted being rescued but refused to testify in the trial of their kidnappers. *I'm defending Victoria's bad behaviour to people, trying to find a new assistant who'll cater to her every whim, following in her footsteps so I can be where she is one day . . .*

Lost in a momentary reverie, a dream of editing her own magazine, Coco was jerked back to reality by the sight of Victoria's sleek blonde head rising into her eyeline; Victoria had stood up, was walking towards the door. Coco jumped out of the way, and was pleased to see that Zarina did the same.

'No time like the present,' Victoria observed, with a malicious little smile, as she trod elegantly into the corridor and turned down it.

Coco's eyes widened. She knew exactly where Victoria was going. And so, from the agonised glance that Zarina darted at her, did the other girl.

'Mireille's in a meeting,' Zarina hissed at Coco. 'She can't just go in there!'

'Are you joking?' Coco hissed back. 'You never say "can't" to Victoria!'

Zarina hurried away, the narrow suede sheath hobbling her. Coco watched her with great amusement: the skirt was so tight that Zarina's knees snapped awkwardly against the hem of the dress with every short darting step.

'*Le drama*!' said a girl in an exaggerated fake French accent, emerging from an office a little further down the corridor, watching Zarina rush off in Victoria's wake. '*Ooh la la!*'

Coco giggled, relieved to have some release from all the tension of the morning. The girl was Chinese-looking, with matte skin the colour of parchment, big bright eyes and a heavy, choppy bob with an asymmetric fringe. Her flat-chested, boyish figure was perfect for her silk shirt with its big floppy, pussycat bow at the neck, tucked into wide-legged tweed trousers.

'She's trying to get past to warn Mireille,' the girl said, craning her head to see. 'Oh, Victoria's blocking her – she's not letting her pass . . .'

Coco didn't even need to look. 'Victoria'll elbow her in the face if she gets too close,' she said.

'Hah! She tackles . . . Victoria's gone in . . .' The girl nipped down the corridor for a better vantage point. 'She blocks – she's shut the door in Zarina's face!' she reported back breathlessly, as other heads popped cautiously out of their offices to hear what was happening. 'Zarina's livid. Ooh – outcoming missiles . . .'

Two smart young women came shooting out of Mireille's office and down the corridor as if they'd been fired from a cannon, their faces flushed, on the verge of tears.

'She just stormed in and yelled at us to get out,' one of them said to the girl, her voice choked. '*So* rude!'

'*No* couth,' agreed the other one, gulping hard in an attempt to hide how much her voice was trembling.

'And now I've left my rail in Mireille's office,' Girl Number One wailed.

'I've left my *bangles in* there,' Girl Number Two chimed in, managing to make this sound even more serious.

'Oh God, I *so* need a wheatgrass shot,' Girl Number One said. 'This is worse than when my houseshare in the Hamptons fell through at the last minute!'

They disappeared into a side office, their high-pitched voices rising and falling like birds in an aviary terrified of a cat stalking round the bars.

'You're Victoria's assistant?' the girl with the bob said to Coco, strolling back to her own office now the flurry of activity had died down.

'Just till I hire someone to do it,' Coco said defensively. 'Then I'll be running the fashion cupboard.'

'Wow.' The girl grinned, and held out her hand. 'I'll get in early with the sucking up, then. Always good to be friends with the queen of the cupboard! Plus, you came over with our new editor, you'll know all the dirt, right?'

Coco shook her hand, noticing that the girl, like most of the other Stylites she had seen so far, didn't seem to be wearing a scrap of make-up.

'I'm Lucy,' the girl said. 'Lucy Lee. I know, sounds like it's something out of a comic, doesn't it? But everyone remembers it, so that's a plus.'

'Coco Raeburn,' Coco said. She paused, then blurted out: 'But that's not my real first name. Victoria renamed me. She didn't think my real name was "fashion" enough.'

'O-*kay*.' Lucy blinked hard. 'So I guess all the stories about her are true.'

Coco nodded. 'Most definitely.'

'Still, my money's on Mireille,' Lucy said, gesturing down the corridor to the fashion director's office. 'She's seen three editors come and go.'

'Victoria's really scary,' Coco said doubtfully.

'Yeah, but look what just happened,' Lucy said. 'Mireille got Victoria to go to her! Now they're going at it on her turf – she's got the home field advantage.'

Coco looked at her, taking this in.

'Battle of the Titans,' Lucy said. 'There's a Chinese curse – "May you live in interesting times".' She grinned. 'Well, here we are! Want me to show you where the canteen is? They'll be in there for a while, so you've got time to grab a quick coffee. Or a wheatgrass shot, if you want to try that. Be careful, though. That stuff goes straight through you . . .'

Victoria

As soon as Victoria stepped into Mireille's office, she knew she had made a mistake. Idiot, she snapped at herself. It wasn't a consolation to anyone who suffered under Victoria's lash, because they didn't know it, but Victoria was, if possible, even harder on herself than she was on others. As the two junior editors fled the scene, flapping like sheets on a clothing line, Victoria mentally excoriated herself for being so stupid.

You should have made her come to you! Instead, you let her get you angry and you let down your guard. Fool! You just acted like a total amateur!

She took a deep breath, trying to regain control. Mireille was sitting behind her desk, one eyebrow raised, looking supremely elegant in that annoying French way. She had perpetual dark shadows under her eyes that she disdained to cover with a stroke of Touche Éclat, and which her red lipstick actually emphasised; those circles would look ghastly on anyone but a Frenchwoman, Victoria thought crossly. But this bitch manages to look like a world-weary film star.

Memories of working at *US Style* years ago, presenting edited selections of clothes to Mireille the way the fluttering editors had been in the middle of doing, flashed vivid in

Victoria's mind. She had been hired as a features editor, but Victoria was no writer, had no gift for it, and though her ideas had been excellent, her copy had always been rewritten. Unable to sack her, because of Jacob's patronage, Jennifer had switched her to the fashion desk – reluctantly, as she feared that this would put Victoria in more direct competition with her. She'd been absolutely right. Victoria had used her transfer as a lever to get *Harper's Bazaar* to make her an offer; no one had ever breathed a greater sigh of relief as Jennifer had done when Victoria announced she was leaving.

This should have been Victoria's moment of triumph: back in Mireille's office, but in charge now, no longer needing Mireille's approval. They had crossed paths since Victoria had left *Style*, of course: at the collections in Paris, London, Milan, New York, at galas and benefits, at private viewings in designers' ateliers. Victoria had always treated Mireille with a wary respect; her reputation was legendary. But Mireille was currently making it clear that she considered herself in no way subordinate to Victoria. She had already played this perfectly. One-nil to Mireille.

'Victoria, my dear. What an unexpected pleasure,' Mireille said, smiling. But she did not get up, nor did she offer Victoria a seat.

Victoria's eyes narrowed. Sit down, or keep standing? She swivelled on her high heels, walking over to the far window, turning her back on Mireille in a deliberate ploy to gain some control of the situation.

'I hear you have been firing away with merry abandon,' Mireille said, considerable amusement in her voice. 'You have certainly made your point, *ma chère*. Everyone is terrified of you.'

Except you, Victoria thought irritably. She studied her reflection in the glass window: her Prada dress, which she had had shortened to show off her legs, was in a cream and caramel print, and her arms were loaded with wide tortoiseshell bracelets. She was currently obsessed with shades of brown; it felt very directional. Turning to face Mireille, she noticed with great annoyance that the trays of bangles and cuffs brought in by the accessories editor were bang on trend; she could find nothing to criticise. In fact, her hand itched to pick up one particularly attractive gold-chased Galliano mesh wristlet . . .

'So modern, that cuff,' Mireille said, giving it the ultimate fashion insider's stamp of approval: to describe something as 'not modern' was to consign it, instantly, to oblivion. 'That would be perfect with your Chanel tweed jacket,' Mireille added thoughtfully. 'The grey one with the piping. Karl told me he was customising it for you.'

Victoria's head snapped back. Mireille had just landed a series of body blows. Victoria had only picked out that jacket a couple of weeks ago, on a lightning-fast Eurostar trip to Paris to select her New York wardrobe from the advance collections: Mireille was not only making the point that she had discussed Victoria with Karl Lagerfeld, but that she could style Victoria with pinpoint accuracy.

Damn her, she's right, Victoria thought furiously. She had made only the tiniest of movements towards the Galliano wristlet. Mireille's eyes must be sharp as needles. Two-nil to the Frenchwoman.

'Jacob's very excited at the idea of us working together,' Mireille said, smiling. 'Oh please – do sit down.' She gestured with the grace of the ballerina she had once been to the chair in front of her desk. 'Adorable of you to wait to be asked, *ma chère*, but quite unnecessary,' she added with a sweet smile.

Three-nil. *Fuck! If I sit down, I'm doing what she's told me to – but if I don't, I look sulky* . . .

Thinking quickly, Victoria chose instead to stroll over to the rack of clothes the other editor had brought in, pretending a sudden interest in the flimsy bikinis and cut-out one-pieces that were suspended by padded clips from metal hangers.

'Ugh, I loathe these,' she said, flicking them with a finger tipped in gunmetal YSL varnish. 'So gaudy.'

'*Oui, c'est vrai,*' Mireille replied with the utmost sincerity. 'She has completely misunderstood me. I specified Missoni in the Caribbean, and she brings me the Rio Carnival. The beading in particular is absurd.'

She pushed back her chair and stood up in a fluid movement that belied her age. Joining Victoria at the rack, she lifted out a heavily-embroidered bikini top that no one would ever dream of taking near the water.

'But this,' she said, draping it over her other hand to display it better, its bright rainbow hues even more attractive when viewed in isolation, 'I thought, perhaps, under the Nina Ricci mohair cardigan that Lucy just called in. Have you seen it yet? It's a particular shade of limoncello that would be perfect to set off the lime greens in this. I thought perhaps we'd unbutton the cardigan just enough to let this chartreuse flash through . . .'

She was absolutely right. Victoria knew exactly the cardigan she meant; it was stunning, and the bikini would look perfect underneath it. Besides, they needed to feature at least two Nina Ricci pieces in the next issue. One aspect of being the editor of *Style* which Jennifer Lane Davis had neglected was the crucial issue of relationships with the advertisers. Victoria's first task, after restructuring the staffing at the magazine, would be to schedule a whole series of lunches and dinners with the cream of New York's ad sales executives, making clear that their designers and products would be featured extensively from now on in their fashion spreads and beauty articles.

'Perhaps,' she said coldly. 'I'll have to see the photos before I decide.'

'*Mais bien sûr.*' Mireille smiled even more sweetly, returning the bikini top to the rack. 'You are the editor – of course the ultimate decisions are yours.'

'Well. Yes. I'm glad that's clear,' Victoria said gruffly, feeling completely wrong-footed by this statement. It should have been a point for her, but it didn't feel like it; in fact, it felt like four-nil to Mireille. How was this *happening*?

'I'm very busy,' she continued, 'but I'm pleased to see that you're pushing ahead here. We have a lot to get accomplished. I've brought some people over from London, and Clemence is joining us from *Harper's*. Plus Dietrich from *Vogue*. They'll all need to settle in.'

'How delightful.' Mireille looked utterly enchanted at the news that two of the biggest and most spoiled egos in fashion magazines were about to arrive at *Style*. 'I cannot wait. What a wonderful team you are assembling, *ma chère*.'

'Yes. Well.' Victoria cleared her throat. 'It will be. Definitely. And now I must be going. I'm having lunch with Jacob. He's due to pop down and pick me up at any moment.'

' "Pop down and pick me up".' Mireille echoed, clapping her hands once, gently. 'How charming! I adore your little English expressions. *Alors*, I will keep you no longer, in that case. *À bientôt*, Victoria.'

She returned to her chair, swinging it back to face her book-cluttered desk, which had the effect of turning her shoulder to her new boss. It was, Victoria recognised with mounting fury, the same technique she herself used, and what was even more galling was that she realised she must have unconsciously copied it from Mireille, back when she had been working for *Style*. Victoria's brush-off was much brusquer, more Anglo-Saxon, whereas Mireille did it in a breezy, casual French style, which somehow made it even more effective. The hairs stood up on the nape of Victoria's neck with anger as she stalked towards the door.

Five-nil.

'Do give Jacob my best love,' Mireille called lightly after her. 'I will be much too *occupée* to see him today, but I'm sure you will have a delightful lunch *à deux*.'

Six-nil: victory to Mireille. Whatever game they were playing, she was definitely the winner.

Victoria fumed as she stormed through the outer office. *How dare she tell me she's sure I'll have a delightful lunch with Jacob – she's so patronising!*

Mireille's assistant was cowering behind her desk, not lifting her head to meet Victoria's eyes. She's no fool, Victoria thought furiously. I'd have bitten her head off if she dared to even look at me, let alone say a word.

Victoria would have been even more annoyed if she had known that a mere five minutes after she left Mireille's office, Mireille had summoned the junior fashion editor and told her with great regret that the bikini shoot would have to be scrapped.

'It is a great pity,' she sighed. 'You have assembled a beautiful selection here, absolutely exquisite. But what can you do? Victoria's taste is very banal, very limited. All that beautiful beading, she completely dismissed it.' She shrugged philosophically. 'We will at least be able to use that superb Etro bikini, so we can salvage something. *Tant mieux*. And do not worry.' She smiled at the still-petrified fashion editor. 'You have done an excellent job, and I will protect you.'

'Thank you, Mireille,' the editor breathed, some colour returning to her cheeks.

'*De rien, ma petite*,' Mireille said fondly. 'We must all stick together, mustn't we? Victoria is a little rough around the edges, but we will polish her up and make her shine. Show her how things are done here.'

Mireille turned to the mirror, automatically surveying herself, pleased to observe that she was as immaculate as ever, even after that crucial scene with Victoria Glossop. Her face was thoughtful, myriad ideas and schemes running through her mind. Mireille was extremely visual; she thought in images, and it was as if a photo display were scrolling at lightning-speed through her mind, spinning past, until one image clicked into place and hung there, filling the screen.

The crow's feet around her eyes fanned deeper as she smiled like a cat with a whole saucerful of cream. Mireille operated on instinct, trusting that her first, swift intuition would always be guided by the steely scaffolding framework she had constructed during the many years she had spent in the cut-throat business of magazine publishing.

'*Peut-être,*' she said slowly. '*Oui, peut-être . . .*' Her smile widened even further. 'I may well have an idea that will deal very satisfactorily with Victoria. Very satisfactorily indeed.'

Coco

Oh God, Victoria's going to loathe working with Mireille, Coco thought unhappily as she selected three candidates for the assistant's job and stacked their CVs in a small pile next to the much larger one of rejects. *And I'll bear the brunt of it. I just hope to God I pick a decent assistant to help me out.*

After the first cull of girls who didn't have enough fashion experience to cope with the high level of knowledge the job required, Coco had selected the three who looked as if they were used to hard work. Girls who'd got to college on scholarships, who'd put themselves through by working part-time, and had still managed to not only join, but run, a whole series of impressive-sounding clubs and party-planning committees. Girls who had interned at fashion magazines or local papers every summer.

Girls who were hopefully tough enough not to burst into tears the first time Victoria swore at them.

'I see you've found the canteen already,' said a male voice. Coco had been so absorbed in her search, had so much invested in the need to replace herself at this desk as quickly as possible, that she hadn't even noticed his approach. She looked up, and knew instantly who was standing in front of her.

The man with his name on the doors of the office, on the masthead, the letterhead, so many of the things she saw here a hundred times a day. It was like having William Randolph Hearst or Condé Nast himself walk into her office; and, to her, he was more impressive than any photographer or supermodel. With Mario Testino, Gilles Bensimon, Naomi Campbell, Kate Moss, she could have coped perfectly fine, had already done so at *Style* in London. But the big boss, the man who pulled everyone's strings, who could directly influence her career . . . that was very different. Coco was dumbstruck.

He was more impressive in person. That didn't help at all. He wasn't that tall, but he was so imposing that it didn't remotely matter. There was an air of confidence about him, an effortless charisma, that she had never known an Englishman to possess; they tended to be more self-deprecating, less comfortable in their own skin. No wonder – their skin was never this glorious shade of golden-tan, their teeth never flashed so white and perfect when they smiled. Jacob Dupleix, in his perfectly-tailored navy Valentino suit, his Savile Row shirt and handmade Italian shoes, looked like . . . like the name Tom Wolfe gave the bankers in that 1980s novel, Coco thought; she was reading every book set in New York she could find. *Masters of the Universe*.

No wonder I can't get a word out, with a Master of the Universe standing in front of me.

'So – how's the coffee?' asked Jacob Dupleix, nodding at the paper carry-out cup on her desk. 'Be honest with me, okay? If you don't like it, I'll go right downstairs and bawl out the canteen manager.'

Coco knew, of course, that he was teasing her. She had a split-second to decide how to handle this, how to make an impression on the man who was her ultimate boss. Normally she wouldn't have found it hard at all: it called on one of her best skill sets, one at which most British girls excelled – witty banter. Even in her brief time in the US, barely a fortnight, she had realised it was a real asset here, being able to banter. Most Americans couldn't do it, not even the New Yorkers, which was a surprise. You'd think, with all their witty sitcoms set in Manhattan, where no one was ever at a loss for a wisecrack, people here would be even funnier and faster than back home in the UK.

But no. The combination of British quick-thinking repartee, plus an English accent, made everyone here fall over backwards with admiration and then rush forward again to help with anything she needed. Coco was embarrassed to admit it, but she had already started to posh up her accent over here. The plummier she sounded – the more like Victoria – the more tough, stony-faced New Yorkers melted into goofy friendliness and asked if she lived in a castle back home and knew the Queen.

I'm going to have to be really careful I don't go home talking like a stuck-up cow and have everyone take the piss mercilessly, she knew. But right now, with the head of the publishing company smiling down at her, she took a deep breath and drawled, as best she could; 'Actually, it's pretty frightful swill. Any chance you could pop out to Starbucks for me?'

Jacob's eyes widened, just fractionally. His full, sensual lips drew together, and every muscle in Coco's body tensed, terrified that she had seriously miscalculated how to handle the situation. Jacob's hands had been in the trouser pockets of his suit as he strolled into the office: now he withdrew them, lifted the back flap of his jacket, so it wouldn't get wrinkled, and propped his bottom on the edge of Coco's desk, sitting right on the small pile of CVs she had just selected. It brought him closer to her, but more importantly, it invaded her territory, putting him in a position of domination. His wool-clad thigh looked huge; he loomed over her. Even his scent – a mix of cigars, leather and a dark, seductive cologne – imposed itself forcefully on her senses.

'So,' he said, looking down at her, his lips now curving into a smile. 'Pretty *and* funny! Victoria sure knows how to pick 'em. What's your name, honey?'

'Coco,' she said, moving a little back in her chair, needing to put a fraction more distance between them. It was like being too close to a fire. She was instinctively afraid of getting scorched.

'Cute,' he said appreciatively. 'Like the drink, or Chanel?'

Coco realised she was smiling back at him. 'Chanel,' she said. 'It was Victoria's idea, to be honest. I was called something else before.'

His grin deepened. 'You like it?' he asked.

Coco's smile became demure; she looked down, then up at him under her eyelashes. 'What's that got to do with anything?' she asked back. 'I thought I said it was Victoria's idea.'

Jacob Dupleix threw back his head and laughed. 'You're a pistol, honey,' he chuckled.

'Is that a good thing, Mr Dupleix? I haven't quite got used to all your American expressions yet.' Coco was still looking up from under her eyelashes; she felt sure that she was overdoing it, but her body was completely out of her control. It wanted to flirt with him, and it wasn't listening to her brain when she told it to stop, that it was acting really cheesily.

'Oh,' he said, gazing at her intensely, his eyes dark as coals. 'It's a *very* good thing. And please.' He leaned towards her, and she found herself leaning in too, hanging on his every word. He lowered his voice a little, deep and confidential, as if he were telling her a secret, and it made her breath catch in her throat. 'Call me Jacob, won't you?'

Coco couldn't say a word.

'Aw, please,' he coaxed, and he reached out with one finger and tipped her chin up, fractionally, so she was looking him straight in his dark, knowing eyes. 'Let's hear you say it. Come on. Say my name.'

His finger was wide and warm, still pressed against the soft underside of her jaw, and he stroked it back and forth caressingly as he waited for her answer. He was halfway across her desk, his body almost sprawled over it now, a big lazy cat. Power and money rolled off him in effortless waves.

Coco's lips opened, and it took every atom of resolve she had for her to whisper: 'Jacob.'

He gave a tiny nod, looking down at her intently, his hand not leaving her chin. His approval affected her so strongly that her lower body began to melt into her chair, her thighs loosening . . .

'Jacob!' Victoria's sharp accent sliced like a knife through the sexual tension that was flooding between Coco and Jacob. His finger slipped from Coco's chin, his body lifted away from Coco's desk as he turned towards his new editor, who came sweeping into the office like a particularly vicious tsunami. Coco felt utterly bereft as his attention left her. She stared at the back of his head, the tight dark curls liberally streaked with silver, the narrow sliver of warm golden-brown skin that showed above the collar of his jacket. Coco shivered just remembering his leg on her desk, so close she could have reached out and touched it.

But it was him who touched me. She raised a hand to her jawline, where Jacob had placed his finger, feeling colour rise to her cheeks. Victoria was speaking, a stream of spiked words, but Coco couldn't make out a single one of them. Victoria went into her office, emerged with her Versace eelskin bag caught in the crook of her elbow, and rejoined Jacob, sliding a hand familiarly over his arm, linking them as she tossed over at Coco: 'So! You'll have that all done by the time I'm back from lunch.'

'Of course, Victoria,' Coco said swiftly, though she had absolutely no idea what she had agreed to do.

'Nice to meet you, Coco,' Jacob said as Victoria towed him to the door, a small impatient tug-boat pulling a majestic ocean liner. He turned his head and caught Coco's eye. Bastard, he's so sure of himself, she thought, blushing more deeply.

Jacob was smiling at something Victoria was saying. But as he glanced at Coco, his eyelid dropped momentarily in an unmistakable wink of complicity.

Electricity shot through Coco. She realised, with huge embarrassment, that her hand was still on her chin where Jacob had touched it, and she whipped it away, much too late, because he must have seen that already, must have realised the effect he had had on her . . .

And then she realised something else. Her knickers were damp. Soaked through. When had it happened? When he touched her, when he winked at her?

No, she thought. *When he made me say his name*. The memory alone made her even more excited. Her upper thighs clamped together instinctively, her pelvis tilting down on the chair, hard, provoking a mini-surge of release; her eyes closed for a second as it snapped through her.

And then she imagined Jacob watching her, perched on her desk, smiling his lazy smile as he saw the effect he had had on her, and again, the breath caught in her throat and the soft cotton of her knickers, twisting at her crotch, grew even damper with arousal.

She wasn't supposed to leave her desk, not for a moment, not unless she organised a replacement to answer the phones. But she couldn't resist, couldn't even take the time to buzz Emily to come in for her. Heart pounding like a tom-tom in her chest, she stood up and dashed into Victoria's office, into the private bathroom which Coco kept stocked with Victoria's favourite Acqua di Parma toiletries and Frette checkerboard-motif hand towels, but which she was never supposed to use herself. Locking the door behind her, she pulled down her knickers, catching a nail on the lace trim in her haste, and shoved her hand roughly between her legs. Her eyes closed: she saw Jacob Dupleix's face in front of her, his dark eyes focused on her intently, his wide lips parting, instructing her to call him by his name, and, imagining that it was his hand working on her, his warm wide fingers sliding inside her, she came immediately, her hips juddering back against the rim of the marble sink.

'Jacob,' she whispered to herself. 'Jacob, Jacob, Jacob . . .'

She came again and again, working feverishly on herself. She'd been so busy at her job day and night that she had had no time for her own needs at all; she'd been dieting hard, tearing round the city running errands for Victoria, exhausting her body and mind so much that every night she'd collapsed into bed too tired to do anything but sleep. She didn't even know how long it had been since she'd last given herself an orgasm.

I needed this so badly, she thought with huge relief. She was sweating with effort and excitement, her back damp, her hand coated lubriciously in her own moisture. It was as if Jacob Dupleix had turned on a tap, let loose all her pent-up physical frustration, and now all she needed to do, hopelessly, deliciously, was to close her eyes, picture his face and say his name and she would come.

As if he were a magician, granting wishes. Knowing what I need, even when I don't myself. Giving it to me – oh God . . .

The thought of Jacob Dupleix actually having sex with her pushed her right over the edge; if the sink hadn't been behind her she might have tumbled to the floor. After that shattering orgasm she dragged in her breath and forced her hand away from her crotch, snatching some tissues to wipe herself down. She turned to look at herself in the mirror above the sink: her eyes were bright, her cheeks pink, her skin dewy.

If he could see me like this, she thought, would he want me? Would he—

She had to get back to work. *Had to*. She could hear the phone at her desk ringing insistently. *I have to stop thinking about him, or I'll never get anything done, and I have so much to do*.

But how can I, when his name's on everything I look at in this entire building?

She had to laugh. *It's like he's haunting me.*

Don't say America, say the States. Don't say Avenue of the Americas, say Sixth Avenue. Don't say Street after the street name. Don't say overseas, pavement, lift, cutlery: say abroad, sidewalk, elevator, flatware or silverware. Don't say Spanish, say Hispanic. Don't *ever* say Oriental, it's racist: say Asian.

That last rule had been drummed into Coco by Lucy, who was her new best American friend.

'But Asian for British people means Indian or Pakistani,' Coco protested. 'It's really confusing for us.'

'You just gotta suck it up,' Lucy said cheerfully, an American expression that Coco adored. 'Here if you say Oriental you mean a carpet. And I'm not a rug.' She pursed her lips around her straw and took a slug of her whisky sour. 'Having said that,' she added, 'you can pretty much get away with anything if you've got an English accent.'

'I worked that out already,' Coco said, smiling.

'Oh, God, yes.' Emily chimed in. 'I've had tons of people ask me already if I'm friends with "Princess Kate"!' She pulled a face. 'I do keep saying that it's actually "Catherine, Duchess of Cambridge", but no one cares.'

'And what do you say when they ask you?' Coco said.

'Oh.' Emily giggled and drank some more vodka and diet tonic. 'I say yes, of course I know her. I do sort of know her sister Pippa actually,' she added. 'From Mahiki and Boujis.'

Lucy's brow furrowed, not recognising the names: a typical aristocrat, Emily always assumed that everyone else went to the same places she did, or at least knew exactly what she was talking about.

'They're the clubs where the Sloanes – the posh people with tons of money – hang out in London,' Coco explained to her. 'They drink cocktails out of treasure chests that cost a hundred pounds a go and then they go red and dance to Abba. Really badly.'

'Oi, that's a bit unfair,' Emily said, pulling a face. 'Not everyone dances badly.'

'I bet Pippa dances well. What's she like?' Lucy asked eagerly.

'Well,' Emily said with an expression of extreme seriousness, setting down her drink, 'she has *awfully* good hair.'

Over Emily's head, Lucy's dark eyes met Coco's, brimming with amusement. Much as Coco liked Emily, she had to admit that the more time they spent together, the fewer brains she noticed rattling around underneath Emily's own lush head of hair. Emily was a brilliant fashion editor, had an excellent eye, and was already putting together some eye-catching spreads, but Lucy, a feature writer, was smart as a whip, and the difference between the two girls was increasingly noticeable.

'She *does* have very good hair,' Lucy agreed gravely. 'Oh look! X!' She waved an arm back and forth in a half-semaphore, gesticulating at someone across the bar. They were in Luxe, a bar around the corner from the Dupleix building, which was the current fashionable watering-hole for its employees to hang out after work – if, of course, they weren't heading off to launch parties and openings for the free drinks and networking, or hitting the gym, which were the main two after-work activities for Dupleix staffers.

Tonight was a Friday, which meant neither launch parties nor openings, which were always mid-week; the girls, exhausted from a gruelling week of work, had chosen the easiest spot to come drinking. Luxe, as befitted its name, was plushly decorated, its dark purple carpet scattered with cosy groups of small velvet tub chairs and matching velvet pouffes arranged around low polished tables. The owners had been unable to resist stripping the walls to bare brick – decades after the style was first pioneered in SoHo lofts downtown, it was still hugely fashionable – but had at least tempered their starkness by draping huge swags of matching velvet along the upper half and softening the lower part with hundreds of tiny candles.

'X!' Lucy hollered, half-lifting herself from her velvet seat. 'Over here!'

Lucy's such a tomboy, Coco thought. She doesn't have an inch of guile or girliness. The floppy-bowed blouse, the wide tweed trousers that Lucy had been wearing the first time they'd met were absolutely typical of her style; she was like a chic 1920s flapper, with her dramatic bob and her narrow body that wore men's tailoring so perfectly. This evening she was in a tight pinstriped waistcoat over a boatnecked silk Jil Sander T-shirt and cuffed wool trousers, with four-inch-heeled pumps. It was a look that Coco could never have pulled off, but it looked wonderful on Lucy.

It was initially hard to tell who Lucy was waving at, there was such a crush of people at the bar. Besides, its illumination mostly came from the miniature candles set into copper-backed niches in the walls, which reflected the flickering light; ideal for intimacy and romance, less so if you were trying to see someone more than four feet away from you.

'Ooh!' Emily breathed. 'Yummy!'

Coco saw exactly what she meant; the guy weaving his way through the crowd towards them, his drink held high, was tall, dark and extremely handsome. He raised his other hand in greeting, flashing Lucy a ridiculously sweet smile.

'X works at *Men's Style*,' Lucy said, as he arrived at their table. 'Junior fashion and grooming editor.'

'Hi,' Emily said enthusiastically, as he pulled up a stool and sat down. 'I'm Emily.' She did her best, big, theatrical swoop of blonde hair, tossing her head so the entire mass cascaded from one side of her neck to the other. 'It's lovely to meet you! Are you really called X?' She giggled. 'I must say,' she added coquettishly, fluttering her eyelashes, 'X certainly marks the spot.'

Oops, Coco thought. Emily, he's pretty much bound to be gay. He's gorgeous, perfectly dressed, really fit, and he's the grooming editor on *Men's Style* – you may want to take a deep breath and back away, because he almost definitely bats for the other team.

Lucy caught Coco's eye again, pantomiming, her mouth open wide in a comical O. Coco grinned back, enjoying the entertainment. She took another tiny sip of the one vodka and diet tonic she was nursing, making it last all evening; she would pick up some sushi from the Japanese takeout two doors down from the tiny apartment she shared with Emily in Fort Greene on the way home. She had worked out at lunchtime in the corporate gym, and she felt in control. A little light-headed from hunger, but she was used to being hungry now; she fell asleep to a lightly-rumbling stomach and awoke to one grumbling even louder. She understood now why film stars and models were always photographed with cups of coffee in their hands. Skim-milk coffee, with sweetener rather than sugar, was practically calorie-free, and it filled you up, the caffeine buzz carrying you along, distracting you from craving solid food.

'I'm Xavier,' the guy said, shaking Emily's hand. 'Xavier Fan.'

'What a fabulous name,' Emily gushed. 'Now, Lucy's just been telling us not to say Oriental – so what are you, exactly?'

Lucy's O opened even wider.

'Chinese-American,' Xavier replied politely. 'My folks are from Singapore, but they moved here before I was born.'

'But you're so tall!' Emily looked him up and down with lustful appreciation. 'I didn't know Chinese people got so tall.'

Lucy cracked up. 'It's all the protein in the States,' she said, giggling. 'It makes us tiny little Asians grow big and strong.'

Xavier smiled at Emily. 'You have such nice teeth,' he said gently. 'I didn't know English people had such nice teeth.'

Emily squealed with amusement. 'Oh God, that's hilarious! You're funny too.' She patted his arm flirtatiously. 'I have nice teeth,' she said, 'because Mummy and Daddy have lots of dosh and got mine fixed. Most British people don't, so you're not completely wrong.'

Coco closed her lips over her own teeth, which were wonky. The ones on her lower jaw overlapped at the front; she'd barely been aware of the flaw before she started at *Style* in London, but Victoria had commented on it, and of course, in America, everyone's dentistry was so much better. She remembered her mum pointing out to the NHS dentist ten years ago that fourteen-year-old Coco's – Jodie's – teeth were a bit crossed. The dentist had answered that Jodie had plenty of room in her mouth for all of them; there was no need to give her braces.

I was so grateful not to have braces then, Coco thought, miserably. But now I really wish my parents had been like Emily's.

'Hey,' Xavier was saying, reaching out his hand to hers; he had lovely manners. 'I'm Xavier. Or X, if that's easier.'

'Coco,' she said, smiling at him, but very carefully, to avoid showing her teeth. 'Lovely to meet you.'

'You work at Dupleix, don't you? I think I've seen you round,' he said. 'Maybe in the canteen?'

'I'm always shooting through,' she said ruefully. 'I never have time to sit down and eat.'

'Coco's Victoria Glossop's assistant,' Emily chipped in, eager to reclaim Xavier's attention.

'Whoah,' Xavier said. 'I've heard some of the stories about her. That's got to be hardcore.'

'Was,' Coco corrected. 'We're celebrating my promotion. I was her assistant. I got a new slave past the interview this week – Monday, I'm off to the fashion cupboard.' She raised her glass. 'To freedom,' she said happily. 'Well, sort of freedom.'

'And lots of free stuff!' Lucy chorused, clinking her glass with Coco's.

Emily and Xavier raised their glasses too, though Emily was staring at Xavier the entire time they toasted Coco. Coco couldn't blame her; he was utterly gorgeous. Skin as smooth and matte as Jersey cream, his face like a sculpture, his cheekbones high and strong, his long dark eyes sparkling with amusement and charm. His tightly-fitted shirt and flat-fronted black trousers showed off his long, lean figure, and they contrasted stylishly with the steel piercings in his ears, three on the side Coco could see. Actually, his shirt was snug enough that she thought she could make out the tell-tale lump of another piercing on his right pectoral.

'I did a stint in the fashion cupboard on *Uomo Vogue*,' he said, sipping his drink, which was a tall orange concoction garnished with three maraschino cherries. 'Toughest gig I ever had. I'd go to sleep and dream of opening boxes all night.'

'Coco's super-organised,' Lucy said.

'Oh wow! *Uomo Vogue*!' Emily cut in. 'You've worked in so many cool places.' She touched his arm again, did her hair-toss, and flashed the teeth he had complimented all at once; it was flirtation overload, and Xavier flinched fractionally from the onslaught.

'Steady, tiger,' Lucy said, laughing.

'Hey,' Xavier said, looking around the three girls, clearly wanting to include them all in the conversation, to avoid being trapped in a tête-à-tête with the over-enthusiastic Emily. 'Can I ask you all something?'

'Anything!' Emily said loudly.

'I've been noticing something in the last few weeks,' Xavier continued. 'All you girls at *Style* look different than you did before. It's not just me – tons of other guys in the building've been commenting on it too. Are you, like, wearing more make-up or something? Or higher heels?'

All three *Style* girls looked at each other and burst out laughing.

'Oh, now I know I've said something funny,' Xavier said, eyes bright. 'Come on, what is it?'

'It's Victoria,' Coco said. 'Everyone's trying to look like Victoria.'

'Before, when Jennifer was editor,' Lucy explained, 'she wore flats and had her hair loose and never used any make-up, so everyone sort of copied her. And she was very fashion-forward. She'd wear whatever was the latest thing, even if it didn't suit her, so we all felt we had to do the same.' She rolled her eyes. 'I'm *so* glad I can wear mascara again. And blusher. I hated not wearing make-up at work.'

'But Victoria's really different,' Emily chimed in. 'She's, like, super-chic and has her own style, so we all need to find our own. But she loathes it if you don't wear make-up or high heels, so we all have to do that.'

'And bangles,' Coco added. 'Everyone's got their Victoria bangles.'

In unison, she, Emily and Lucy raised their arms and jangled their big cuff bracelets, making a rattle that could be heard even in the noisy bar.

'That's hilarious!' Xavier exclaimed, laughing now. 'Hey, if I want a job on *Style*, should I get some bangles too?' He shot back one cuff of his tightly-fitted shirt, baring his wrist.

'Wow, you're so smooth!,' Emily slurred appreciatively, reaching out to try to stroke him.

Well, her gaydar may be faulty, but her taste isn't, Coco thought. He's lovely. She watched Xavier politely fend Emily off, launching instead into a conversation with Lucy about getting tickets for an upcoming revival of a musical called *Flower Drum Song*.

Definitely gay, Coco thought. Shame for Emily, as he's gorgeous, but honestly, he works on a fashion magazine. What are the odds? He was around the same age as them, in their mid-twenties. *Too young,* Coco suddenly realised. *Or – much too young for me*.

The wavering shadows of the candlelit bar hid her blush as the memory flooded back of Jacob sitting on her desk a few days ago. Since then she had thought about him incessantly, endlessly checked Victoria's schedule to see if she had any more meetings where Jacob might conceivably be present and Coco could arrange to bump into him. He had to be thirty years older than her; she had never remotely been attracted to someone of that age before.

But then, I've never really had anything serious before, she reflected. She had had flings at college, and a brief relationship with a sales rep at *Wow*, but no one that she could seriously call an ex-boyfriend. Coco had always been more focused on her work, her ambition, than she had been on having a boyfriend. There'll be plenty of time for that, she'd thought, and there still was; she was only twenty-four, had her whole life in front of her to get serious and settle down.

But now all I can think about is Jacob Dupleix touching my chin. Stroking it. Telling me to say his name.

Emily was reaching playfully for one of the maraschino cherries in Xavier's glass, and he was holding it out of her reach, rolling his eyes at Lucy and Coco, mouthing, 'Help me!' to them.

'Emily! Going-home time,' Coco said, leaning forward, seeing her flatmate's eyes now glassy with alcohol. 'And we'll grab something to eat when we get back, okay?'

'Good idea,' Xavier said, winking at her in the friendliest of conspiracies without making Coco feel that he was criticising her friend. He had lovely manners, and he was ridiculously cute.

And he looks like a boy, her inner voice said. *A boy my age.*

When Jacob Dupleix is most definitely a man.

Victoria

Victoria's Town Car set her down outside the Lipstick Building, the driver zipping round to open the door for her, ignoring the frenzied klaxon of honks from the Third Avenue bus, which had had to apply its brakes as the car cut in front of it and pulled to a halt.

Victoria swung her legs out with a contented smile. Her lunch meeting at Da Silvano with the Lancôme people had been hugely successful; they had agreed to practically double their current advertising spend, which Victoria had finagled with assurances that she would radically increase namechecks for their brand. Da Silvano, a famous downtown restaurant on a fashionable block of Sixth, was a meeting place for actors, models, and film people, and the Lancôme reps had been hugely impressed by the number of celebrities who had come over to greet Victoria. The food was no better than average, and the prices sky-high, but then few customers were actually eating anything, and they were all on expenses anyway, so no one cared.

Another triumph under my belt, Victoria thought complacently. And I simply adore coming back to the office; it's my favourite building in the whole of New York. She loved the

Lipstick Building, so-called not only because its post-modern design was oval, stacked in three layers like a lipstick tube, but because its glittering, shiny red granite, banded with equally shiny stainless steel, resembled designer cosmetic packaging much more than it did a traditional office block. We should do some sort of *Style* tie-in with the building, she reflected. A cosmetic line. Lipstick, obviously, and perfume. I must tell Special Projects to get on with that.

She swept across the lobby's carnelian granite floor, past the colonnade of granite, steel-trimmed pillars that reminded her of Italian baroque architecture, over to the bank of lifts. Victoria loathed being in a lift with anyone else; if she could, she would have sequestered one entirely for her own use. She had achieved the next best thing, however – there was a bank of elevators that served only the ten floors of the Dupleix publishing empire, and everyone at Dupleix knew better than to enter a lift behind Victoria. Employees who walked in, too busy BlackBerrying to notice her presence, would immediately jump out again, mumbling apologies.

Victoria was absorbed in thought on the journey up and the brisk walk back to her office, down the corridors that she had had painted in her signature shade of greige. One of the concepts that she had suggested to the Lancôme people had been perfume-matching to various outfits in fashion spreads, a way of increasing their editorial coverage, which was always an advertiser's dream. She was mulling over whether an upcoming shoot of Mireille's – cruisewear on gondolas in Venice – would dovetail successfully with the Lancôme perfume line. Mireille would loathe it, Victoria thought contentedly. Always a bonus. She simply doesn't get the business side of publishing at all. But I must be careful not to force through ideas just to annoy her. They still need to be right for the magazine . . .

She was so deep in thought that she didn't even notice her new assistant, Alyssa, jumping to stand behind her desk, trying to catch her boss's attention as Victoria blew through and into her office. And for a few moments, she didn't notice the girl on the far side of the office, in the curve of the windows, sitting on one of the two bone-white Le Corbusier leather chairs, slung on chrome frames. Very uncomfortable, very expensive, and exactly the same colour as the girl herself, which was partially why Victoria didn't immediately see her; she blended into the furniture.

But as the girl rose up – and up, and up, because it seemed to take her forever to unfold her long frame – it was impossible not to notice her. Victoria, in the act of dropping her bag on her desk, stared over, thinking for a second that it was an optical illusion; she knew she wasn't drunk. And then she thought of nymphs and sylphs, wild mythical river or woodland creatures who lived in half-light or in the depths of oceans, because the girl's pallor was extraordinary, as if she had never seen the sun.

'Victoria!' Alyssa, in the doorway behind her, was wringing her hands. 'I'm so sorry! She's on a go-see, and I let her sit in your office because Clemence and Dietrich were out here shouting at each other, and I meant to move her out to the waiting area when they went, but I forgot because Clemence stormed off, and Dietrich wanted me to call Mario in Brazil and I was explaining about the time difference, and then *he* stormed off, and anyway, I completely forgot, I'm *so* sorry . . .'

Coco would never have let this happen. No one Victoria didn't know, and practically no one that she did, was supposed to wait in her office. It was her sanctum, her eye of the storm. *God, I miss Coco guarding my door. She was a bloody star.*

And this reminded Victoria that, again, she needed to do something about Coco. The girl had been running the fashion cupboard for two months now with total efficiency, while simultaneously training up Alyssa, and she had still found time to assist Mireille with the cruisewear shoot. Mireille had apparently, according to Clemence, called Coco 'invaluable', which was true – but an absolute bugger. Coco was on her way up, and Victoria wanted her loyalties to be undivided. There were so many politics in this job. She needed Coco to be 100 per cent on her side, and if Mireille was making a play for her, then Victoria would have to reward Coco's hard work by promoting her to junior fashion editor – which, frankly, she deserved, Victoria had to admit. It would be a very fast climb up the career ladder, but scarcely unprecedented: Victoria herself had shot ahead just as rapidly.

Okay, then – junior fashion editor it is, Victoria decided. She'd better not start getting too ambitious, though. Coco might only be in her mid-twenties, but career-driven girls that age were already looking high up to the top of the ladder, to *Style* and *Vogue* and *Elle*, the ultimate glittering prizes. She's my protégée, not my rival, Victoria thought grimly. She'd better not forget that, or I'll slap her down so hard her head will spin like that little girl's in *The Exorcist*. Green vomit and all.

And in the meantime, Victoria had an assistant to ream out. She opened her mouth to tell Alyssa exactly what she thought of the fact that Alyssa had countermanded her strict instructions never, ever to let anyone into her office when she wasn't there; and then the girl shifted, adjusting the portfolio she was holding under her arm, and Victoria's gaze was irresistibly drawn to the girl's irises. They reminded her of husky dogs: their colour was an eerie and otherworldly pale blue, and, like huskies's eyes, they were ringed with dark borders that were a striking contrast to the pale aquamarine.

'*Vogue Russia*, last October,' Victoria commented, looking the girl up and down. She had an encyclopaedic memory for not only her own magazines, but everyone else's too. It was one of the sources of her power. 'The cover. I'm right, aren't I?'

The girl nodded. It was like watching a flower on a long stem moving gently in a breeze. She had to be almost six foot tall in her bare feet, but in her stack-heeled boots, she towered over Victoria. She was wearing a white jersey catsuit with a long gilet over it, and the fabric of the catsuit was no paler than her skin. Her hair was pulled back tight to her skull, the ideal style for a model on a go-see, and it cascaded down her back in a corkscrew-curling ponytail. She wore not a scrap of make-up – again, utterly appropriate for a model on a go-see – and her blonde-white eyebrows and lashes were almost completely invisible against her skim-milk skin.

'I don't see models,' Victoria said curtly, both to Alyssa and to Miss *Vogue Russia October*. 'I'm much too busy.'

'Mireille sent her in,' Alyssa explained. 'She had to rush out because Clemence couldn't make it to the Alaia private show because she was fighting with Dietrich, and Mireille told me—'

'Too much information!' Victoria snapped at her assistant. 'You're boring me.'

Alyssa heaved in a long, gulping cry.

'Oh, piss off,' Victoria said crossly. 'And call in those skirts for the circus shoot.'

Alyssa fled precipitately, grateful not to have been fired. *Vogue Russia October* was still standing there, her portfolio under one arm, a suede drawstring Hayden Harnett hobo slung over the other shoulder. Hayden Harnett didn't advertise in *Style*, but it was a brand models loved: Victoria had noticed that before.

'You photograph very differently,' Victoria said, still staring at her. 'I remember your cover very well.'

The girl extended her portfolio to Victoria. 'Everyone says that. Do you want to look at my pictures?' she asked, her voice soft, yet carrying. 'I know you don't usually do go-sees . . .'

Victoria paused. But the girl wasn't pressuring her in any way, wasn't apologising, wasn't eagerly pushing her portfolio at Victoria; she was simply standing there, over six foot of white, intriguing skin and bone barely padded by flesh . . .

'All right,' Victoria said, flicking her fingers out, waiting for the girl to place her photo book in her hand. The girl flowed forward like the river nymph Victoria had initially compared her to, obeying silently, and Victoria flicked through the book, her eyebrows rising as she did so.

'I used to be a dancer,' the girl said, answering the unspoken question. 'But I grew too tall.' Her solemn face flickered momentarily into a smile. 'Much too tall.'

'You jump very well,' Victoria observed; it was one of her highest compliments. Mireille thought her vulgar, but Victoria knew what sold in America. Her girls had to jump, run, dance, hail cabs, whirl in motion, smile joyously, not drape themselves over the furniture like bored mannequins. This was the New World, and Mireille would have to put a rocket under her arse and start shooting dynamic, energetic models or watch her spreads being slashed.

Victoria closed the portfolio and handed it back to the girl, reading the name on the cover. 'Lykke,' she said. 'What are you exactly?'

'The name's Danish, from my grandmother,' Lykke said. 'But I'm Finnish.'

Most models, granted the honour of a one-on-one with the most influential women in fashion, would have been unable to resist prattling away, desperate to impress on Victoria what a great personality they had, how positive and fun they were. But Lykke stood simply there, looking absolutely perfect, and limited herself to direct answers containing only the information Victoria wanted and not a word more.

Victoria made a snap decision. 'Alyssa!' she called through the open door. 'Get me a studio, now! And have a Polaroid waiting for me in it.'

She nodded briskly at Lykke.

'Follow me,' she commanded. 'I want to do some test shots.'

I haven't done this in years, she thought, striding out of the office, Alyssa scrambling to obey her commands, Lykke duly high-stepping after her with the show-pony gait of a catwalk model. But it was fun to break routine every now and then, remind herself of what it was like being a fashion editor, spotting new talent. By the time she and Lykke had taken the lift down to the floor on which *Style* maintained two photographic studios, a trembling intern was waiting by the doors, a Polaroid camera in her clammy hands. Victoria took the camera without a word of acknowledgement and swept through the door the intern was holding open.

'Do you—' the intern started bravely.

'No,' Victoria said tersely, and the girl disappeared as Victoria turned to see Lykke putting down her portfolio and bag on a trestle table, long-fingered hands poised at the lapel of the gilet, her near-white eyebrows rising to enquire whether she should take it off.

'Leave it on,' Victoria said crisply. 'I like the contrast of the fake fur.'

She positioned Lykke so the light flooding in through the north-facing windows was full on her face, and snapped a couple of shots. Lykke was one of those rare models who look very different, but equally beautiful, from real life in their photographic image.

Many times Victoria had seen girls who were nothing in person, but lit up like 100-watt bulbs in front of a camera, or vice versa: gorgeous creatures who were very unphotogenic. Then you had the ones who you recognised instantly, exactly like their photos. This one, however, became someone else entirely. Maybe it was the translucent skin; her veins pulsed blue beneath it, haunting and delicate and more visible in the photographs.

'Can you take your hair down?' Victoria said, an order phrased as a question, still looking at the Polaroids. 'It's not naturally that curly, is it?'

'No. They did this for a shoot yesterday, and I liked it,' Lykke said, taking out the elastic that had been holding back her long mane of hair.

Victoria put down the Polaroids and walked briskly towards

her, lifting the curls and arranging them over Lykke's shoulders to her satisfaction. It was the most extraordinary hair. In the clear pure daylight of the studio, Victoria could see that it did not have the slightest hint of blonde at all. It was as white as snow, and soft as silk. Like something out of a fairy-tale.

'I'm half-albino,' Lykke said, pre-empting the question Victoria was about to ask. 'Even Finns aren't this pale.' She smiled fleetingly again, and Victoria noticed that even her lips had hardly a touch of colour. 'I was very lucky I didn't get the pink eyes.'

'That would have looked . . .'

Victoria was about to say 'amazing', but she met Lykke's eyes, her hands still in Lykke's extraordinary hair, and the sentence died on her lips. Lykke was like a watercolour, painted with just the faintest hint of colour on the brush. The blue of her eyes was so delicate, the rings around the irises so defined, that Victoria, who had been equally close to every single one of the most beautiful and famous models in the world, was utterly hypnotised. She stared up at Lykke, at the silky white eyelashes that framed those pale blue eyes, and could not say a word.

Nor did she move. It was Lykke who lowered her head, like a blossom folding over, her hair the petals that fell around Victoria's face as Lykke's lips met hers.

Victoria's entire body went into shock. Lykke's long, reed-slender body was pressed against hers, the points of Lykke's hipbones digging gently into Victoria's flat lower belly, and the light pressure sent a kaleidoscope of sensation through that precise area, bright swirls of colour, light and heat. It was such a dizzying feeling that it took her a while to realise that her eyes were closed, her mouth opening under Lykke's, that Lykke's arms had come round her, and Lykke's hands were in the small of her back, holding her tilted up to meet her kiss.

Wait! Victoria thought frantically. Later, she would

remember that her objection had not been to kissing a woman; that hadn't even registered as what was wrong, what was triggering her panic. It was that she had entirely lost control of herself. Lykke was kissing her, stroking her up and down her spine in long, lovely caresses, and Victoria was responding eagerly, kissing her back, arching her pelvis into Lykke's narrow frame, wanting more and more of those spirals of delicious sensation.

Only Victoria's brain – used to dictating terms and conditions for absolutely everything – was resisting, utterly panicked by being overridden. *Stop!* it yelled. *Wait! I need to process this, I need to decide what comes next, I need to be in charge . . .*

It managed to connect to Victoria's hands, telling them to push Lykke away, to catch her breath. Victoria complied, but when her hands sank to Lykke's shoulders, she found herself clutching on instead. She couldn't obey her brain, couldn't push Lykke away. Her fingers sunk in, entranced by the lean, steel-fine muscles of Lykke's arms, her back . . .

Her brain gave up, overmatched. Victoria's tongue twisted around Lykke's, wet and hot, her hands tangling in Lykke's amazing hair, pulling her even closer. She groaned as Lykke ground her pelvis against hers; it was too high, Lykke was too tall in her heels, she needed it lower down, between her legs, and she needed it *now*. Everything was rising inside her, churning, swirling, and she would explode if she didn't get what she wanted right now . . .

She had never felt like this before, ever. She had barely had sex with Jeremy since they came to New York; she'd just been too busy. And she certainly hadn't missed it. She had never thought, in fact, that she had much of a sex drive at all. It had never been anything like a priority for Victoria; she'd always got her thrills from power, not sex. She had done what Jacob wanted her to do during their affair, had kept the entire thing secret from Jeremy, simply because it was the fastest way for her to get where she wanted to be. And she had enjoyed almost all of it; Jacob had always made sure her needs were met, even if his own were fairly risqué.

But she had never melted like this in his arms, never kissed him back with this passion and sheer, driving *need*.

Victoria wrenched her mouth free, her lips damp and swollen, her chignon coming loose.

'I—' she began, a typical Victoria opening to a sentence, but Lykke already knew, was backing her against the trestle table. The two women, in their high heels, moved like a beautiful, conjoined, mythical creature as they staggered back and Victoria's bottom hit the edge of the tabletop. She dragged up the hem of her mini-skirt, so short and tight that she needed to wriggle a little to get it up to her waist, and was shoving her hand between her legs to give herself the satisfaction she so desperately needed when Lykke's hips slammed into her, widening the opening of her thighs. Lykke's pelvis swivelled against her expertly, driving the lace of her g-string into her crotch, an extra little rub of friction that sent Victoria's eyes rolling right back in her head as she arched back and started to moan: 'Fucking Jesus God, fucking Christ, that's so bloody fucking good, oh God, yes, fuck me there, fuck me really hard, do it, do it *now* . . .'

Her hands were grabbing onto the edge of the tabletop, bracing herself, her hips thrusting up to meet Lykke's. Her thrice-weekly Pilates classes gave her complete control over her core, her tight abdominal muscles curling her into a crunch that sent her wet, hot pussy exactly, precisely, into the seam of Lykke's catsuit, their bones grinding together, Lykke's hipbones digging into the soft inside flesh of Victoria's bare thighs, her crotch rubbing and rubbing in circles and hard fast strokes just where Victoria was so desperate to be touched.

'Fuck!' she wailed. 'Don't fucking stop, don't you fucking *dare!* Fuck my cunt like that, I'm – Jesus Christ, God yes, that's it, that's bloody *it*, yes, fuck you, fuck you, fuck *me* . . .'

Lykke's palms were flat on the table, wide on either side of

Victoria's body, her white hair spilling down, her gilet falling open, revealing the outline of her nipples, hard little stubs thrusting against the fabric of her catsuit. Her milk-white cheeks were flushed, her mouth almost red with kisses, her eyes aflame, and the sight of her, so beautiful, so extraordinary, fucking her so perfectly, sent Victoria into spasms of ecstasy.

'Are you fucking coming?' she panted, the first time in her life that she had actually asked a partner what they were feeling. 'I want to watch you come – fucking *come!* I want to bloody watch you fucking come, fuck my cunt and come—'

Desperate, suddenly, to touch Lykke's pointed nipples, to feel her breasts, Victoria managed to drag her hands free, to sit up and close her palms over them. Lykke's breasts were tiny soft swells of flesh, almost flat to her chest, the sharp hard nipples in exquisite contrast to the softness that cushioned them, and Victoria rubbed her palms over and over them, making them even harder, even more pronounced, as Lykke moaned at the back of her throat and jerked frantically into the spread V of Victoria's legs. Victoria wrapped her thighs tightly around Lykke, her ankles locking in the small of Lykke's back, and gave herself completely up to the endless stream of orgasm. Lykke was coming in waves and waves; Victoria closed her eyes, sank her hands into Lykke's shoulders and held on for dear life, a constant stream of obscenities pouring from her mouth, shoving herself into the woman in her arms, between her legs. She had no idea which one of them was coming from one moment to the next; it was as if they were both in stormy seas, battered by the waves, clinging to each other like life-rafts, tossed up and down, gasping in breaths, moaning them out again as they came again and again on the cross of each other's bodies.

Eleanor, Victoria thought suddenly, a name from the past flooding into her consciousness, a pretty little face, a girl from school she hadn't thought about for years, almost decades. *Eleanor Johnson-Smythe. My God, Eleanor.* They'd been fourteen, obsessed with boys and romance at their all-girls' boarding school in the middle of the Shropshire countryside, marooned miles away from anything resembling testosterone, and they'd turned to each other, best friends who spent every break they had acting out complicated and elaborate romantic stories culled from the Regency romances with which they were obsessed, taking it in turn to play the male hero, pressing themselves against each other, kissing excitedly with closed mouths.

It had never gone beyond that, never even turned into French kissing. Never had one of them climbed into the other's narrow dormitory bed, or touched each other beyond dry presses of lip to lip, or inexpert, enthusiastic caresses of hair and upper arms. But it had been enough to attract the attention of their form teacher, who had spoken, Victoria had the vague memory, to Eleanor's parents. Probably, Victoria thought now, she didn't dare speak to mine. Judge Glossop would have given short shrift to any teacher why had even mentioned to him that his beloved daughter might not have been completely 'normal', as he would have considered it . . .

And when Victoria had come back after the summer holidays, Eleanor was no longer there. She had been sent to another school – a mixed one this time. They had kept in contact, but not for long. Victoria didn't even remember being that upset. She hadn't understood why the teacher had even bothered to mention their silly, childish games; if anything, she'd been a little embarrassed by the idea that they'd been seen acting out romantic stories. That the teacher might have been concerned that she and Eleanor would have ended up hiding in a broom cupboard, fucking as madly as wild animals on heat, had never even occurred to her.

But now – now that she was jamming her pussy frantically against the pussy of a six-foot, half-albino, Finnish model whom she had barely met ten minutes ago, coming harder than she ever had in her entire life – now Victoria was remembering Eleanor, for the first time in so many years, and wondering if that teacher might have had a point, after all . . .

'*Fuck!*' she screamed, as Lykke, with a last, powerful thrust of her hips, collapsed on top of her, dragging in long, agonised breaths. Victoria's body jerked under Lykke's, her buttocks beating a slower and slower tattoo against the trestle table, until she finally came to rest.

'Not on top of me,' she muttered, and Lykke rolled sideways, removing her weight from Victoria's.

'You remind me of someone,' Victoria said, turning to look at her, amazed at the words that were coming out of her own mouth. It was as if her brain wasn't filtering her thoughts, her actions, any longer.

'Oh yes?' Lykke smiled. 'Some other girl you fucked before?'

There was a pink flush down her neck, to the opening of her catsuit. The flush would stretch beyond, down perhaps to her breasts. Victoria wanted to drag down the zipper, expose her chest, see the colour of her nipples – pink, she thought. Pale, pale pink. The idea made her sit up, pull her own skirt down, frightened that she would do that, would bare Lykke's tiny breasts. And that would make it all start once more. They would fuck again and again, stay in this studio for hours, not leave until night had fallen and they were too sore to move . . .

'No,' Victoria said, looking away from Lykke to regain control. She reached behind her, gathering her hair back into its chignon. 'I never fucked another girl before.'

Lykke's eyes widened, the ring around the pale blue iris seeming even more vivid with her surprise.

'Oh,' she said softly.

Picking hairpins off the table, securing her chignon back into smooth elegance, Victoria waited to hear if Lykke would say anything more, but she remained silent as she pushed herself up off the table, drawing her gilet over her chest again, concealing the still-hard thrust of nipples against the thin white jersey covering. Victoria stood back up too, grateful again for the demanding exercise programme that gave her the ability to balance on her high heels, her core contracting to keep her upright even though her legs wanted to wobble and her pussy was still throbbing. Not just her pussy; Lykke's narrow, prominent hipbones had driven into her inner thighs again and again. She'd have bruises tomorrow morning.

The memory was overwhelming. Victoria glanced down swiftly at the table, and then headed for the door.

'You're Elite?' she said, though it wasn't a question: the name of Lykke's modelling agency was clearly marked on the portfolio. 'Good. You can see yourself out. I'll be—'

She had been going to say 'in touch', but she couldn't get those words out.

'We'll—' she started again.

No, 'we' was all wrong too. Victoria was at the door by now; they hadn't even locked it. *My God. What the hell had come over her? What the fuck just happened*? She wrestled it open, and couldn't resist a last look back over her shoulder. Lykke was collecting her portfolio, her hobo bag, pulling her flood of white curls back into its elastic again. The pink was still in her cheeks, over the narrow rise of her collarbones, down to the V of her chest where the tag of the zipper was resting, the zipper that Victoria could so easily pull down . . .

Victoria shot out, rushing down the corridor to stab the Up button of the lift, in a tearing hurry even though she knew that Lykke would wait. Lykke wouldn't follow until she was sure that Victoria had gone back to her office. Lykke would do what Victoria wanted her to do. Just as Lykke had done, this afternoon, exactly what Victoria had wanted – even though Victoria hadn't even known that she wanted her to do it.

Eleanor and I used to hide behind those big oak trees in the school grounds, Victoria remembered suddenly. The bark of the trees dug into my back, through my uniform shirt, when it was my turn to be the girl and Eleanor was kissing me. Were they oaks? The bark was terribly rough, but I never minded. In fact, I only noticed afterwards that my back was all scratched up.

Victoria had never been more grateful to hear a sound than she was at the overhead pinging that announced the arrival of the lift which would carry her back to normality. To her office, her magazine, her office at the centre of it all.

To being in control once again.

Coco

Almost finished. Coco had been working her way through the various sections of the fashion cupboard, which was really a whole suite of open rooms, a seemingly-endless Aladdin's cave of bright glittering jewellery and accessories, soft silky fabrics, feather and furs and shearlings, all now perfectly arranged and organised, each rack labelled, the dry-cleaning hung up and classified.

Just some shoeboxes to sort through, and then she could go home; it was already past nine o'clock. She opened up a Gucci box and drew out a pair of suede heels, palest pink and so soft she couldn't resist drawing the back of one against her cheek; until you started handling luxury goods on a regular basis, you simply couldn't believe the quality of materials that were available to the rich. The suedes and leathers, the silks and velvets that the really high-end designers used were so exquisite to the touch that they made anything Coco had owned before coming to *Style* look like pleather and polyester by comparison. These heels, which she placed on a narrow shoe shelf, careful that her hands weren't leaving any faint traces of sweat or moisturiser on the delicate suede, were a perfect example of how cocooned in comfort rich people really were.

Us plebs think we're wearing cashmere – we buy it from Uniqlo or M&S and feel glamorous, she thought. But then you pick up a Loro Piana cashmere sweater, and you realise that you might as well be wearing some cheapo acrylic blend, compared to the really good stuff.

And the sizes were so much smaller in designer clothes! That had been another shock to Coco. A high-street medium was much more generous than a designer one. Although Coco was now an American size 4 in a chain like Zara or Club Monaco, she could barely squeeze into a designer size 6. It meant that she'd missed out, to a large extent, on one of the huge perks of running the fashion cupboard – borrowing clothes. The size 4-and-under girls ran in and out, pulling outfits for themselves on a regular basis, according to how much status they had at the magazine and how nice they were to Coco. She'd watched them trying on dresses and trousers and fitted tops with sheer jealousy: those were items that you couldn't cheat on, that looked awful if they were too tight. She'd had to limit herself to knits, which had a forgiving amount of stretch, or jackets. The trick about jackets, she'd worked out, was that you didn't have to do them up. You could just wear them open, and if it got chilly, you pulled out a feather-light vicuna-silk blend wrap and draped it cleverly in the gap.

God, who'd have thought it back in London? Coco wondered ironically as she opened more boxes and stacked their superb contents on the shoe shelves. I'm the thinnest I've ever been in my life – I'd be a size 8 back in London – and here I am, too fat for the fashion cupboard at *Style*. She was doing regular cardio at the gym – in addition to the Dupleix one, she'd joined a local branch of Crunch – 500-calorie workouts, which took her at least forty-five minutes a time. Plus classes at Core Pilates, down on University Place, below Union Square; it was on the way home, just a couple of stops on the Q train to the flat she shared with Emily in Brooklyn. Everyone at *Style* raved about the studio, and it was true, it was amazing.

The teachers were all brilliant, every single class was different, and they had a range of equipment that was frankly daunting. Yesterday Coco had, along with two other women, been lying on her side on something they called a chair but she'd secretly nicknamed the 'torture stool', trying to stay completely balanced while pumping its weighted pedal up and down with one arm and then the other. Her obliques and biceps were agonising today; she winced a little every time she picked up a shoebox. That was the thing about studios which varied their classes – they got you in a different muscle group every time. Some part of her body always hurt from Pilates.

It's so hard! she thought gloomily, rolling back her shoulders in an attempt to bring some relief to her aching muscles. The amount I'm working out, I'd really think I'd be a designer size 4 by now . . .

That still wouldn't make her a model size, of course. Models were an 0-2 nowadays. Skinny bitches, Coco thought enviously, they can slip in and out of anything. Plus, they have no boobs. She was beginning to resent hers, now smaller, but still frustratingly present, along with her curvy hips – you can take the girl out of Luton, but you can't completely take Luton out of the girl. Her mum, her sister, were both big, curvaceous women, and no matter how Coco dieted and worked out, she couldn't change her basic bone structure, or the DNA that gave her padding in those precise areas where most clothing designers loathed women to have them. The Russian and Eastern European girls who were so popular at the moment were ridiculously long and thin, with hips as straight as a boy's, concave stomachs and almost-flat chests. Of course, it helped if you got the models at fifteen, ideally before they'd even started their periods.

Contemplating the shoes she'd lined up, Coco thought snarkily, Oh well, they may be tall and thin, but they've all got feet like boats. Five-foot-ten or eleven models wore American size nines or tens, UK sevens or eights; even with the steep heels – which disguised large feet to some extent, making them look a little shorter – it was undeniable that the shoes would look prettier if they were a couple of sizes smaller. A casting for a Miu Miu runway show last year, determined to showcase its latest shoes in a size 8, had famously had models sobbing as they fought, Ugly Sister-like, to cram their feet into shoes a whole size too small for them and then do their best walk as if they weren't in screaming agony.

Complacently, Coco looked down at her size 5 feet with their perfect pedicure. Manhattan might be stressful, its inhabitants tightly packed onto a small island like grumpy sardines, but it did offer wonderful perks. Round the corner from Coco and Emily's apartment was a choice of nail salons where a mani-pedi cost $35, with whirlpool massage chairs and UV-drying lights to harden the polish as fast as possible. The girls had quickly learned the New York trick of walking to the salon in flip-flops, so that, after your foot soak and massage, you could put your flip-flops on again and have your polish done while you wore them; that way, you walked back home again without smudging your polish by slipping shoes over it.

'I thought I'd find you here,' came a deep male voice, almost a purr, and Coco jumped.

It was late; most of the *Style* staffers had left for the day, but Coco had stayed on to get the fashion cupboard in mint condition before she started her junior fashion editor job the next day. It wasn't just that Coco was a perfectionist; she was learning from Mireille the strategy of mentoring people who were junior to her at work. Nadege, who was taking over the running of the cupboard, would eagerly turn to Coco for advice, be hugely grateful she didn't have to sort out any messes Coco had left behind, would keep an eye out for items that Coco might want to borrow and let her know when they came in. Alyssa, Victoria's new assistant, was the first of Coco's growing network of junior girls indebted to her, and Nadege would add to that count.

Coco was watching both Victoria and Mireille acutely, copying their strategies for success. As a career-boosting tactic, it seemed to be working very well.

And now, looking at the man who had just walked into the cupboard, she went bright red. Thinking of what both Mireille and Victoria had reputedly done with him, and which certainly hadn't done their careers any harm . . .

'Hi, again.' Jacob Dupleix smiled, his teeth flashing white. 'It's your last day here, isn't it? And then you move on and up.'

Coco hadn't touched up her make-up for hours, or run a brush through her hair. And the lighting in here was cruel, white and clear, simulating daylight so editors could ensure they were seeing the colours of the clothes they picked out as they really were. She was sure she looked horribly scruffy, every imperfection emphasised by the merciless lighting. Whereas Jacob Dupleix – his dark suit as smooth as if he had just slipped it on, his eyes sparkling, his skin buffed and scrubbed and moisturised, carrying a spicy bergamot and amber scent – was as intimidatingly, perfectly groomed as ever.

'How did you know?' Coco asked, feeling stupid even as the words left her lips.

Victoria, of course. Victoria told him.

'Victoria says you've done a really kick-ass job here,' Jacob commented, looking round him. 'I've gotta say, it looks in really good shape.'

'Thanks,' Coco managed, her brain racing with speculation. What did he want? Why had he made a special visit to the cupboard to see her?

'I wanted to swing by and congratulate you,' he said, propping his shoulders against the shelves, leaning back, looking at her with frank approval. 'You're shooting up the ladder, Miss Coco. From Vicky's assistant to fashion cupboard to junior editor in just a few months. Pretty meteoric rise so far. I look forward to seeing some of your layouts.'

Coco flushed even deeper.

'Oh, I've got so many ideas,' she said eagerly. 'I love Victoria's aesthetic. You know, she likes things to be really dynamic, lots of movement and fun. But,' she added quickly, to show Jacob that she could be flexible, 'Mireille's got the most incredible eye. She's so artistic. I want to learn a lot from her as well.'

Jacob's smile deepened. 'Smart girl,' he said. 'Learn from the best, and learn it fast.'

'Oh, I will,' she assured him fervently.

'I always like to take an interest in my rising stars,' Jacob said, the last two words making Coco's heart pound against her ribcage. 'I hand-picked both Mireille and Vicky, did you know that? Mireille was a dancer, but that's a tough life, and a damn short one. I saw what a great eye she had, encouraged her to take up fashion styling. And Vicky was a pistol from the word go. Like you, I think. I called you a pistol the first time we met, didn't I?'

Coco nodded. *And then you stroked my chin, and told me to call you by your first name* . . .The memory was paralysing. She'd been cockier before, more able to banter and be funny; once he'd touched her, activated something deep within her, that part took over. Now she was remembering, all too clearly, what it had been like to be touched by Jacob's wide index finger—

He pushed off the shelving wall and strolled towards her, his footsteps silent on the carpeted floor. Coco tightened every newly-worked muscle she had in the effort not to back away; she had to tip her head up to look at him, even shorter without her heels. Despite Jacob's colouring being so dark, and his hair so thick, his jaw was perfectly smooth, not a trace of stubble or five o'clock shadow. His skin glowed with vitality.

Like all the rich people, she thought, having some experience with them now. It's not just the clothes they wear, the cashmeres and suedes and silk suits. It's their skin, too. They can afford the best nutrition, the best dermatologists, the best moisturisers and procedures . . .

'Remember what I told you to call me, when we met before?' Jacob said gently, so close now she could feel his warm breath on her face.

'Jacob,' she managed, in a very small voice.

'Good girl,' he murmured, and she found herself leaning in to catch every word. He's like a snake charmer, she thought, hypnotised.

She knew her eyes were wide, that she was staring up at him like a pathetic schoolgirl with a crush on the teacher. Desperately she told herself to say something funny, snappy, to remind him of why he'd liked her in the first place, to show some personality and not just act like a stupid sixteen year old.

And then he lifted his hands, turning their palms upwards, and cupped them on each side of her head, under the ends of her hair, bouncing the long bob up and down. He wasn't touching her skin at all, but every nerve-ending in her body fizzed, rose, wanting to push herself against his hands, feel his skin on hers.

'Will you take a little advice from a man old enough to be your father?' Jacob said, his lips quirking in amusement.

Coco nodded again, her own lips parting.

'Your hair doesn't suit you like this,' he said, considering her carefully. 'It's too long. It should only skim your shoulders, to show off your neck better. Then you can push it back,' he suited the action to the word, 'perhaps even fasten it back here . . .' His big hands took her hair to the nape of her neck, holding it there. 'Mmn,' he said. 'Much better. I like this. Will you do that for me? Cut it and pull it back like that?'

'Yes, Jacob,' Coco managed to say.

He closed his eyes for a brief moment in satisfaction. One hand clasped the back of her neck, so warm that she arched into it, pushing against him like a cat wanting to be stroked. She felt his fingers, splayed across her nape, closing around it just enough to encircle it before he released her; it was all she could do not to gasp aloud in frustration as his touch left her.

'Girls on the way up should look their absolute best,' Jacob said seriously, his tone abstract, almost impersonal, the boss giving an employee. 'If I may . . .'

He slid his hands down, touching her hips with one finger on each side of her body, through her heavy cotton pencil skirt. Coco jumped, and Jacob huffed out a little laugh of amusement.

'There's still a little too much here, isn't there?' he said, tracing little circles on her hips with the tips of his fingers, melting her insides like wax. 'I can see that you've been dieting, but you need to keep going, I think. Don't you?'

Coco was so panicked that he would bring his fingers up, feel the slight roll of fat below her waist that not even the Spanx could completely suppress – or, even worse, feel the Spanx itself! – that she couldn't think straight. It seemed the most important thing in the world that Jacob not touch her there, not sense that gross imperfection. And yet, simultaneously, she wanted him to touch her everywhere, to feel his hands all over her body, to pull him down to the carpet and have his entire weight on top of her, letting him do whatever he wanted, as long as he would keep casting this spell on her . . .

Almost at random, she nodded, so distracted by his caresses that she couldn't think straight. He was so close to her pelvis, so close. If he'd just slide his hands along, between her legs, touch her where she wanted him so badly . . .

Her mouth opened, but no words came out.

'Good,' Jacob said, smiling in contentment, allowing her a brief squeeze to either hip before he let go. 'Keep on with the diet. Watch what Victoria does. She's wonderful about maintaining her weight. And she's your role model, isn't she? You want to be where she is one day?'

This was what restored Coco's voice. Ambition, her most powerful driver and motivator, cut through the sensual enchantment that Jacob, like a sorcerer in a fairy-tale, had wound around her.

'Yes,' she said, her voice so clear and resolute she even surprised herself. 'Yes, I do.'

He nodded. 'Excellent. I knew it from the moment I saw you. That light in your eyes. It can't be faked – you either have it or you don't. And very, very few people do.'

Jacob leaned down, bringing his face closer to Coco's than it had been so far. She trembled, her whole body shaking, as he said softly, 'Be good, Coco. I'll see you soon.'

And then he pulled back. Shooting his shirt cuffs, so they once more hung perfectly just below the hems of his jacket sleeves, his heavy Cartier watch flashing a bright gleam of gold, Jacob Dupleix turned away and left the fashion cupboard without another word.

She watched him go, all the way down the corridor, his step as light and easy as if he hadn't just deliberately driven a junior employee of his into a haze of lust, her legs shaking, so wobbly, even in stockinged feet, that she had to clutch onto the edge of the shoe shelf to steady herself.

Oh my God! she thought, dazed, her head spinning. What just happened? I can't believe that he barely touches me and I have this kind of reaction to him. I lose all my willpower, all my commonsense. I'm scared I'd say, 'Yes,' to absolutely everything he asks me to do.

And Jacob's my ultimate boss, he can even tell Victoria what to do. He could get me promoted even faster than she's doing now . . .

Bright dreams of power and possibility filled Coco's head. In that moment she felt that anything could happen, that she just had to reach out her hand and grab her opportunity to make her wildest, most dazzling ambitions come true.

I'll book a hair appointment tomorrow. I'll diet even harder. I'll make myself into the person Jacob wants me to be – a future editor of Style . . .

'Coco? Coco, you in there?'

It was a male voice, but there the resemblance to Jacob ended. A light tenor to Jacob's deep bass, friendly and easygoing, it was the tone of an equal, not a superior. Unlike Jacob, this man wasn't asking a question to which he already knew the answer.

'Hey!' Xavier appeared at the end of the corridor. 'There you are. Wow, this place *rocks*.' He stared around him, eyes widening as he took it in. 'It's like a girls' paradise, isn't it?' he said, reaching out to lift with great caution a feathered tulle Dior skirt. 'Do you, like, just spend your entire time in here trying stuff on?'

Coco took a deep breath and mustered up control of herself. 'Most of it doesn't fit me,' she admitted, pulling a face. 'My hips are too big.'

'Oh, come on.' Xavier, slim in a red T-shirt and black jeans, a pinstripe waistcoat over them with a dandy-like fob watch strung across it, batted this away. 'You look great,' he said, grinning at her. 'All you fashion girls think you're, like, gigantic, and actually you're all way too skinny.'

Coco knew it wasn't true, but she couldn't help smiling at him anyway. She, Emily and Lucy had been hanging out with him regularly over the last few months. Emily had been politely rebuffed by Xavier enough times for her to turn her attention to more available men, which leached any awkwardness from the situation, and Xavier was really good company. Coco liked him a great deal.

'Lucy said you were working late, and I was too – I only just finished up. So I came to get you,' he said cheerfully. 'She's already getting her groove on at Urge with Emily – want to come along? We should totally celebrate you getting your own desk!'

Coco hesitated for a moment. But X was right, Lucy was right: she should celebrate. She'd had a long, tiring day, packing, unpacking, running round moving rails and re-sorting tons of stuff; she'd been planning to crawl home and fall into bed.

And if it hadn't been for Jacob Dupleix's visit to the fashion cupboard, that was exactly what she would have done. Gone home and crashed. But now – now she was all worked up, her head buzzing with ambition, her body with sexual excitement. He had awoken so much in her that Coco knew she couldn't fall asleep yet. Not until she'd had some drinks, burned off some brain cells and all this excess energy.

'Can we go dancing?' she asked, looking round for her shoes. 'I need to let off some steam.'

'Sure.' Xavier looked surprised. 'You haven't been to Urge yet? It's a gay bar, there's a big dance floor – you can shake your booty all you want.' He looked her up and down appraisingly. 'You got anything you can change into? I mean, I'm digging the sexy secretary thing,' he gestured at her pencil skirt and little short-sleeved, Peter Pan-collared sweater, 'but it's not exactly dancewear.'

Coco grinned. She always felt ridiculously at ease with X.

'What do you think I should put on?' she asked. 'A leotard and leggings?'

'Actually,' Xavier said, 'that would be deeply cool. But no. I was thinking more . . . this.' He was rifling through a rail of clothes due to go back to their respective PRs; with triumph, he produced a black, sequinned Max Mara dress, sleeveless and scoop-necked. 'Here,' he said, approaching Coco. 'Put it on.'

'That won't fit,' Coco started to object, but as Xavier handed her the dress, she tailed off. 'You know,' she said thoughtfully, looking at the cut, 'it actually might.'

'I do this for a job, you know,' Xavier said, mock-indignant. 'What, you think only women can be stylists? You girls are so sexist! We have plenty of women modelling in *Men's Style*.' He grinned. 'It makes the hetero guys feel okay about buying the mag. Go on, try it. Bet it fits.' He nodded to the far corner of the cupboard, where a makeshift changing room had been rigged up with a curtain thrown over a clothes rail.

The Max Mara didn't just fit; it looked fantastic, clinging to the curves Coco had left, making her breasts look enticingly full as they swelled against the neckline. She'd thought she was too big to carry off sequins, but the designers knew what they were doing; the paillettes were large and dull, sewn flat to the knit fabric, shining discreetly, instead of glittering so brightly they added bulk to her figure. Her skin was pale against the black, gleaming mother-of-pearl, and her arms were lightly toned now from the Pilates lessons. Luckily, her beige patent shoes just about worked with the dress, as she couldn't have borrowed a pair from the cupboard; the sizes there were all too big for her. She'd pulled her hair to the nape of her neck, as Jacob had done, and added dark coral lipstick: Xavier gave a wolf-whistle of admiration when she emerged, doing a big theatrical twirl for him.

'God, I'm good,' he said. 'You look like a million dollars. Come on, Cinderella, I'm busting you out of here. All the gay guys are going to eat you up with a spoon.'

He turned towards the door, crooking one arm like an actor in a 1940s film, and, laughing, Coco grabbed her jacket and ran up to hook her own arm through his.

'Thank you, X,' she said in heartfelt tones as they proceeded out of the cupboard, pausing so she could switch off the bank of lights by the door. 'I can't tell you how much I needed this.'

'I bet,' he said, grinning down at her affectionately. 'You work too hard, Coco-puff.' He flicked her ponytail. 'You gotta let your hair down a little sometimes.'

No, Coco thought instantly. I need to cut it and pull it back, like Jacob said. And at the memory of her recent encounter with Jacob Dupleix, she felt a flush rising right from between her legs, up her body, heat flowing with it, bringing bright colour to her cheeks.

Victoria

'You're pregnant!' Jeremy ran out of the bathroom, waving the test stick. 'Oh my God! You're – *we're* – pregnant!'

His curly hair was sticking right up, his eyes wide behind the lenses of his round-framed glasses, his mouth in a big O of excitement and happiness.

'Vicky! Did you hear me? It's the most amazing news,' he yodelled to his wife, who was sitting in bed, wearing one of her favourite Jenny Packham silk nightdresses, a pile of the most recent Italian, French, Japanese and Russian fashion magazines around her, busily ripping out pages that interested her. She looked up, her blonde hair falling around her bare shoulders, her expression distracted, in a haze of glossy images, neon-bright make-up, faux-Afro blowouts.

'Yes, I thought I might be,' she said. 'My boobs feel different already. Hmm.'

Pushing the magazines away, she stared straight ahead, processing her reaction to the life-changing news. She was surprised to realise that she felt quite triumphant. Her body had done exactly what it was supposed to with the same efficiency with which her brain processed the complex decisions she had to make every day at work. Every part of the machine was working successfully. It was actually very satisfying indeed.

I can't quite imagine having a baby yet, though. I suppose the reality will gradually dawn on me as I get bigger . . .

Victoria wouldn't get much bigger, though. That wasn't the plan at all. Already she had a nutritionist working with her on a pre-conception diet, and now they would swing fully into action, with daily meetings to check her weight on the scales and assess her fat gain with callipers. Plus, and she'd be eating specially-prepared small meals, six a day, to ensure maximum nutrition for minimum calories.

And thank God, at least this means no more sex with Jeremy . . .

Completely unaware of the tack his wife's thoughts had taken, Jeremy plopped happily onto the bed, sending some of the magazines shooting away; their covers were so shiny that they slid right across the coverlet and straight onto the carpet.

'You know I'll do all the looking-after,' he burbled. 'I'm so excited, I can't wait!'

'Well, that's obvious,' Victoria said dryly. But she smiled at her husband, whose enthusiasm was infectious. Setting down her copy of *Vogue France*, she reached out to ruffle his wild tangle of curls.

'I'm so glad you're happy, Jeremy,' she said affectionately. 'I do love to see you like this.'

Jeremy beamed, his smile almost as wide as his face.

'Moving back to New York, getting pregnant – it couldn't get any better,' he sighed blissfully. 'I'll zoom things along with the realtor. I want us to be all moved into a nice house well before the baby's due. That way I can sort out the nursery, make sure we have absolutely everything we need.' He grinned, a little abashed. 'I've already started making lists. I've been on all the websites, working out exactly what we ought to get.'

'And interviewing nannies,' Victoria specified firmly. 'That's the most important thing of all.'

Jeremy pouted. 'You know I want to do a lot of that myself,

sweetie,' he said. 'I've checked out everything with Carpenter, de Vere – they're absolutely fine with me taking extended paternity leave. I must say, HR thought it was utterly hilarious. No bloke who works there's ever asked for paternity leave before. They're awfully keen on it, actually. Makes them look good for PR.'

'We definitely need a night nanny,' Victoria said even more firmly. 'You can't do the whole thing yourself. You'll be shattered.' *And if you're shattered, you won't do a good job of running the house and supervising the staff, which will drive me mad.*

'All right,' Jeremy conceded. 'I'll look into night nannies. Ooh, it's going to be so amazing! A little baby to look after!' He actually clapped his hands together in glee.

'Honestly, Jeremy, I so wish you could carry it,' Victoria sighed, pushing the magazines away. 'You're the one who's madly keen on this whole baby idea – it does seem unfair that you can't be the one to get fat and go through the awful messy horror of it all.'

'Oh, you won't get fat.' Jeremy squished his bottom along the coverlet so he could get closer to his wife, his blue eyes anxious to reassure her. Grabbing both her hands, he pressed them comfortingly between his own. 'You're so careful with your weight, I'm sure you'll be fine. Not that I'd mind, darling, you know. I actually like you with a bit more chub on you.'

Victoria shuddered, a ripple that ran through her entire body.

'Sorry.' Jeremy grimaced. 'Not chub, obviously. I just meant, I think you look even lovelier when you're a little – a little more . . .' He floundered, unable to come up with a single word that would be acceptable to his pencil-thin wife.

'Well, I will be a "little more",' Victoria said grimly. 'Oh well, supermodels and actresses do it all the time. You barely need to eat any more at all when you're pregnant, according to my nutritionist – that whole eating for two stuff is total bollocks. I've put a trainer who specialises in pre- and post-pregnancy workouts on retainer. I'll work out like a maniac as soon as the baby comes.'

'You're terribly efficient, darling,' Jeremy said admiringly, but even his self-obsessed, hyper-driven wife could see his expression was a little clouded. In a surge of empathy that was very unusual for her, she slid her hands out from his grasp and reached up to stroke his cheeks caressingly.

'*I am* happy about this baby,' she said.

'You'll be a really good mother,' Jeremy assured her earnestly.

'I don't know about that,' Victoria said honestly. 'But I do know that you'll be a really good father. The baby'll be lucky to have you.'

She swallowed.

'*I'm* lucky to have you,' she added, knowing that she was. Many husbands of her contemporaries had lost interest in them once the children started to come, left them for younger models. Jeremy, bless him, was quite the opposite. Right now, his blue eyes were welling up with tears.

'Oh, darling,' he gulped, enfolding her in a hug, pulling back to shower her face with kisses, then hugging her once more, his much-washed flannel pyjamas soft against her skin. It was the kind of display of affection that Victoria would usually have been uncomfortable with, would have terminated before it really even got started; but for some reason, with her husband's arms around her, his tear-damp face pressed into her hair, she found herself – not exactly relaxing into his embrace, but certainly quite able to tolerate it.

God, she thought. Maybe getting pregnant really is going to make me a nicer person.

But then a rush of guilt swept over her. Guilt and utter confusion. It had been a couple of weeks since the 'encounter' – this was the word she used to describe it to herself, though she knew what a cowardly euphemism it was – that 'encounter' with Lykke in the Dupleix studio. Her eyes closed for a second or two as she remembered Lykke, her wonderful mane of white hair, those otherworldly pale eyes and skin, that incredible, long, beautiful body, her tiny breasts . . .

Victoria hadn't seen Lykke since, and she didn't intend to. For Victoria Glossop, a judge's daughter, who prided herself on her extreme self-control, it would be much too dangerous to ever again place herself in a situation where she lit up like a firework as soon as a half-albino Finnish model came anywhere near her. But Victoria had memoed Mireille, Clemence and Dietrich the day after her 'encounter' with Lykke, instructing them that she wanted to use Lykke in the issue of *Style* they were currently putting together; just yesterday, Mireille had informed her that Lykke had been booked for a directional shoot the French woman was planning under the famous St Louis Arch.

It wasn't a pay-off, Victoria thought now. But she writhed a little, knowing she wasn't being completely honest with herself. All right, maybe it was a pay-off, in a way. Lykke's been completely discreet. I know she hasn't said a word about what happened between us: gossip spreads like wildfire in this industry, and I have a net of contacts that extends all over the world. I'd have heard if Lykke had even breathed a hint to anyone that she fucked the editor of *US Style* over a table in her own studio.

Oh God. I have to stop thinking about Lykke. This is no bloody good.

Victoria had never been unfaithful to Jeremy in their entire time together. Despite her abrasive personality, she had a strong moral code, instilled in her by parents to whom the idea of infidelity, let alone divorce, was anathema. You made a choice and you stuck by it, was Judge Glossop's firm belief, and to Victoria, his favourite child, her father's word was gospel.

It hadn't been difficult, not at all. Before meeting Lykke, Victoria had never even been tempted to stray. The formula on which she and Jeremy had settled was enough to satisfy them both. She liked being in charge, making herself come, and Jeremy, a born voyeur, loved, above all, to watch; apart from when they had been trying to get her pregnant, Jeremy had barely ever actually fucked Victoria, and he didn't even mind – as long as she let him see everything she did to herself.

Although the fashion world was rampant with sex and drugs, Victoria was so controlled, so self-possessed, that no one had been brave enough to make a serious attempt to crack her icy façade – well, no one except Jacob. And though she'd been with Jeremy then, they weren't yet engaged, let alone married. It had been Victoria's one slip from perfect morality, and only in the service of her career; it had barely felt like cheating at all, more an extra-curricular service which the boss required from her. Though of course, she had never breathed a word to Jeremy.

Jacob wouldn't have dreamed of expecting anything sexual from Victoria now. He had his affairs with women barely out of their teens, as Victoria had been when Jacob first spotted her at *US Style*, singled her out for special attention, groomed her – *literally*, Victoria thought, amused. It was Jacob who told her to lose seven pounds and to do her hair in a chignon; Jacob who seduced her, bought her gifts, mentored her career, and ensured she rose with lightning speed from one job at Dupleix to the next. Victoria's editor had accepted this, aware that it was Jacob's modus operandi, just as Victoria would accept it now for Coco, who was clearly the latest twenty-something to be picked out by him as a special protégée. He had been keeping tabs on Coco ever since he'd chatted to her outside Victoria's office, had rung Victoria that day to check that Coco would be starting as junior editor from tomorrow.

Oh yes. Coco's definitely next, If everything goes according to pattern, he'll be telling me to bump her up a rung on the ladder in a few months' time . . .

Victoria took this for granted, as did everyone else who knew of Jacob's habits. It wouldn't have occurred to anyone at the Dupleix publications to consider this sexual harassment. Older men with much younger women was a combination so familiar in the fashion world that Jacob's behaviour didn't raise an eyebrow. There was no coercion, no insistence that a girl he'd chosen duly spread her legs for him or face the sack; Victoria knew perfectly well that if she'd turned Jacob down, he would have shrugged and moved onto the next prospect, without harming her career in any way to punish her for refusing. She would still have done well, been promoted, because she was bloody good at her job.

But it wouldn't have happened as fast, Victoria acknowledged.

Briefly, Victoria wondered whether any girl had ever turned Jacob down. She doubted it. He was hugely seductive, his charm legendary, his charisma overpowering to the young women he selected for particular attention. It was a great compliment if Jacob picked you out from a whole host of other ambitious young aspirant editors; he was highly selective. Victoria could only think of a handful of other women who had been through Jacob's elaborate reward programme. If he didn't see that particular light in the eyes he looked for, that gleam of real personality and ambition, he'd happily confine himself to working through the latest crop of up-and-coming models until another candidate for career advancement eventually, unwittingly, presented herself.

And it's not like he makes you do anything in bed that you don't want to do, she remembered with amusement. My God, he works you up till you're absolutely begging for it. Coco's in for the time of her life.

Victoria had certainly enjoyed her stint as Jacob's mistress, but she hadn't missed it since. Jacob knew exactly how to manage his affairs, how to bring them to a graceful finish, leaving his girls not only grateful for his attention, well rewarded for their time, but styled much better than they had been when he met them. Victoria knew all of Jacob's protégées, and every single one was not only highly successful now, but on the best of terms with their ex-lover, able to call on him whenever they needed help or advice.

We should really form a dining club, she thought. Jacob's Angels, we could call it. We'd meet once a year and have a nice catch-up . . .

And then she rolled her eyes. *What am I thinking? We'd have to include Mireille. She'd probably be the founder member of Jacob's Angels – she must have been his first protégée.*

Victoria's relationship with Mireille was still rocky; she had no wish to socialise with her fashion director, and managed to avoid spending any time alone with her if she could help it. Mireille's attitude of effortless superiority grated on Victoria, as it always had. But she did have to admit that Mireille was doing an excellent job of following Victoria's new diktats for *Style*.

And she booked Lykke as soon as I asked her to.

Oh God, Lykke. It was going to be hard enough seeing her pictures, Victoria knew. Even saying the girl's name in her mind, let alone imagining her body, sent a rush of yearning through Victoria, stronger and more powerful than anything she had ever felt before. No man had swept Victoria away like this, not even Jacob, with his sophisticated games, his elaborate, exciting scenarios that had always left her drained and satisfied. One kiss from Lykke and Victoria's entire world had broken open.

My God, anyone could have walked into that studio and caught them at it! She'd never taken a risk like that in her entire life.

And she couldn't ever do it again.

Jeremy pulled back from embracing his wife, wiping his tearstained face with the sleeve of his pyjama jacket.

'I'm just so happy,' he said, gulping. 'I have everything I ever wanted in the world. We're so lucky!'

'We *are*, darling,' she said, dabbing at his damp cheeks with genuine fondness.

'Oh Vicky, I do love you so,' he gushed. 'And darling, you're being so sweet to me – I do adore you.' His expression grew very serious. 'I really do think that you're going to be a corking mother, darling.'

To her surprise, Victoria felt herself grow a little tearful at this too. She realised, with even greater surprise, that her hands had fallen, and were now cradling her still completely flat stomach. There's a baby in there, she thought. Goodness! I still can't quite believe how happy I am about the whole prospect.

And then she realised why: because now, Victoria Glossop, editor of *US Style,* queen of the New York media scene – which was the only scene in New York worth a damn – really did have it all. She was making a huge success of the job she had coveted for so long, she had the approval of her boss, an utterly loyal and supportive husband, and now, a baby on the way, conceived with what was really a minimal amount of fuss or trouble.

Even though Victoria always wanted to believe that everything she possessed had been achieved through hard work, talent and tightly-focused ambition, she did have to admit that Jeremy might be right as well. For the first time in her life, surveying the empire of power and success that radiated from this huge bed, high up above Manhattan, the windows beyond her giving an unparalleled view of Columbus Circle and Central Park beyond, she conceded his point.

We are lucky, damnit. And it feels bloody wonderful.

Coco

As soon as she climbed out of the cab that had brought them down to the East Village, Coco could hear the pounding of the bassline from Urge. Her heart soared. She hadn't realised how much she needed to go out clubbing until Xavier had come into the fashion cupboard to sweep her out into the warm, enticing Manhattan evening. X was absolutely right, she reflected happily. I needed to let my hair down a bit. She flashed a huge smile at the bouncer on the door, a big butch guy in a muscle tank. He looked taken aback at first – New Yorkers were usually much too cool to smile at bouncers or doormen – but Coco's excitement was infectious, and he grinned back at her as he stamped her hand.

'Love the frock, honey,' he said as she passed.

'I picked it out for her,' Xavier said smugly. 'Told you, didn't I?' he added to Coco, his voice rising to compete with the sound system as they walked through the entrance passage and into the club itself, opening up before them like a very decadent Pandora's Box of delights. Urge's décor, Coco was delighted to see, was much like the clubs she'd been to in London: basic, black-painted, not one of those places where so much money had been thrown into the décor that there was a huge entrance charge and extortionately priced drinks so the owners could claw back what they'd spent doing it up.

Coco hadn't been out dancing once since she'd come to the city. She'd heard that the Manhattan megaclubs, in Chelsea and the Meatpacking District, were vile, huge shiny discos on multiple levels where bankers and stockbrokers stood around the bar, buying twenty-dollar cocktails for their bored dates, who were wriggling cautiously on the brightly-lit dance floor, worried that they'd slip on their Louboutin knockoffs. The music was apparently generic, the atmosphere dull as ditchwater.

But Urge was utterly different from how the megaclubs had been described. Its black walls were slightly damp already with condensation, and a gigantic screen at the back was showing the latest episode of *Project Runway*. Avid watchers clustered on divans and banquettes, ooh-ing and aah-ing as each new outfit came down the catwalk. There was a big square central bar with glitterballs, half-naked barmen – and fully naked men dancing on top of it, Coco noticed, her eyes growing wide. Well, okay, not fully naked – they were all in work boots.

'Coco! Isn't this *fabulous*!' Emily ran towards her, already fairly merry, her blonde mane bouncing on her shoulders in a way that made several of the gay guys clustered around the bar turn and look at her appreciatively.

'You work it, girl,' one said approvingly. 'Love a bitch who knows how to do the hair run.'

'Look at all the hot guys!' Emily exclaimed. 'God, it's like *paradise* in here.'

'Emily, you know this is a gay bar, right?' Coco yelled back.

'That one up there's definitely giving me the eye.' Emily gestured to a gyrating naked dancer, black and muscle-bound, who winked back at her and pumped his hips in her direction. 'Look at his cock! It's absolutely huge!'

There was no denying that the dancer's cock was, indeed, enormous.

'I'll get you a drink,' Emily said. 'The barman's being lovely, he's barely charging me anything.' Wiggling her fingers flirtatiously at the go-go dancer, her slash-neck top falling off one shoulder, her mini-skirt hiked up even further than it was supposed to go, Emily headed for the bar, swaying in her heels.

'At least here she can't get into too much trouble,' Coco said close to Xavier's ear.

'Oh, you'd be surprised,' Xavier said back. 'Quite a few straight guys hang out here, including more than a couple of the dancers. They get great tips from gay guys, plus lots of admiration, *plus* they get to pick out the prettiest fruit flies and take them home.'

'Fruit flies?' Coco echoed, confused.

J-Lo's latest single came on, and a cluster of guys by the bar whooped and threw their hands up as Emily's favourite dancer widened his stance and popped his firm, round buttocks, his thighs rippling, his quads defined, his calves bulging as he bounced his bottom right down to the bar and up again.

'Shake it, girl!' screamed one, leaning forward to shove a twenty-dollar note in one of his boots. 'Work it out!'

'Here, you gotta meet the queen of the fruit flies.' Xavier grabbed Coco's hand and pulled her over to one of the banquettes, where a stunning slim blonde was holding court, surrounded by a bevy of handsome gay men. 'Jamie, this is Coco. She works on *Style* with Emily, and she wants to know what a fruit fli is.'

'Dulling,' drawled Jamie, looking Coco up and down. '*Love* your sequins. Here, Travis, make some room for X's friend.'

The guy called Travis, shirtless and ripped, his eyes a stunning bright blue, his chest perfectly smooth under his linen waistcoat, flashed Coco a smile and obediently squished up to the man beside him, a tall, dark Latino in a Top Gun jumpsuit.

'Ow! You squash me, you big queen,' the Latino complained, pouting his full lips theatrically.

'Oh, Marco, you love it, you dirty boy.' Travis bumped his hips into the Latino's playfully as Coco sat down dutifully, next to Jamie.

'Okay,' Jamie started, tilting her head close to Coco's, her hair a smooth straight blonde fall, her make-up perfect, her dark eyes glinting. 'Here's the rundown. A fruit fli – with an i – is a girl who loves her gay boys, but she's *more* than a hag, okay? I've seen so many damn hags who think their gays are their boyfriends, you know – the ones who get jealous and throw hissy fits when their best gays start making out with some hot boy at the gay club?' She rolled her eyes. 'So. Fucking. Tragic. So I invented the whole fruit fli thing. Because the guys are fruits, and we buzz around 'em, but we don't want to fuck 'em. We've got our own guys to fuck.'

'You *do* want to fuck us,' Travis squealed coquettishly. 'You know you do! Look at this!' He threw his arms wide, showing off his perfect physique.

Jamie ignored him with magnificent aplomb. 'Make sense?' she asked Coco.

'Totally,' Coco nodded. She had been watching Jamie as she explained, hypnotised; now she said, 'Do you mind my saying something? You have the prettiest teeth I've ever seen in my life.'

They were truly beautiful. Coming from England, Coco was used to being impressed by American dentistry, but Jamie's teeth were like a string of perfect pearls, with a sheen to them as if they had all been individually polished and buffed to perfection.

The boys hooted.

'Girlfriend!' The Latino leaned forward. 'Check out mine.' He flashed Coco a huge white even smile. 'Jamie does PR for the best dentist in the city – the bitch got me into those invisible braces for two years. Hurt like hell, but look at them now.'

'They're lovely,' Coco said sincerely, as Emily came up and thrust a tall frosted glass into her hand, mint leaves clustered at the bottom, a straw sticking out of the top.

'I got you a mojito,' Emily carolled. 'Yummy yummy. Cheers!' She clinked her own mojito with Coco's, then looked at the group of guys clustered around Jamie, their queen. 'Ooh,' she added naïvely. 'Everyone's so hot here.'

'I love you already,' Travis said. 'Who are you, honey?'

Coco looked down at her drink, aware of how many calories there were, how much sugar, in a mojito. *I should really get myself a VLT instead. Especially after Jacob telling me that I need to lose more weight off my hips . . .*

And then she looked around her at the gorgeous people, the laughing happy faces with their perfect teeth, the TV viewers beyond cheering as the *Project Runway* credits rolled, and she thought, Fuck it! I deserve a night off from everything – from dieting, from being careful, from trying to be perfect all the time.

She took a long, delicious drag at the straw, an instant rum and sugar high flooding through her bloodstream.

'Oh God,' she sighed almost orgasmically. 'This is delicious.'

The music, which had been kept lower while the TV show was on, now soared to a deafening pitch, its beat pumping like a tribal drum. The alcohol, the music, the laughter, the whoops as clubbers flooded back onto the dancefloor, all combined to make Coco feel incredibly, exhilaratingly . . . young.

She had barely been out in the last few months, she realised. Between the long hours the fashion cupboard demanded, her determination to do any job she was given better than anyone had done it before, the exercise programme that sent her to Pilates or the gym after work, the diet that made her wary of drinking in bars, she had been living almost like a hermit.

Fuck it! she thought again, drinking more of her mojito. I'm only twenty-four, I'm single in Manhattan, I'm wearing a fabulous sequinned dress, I've got a lovely gay friend to dance with, and I'm going to drink mojitos and dance till I can't stand up any more.

Finishing the mojito with a last, heroic slurp, she wiped her mouth, grabbed Xavier's hand and dragged him onto the dancefloor. He followed her more than willingly, laughing at her enthusiasm, shaking his hips as she gyrated round him, the other guys on the dancefloor giving them room to move. High above them, around the bar, the near-naked go-go boys popped their bottoms out, their arms folded behind their heads to make their impressive biceps bulge even more. As Coco looked over, one of them squatted down right in front of an eager guy, the dancer's thighs swelling, the definition of his quads sculptural: the guy tilted his head back, his expression ecstatic as the dancer rubbed his private parts over his face. The guy's group of friends whooped and hollered, yelling, 'That's right! Teabag him, the dirty slut!' stuffing more and more notes into the dancer's boots to keep him going. His thigh muscles strained impressively, veins popping out with the effort of keeping himself in the deep squat, pumping his hips back and forth.

Oh God, I really hope Emily doesn't get that done to her! Coco thought, spotting Emily, who was standing below her chosen dancer, imitating his dance moves to the best of her ability, flicking her hair, wriggling her body at him in a blatant come-on that he seemed to be enjoying immensely: he turned round, shaking his firm, plump buttocks at her, the colour of rich, dark plums, and Emily, giggling like a hyena, went up on tiptoes to slap his cheeks, back and forth in rhythm to the pound of the baseline.

'Whee! Give it to him, girlie!' someone yelled hysterically, and the barman waggled his finger at Emily, reproving her.

'No touching the meat,' he said, but even he couldn't help laughing as Emily put her finger in her mouth and cocked her head sideways, pantomiming apology.

'Awfully sorry,' she said in her high, posh voice, and at least ten gay men echoed back, 'Awfully sorry!' in an appreciative echo.

Xavier shouted something to Coco, but she couldn't hear it;

she threw her arms around his neck and pulled him closer, dragging his head down so that his lips touched her ear, his thick dark glossy hair falling in her face.

'I said, girl gone wild,' Xavier repeated, his breath warm on her skin, and though Coco knew that he meant Emily, she felt herself surge in recognition.

'Me too,' she yelled back, knowing that her eyes were bright, her cheeks pink, her hair starting to come loose. 'I'm going wild too!'

Xavier's smile was dazzling. 'Hey, it suits you,' he said. 'About time you went crazy. Want another mojito?'

Coco nodded vehemently. She had had nothing to eat since lunchtime, and even that had only been a spinach salad with feta cheese, no dressing, the Dupleix canteen's menu option for skinny minnies. The first mojito had taken away any hunger pangs, distracted her completely from her growling stomach; after the second, drunk with Xavier at the bar, his arm companionably round her shoulder, giggling with him as they watched Emily now dancing with Travis, who was happily groping her boobs, Coco was on top of the world.

And then a Britney remix came on, and Coco squealed like a six year old. Dashing back to the dancefloor, she promptly tripped over her feet as she caught her toe on the metal edging that separated the carpeting from the wood of the dance area. The mojitos had gone right to her head; she would have tumbled flat on her face if an arm hadn't caught her, wrapping around her waist, dragging her to her feet again. Howling with laughter, drunk enough by now to think everything funny, she looked down at the arm round her waist: creamy matte, lean with muscle.

'You really aren't hairy at all,' she observed, and put her hand out to stroke Xavier's forearm. It was surprisingly strong, corded like rope, his muscles standing out from the effort of catching and supporting her, and her head span as she made contact with his smooth skin, closed her hand around his arm.

Involuntarily she felt a rush of excitement build in her; it had been a long time since she'd had sex, and though she'd suppressed those impulses, redirected them into work, throwing all her energy into building her career, sex was something that you couldn't repress forever.

Not only that, she thought suddenly, feeling such a flood of lust run through her that she shivered from head to toe. It's like pushing a ball underwater – you can shove it down, under the surface, and you can even hold it there for a while. But when you finally can't keep it underwater any more, it shoots up to the surface like a torpedo. It bursts right out and flies into the air, and splashes you in the face . . .

Coco was drunk enough to start to giggle at this thought, at the sexual innuendo of being splashed in the face, and her whole body vibrated against Xavier's, which was still pressed against her back, holding her steady, tall and warm and strong. She leaned back into him; she couldn't help it. For a moment, she pretended that he was straight, that he fancied her, that she was going to have sex with him tonight. The encounter with Jacob earlier that day had worked her up to a pitch of excitement and frustration that came rushing back now, and she felt her eyes closing, a soft moan coming from her lips, barely audible even to her with the roar of the music and the bustle of the club.

Oh God, she thought, realising that she was unsteady on her feet, that her thighs were clenching tightly together, her body hot and fizzing with sudden desire. *I should really go home now. I'm all worked up and I'm in a gay club, practically grinding against a gay guy who's probably totally and utterly embarrassed at me grabbing onto his arm and shoving my bum back into his crotch*.

And then her entire body stiffened in shock as she realised what she was feeling back there. Her brain, fuzzy and happy and slowed down by strong drink, had finally caught up to what her body knew already.

No wonder I'm so turned on. No wonder I'm feeling suddenly desperate to have wild crazy sex. No wonder I'm feeling like I want to turn round right now and wrap myself around X and shove my tongue down his throat.

Because pressing insistently into her bottom, its shape and size unmistakable, hard as an iron rod, was Xavier's very large erection.

He felt Coco freeze in his arms. The next thing she knew, he was jumping back, to her great disappointment, and when she swivelled round to look at him he was grimacing in embarrassment and apology.

'I'm so sorry,' Xavier blurted out, words tumbling over themselves in his haste to make amends. 'That was totally gross. I'm really sorry, I just couldn't help it – it just sort of happened.'

He shoved both hands into his thick hair, dragging it back off his face, the flashing coloured lights that spun over the dancefloor catching bright shards off the glitter ball, casting light and shadow over his strong bone structure, the high wide cheekbones and long dark eyes.

'I know you're not interested in me like that,' he went on swiftly. 'I never meant to make a move – it's fine just being friends, I never meant to push for more . . .'

Coco was goggling at him, her mouth open wide like a fish's. 'I thought you were gay!' she yelled incredulously.

'You what?' Xavier goggled back at her, his face a comical mask of disbelief. He leaned in, careful not to touch her, worried about offending her with physical contact. 'Did you say you thought I was *gay*?' he said.

She nodded frantically, her head bobbing up and down.

Xavier cracked up. He had been drinking too, he wasn't sober either; he howled, tears coming to his eyes, doubling over, hands on his thighs. Coco, tipsy and sensitive, became instantly offended.

'Look,' she shouted crossly. 'You work for *Men's Style*, you have all these girlfriends but you don't date any of them, and you brought me to a gay club tonight. What was I supposed to think?'

Xavier was still laughing, but he straightened up and managed to say, 'I come to gay clubs a lot. They have the best music, no bullshit straight guys acting like asses, and the girls are really pretty. Right, Marco?'

The Latino guy in the Top Gun jumpsuit, who was shaking his stuff on the dancefloor close by, heard his name and came shimmying over, throwing his arm round Xavier's shoulder.

'What's up?' he yelled.

'Marco's straight too,' Xavier said to Coco.

'Oh yeah.' Marco leered cheerfully at Coco. 'Very straight! We're the big macho studs of the gay clubs, eh, X? Whee!' He took hold of the zipper of his jumpsuit and pulled it down to his waist, showing off an impressive chest.

'Marco, you big whore!' Travis called from where he was dancing with Emily.

'*You* the big whore!' Marco took off towards them, leaving Xavier and Coco staring at each other.

'So, um, you're not gay,' Coco managed, her breath suddenly short.

He shook his head.

The mojitos giving her Dutch courage, her whole body still surging with excitement, Coco took a step towards him, wrapped her arms around his neck, practically threw her whole body against his, and pulled his head down towards hers. For a brief second, he held back, but drink made Coco persistent; she found his lips with hers, ground herself into him insistently, and with a huge swell of relief she felt him, hard as before, pressing against her; the heels made her tall enough to twist and wriggle so she could position him where she wanted him so badly, where she was desperate to have him, against her crotch, between her legs, and as she did so she felt him moan into her mouth. His hands came up to the small of her back, pushing her into him even more, and she came up on tiptoe, meeting him, his cock like a rod between them, the sequins on her dress cutting into her with the pressure.

'Coco . . .' Xavier groaned against her mouth. 'Don't do this unless you mean it, okay? I can't hold out much longer.'

'I mean it.' Dizzy, delirious with sexual desire, Coco kissed Xavier long and hard. 'I really, really, mean it. I want you to—'

'Jesus, don't say it!' He dragged his body away from hers. 'You want me to come in my pants?'

His eyes were shining, his skin glowing with anticipation. Grabbing her hand, he set off at a near-run for the door of the club. They passed Jamie, now bumping and grinding seductively into Marco, her long fall of blonde hair gleaming in the spotlight, her little black dress tight on her slender body.

'Have fun, kids,' she drawled, raising a hand to wave them goodbye as they hurtled past and out of the door, past the smokers gathered in a cluster by the red velvet rope, across the sidewalk to Second Avenue, Xavier hailing a cab that screeched to a halt, dragging open the door, tumbling Coco in and falling in himself after her, pulling her onto his lap.

Her skirt was already hitched up to the tops of her thighs, and as she climbed onto his lap it rode up to her waist, the sequins slipping against each other, bunching up, a tiny strip of lace thong the only piece of fabric now between her and total nudity below the waist. Eagerly, she wound her arms around Xavier, pressed herself down on his crotch, her eyes closing, a gasp of release sighing out as she found the tip of his cock, pressing insistently upwards through his trousers, and drove herself down on it, working it right to where she wanted it, feeling him slide past the lace of her thong, trying desperately to slip inside her, butting against the fly of his trousers. Over her shoulder she heard Xavier, in a strangled voice, giving his address to the cabbie, but she paid no attention; she was blind, almost deaf, utterly focused on what she wanted, what she needed so urgently, what she thought she would die if she didn't get now, now, *now* . . .

Xavier was kissing her frantically, his tongue filling her mouth, mimicking what his cock wanted to do to her so badly, plunging in and out so that she could barely breathe, but it didn't matter; all that mattered was that she had manoeuvred him exactly where she wanted him, was gripping onto the old ripped leather of the headrest behind him to balance herself, her fingers sinking into the filling of the padded cushion, knuckles white, the beaten-up suspension of the cab jouncing up and down on the potholes, rubbing the swollen tip of Xavier's cock high up between her legs, against her pussy, sending a hot rush of orgasm up right through her, stabbing up through her, rising on a climax that came screaming out of her mouth as Xavier kissed her so passionately that the pressure of his tongue against hers, his cock big and hard between her legs, made her come again and again, throbbing and bouncing on top of him as the cab tore through the narrow streets of the Lower East Side, honking, tyres squealing, brakes crunching, racing as fast to its destination as Coco was to hers, Xavier's hands on her hips holding her clamped to his lap.

A final metallic grind of brakes, and the cab screamed to a halt with a series of bounces against its shocks that gave Coco an orgasm that reverberated through her so powerfully it was like an electric shock. She spasmed so hard that she collapsed on top of Xavier, her whole body jerking with the aftermath, so consumed by it that she barely felt him tilting her sideways, reaching into his trouser pocket for his wallet, lifting her gently off him so he could lean forward through the gap in the Plexiglas and settle up with the cabbie.

Xavier got the door open and helped her out. She stumbled on her heels, pulling down her skirt past her bottom, as the cabbie shouted, 'Too late, lady, I got the full show already!' as he pulled away from the kerb.

Coco fell against Xavier, so drugged with lust and rum that she could barely stand.

'I want you to fuck me,' she said, grabbing his arm. 'Please tell me you're going to fuck me now.'

They were climbing a stoop, Xavier fumbling his keys out of his pocket, unlocking a huge iron grille of a door, pushing open an ancient brown metal door beyond it, pulling her through and down a narrow, stinky, linoleum-floored corridor, up a flight of stairs so rickety they looked as if they had been chewed by rats, coming to a halt in front of another door with not one, but two peepholes set into it. Coco held onto the wobbly stair railing for support, her legs weak as jelly, Xavier turning the wards in a whole series of heavy locks, finally pushing open the door and ushering her into a tiny kitchen, Coco bumping her hips on the countertop as he slid a big metal bar back across the door again and turned the lock to bolt it behind them.

'It's like Fort Knox in here,' she said, bracing herself back against the counter.

'Better safe than sorry,' Xavier said over his shoulder, and then he turned to look at her and his face flushed with lust. She was dragging off her thong, or at least getting it down to her feet; too tipsy to manage to manoeuvre it over her high heels, it ended tangled around one ankle.

Coco stared at him, her lips parted, her hair now completely loose. She knew she looked like a complete and utter slut, and she didn't care. She had been good for so long, kept her impulses under such tight control, and now all that self-restraint had washed away. She didn't care what Xavier thought of her; she didn't care if he thought she was the biggest tart in the universe. Jacob's hands on her that evening had worked her up, got her heart pounding, made her wet and horny, and Xavier, so young and handsome, with his big hard cock and his dark eager eyes, was about to reap the benefits. Never fuck on the first date was the New York rule, she knew that by now – you had to wait until at least the third one so a man would respect you.

Well, sod the fucking rules. She didn't give a shit about dating, about presenting a ladylike façade so that Xavier would think she was good girlfriend material. At that moment she didn't even care if she never saw him again after tomorrow, just as long as he gave her what she wanted tonight.

'You've got condoms, right?' she said breathlessly. 'Please tell me you've got condoms!'

Xavier reached into his wallet, dragging out a strip of shiny foil squares. He paused for a second, staring at her, his breathing hoarse and ragged.

'We should go to the bedroom,' he started, but Coco couldn't even wait for that, was too impatient, needed him inside her right now, this second: she stretched out her hands, the galley kitchen so narrow that his belt was in easy reach, and dragged the leather through the buckle, whipping the belt back against the metal buckle to release it, pulling it open, unbuttoning his trousers, unzipping them, shoving them down and reaching for the slit in his boxers.

'Oh my God,' Xavier moaned as her hands closed around his hard dick, pulling it through the opening, wrapping her fingers up and down its length, working him up as he ripped open one of the condoms and rolled it onto the tip, his hands shaking with the urgency. 'Coco, you're driving me mad.'

She was hoisting herself up onto the counter, spreading her legs, her skirt up around her waist once more, one hand gripping his cock still, pulling him towards her, her other hand between her legs, where she was already dripping wet, guiding him in. Xavier pounded into her with one deep thrust, slamming her back against the counter.

'I can't go slow!' he gasped, eyes rolling back in his head. 'I can't slow down, I can't.'

'Fuck me!' she panted, grabbing onto the counter for dear life. 'Fuck me really hard! I want you to!'

It was all he needed to hear. He fucked her like a runaway train, hard and fast, all his pent-up young energy boiling up, sending her head banging against the cabinet door behind her, her legs wrapping around his waist so he could plunge harder, deeper, as if he were trying to pound his cock right through her.

Coco couldn't even scream; it was too wild a ride. She was gasping for breath, clinging onto the counter, trying to keep her head from hitting against the cabinet and only partially succeeding, the sensations slamming through her so powerful and overwhelming that she thought she might faint. Xavier barely managed a couple of minutes more; with a last frenzied thrust of his hips, he exploded inside her, yelling what sounded like a war cry before he collapsed forward, his cock pulsing over and over again, big enough so that Coco felt every single spasm, each one an exquisite extra pulse and surge of strength.

She truly hadn't known how frustrated she'd been feeling, how desperate she'd been for sexual release. Apart from that time she'd masturbated in Victoria's bathroom, she'd crashed every night when she got back from work and her exercise classes, utterly drained. When her alarm went off in the morning, all she could think about was the crazed rush of putting together a stylish outfit, running for the Q train, getting into the office before Victoria to make sure Alyssa had Victoria's chilled water, goji berry plate and non-fat chai tea all ready and waiting, arranged exactly as Victoria wanted . . .

'God, I needed a fuck so badly!' she exclaimed, and didn't realise until the words had escaped her lips that she'd said them out loud.

Xavier, who was reaching down with both hands to make sure the condom didn't slip off, grimaced involuntarily.

'Wow,' he said ironically. 'That makes me feel really good.'

'Oh.' Coco bit her lip, shudders running through her as Xavier's still-firm cock slid out of her. 'I didn't mean . . .'

But she had meant it, she knew she had. She really had

needed a fuck, more than she'd realised; she'd been absolutely desperate for a man, a stiff cock, the sensation of losing herself utterly and completely in the physical needs of her body, which she had been starving and working out and barely allowing any pleasure at all. And even though Xavier had just fucked her with extreme thoroughness, she knew that she wanted even more. She wasn't ready to wipe herself down, pull up her thong again and get a cab home; now she'd had him once, she wanted him again and again. For tonight, at least.

She was still drunk, still high on the thrills of dancing and sex and the wildness of the night. Looking up at him, she saw his handsome face had fallen.

He's such a nice guy, she realised. He doesn't want to think I'm just using him for sex.

And I am. She had to admit it to herself. She liked Xavier a lot; he was a lovely guy, funny, supportive, a good friend. *With a really big cock*. She blushed. *All I can think about right now is sex. I don't want to curl up with him and have a conversation about our hopes and dreams. I want to take all our clothes off and have us do unspeakably filthy things to each other.*

'Coco . . .' Xavier began, and his voice was soft, his dark eyes gentle as he gazed down at her.

She panicked. *I can't do this. Not right now. I can't do soft and gentle and tender. I'm in crazy party mode, and I can't get out of it.*

And also, she was remembering Jacob Dupleix. His touch on her hair, her hips. His knowing, experienced eyes looking her up and down, assessing her, passing judgement on her appearance, making her feel chosen, beautiful, special . . . and incredibly turned on. She knew that in a way, Xavier was reaping the benefit of what Jacob had started and deliberately chosen not to finish. Jacob had played cat and mouse with her, worked her up, and left her fizzing with sexual excitement; she had been desperate for a man after that, and Xavier had turned up – and turned out to be straight – at exactly the right moment.

She shivered, thinking of Jacob's sexual magnetism, the way he had been able to turn her on so effortlessly with just a few words, a bare touch of her body.

I can't possibly give Xavier anything more than a fuck right now. Because I can't stop thinking about Jacob.

Xavier had thrown the condom in the bin, washed his hands at the rust-stained sink, and, drying them on an ancient tea towel, came back to her, cupping her face with both his hands, looking down at her. He pushed a strand of hair gently off her cheek, and it reminded her, again, of Jacob, touching her hair, telling her to cut it. Another shudder ran through her.

'Coco,' he said again. 'You're so beautiful. I've been wanting to tell you for ages how beautiful you are.'

He bent to kiss her, his lips soft now; it was a sweet, loving kiss, a caress, not the full-on, passionate, driven kisses of the club, which had been an instant promise of sex. This kiss was tender, and it felt wrong. Coco couldn't bear it. The wrong man, the wrong kisses. Ridiculous as it was, if she kissed him back like this, she'd be leading him on. He might be one of those guys who made love to you for a night, acted as if they were falling for you hard, as if this was the start of something amazing, and then dropped you like a stone the next day when they'd got what they wanted. But somehow, Coco didn't think so.

I should leave right now, she thought. Get out of here while I still can.

But instead, she wriggled forward, reached behind her and unzipped the back of her dress, letting the expensive sequinned Max Mara fall to the grungy floor of Xavier's kitchen as if it were a cheap rag, undoing her bra and letting that fall too. She kicked her thong, finally, off her heel; she was naked now apart from her shoes.

'Jesus,' Xavier said devoutly, his eyes eating up the sight of her. His hands closed over her breasts, small enough now to fit into his palm completely, and the sensation of his skin on hers made her shiver and gasp. He bent to lap her nipples with his tongue, and she moaned as they stiffened instantly, burying her hands in his thick, heavy hair, pulling him even closer.

'I want you to fuck me again,' she said, bending her head to his. 'I want to suck your cock and have you fuck me again.'

She felt his whole body jerk at the words, knew that he was getting hard, even though he'd come a bare ten minutes before.

'Sound like a plan?' she whispered into his hair.

'Hell, yeah,' he sighed against her breasts.

'Where's the bedroom?'

Xavier raised his head, his expression comically distressed. 'Close your eyes, okay?' he said, taking her hand. 'Don't look at anything. I wasn't expecting company, especially not a beautiful naked woman.'

But she had to peek, of course. She couldn't help it. Especially after, dragging her in his haste, he whacked her bare hip against the jamb of the kitchen door; the paint was clearly flaking – she felt it scrape and peel off against her as she hit into it. Opening her eyes a little, she saw a small, messy living room, Ikea bookshelves teetering under the weight of art books, a sofa that looked as if it had been rescued from a skip, game consoles lying on the rickety coffee table. Floorboards creaked underfoot as they wove through the piles of photography books on the floor, through a doorway with no door, and tumbled onto a bed which almost filled the entire room beyond.

'I need to do it up,' Xavier said apologetically, 'but it's all my own. A one-bed. I don't share with anyone.'

There was pride in his voice now, and Coco knew what he meant. Xavier had his own sitting room, his own bedroom; that was a huge deal here. She and Emily had managed to find a small, two-seater sofa, what Americans called a loveseat, to squash in their kitchen next to the breakfast bar, filling the space where stools should have been, so they could pretend they had a sitting room; but they did have separate bedrooms, which for New York, was a luxury. Style interns and junior editors who didn't come from moneyed families were sharing one-bed apartments, taking it in turns to have the bedroom, one month on, one month off, as the other one slept on the sofabed – or just the sofa.

It had turned out that Emily's family had history, pedigree, and a crumbling old house, but barely any cashflow; Emily would have to marry money if she wanted it, not being bright enough to make it herself. She had no private allowance, no extra income to help afford a nicer apartment; she had apologised to Coco profusely, which had been a source of great amusement to Coco, who, being a down-to-earth Luton girl with no expectation of any help from her family, hadn't assumed that Emily would have anything of the sort. Coco and Emily had lucked into their place, though it was technically an illegal sublet. And they were in a trendy area of Brooklyn, just a ten-minute cab ride to Manhattan; other girls she knew were miles out in Bed-Stuy, Forest Hills, Bay Ridge, hour-long journeys on the subway to get into the city.

'Is that a door?' she asked, staring at the wall beside the bed, behind which was the stair landing. Then she noticed another one on the far wall, blocked off by the bed. 'Wait, two doors!'

'The building used to be an SRO – single room occupancy,' Xavier said, stretching out beside her. 'You know, single rooms for working men, with a shared hotplate and bathroom. There are two apartments each floor now, but they didn't take the doors away.'

He grimaced. 'Cheap conversion. But hey!' He stroked her hair. 'Not to boast too much or anything, but it's rent-stabilised, and I'm fixing it up slowly. Did you see the kitchen cabinets? I put those in a couple months ago. Ah, shit! I have a gorgeous naked woman in my bed and I'm talking about kitchen cabinets?'

He whacked himself theatrically on the head with his hand. 'What a dork!'

Coco giggled, straddling him and unbuttoning his shirt. 'It

wasn't a dork who just fucked me so hard I saw stars,' she said, her eyes widening as she saw his firm pecs and taut six-pack.

She dragged his shirt-tails out of the waistband of his trousers. Eagerly, he lifted his hips as she pulled down his boxers, his cock, hard again, springing free, bouncing up towards her as she leaned over it, taking him into her mouth, sucking him like a lollipop, too excited to go slowly, to use any clever tricks or techniques. She licked and tugged and stroked him, hard, feeling him respond, seeing that he didn't want to take it slow any more than she did; the harder she worked him, the more he groaned and thrust his hips up at her, showing her how much he loved it. His hands wove into her hair, and finally, reluctantly, slid to her shoulders, pushing her away.

'I don't want to come yet,' he muttered, barely able to speak. 'I came too fast last time. I want this to be all about you . . .'

It was dark in the tiny room, the bed right next to the window that gave onto the airshaft at the centre of the building. The sounds of the Lower East Side flooded over them, shouts, honking horns, screams of laughter, people smoking on the sidewalks, yelling at each other, music from the many bars that filled the area competing, jazz and rock and R&B beats rising up into the night. The sounds Xavier and Coco made as they fucked blended in, barely any words, just urgent moans, gasps of pleasure, involuntary grunts and cries, and the frantic creaking and groans of the bedsprings below them. Still tipsy, still overwhelmed by the excitement of the day, her meeting with Jacob, the unexpected, amazing connection with Xavier, Coco let herself go completely.

They wound round each other, sweat slipping over their limbs, only the light from the windows of others up late filtering in through the airshaft for illumination. By the time she ended up sitting in Xavier's lap, his feet propped on the floor for traction, rocking her back and forward, her back arching so she could feel every inch of him as he slid in and out of her, she was completely beyond words, had come so many times that she wasn't even sure she could come again, but completely lost in sensation. She arched even more, and her newly-strong, Pilates-toned thighs sent her further than she'd meant, back off the bed; Xavier shot forward to grab her, stop her from flying into the wall beyond, into the locked old door with its bolts and bars, and he tumbled off balance too. Half-in, half-out of her, they crashed onto the rug beside the bed. Coco managed to twist, to get her hands under her to break her fall, and though she landed awkwardly, the rug was thick and the worst that happened was an 'Oof!' of expelled breath as they landed in a tangle of limbs.

'Are you okay?' Xavier gasped, as she said simultaneously, 'Don't stop – don't stop.'

He was so close he needed no extra reassurance; on hands and knees, she thrust back against him as he pushed fully into her, hard and fast, and she heard herself cry out every time he plunged into her, faster and faster, losing all his own control now after maintaining it for so long, coming in a long stream of heat that flooded through her. He slammed one arm into the wall for balance, to stop his entire weight collapsing on top of her, lean muscle knotting with the effort, his hips throbbing against her bottom as he came.

Coco's knees hurt, her back ached from arching so much. She was utterly spent. Xavier eventually hauled himself to his feet, reaching down to help her up, back onto the bed.

'I'm just going to clean up,' he said, kissing her shoulder. 'Then I'll come back and we'll cuddle.'

In the distance, Coco heard water running in the bathroom. Far away, beyond the ebbing rush of hormones that were flooding through every nerve-ending, drugging her into a state of total relaxation, she knew she needed to use the loo, but she couldn't move. Beside, getting up and going to the bathroom with Xavier in there, being naked, post-sex with him, was so intimate, in a boyfriend/girlfriend way. She didn't want to do that yet. Maybe not ever.

I did really need a fuck. Or three, she thought, her mouth curving into an exhausted, satisfied smile. And that was a really good one.

But as she heard Xavier padding back from the bathroom, as she managed, with the last little shred of energy she had left, to roll over towards the window, giving him room to lie down, she had to admit something to herself. It had been an amazing night. Probably the best sex she'd ever had.

And every so often – well, maybe a little more than that – when Xavier had been behind her, when she couldn't see his face, she had pictured, not his long, smooth limbs, his hairless chest, but Jacob Dupleix's stocky body, his hands on her, his hairy, thick arms. His face, watching her as he moved her as he chose. His voice, telling her what to do . . .

'Wow!' Xavier flopped into bed beside her. He had splashed water over himself to cool down, and his skin, beaded with wet drops, was deliciously fresh. He kissed her and their bodies naturally spooned, Coco turning away from him, towards the window. The night air was light on her bare skin, Xavier warm behind her, his now-soft penis and balls cosily pressed against her bottom.

'That was wonderful,' he said sleepily, pressing a kiss on her shoulder. 'Just wonderful.'

'Mm,' Coco murmured back, already half-asleep.

Xavier is perfect boyfriend material, she thought. My age, with a good job, his own place in the city . . . Then she remembered something she had thought before. *Xavier's a boy. But Jacob's a man.*

A shiver ran through her as she thought of Jacob. Xavier, misunderstanding, thinking she was cold, threw an arm over her waist, pulling her closer to him, warming her up.

I'll have to sneak out before he wakes up. It'll be too cosy, too couple-y, if we get up, have breakfast, go into work together. And I can't be a couple with Xavier. I should let him down now, before things go any further.

And so, despite the incredible sex she'd just had, despite the fact that every muscle in her body was deliciously relaxed, Coco fell asleep feeling horribly guilty.

Victoria

Victoria was getting fat. Horribly, revoltingly fat. Slumping into the limo seat, she was all too aware that her stomach was beginning to fill out; if she didn't suck it in tightly, it protruded fractionally into what was without question a tiny roll above her lap. That morning, staring at herself after her shower, she had angled the three full-length mirrors of her bathroom to see herself, mercilessly, from every angle, something she had been avoiding for the last couple of weeks. And yes, her stomach was no longer concave, which had been a great source of pride to her; it had a perceptible swell to it.

Her breasts were definitely fuller, too. She had barely ever needed to wear a bra before the pregnancy, only for certain clothes that required a particular silhouette, but now she was beginning to feel uncomfortable if she didn't have support for them every day. Instinctively, she'd raised her hands to cup them, not because she liked the feel of them larger – God forbid! – but because they felt heavy, and she was terrified that they would start to sag if she didn't protect them against the tug of gravity.

She was sure her bottom was beginning to spread, too. Still

holding her breasts, she'd swivelled, staring into two mirrors at once to get a view of it. By anyone's standards, it was tiny, and relatively flat; fashionable as it might be nowadays to have a round, projecting bottom, Victoria had always been grateful that hers was as minimal as her breasts. It made wearing clothes so much easier; nothing to interfere with the line or the cut. But what if her arse was going to widen out? She'd stood there, horrified at the mere idea. *Oh God, a flat, wide arse! The worst of all worlds – the classic Sloane girl's bum, flat as a pancake and big as the fucking moon!*

Well, if that happens I am definitely having lipo, she thought. No question. I don't care if I can't sit down for weeks and have to stand up at my bloody desk all day. I'll get a damn lectern and work off that. I am not tolerating a wide arse.

It was all over, the weight gain. Her face looked rounder, her jawline softer. The changes might be tiny, imperceptible to anyone who lived a normal life, but in Victoria's high-pressure world, where appearances were literally everything, nothing went unnoticed. She had spotted Mireille glancing knowingly at her chin, which had the faintest pouch of flesh forming underneath it, something Victoria couldn't hide. She was managing to conceal her stomach with an extra-tight pair of Spanx, but no one made Spanx for the chin, damnit.

They bloody well should, Victoria thought savagely, tapping her fingers under her jaw like women did who were worried about a double chin in 1930s movies. *Maybe I should strap it up at night with elastic bandages*. Pulling out her BlackBerry, she messaged Alyssa to go to the pharmacy and buy her stretch fabric bandages in every size they carried. Victoria was undergoing a series of light-pulse treatments, plus lymphatic draining massages for water retention, but nothing was slimming down her face to where it had been a mere three months ago. Before she'd got pregnant.

It was loathsome. She sighed deeply. Why couldn't Jeremy have this baby for her? He'd love that! God, if he touched her stomach one more time and said he could feel it getting bigger, she was going to slap him!

She'd heard the latest celebrity baby gossip from Clemence a few days ago: a famous actress was secretly having her baby by a surrogate so she didn't put on the weight herself. That happened all the time nowadays, but in this particular case, people were gossiping madly because the actress wasn't doing a good job at gradually increasing the padding under her clothes. She had even been caught, on video, sitting down for a TV interview with a very noticeable crease right in the middle of her stomach, where no truly pregnant woman's baby bump could ever possibly fold in half.

With the extra spotlight on her, the actress had started to panic: she was planning to sell the baby photos for a lot of money, and then pose in a bikini on the cover of *People* in two months' time with the headline: *How She Lost the Baby Weight – and How You Can Too!* for an even bigger payout. If people didn't believe she was really pregnant, she could kiss goodbye to millions. The rest of her – which wasn't padded – was looking too thin to be convincing, and not only did she want to avoid putting on a pound, you never knew when you put on weight exactly where it would go.

Her doctor, however, had come up with a miracle solution. Apparently, he had started giving the actress large doses of corticosteroids, whose main side effect was gaining weight, especially in the face and neck and abdomen. She had had to take them years before, and had hated what they did to her face: now, however, they were ideal. Her face and neck were already swelling up, and the rumours about her pregnancy being fake were receding fast. Clemence had heard all the juice because she was best friends with the actress's stylist, who of course was in on the entire conspiracy.

Looking down gloomily at the tiny roll of fat distending her Spanx, Victoria took some comfort in the insanity of Hollywood actresses and world-famous singers. At least I haven't actually lost my mind, she thought. At least I'm having my own baby. Though by the standards of the world I live in, it's actually terribly old-fashioned.

The thought amused her so much that she was smiling as Jeremy slid into the limo beside her. She had shot out of the appointment to work on her BlackBerry in the limo while he waited to pick up the photo of the scan they had just had done – *well, so much for that*, she thought, cross with herself at having neglected to check her messages or do anything beyond instructing Alyssa to buy her bandages to strap up her chin. Jeremy was clutching a large envelope with great excitement; the driver had barely closed the door behind him before he was pulling the ultrasound photo out and waving it under Victoria's nose.

'Our baby,' he sang out happily. 'Our little peanut.'

The grey, smudged fan shape was familiar to Victoria; she'd seen it often before, in films and on television. It had been hard for her to connect with the reality, that it was showing the burgeoning baby inside her. At about eight weeks along, it wasn't possible to hear the baby's heart, which had been a great disappointment to Jeremy; they had watched the ultrasound pulse with the regular thump of the heartbeat, but the lack of audio had meant that Victoria still didn't feel fully connected to what was happening to her body.

'Look – there's the head!' Jeremy tapped excitedly in the black oval area highlighted in the scan, a pale greyish peanut-like shape floating inside it. His finger indicated the little blob at the smaller end of the peanut, then moved onto the larger end. 'And the body . . .' He traced along. 'And the yolk sac, that circle there.'

'Ugh – yolk sac! It makes me feel like a chicken.' Victoria shuddered.

'It goes away when the placenta's formed,' Jeremy said earnestly. 'The gynaecologist said it's just a temporary thing.'

'Still – *yolk* . . .'

Victoria realised that she had both hands over her stomach, feeling the faint swell of it, pushing against the Spanx. They had been very hard to pull back on after the scan; she'd thought that was the gel they'd put on her for the ultrasound, but maybe it was time to start wearing two pairs of them, one over the other. Gwyneth Paltrow had admitted to wearing two pairs after she gave birth – why shouldn't Victoria try it before?

Victoria had already, of course, set up secret meetings with her favourite designers, who had all agreed to work on maternity outfits for her: Miuccia Prada, Alexander Wang, Alber Elbaz from Lanvin, Jil Sander. It was an extraordinary privilege, but Victoria's position in the world of fashion was equally extraordinary, her power and influence unique, and it meant that designers who would normally never have dreamed of accommodating the very un-model-like proportions of a pregnant woman had jumped at the opportunity of doing the editor of *US Style* a favour.

But maternity clothes, even by Prada and Lanvin, were still maternity clothes, Victoria thought gloomily. Made to fit big tummies, big bosoms . . .

'You don't look terribly excited,' Jeremy said, leaning forward to look at his wife, who was staring straight ahead at the glass partition that separated them from the driver. 'Darling, what's wrong?'

Victoria heaved a long sigh. 'I don't want my boobs to get saggy,' she said in a small voice. 'Apparently big ones actually recover better after breastfeeding – small ones can get all deflated, like fried eggs. And mine are tiny.'

She felt something pricking at the inner corners of her eyes, an irritating itch. Was she allergic to something in the cab, a cleaning product? Air freshener? But she couldn't smell anything unpleasant, and the itch was getting worse. Raising one hand to rub her eyes, carefully, to avoid smudging her make-up, she realised, in absolute astonishment, that her fingertips were damp.

What on earth is going on?

Oh my God! Those are tears! I can't believe it! Victoria simply could not remember the last time she'd cried. No wonder the sensation was so unfamiliar to her.

'Darling! You're crying! Please don't worry – you'll always be beautiful to me.' Behind the lenses of his glasses, Jeremy's blue eyes blinked sincerely. Taking Victoria's hand, he pressed it devoutly, saying, 'How could I ever criticise the changes in your body, when they've happened because you're carrying our baby? What kind of man would do that?'

Victoria's aristocratic features creased in frustration as she pulled her hand away from her husband's, searching in her bag for a tissue that she could use to carefully blot the moisture in her eyes.

God damnit, I'm crying because I like my boobs just the way they are, Jeremy – can't you understand that!

'*I'd* criticise the changes in my body,' she snapped. 'I'd got it exactly as I wanted it, and I don't want tiny little fried eggs for a chest!'

'You are going to breastfeed, aren't you?' Jeremy said, concerned. 'It's so much better for the baby.'

Victoria pulled a face. 'I don't want to,' she admitted honestly. 'But I know it'll help me lose the weight after the birth.'

'You can express the milk,' Jeremy suggested. 'The nanny and I can do the actual feeding, if you don't want to.'

'And, talking about losing weight after the birth, I'm scheduling a caesarian with a tummy tuck,' Victoria said quickly, knowing that he wouldn't like this news. 'For a couple of weeks before the due date. It's all terribly standard nowadays, everyone does it.'

It took Jeremy a while to take in this piece of information, exactly as Victoria had been hoping. Their appointment had been at Columbia Presbyterian, and the limo was supposed to drop Jeremy off first, at the realtor's office on the Upper West

Side, where he had an appointment to view a shortlist of town-houses. He'd been refining his and Victoria's requirements over the last couple of weeks, and was hoping to put in an offer on a property soon. It wasn't a long ride to the realtor's – down Riverside Drive, past the Palisades and the New Jersey shore-line on the right – a hundred blocks or so, but powering fast down the west side of Manhattan with an expert driver, it would only take a few minutes.

Just enough time to tell Jeremy what I've planned, Victoria thought, then drop him off and drive away to the airport before he can get his breath back to complain . . .

'A couple of weeks before the due date?' Jeremy repeated blankly. 'But why? That doesn't make sense.'

'That way, I don't put on the last few pounds,' Victoria said. 'Apparently they're the worst ones to get rid of. And it stops my stomach muscles completely losing their elasticity as the baby settles low in the pelvis. Really, it's all very straightforward.'

'But what about the *baby*?' Jeremy protested, twisting his whole body round on the leather seat, reaching for her hands, trying to turn his reluctant wife round to face him. 'Surely the baby's supposed to be born on the due date. That can't be good for him – or her.'

'They do all sorts of checks to make sure it's safe,' she said firmly. 'I mean, obviously they wouldn't do that sort of operation if it was dangerous for the baby. You wouldn't believe how common it is. How do you think all the film stars and pop singers get their figures back so quickly after giving birth? Believe me, it isn't just because they start Pilates again two weeks afterwards. A tummy tuck's abso-lutely standard nowadays.'

She rattled off a list of four A-list celebrities who'd had the combined operation and pretended that their rapid weight loss, post-birth, was entirely down to diet and exercise.

'And,' she threw in to distract him, 'if my boobs do collapse after breastfeeding – or expressing – I'll definitely get them perked up again to where they were before. I mean, everyone does that.'

'But what about the second one?' Jeremy almost wailed. 'If you get a boob job, that might mean you couldn't breastfeed the second one.'

'The *second* one?' Victoria flinched. 'Jeremy, give me a chance to have this one first!'

'We always said we'd have two.' Jeremy looked like a distressed little boy, his wild curls bobbing as he pulled back from Victoria, pushing his glasses up his nose.

'No,' Victoria said unfairly. '*You* said that. I never actually did.'

She knew that wasn't completely true; she knew that she probably had agreed to have two children, if they could – had certainly gone along with Jeremy when he repeatedly talked about 'kids' in the plural. Going back on that now was cruel of her, throwing him into complete upset and disarray, especially as the limo was now pulling to a halt in front of the condo building on Amsterdam Avenue which housed the realtor's office.

'Victoria!' Jeremy frowned indignantly at his wife. He was by no means a pushover, though he was happy to let her demanding career rule where they lived, accept her long hours at work and her very specific rules for how their sex life was conducted. Those were all concessions that he had accepted, going into the marriage, had been prepared to give. Letting her go back on her word was something else entirely.

The driver had double-parked the limo and was coming round to open the door for Jeremy. There was no time to continue the conversation, and Jeremy knew it; he glared at his wife, letting her know that he was perfectly aware she had set him up.

'I'm very angry with you,' he said, as the door swung open. 'Very angry indeed. This is not how we have a serious discussion about our future, our children. Don't think you can just shoot off to St Louis and think that it's all been decided, because it hasn't. Not at all!'

His blue eyes were flashing, his arms gesticulating wildly. Victoria had never seen her husband this passionate about anything, and she was taken aback; she hadn't known Jeremy was capable of such strong feeling. Quickly she glanced to the open door of the limousine. The driver, who was discreetly averting his gaze, was still holding the door, which placed him well within earshot.

'Jeremy,' she hissed, her eyes flicking to the driver and back to her husband. '*Pas devant les domestiques!*'

'I don't give a damn about whether the staff can hear us!' Jeremy yelled. 'This is much more important!'

Victoria recoiled in shock. Her quiet, discreet, geek of a husband, usually so British-reserve-and-stiff-upper-lip, yelling like a stevedore on the docks in front of a driver hired by Dupleix, who would almost certainly gossip about what he'd overheard . . .

'Jeremy,' she hissed again. '*Please!*'

'I don't want you to go to St Louis,' Jeremy shouted. 'Ring the office and cancel the trip. Your bloody work can wait for once!'

Victoria panicked. It was such an unfamiliar sensation for her that she was paralysed by it for a moment, cold fear freezing her to the leather of the car seat. Jeremy took her silence for consent, and reached out to grab the handle of the door, about to close it again. That finally snapped Victoria into a thaw; she came to life again, exclaiming, 'No, don't!' Her heart was racing, her breath short. 'I really have to go to St Louis, Jeremy. I'll miss my flight—'

'Why is it so bloody important?' her husband bawled, swinging round to look at her again, so furiously that the movement dislodged his glasses from his nose. He forced them back on, glaring at her through them.

'It's a cover shoot.' Victoria heard her voice, thin and weak. 'This is a really important issue – I have to get the cover just right.'

'You're not even styling it – Mireille is,' Jeremy argued. 'This is all just an excuse to avoid talking to me.'

Victoria, to her horror, realised that her voice had risen, was almost imploring in tone. She was positively pleading with him now.

'I don't trust Mireille,' she wailed. Which was true, if not the reason she was so desperate to get on the plane. 'You *know* I don't trust her. Please, Jeremy, get out of the car, go to your appointment. I'll be back by lunchtime tomorrow. I just can't miss this shoot.'

Jeremy drew a long breath. Victoria was practically wringing her hands now. Like an Irish widow in a Synge play, she thought hopelessly. I'm being absolutely pathetic.

'When that plane lands tomorrow, I'll be in the limo to meet you,' Jeremy said with martial resolve. 'We'll go round the houses I've seen today and make a final decision on one. You're not to go to work tomorrow until we've agreed on a house and thrashed out the whole children thing. *Children* thing!' he repeated for emphasis, waggling his finger at her.

'All right, all right – anything. I promise.' Victoria glanced at her watch, its diamond-studded face set into one of her huge tortoiseshell signature bangles. 'I really have to rush if I'm going to make the plane. Jeremy, please, I promise!'

Her bangles clattered as she made frantic, flapping gestures at him to get out of the car; sighing, Jeremy obeyed.

'Don't think you can get out of this,' he told her.

'No!' she practically screamed. 'I don't. I won't.' She waved at the driver. 'Get in – drive! I have to be at LaGuardia in thirty minutes.'

Jeremy folded his arms, frowning deeply, watching the car as it pulled away. His wife slumped back into the car seat with relief, not even caring that collapsing might mess up her hair – extraordinary behaviour for her. Victoria got up at five a.m., worked out with her trainer in the private gym at the Columbus Circle condo, showered, dressed and sat down in her boudoir for her waiting hairdresser to put up her blonde locks into her sleek chignon. After that, she never rested her head on anything for the entire day, sitting up as straight as if she had an iron bar glued to her spine, ending the evening with her hair as smooth and perfect as it had been when she left for the office.

But now, as the limo sped across Manhattan, leaving a trail of blaring horns in its wake, scything round jaywalking pedestrians, Victoria's chignon was smushed into the leather headrest, her eyes closed. She couldn't bear to look out of the window, to see what progress they were making. *What if we don't get to LaGuardia in time? What if I don't make my flight?*

Of course there would be other flights to St Louis that day. Of course the Dupleix credit card would buy her a first-class seat on any one of them. But she had waited weeks for this trip, couldn't bear to wait even an hour or so longer . . .

She positively threw herself out of the limousine as it pulled up outside the American Airlines entrance, slinging her oversized Bottega Veneta bag over her shoulder, running so fast into the terminal and to the security line in her four-inch-heeled Alaia ankle boots that she could have won a race against a drag queen. Her overnight luggage was already in St Louis, had been packed and taken there by the fashion assistants on Mireille's shoot two days before, so that Victoria wouldn't have to suffer the stress of travelling with it herself.

She was so frantic to make the flight that she barely even flinched in disgust at having to put her exquisite bag in a dirty grey plastic security tray, at unzipping her delicate suede studded boots and putting them in another, equally dirty tray, at stripping off her precious bangles and hurrying on tiptoes in stockinged feet through the metal detector, averting her gaze from the enormous female security guard whose bright blue plastic-gloved hands looked menacingly ready for a full-body cavity search.

Every head in the terminal swung round to watch Victoria Glossop, exquisitely and expensively dressed, her pale blonde hair pulled back to display her elegant features, lips a bright slash of crimson, dashing along the cheap grey carpet tiles, her three-thousand dollar purse swinging from her arm like a grocery bag, heading for the finish line, the gate from which the American Airlines flight to St Louis was due to take off in fifteen minutes. She made it just as they were closing the doors, but the combination of her aristocratic demeanour, English accent and first-class ticket allowed her through them and onto the jetway. Very fit from her daily exercise sessions, Victoria was scarcely out of breath as she sank into the pale blue seat, tucked her bag in behind her – she certainly wasn't putting it on the floor, which was probably filthy too – and fastened the seatbelt.

Thank God, she thought, her head spinning. *Thank God.* She was so elated to have made the flight that she barely even noticed the ancient plane, the fading, scratched leather of the seats, the fact that the cringingly apologetic stewardess didn't have champagne to offer her, only warmish white wine in a stumpy-stemmed glass. It was a bumpy flight, but Victoria was not even aware of the choppy air rocking the plane, just sipped a sour-tasting Pinot Grigio and stared blindly out of the window. The view of the Upper Bay of New York Harbour and the Statue of Liberty, the shoreline beyond, sunshine flooding over grey water, the little green islands and inlets of wetlands dotted along the coast, so charming that it had the other business travellers murmuring in appreciation, was invisible to Victoria; she might as well have had the blinds drawn.

She was in a state of suspended animation. American Airlines, which had filed for bankruptcy last year, was so cash-strapped that there weren't screens in the seatbacks, even in first-class; other travellers pulled out laptops and magazines and PDAs and absorbed themselves in work or leisure, but Victoria simply sat there, her gaze on the window, wordlessly holding out her wineglass in one pale, heavily-bangled hand any time that the stewardess bent over her, offering a top-up, sipping continually for the two-hour flight. By the time they bounced down onto the runway at Lambert-St Louis airport, her nerves were calmed, but excitement danced and sparkled along her skin like sunlight on the water of the Upper Bay.

Nearly there, she thought, the wine she had drunk keeping her just serene enough to 'deplane', as the Americans called it, without any more undignified rushing. *Oh God, what was I thinking, drinking that revolting wine? I completely forgot I was pregnant! What on earth is* happening *to me?* She knew she should be feeling guilty, but she couldn't access anything but the rush of anticipation that was racing through her veins. Ironically, now that she was so close to her goal, she didn't need to hurry any longer.

I mustn't seem too eager. I must be very cool, as if she means nothing to me at all . . .

Emily was waiting for her at the gate, her blonde hair tossed over one shoulder, her face contorted with embarrassment as she saw Victoria emerge from the jetway.

'I'm *so* sorry you were booked on American, Victoria,' she said in a rush, words she had been planning to say for hours now spilling out of her. 'I know you hate it. I can't *think* what Travel were doing!'

'It was the most convenient time,' Victoria said casually.

'The hotel isn't quite what you're used to, either,' Emily said apologetically, scurrying ahead of Victoria to show her the way, scuttling sideways like a crab in an effort to look her boss in the face while she talked to her, a considerable achievement in Miu Miu Mary Jane stilettos. 'But you're in the Presidential Suite. Apparently it's the best in St Louis.'

Victoria flapped a hand at her, indicating that she should shut up. Emily went white, red, and then white again, biting back tears, and obediently fell silent; she was so intimidated by Victoria that she didn't dare to say a word from then on, not even to indicate where the limousine was waiting for them. Instead she did her best to convey everything by gesture, which would have been very entertaining if Victoria had been in the mood to be amused.

But I'm not, Victoria thought. Her body was on tenterhooks, her guts churning as if she had food poisoning, twisting and writhing like a pit of snakes; she hadn't eaten a thing all day, couldn't have managed solid food, had existed on skim-milk cappuccinos and white wine, and was feeling positively light-headed as a result. Her iron self-control, however, meant that Emily had no idea that Victoria was any different from normal. Victoria either overwhelmed her underlings with a barrage of questions, or ignored them completely, so the fact that she was sitting silently in the limo, staring straight ahead, taking regular sips of Fiji water from the glass that Emily had eagerly poured for her as soon as the car pulled away, meant only that Victoria was pretending Emily simply didn't exist, something she did in the *Style* offices on a daily basis.

This water isn't 12 degrees, Victoria noticed. And the lime isn't cut how I like it – quartered, not sliced. Coco would have made sure it was exactly right, even on the road. Normally, she'd have taken the opportunity to make that point firmly to Emily, but today, it simply didn't seem to matter.

Emily cleared her throat, wanting to say something, but nervous at her boss's reaction.

'Yes?' Victoria turned her head.

'Um, we're here, Victoria,' Emily mumbled. They had not only come to a halt: the driver had climbed out, and stood ready to open the door.

Victoria started in surprise. 'So we are!' she said, handing the empty glass back to Emily. 'Thank you,' she added absently, and, exiting, completely missed the girl's astonished reaction to her last words.

Across a smooth incline of green lawn, the St Louis Arch rose in front of Victoria, nearly 200 metres tall, a shining, stainless-steel curve like a huge twisted silver ribbon, superbly elegant and utterly incongruous against the background of the standard American city it anchored. Its single, powerfully sleek line, designed by Eero Saarinen, might have come straight from an Ayn Rand novel, a monument one of her heroes or heroines struggled for decades to build, a soaring triumph of the individual will against collective mediocrity.

Through the arch, at the base of the levee on which it stood, the muddy, coffee waters of the Mississippi could be seen, flowing sluggishly along. Huge, ugly, rusted freighters chugged slowly upstream against the current; Victoria could just glimpse a white paddle-steamer riverboat, moored at the base of the steps that led down to the waterfront, clearly a tourist destination.

Not the riverboat, she thought instantly, her razor-sharp editorial brain snapping into gear. The freighters might be rather wonderful, but we can't possibly have that tacky tourist trap in the photos.

And then, picking her way down the looping path which cut through the manicured green grass, she began to make out the details of the fashion shoot, and it was as if a sledge-hammer had slammed into her ribcage.

Because, standing at one of the bases of the arch, was Lykke.

She wore a tiny, abbreviated, deep blue polo shirt which clung to every inch of her narrow torso, a band of milk-white skin showing at its hem, above the waist of her huge, crimson skirt. It was made of layers and layers of stiff tulle, spreading out wide as petals on a cabbage rose, a huge blossom with Lykke's slender body as the stamen, her delicate features at the centre. Her hair was a long white flag spilling down her back; on her feet were high wedge sandals. She was posed standing against one foot of the arch, her spine curved to mimic its shape, a white marble statue in a perfect, formal tableau.

'No!' Victoria said loudly, her cultivated, patrician voice cutting like a diamond through glass across the air between her and the troupe of *Style* staffers. She strode swiftly towards the group, all of whom jumped nearly out of their high heels, swinging round with identical expressions of panic on their faces.

'Wrong!' she continued, closing the distance with a snap of her stiletto boots on stone.

Stretching out one arm to the side, she held out her Bottega Veneta bag, which was instantly removed by Emily, who had hurried up behind her.

'What did I say?' Victoria asked rhetorically, putting her hands on her hips. 'Jumping. Running. Girls in movement. This is America, not bloody *France!*'

She swivelled to fix Mireille in her sights. Annoyingly, Mireille was the only one of the *Style* employees whose expression had barely changed on hearing Victoria's emphatic 'No!' Standing with her Italian-shod feet in third position, her pencil skirt and twinset fitted perfectly to her slim frame, her high bun and Hermès scarf were the final touches that made her look entirely French, in a town so American that the correct pronunciation of its name emphasised the final 's' in a way that totally contradicted its French origin.

'I've *told* you, Mireille,' Victoria said crossly. 'Why is she standing still? This is an American shoot – my first American cover. That's the whole point! Iconic American . . .' she waved at the arch . . . 'edifice, monument – what the hell is that thing? Anyway, iconic American *thing*, and American sportswear, red and blue – and look at her, she's white as a sheet of paper! She *is* the American flag! And what the hell does a flag do? It bloody well *moves!*'

Victoria could barely look at Lykke, let alone say her name in public; she confined herself to swinging her arm briefly in the model's direction. Lykke had relaxed from her pose and stepped off the grass to spare the suede of her shoes. Hands folded in front of her, those incredible blue eyes regarded Victoria as gravely as a young nun in front of the Mother Superior.

'America's in *motion!*' Victoria swept on, instantly averting her gaze. 'This girl,' she still couldn't say Lykke's name, 'was a dancer – that's partly why I told you to book her. I want to see her moving.'

And then a red flush swept over her face as, despite her most rigorous efforts, she failed to repress the memory of Lykke, moving between her splayed legs, jamming her pussy against Victoria's, humping her, hard and furious, against the trestle table in the studio, her hands wedged against the top of the table to let her grind even harder against Victoria's . . .

She knew the blood had risen to her cheeks, and hoped desperately that they'd take it for a surge of anger. Mireille's eyes were quizzical as they took in her editor's arms-akimbo stance, but she replied, with her customary poise, 'Of course, Victoria. We did, *naturellement*, plan out many of the shots in motion that we know you prefer. There was the suggestion by Ludovic,' she gestured at the photographer, 'that we shoot just a handful of more sculptural photos for the website. But we will immediately abandon that and return to the more American style, *comme vous voulez*.'

Victoria bit her tongue. But she couldn't go back now.

'Good!' she said curtly. 'You can do some standing shots later, if the light holds out. Now, let's go.' She snapped her fingers. 'Come on! The sooner we finish, the sooner we can get out of this Godforsaken hole.'

'Ms Glossop?' said a small voice. Victoria looked impatiently in its direction to see a large-boned, Midwestern woman, who looked clinically obese next to the skinny *Style* girls, emerge from behind the photographer. She was wearing a navy shift dress, a pink cardigan fastened round her neck with an elaborate brooch, and court shoes.

Macy's finest, Victoria thought dismissively. *Mall wear*.

'It's a pleasure to meet you,' the woman gabbled on bravely.

'I'm Myrtle Robinson, from the St Louis Convention and Visitors' Commission – I was hoping to interest you in a few facts about the Gateway Arch. You know, it's the gateway to the West, it truly symbolises the heroism of those early explorers, Lewis and Clark, we have a real fine statue of them down in the river in a little boat, with their dog Seaman, it sure is real cute and I'd be more than happy to personally escort you down there to take a look if you'd like – it might make a fine background for one of your fashion photographs . . .'

Dead silence had fallen. Every single *Style* staffer was staring at Victoria with agonised expressions, expecting her to first rend Myrtle Robinson limb from limb, and then turn on them for having allowed her to be exposed, even momentarily, to this flood of tourist-board drivel. Even Myrtle herself finally wound down midstream as if her batteries had died, her bright-lipsticked mouth hanging open as she took in the wordless way Victoria Glossop was staring down her long aristocratic nose at her.

Victoria's lips parted. Emily, hovering close, the handbag over her arm, took a full step back in fear.

'Take *her*,' Victoria said, nodding at Mireille. 'She's our fashion director. I'm sure she'd love to see the statue. And don't hurry back,' she added to Mireille.

A small smile curving her lips, Mireille strolled towards Myrtle Robinson, who was pink-cheeked with excitement and pleasure at being able to take *Style*'s fashion director to one of the city's famous landmarks.

'Well!' she could be heard saying as she bustled Mireille away in the direction of the steps down to the river. 'It sure was nice of her to spare you for a little while.'

What on earth is happening to me? Victoria thought briefly. Is the pregnancy making me soft?

The thought was nauseating. Turning to the trembling Emily, she bellowed, 'Coffee! Now!'

And then, fixing Ludovic with a steely stare, she continued,

'Well, what are we waiting for? Come on – action shots! Let's get moving! I want to see her fucking *fly!*'

Victoria had been up since five that morning. She had worked out, dropped into the office briefly, left again for her hospital appointment – which, as far as the office was concerned, was a trip to view a house; she wasn't telling anyone she was pregnant till she passed what the Americans called the first trimester. Then she had dashed to the airport, flown to the Midwest and supervised a crucial cover shoot for four hours. *I ought to be shattered,* she knew, as she stood at the floor-to-ceiling window of what passed, in St Louis, for a decent suite, staring out of the window at the city by night, bright with lights in a regular pattern of lines that signified the centre of a purpose-built American city, laid out to a symmetrical grid pattern. Beyond the sprawlingly-wide Mississippi, now a black swathe of velvet spanned by orange-lit bridges, the factories of heavy industry on the wrong side of town sent up a faint plume of smoke still, though it was past ten at night. The smoke had been there all day, grey and dirty; it would be scrupulously airbrushed out of the final photographs.

An Ayn Rand arch is a fabulous symbol of America, Victoria thought. Those factories are just as Ayn Rand, but rather less photogenic . . .

Or are they?

An image popped into her mind, fully-formed, influenced also by the rusty sides of the passing freighters, their faded and peeling paint. A huge factory, pipes and metal framework, girders and RSJs, high ladders against old brickwork. And Lykke, beautiful and pale as a ghost, halfway up the ladders, draped over rust-stained slabs of iron, her limbs long and slender as the poles of the ladders, spike heels elongating her legs to impossible proportions . . .

Fuck! Victoria slammed a hand into her forehead. Every time she closed her eyes, she saw Lykke's face, her body, her breasts . . . every time she lay down in bed she imagined Lykke on top of her, fucking her as she had that afternoon weeks ago. She had planned the entire cover shoot around Lykke, her white skin and hair that would make such a stunning visual image with the reds and blues that were so on-trend right now, would provide an unearthly, sophisticated vision of Americana that would instantly proclaim Victoria's arrival at the helm of *Style*. She had put Mireille in charge of the shoot, had held off for ages on even booking herself a ticket, had told herself that she wouldn't visit, would leave matters entirely in Mireille's hands.

But of course, she had been completely unable to resist the temptation of seeing Lykke again.

Victoria had left them all after directing the shoot, had said she was tired and would retire to her suite and get room service. But that hadn't been true. She was terrified of being out in public with Lykke in a social situation, afraid that the way she looked at the girl – or maybe even the way she avoided looking at her – would betray her to the watching eyes of her employees, who were used to observing her like a hawk to ensure they were doing things precisely the way she wanted. Even being so close to Lykke, outside, by the arch – she had needed to touch the model, to rearrange the hang of clothes on her body, to show the hairdresser how she wanted Lykke's long silky white hair done for the next shot – had been unspeakably erotic. Victoria's breath had come fast, her hands had trembled; she had blamed Emily, loudly, for bringing her over-strong coffee.

And Lykke had stood there like a beautiful mannequin, only a blue vein in her throat, pumping against the white silky skin, to show that she was moved, agitated, in any way by the proximity of the woman she had fucked so wildly the one and only time they had met before.

Oh my God . . .

Victoria looked at herself in the dark glass of the window as she reached down and slid one hand between the wrapped folds of her robe, parting it slowly, the silk lining brushing exquisitely against her bare legs as she pulled it aside. Her fingers moved up her thighs, even higher, between her legs, slipping her fingers up into the parting of her lips, teasing herself, easing back and forth, her body gradually yielding, relaxing fully, allowing her between those folds, too. Victoria inhaled a little gasp at the sensation, the wetness her finger found inside her, the eager readiness as she pretended that it was Lykke caressing her like this, Lykke's fingers between her legs, Lykke's fingers inside her now . . .

A moan escaped her. And then she heard a series of light, insistent knocks on the door of the suite.

She knew instantly who was there. It wasn't room service; her untouched dinner still stood on its trolley in the sitting room, covered by stainless-steel lids that she hadn't even lifted. It was too early for them to come to take it away again, and besides, room service, or housekeeping, would howl loudly outside the door; it seemed the policy now in provincial hotels, some sort of training code that taught them to whack at the door, throw their heads back, and yodel: 'HOUSEKEEPING!' at the top of their voices. You couldn't call to them to come in any more, either: no, you had to open the door yourself, and then invite them in. Like vampires, they weren't allowed to enter until you had officially told them to do so. It was all so tedious.

The knocks came again, soft and discreet.

There was a moment, poised in time, where Victoria held fire. Where her brain still desperately tried to distract her by running through room service and housekeeping protocol, keeping her away from the main door of the suite for long enough for the person outside to become discouraged and slip away again.

But the next thing she knew, her mules were dashing across the carpet, her silk robe whispering around her as she ran, and she was fumbling at the door, cursing under her breath as she struggled with the security latch, the awkward brass handle. Eventually she dragged the ridiculously heavy door open, her breath stopping, caught in her throat, as she saw Lykke standing there, pale and beautiful, her hair pulled back in a ponytail, wearing the leggings, loose sweater and Ugg boots that were the uniform of the off-duty model.

The two women stared at each other for a few seconds. Eye to eye, almost; Victoria's mules had heels, while Lykke's boots were flat-soled, which helped to even out the height difference. *Lip to lip*, Victoria thought, and then she couldn't help it, she found herself looking up and down Lykke's body, picturing what was under her clothes, and thought, *Breast to breast . . .*

The next moment, Lykke had stepped forward, inside the suite, and the heavy door swung shut behind her as she took Victoria into her arms.

'I had to come to you,' she said seriously. 'Because you wouldn't come to me.'

The breath Victoria had been holding flooded out of her in a great sigh of relief. She threw her arms around Lykke, suddenly desperate to embrace her, to touch every inch of her, to kiss her as passionately as they had kissed before. Even though she had been thinking about Lykke near constantly, fantasising about her, imagining her long, pale naked body stretched on top of hers, she hadn't realised, until her lips and Lykke's met, how intense her yearning had been.

Wrapped together, stumbling in their haste, Lykke crashed back into the wall of the hallway, Victoria pressing her back against it, grinding herself into Lykke, dragging up the girl's sweater, moaning with satisfaction as she discovered that she was naked underneath it, her hands closing over Lykke's bare breasts. Lykke's hands were in Victoria's hair, cupping her skull, dragging her lips to hers, her tongue sliding into Victoria's mouth, claiming it, her breath sweetly tasting of sugary fresh mint. The kiss went straight to Victoria's crotch, like a stab between her legs, a fizzing and buzzing in her pussy as if she had slid one of her many sex toys up inside her.

'Fuck,' she moaned into Lykke's mouth. 'God, you make me practically fucking come just by fucking kissing you . . .'

Lykke pushed off the wall, took a couple of steps forward, pressed Victoria back in her turn against the opposite side of the hallway, a picture hanging there tilting sideways with the impact, luckily failing to hit Victoria's head. Lykke was unbelting Victoria's robe, squeezing her breasts, and Victoria made a choked protest, between pain and pleasure; her breasts were more sensitive than they had been before.

Lykke noticed instantly. 'Are you on your period?' she whispered, kissing Victoria's neck.

'No, I—' Victoria couldn't say the words.

But then Lykke's gaze dropped down past the slightly swollen breasts to the curve of Victoria's stomach, and she drew in her breath as she realised the truth.

'Don't stop!' Victoria heard herself say frantically. '*Please* don't stop!' She writhed towards Lykke, unable to bear the thought of not finishing what they had started, arching her whole body into Lykke's, wrenching the girl's sweater up and over her head, sighing in ecstasy at the sight of her tiny, bud-like breasts.

'You're so fucking beautiful,' she sighed, her hands going down Lykke's smooth back, sinking under the waistband of her leggings, cupping Lykke's small buttocks, throwing herself at Lykke till they crashed back into the other wall once again, ricocheting into it. She dragged the leggings down to Lykke's thighs as Lykke sank her mouth into Victoria's neck, finding the most sensitive points, licking and biting and kissing. Victoria heard obscenities streaming out of her lips, words over which she had absolutely no control, that trailed into a high, wordless wail. She jammed her hand into her mouth, to stifle a scream as Lykke cupped Victoria's crotch with her hand and expertly flicked the tip of one finger three times, just enough to send Victoria into a desperately-needed orgasm.

Her hips slammed into Lykke's with release, her muscles slackening, her eyes closing as she gave herself up to pure sensation. Dimly, she felt Lykke pushing her against the wall behind her once more, giving her something to lean against as the girl sank to her knees, eased Victoria's legs apart, and, her hands reaching up to caress the infinitesimal swell of Victoria's stomach, tilted her head into Victoria's pussy and slid her hot, clever tongue inside it.

Victoria's palms were flat against the ridges of the wallpaper, pressing into it with everything she had, trying to keep herself upright, steady enough so that Lykke could keep doing what she was doing, licking her in strokes and whirls, flicking her with the tip of her tongue, making her come again and again. Victoria's hips bounced back and forth off the wall, a regular, steady rebounding as she rose and fell on Lykke's tongue. Lykke knew exactly how to pace Victoria, not to over-stimulate the highly-sensitive cluster of nerve endings that blossomed between her legs, to take her on a long ride, like a boat sweeping up and down a series of waves, cresting the white foam on each ridge, then dipping, with just enough time to catch her breath, have her eyes focus again on Lykke's smooth white forehead, the delicate wisps at the hairline, as white as her skin – *like swansdown, like feathers*, Victoria thought distractedly before Lykke's tongue twisted around her centre and her eyes snapped shut once more as another orgasm laced through her.

She had no idea how long it went on before she became aware, slowly, her pussy wet and open and throbbing with sensation, that Lykke was on her feet once more, winding an arm around her waist, leading her through into the bedroom of the suite, laying her down on the bed.

'I wonder if you taste different,' Lykke said, her blue eyes wide, 'now that you are pregnant. I wish I had tasted you before, to see the difference.' She was kicking off her Uggs, pulling off her leggings, her naked body even more perfect and streamlined than Victoria had imagined it.

'What do I taste like?' Victoria asked, pulling Lykke towards her, licking her own juices off Lykke's wide mouth.

'Do you think you taste different?' Lykke asked eventually, raising her head. 'You lick your fingers after you touch yourself – do you think there is a change?'

And bossy, utterly confident Victoria Glossop, editor-in-chief of *US Style*, all too used to rapping out commands, with no hesitation, ever, in giving her opinions, found herself wriggling and blushing like a little girl.

She couldn't answer. Instead, she tilted herself up, one hand between Lykke's breasts, pushing her back, watching the serious, questioning expression in Lykke's long, pale aquamarine eyes grow even more serious, even more concentrated, as she stretched out her long legs, lay down in response to Victoria's unspoken order. Like all five-star hotels nowadays, the bed was made up with a duvet on top of the high mattress, for extra softness, extra delicious yielding as one climbed onto it, and Victoria felt as if she were moving through a cloud as she slid between Lykke's legs, her knees sinking into the mattress topper, which was soft as Lykke's skin, as her silky inner thighs, as the faintest, silkiest, down on her mound of Venus . . .

Like feathers, Victoria thought, smoothing it with her hand, hypnotised by the tiny fluff of white pubic hair on white skin. *She's like some mythical creature. I could almost imagine that she'll grow wings and fly away . . .*

Her hands met on Lykke's mound, caressing it, slipping down into the grooves on either side, tracing them with her fingertips, making Lykke groan and thrust her hips up, begging for Victoria's touch further down. Her knees came up, the flats of her bare feet on the coverlet, pushing down, raising her groin to where Victoria's mouth was ready to meet it.

Victoria didn't have Lykke's expert technique, but she had always been the fastest of learners. And the inability to speak was what helped her more than anything else, what forced her to concentrate entirely on listening to the sounds Lykke made, on feeling how Lykke's pelvis pumped against her lips, teaching her how to pace her licks and bites and tongue-flicks as Lykke had done with her, finding Lykke's own particular rhythm, making her dance on her tongue with pleasure, relishing the sweet, salty, sharp-lemon taste, using her hands to cup Lykke, tip her up into her mouth, stroking the creases of Lykke's groin with her thumbs in tickling strokes that made the girl gasp even louder, groan even more.

Victoria had always been entirely selfish in bed. She had considered Jeremy's orgasm something for which he was completely responsible and which she strongly preferred him to keep away from her as much as he possibly could. But this was entirely different, so different that the sexual experiences Victoria had had up to that point, before Lykke, seemed, by comparison, completely unworthy of the name. Victoria was transported, overcome, utterly consumed by what she was doing, the stream of orgasms she was giving; grinding her own pelvis into the comforter, she gave herself a whole mini-string of climaxes that echoed Lykke's cries, the rise and fall of her small, gently-rounded buttocks as she rode Victoria's mouth again and again, growing wetter and wetter, Victoria licking as fast as she could.

Until, finally, her jaw locked, clamping painfully, and she had to pull back, massaging its points with her fingers, looking guiltily down at Lykke, starfished on the bed like an unearthly, wingless fairy fallen to earth.

'I'm sorry,' she said awkwardly. More firsts for her: both the apology and the awkwardness. 'Was that enough?'

Lykke's long white torso started to ripple, from her shoulders to her hips, as if the bed had a heated roller, Shiatsu-massage function. It took Victoria a few seconds to realise that Lykke was laughing silently. One pale arm reached up, finding Victoria's hand, pulling her down on the coverlet beside her.

'For this time, it's enough,' Lykke said, still laughing, turning her head to look into Victoria's eyes. 'Since you have never done this before, I'll let you stop. But the next time, you must do it for at least an hour.'

'Oh!' Victoria realised she was being teased. It was such an unusual experience for her that it took her a little time to process it. Her jaw relaxed into a smile, matching Lykke's. She reached out to stroke her lover's wisps of hair back from her forehead.

'I did not come to see you because you gave me the photo shoot,' Lykke said very seriously, the dark blue that ringed the paler blue of her irises deepening. 'I came because I wanted to.'

'Really?' Victoria said. She wanted to tease Lykke back in return, but the joshing, sarcastic words faded on her lips: she couldn't say them. There was something about Lykke, her calm, centred, pale beauty, that hypnotised Victoria.

'Yes,' Lykke said simply, smoothing back Victoria's hair in her turn. 'I wanted to very much. I was so happy when I saw you today.'

'I was too,' Victoria mumbled, so quietly that Lykke could barely hear her.

Lykke sensed that she had pushed Victoria far enough beyond her normal limits of reserve; she fell silent, gazing meditatively at Victoria, the faint flush that had suffused her cheeks fading again, one blue vein still pulsing in her forehead. Words tumbled through Victoria's brain, a complicated tangle of thoughts and impulses, things she wanted to say and wouldn't let herself. Lykke gave her all the time she needed, watching her lover's face, seeing it contort with confusion.

Finally Victoria said gruffly, 'No one knows I'm pregnant yet. Apart from my husband.'

'I will not say a word,' Lykke promised. Her gaze drifted down Victoria's body; her hand released Victoria's and gently cupped one breast, light as feathers on the sensitive skin. 'I want to see these in a month,' she said thoughtfully. 'When they are a little bigger. And this, too.' Her hand slid to Victoria's stomach. 'It will be very beautiful.'

'Ugh.' Victoria pulled a face. 'Not to me.'

'In my country, they say that pregnant women have even better orgasms,' Lykke said solemnly. 'They feel it more. It is very strong.'

Her hand slid even lower, stroking Victoria's completely-depilated mound, the index finger rubbing just below it, making Victoria arch to meet it.

'One more time,' Lykke whispered, rolling over on her side, rolling Victoria on her side too, pushing against Victoria's back, spooning her. Victoria moaned softly, unable to resist, her legs parting, the upper one falling back a little against Lykke to give her just enough access. 'One more time, to make you sleep . . .'

'Oh *God*.'

Victoria rocked against Lykke as she started to come. Her eyes closed; she realised how exhausted she was, how very much she wanted to fall asleep, coming, cradled against her lover. She had never shared a bed willingly with anyone in her life, never fallen asleep in anyone's arms; but then, she had never been wrapped around by such a sweet, cool body before, never been touched so cleverly by delicate fingers, never realised how much she relished the smoothness of a woman's skin.

She was asleep almost as soon as her last, drugging orgasm slowly subsided, in a deep, blissful trance, her eyelids fluttering gently, her lips parted, breathing regularly. Lykke lay, holding her, for another ten minutes or so; then, very carefully, she slid her hand off Victoria's hip, and gathered the silk robe up, wrapping it around her prone body. She slipped off the bed, pulled on her clothes, and then lifted the edge of the coverlet, folding it over the sleeping Victoria, tucking it under her chin, pausing for a moment to look down at Victoria's serene features, before she trod quietly over to the wall and turned off the light switches, plunging the suite into darkness. Easing open the door, she shut it even more carefully behind her, to avoid making any noise at all that might wake Victoria.

She padded towards the lifts, the Ugg boots soundless on

the garishly-patterned hotel carpet. Hotel corridors were long at the best of times, and seemed even longer when there were suites on each side; fewer doors to pass, because the rooms were so much bigger. So the door that opened behind Lykke, further down the corridor, was far enough away for her not to hear it; the person opening it was just as quiet as she had been, guiding it closed with the tiniest of clicks of latch into lock.

It was Emily, her clothes looking as if they'd been thrown on in a wind tunnel, her long blonde hair tangled and messy. Ludovic, the photographer, had convinced her a couple of hours ago in the bar to slip away to his suite with him; Lykke wasn't anywhere to be found, and if he couldn't have sex with the model after a shoot, a pretty assistant editor was his next choice.

Emily was walking carefully, carrying her shoes in one hand. Barefoot, because her tights had been badly ripped earlier in the evening. She was sore in all sorts of places, with a sour taste in her mouth and stubble burn everywhere: Ludovic's sexual tastes were catholic, and he had insisted on doing exactly what he wanted, in his preferred order of business. A *Style* junior editor had tried to warn Emily away from him, but Emily had assumed the editor was simply jealous because Ludovic was famous, rich, and good-looking.

Well, Emily had found out the truth the hard way. And she would try to warn the next girl she saw being singled out by him, like a gazelle being picked out from the herd by a lion – but she probably won't believe me either, Emily thought miserably. Why should she? I didn't.

Her inner thighs were chafed, and would be bruised tomorrow. Her jaw was stiff, and her lips sore. She had a feeling there would be a bite-mark showing on her breast tomorrow, too.

I'm not going to think about it any more, she told herself. There's nothing I can do – he's famous and rich, and I'm not. All the wagons will circle around him, and I'll never work in fashion again if I say one word about the things he made me do.

Turning to walk away, determinedly blinking back her tears, Emily did a double-take at the sight of Lykke – the model who had been sensible enough to avoid Ludovic's attentions – walking away down the corridor with loose, easy grace, her back turned. It was enough of a surprise for Emily to forget, at least briefly, the unpleasant experience she had just been through.

Where was she coming from? With dawning amazement, Emily realised that the only door from which Lykke could conceivably have exited was the one on the other side of the corridor from Ludovic's, a little further up, and that – she scampered along to check, silent on her bare feet – it bore a brass plaque without a number on it, simply the words *Presidential Suite*.

Oh my God! If anything could conceivably alleviate what had just happened to Emily, this piece of gossip could. *Lykke and Victoria Glossop? There hadn't been a single rumour about Victoria being gay!* Lesbians were two a penny in the fashion world, naturally, but Victoria was not only married, but well known to have had a career-ladder-enabling fling with Jacob Dupleix. This was genuinely juicy, A-class gossip, and Emily clutched it to her chest in excitement.

She was puzzled, however, when she reached the end of the corridor, which finished in a T-junction, and cautiously peeked her head, very carefully, round the corner, to see that Lykke had disappeared from sight. Lykke's room wasn't up on this floor, which was suites-only; models didn't get that kind of luxury accommodation unless they were household names, with their own advertising campaigns.

Emily knew she hadn't heard the ding of the arriving elevator. And there wasn't a fire exit to a staircase anywhere that she could see. Emerging into the T-junction, she looked up and down the corridors on either side: nothing. She pressed the down button, her brain still racing.

She can't possibly have gone into another suite . . .

But Emily was wrong. At that moment Lykke was standing

in the sitting room of Mireille's suite, further down the corridor past the bank of elevators, looking at its occupant. Having let Lykke in, Mireille was re-seating herself on her sofa, her long, white-streaked hair brushed out and flowing over her shoulders. Wrapped in an ankle-length, green velvet dressing-gown, she was sipping from a brandy snifter, the huge emerald solitaire on her left hand flashing richly in the soft lamplight.

'*Et alors*?' she asked Lykke, her finely-plucked eyebrows raising in interrogation. 'You have been with her, *non*?'

Mireille smiled in anticipation, the smile of the Sphinx. She crossed her legs, smoothing the velvet dressing-gown over her thighs.

'Tell me *everything*.'

Coco

Coco was wearing the Max Mara sequin dress for her date that evening. It hung a little looser on her now – she had barely eaten anything for the last few days, ever since accepting the dinner invitation – but still looked wonderful. Besides, when you wore a sequin dress, you didn't need accessories, which meant one less thing to worry about.

She had had it dry-cleaned, of course, since that night at Xavier's the week before; woken up at the crack of dawn, sneaked out, leaving him sleeping, and retrieved her dress, knickers and shoes from his kitchen floor, borrowing a sweater of his to throw over the dress for decency. It was still, quite obviously, the walk of shame, but one of the best things about living in New York was that there was almost always a cab instantly available, and she'd been able to nip home before going into work and change into more appropriate work clothes.

The worst part had been giving Xavier his sweater back. She had seriously considered being cowardly enough to put it in a bag and leave it for him on the *Men's Style* reception desk; if she didn't include a note, that would be a clear hint that she considered the night before to have been a one-off.

But I'd be livid if a guy did that to me, she'd thought, ashamed of herself. I can't be that much of a bitch.

She had been debating what to do all day; should she ring him, arrange to go out for a drink, to at least have the decency to let him know face to face that she didn't want to date him? Of course, she thought hopefully, he might not be interested in dating me either. Lots of guys seem all keen until they've got what they wanted.

But she'd sensed that Xavier was more serious than that, and she'd been right. That afternoon, he'd come up to the *Style* offices, beaming with excitement, trying to act cool in front of Coco and the other junior fashion editors, nonchalantly leaning against her new desk. Coco's heart had sunk at the sight of him.

'I just wandered by to officially congratulate you on your promotion,' he'd said casually, for the benefit of the girls around her, but his dark eyes, lit up and shining, gave her a very different message. 'See where you're hanging out now.'

'O-oh!' she'd stammered. 'Thanks . . .'

And her tone of voice had been all Xavier had needed to understand that things weren't going to go as he had hoped. Anyone used to swimming in the shark-infested waters of the New York dating scene had developed finely tuned antennae that could pick up the merest whisper, the faintest hint that interest was fading and that they should protect themselves by feigning indifference. All of the light had drained from his eyes, leaving them flat and dull as black stones, and he'd pushed back off the desk, standing straight up.

It had been horribly hard to watch. Coco had had to bite the bullet.

'Look,' she'd said, grabbing the bag in which she'd put his sweater, 'let's just walk out to reception for a second.'

'No need,' Xavier had muttered.

She had insisted on following him back to the lobby, where she'd given him the sweater and mumbled a few words about being really busy at work for the foreseeable future.

'I just don't have time for anything serious,' she'd said, a lie so old and hackneyed she was embarrassed to trot it out.

Awfully, Xavier had taken this as a possible opening: looking hopeful, he had said immediately, 'Okay, I get that. You just started a new job. But we could hang out, have fun together, see where things take us. You'll settle in on the fashion desk after a while, and then we could see if you have more time . . .' Then he'd met her eyes, and his voice had tailed off as he'd read the 'No' in them.

'You deserve better than me,' Coco had said, another pathetic brush-off that she'd have groaned at if a girlfriend had recounted a one-night stand saying that to her the morning after.

Xavier wasn't a fool, or a pushy egotist. There had been no more attempts to convince Coco to date him.

'Thanks for bringing back the sweater,' he'd said stiffly, taking the bag, avoiding any further direct looks at her. 'Best of luck with the job, okay?'

'You too,' she'd said stupidly. 'Maybe I'll see you in the canteen sometime.' It was the final coup-de-grace, the 'I'll see you around' that really meant 'I'm deleting your number from my phone. Don't call me'.

As he'd turned away, heading for the bank of elevators, it was impossible for her not to notice the slump of his shoulders, which had been set back so proudly when he'd strolled into Coco's office – the pride of a man who, the night before, had finally got the woman he was after back to his bed, and knew that he'd done a damn good job of satisfying her while she was there.

'Aww, shame!' Lucy had called out as Coco walked slowly back to her desk, her face twisted up into a knot of guilt. 'Did you just kick X to the kerb?'

'I'll have him,' Emily had said excitedly. 'Seriously, Coco, did you just tell him to get lost?'

Coco nodded gloomily. Lucy clicked her tongue, spinning

her chair round, putting her feet up on Emily's desk so she faced Coco.

'No good in the sack?' she asked. 'His yin didn't fit your yang?'

'Oh my God, small willy?' Emily blurted out, wiggling her little finger in the air.

Lucy slapped her finger down. 'Shut up, you racist English cow,' she said affectionately. 'Asian men don't all have small dicks, okay? Why don't you screw a few and find out?'

'I'm rather concentrating on black men at the moment,' Emily giggled. She was having a torrid affair with the go-go dancer from Urge. It was the classic case of a posh white girl sowing her wild oats with a working-class black guy. Emily was destined to settle down with a rich Piers or Toby or Harry, pink-faced and braying. She was taking her fun while she still could.

'X was great,' Coco had said, slumping into her own chair. 'It's just – he's not what I'm looking for, okay?'

'He's one of the good guys,' Lucy had said more seriously. 'And there aren't many of those in this city, let me tell you.'

She's right, of course, Coco knew. But I can't date Xavier while I'm thinking, all the time, of Jacob.

'Coco!' It was Alyssa, dashing over to her desk, looking panicky.

'Oh God, what is it now?' Coco said. 'Has she run out of linting tape? I told you to stock the cupboard with tons of it.'

'No, she wants to see you – now! Come on – oh shit, my phone's ringing.'

Alyssa shot back to Victoria's office, and Coco followed at high speed, glad to get away from Lucy, who was making her feel even guiltier. You never, ever kept Victoria waiting. Victoria was pacing her office, looking even more fearsome than usual, and it was all Coco could do not to run to the built-in fridge and placate her with a glass of Fiji water and lime.

But I'm not her assistant any more. That's not my job. I'm a junior fashion editor now. Alyssa has to get her water.

'You wanted to see me, Victoria?' she said, managing to keep her voice even.

Victoria came to a halt by the big windows, her back to them, the sun behind her making her into a thin dark shadow; it was impossible to read her expression.

'I have my eye on you,' she'd said. 'Remember that.'

Never, ever, tell Victoria you haven't understood something she's said. Never ask for clarification.

So Coco nodded carefully, and waited.

'For good and bad,' Victoria added. 'You can go far. But don't get ahead of yourself, and don't forget that it was me who gave you your first break.'

'Of course not, Victoria!' Coco said swiftly. This is about me working with Mireille, she thought. Victoria's making it clear who I owe, who I work for. I've seen her put down her markers before. I know what's happening.

'And don't get your head turned by any temporary attentions that are paid to you,' Victoria went on. 'You're simply one in a long line of young women. Remember that, too. Don't let it go to your head. I've seen that happen before, and it never ends well.'

'No. Yes. Of course, V-Victoria,' Coco had stammered, at a loss. What on earth was she talking about? Never ask for clarification . . .

'That's all. You can go now,' Victoria had said. 'Tell Alyssa I want my bandages.'

'Yes, Victoria.' *Bandages*? Coco slipped swiftly out of the office.

'She wants her bandages,' she said to Alyssa.

'Oh dear, I hope I got enough!'

Alyssa picked up a Duane Reade bag and nipped into Victoria's office with it. Coco went back to her desk, turning over Victoria's last words, but with little clue to their significance. A week later, however, as she stood looking at her reflection in the full-length mirror of the fashion cupboard, other *Style* girls running back and forth behind her, picking out outfits to wear for their evening dates, she knew exactly what Victoria had meant.

A shiver ran over Coco from head to toe, fear and anticipation making her so nervous she almost thought she might throw up. She had cut and styled her hair exactly the way he wanted; at lunchtime, she had dashed to Blow, the blow-dry bar on Fourteenth and Ninth that many of the *Style* girls patronised. Emily had given Blow a mention on the *It's Happening* page, and in return they gave *Style* staffers a discount; that was how it worked in the city. Junior editors and manicurists and hairdressers and make-up artists and boutique assistants all linked up in a complex mesh of favours, freebies from fashion-cupboard clearouts or launch parties for a head of highlights or a mani-pedi.

Coco had had a mani-pedi too, last night; she only wished that she knew Jacob's preference in nail colour. A French manicure had seemed safe for her hands, and red for her toenails: when in doubt, go for the classics. And he'd been right about the hair, which suited her more than she had expected. The other junior fashion editors had ooh-ed and aah-ed when she'd got back from Blow, commenting on how pretty her neck looked with her hair pulled back and clipped at her nape.

Her bag – a suede Gucci clutch – had been borrowed from the cupboard, but she'd had to put her shoes on a credit card, remembering all too clearly Victoria's scathing dismissal of the ones Coco had been wearing at her interview, and her consequent advice: *always spend money on shoes. People notice*. They were Kandee 'Liquorice' pumps, black suede with 6-inch heels mitigated slightly by the 1.5-inch platforms. She had barely been able to walk across Bloomingdales' shoe department in them, but they looked fabulous, elegant yet dramatic, and the salesgirl had not only assured her that she looked like sex on legs, but snagged her a 20 per cent *Style* discount. Coco had been practising walking in them ever since, and calculated that she could just about make it out of the building, into a cab, and into a restaurant with them on.

I mustn't drink too much – I don't think I can manage going to and from the loo in these shoes, she thought, with a hint of humour, grateful for something that would lighten her mood. She kept checking her appearance over and over again, looking for the tiniest of flaws; she was two pounds lighter than she had been last week, but had it come off her hips, where he'd told her she needed to be slimmer?

In one part of her mind, she knew that she was being ridiculous. That she looked perfectly fine as she was; that she'd already lost more weight than she'd ever thought she could, got down to an American size 4–6, an English 8–10. That, despite all the magazines and papers and local TV stations insisting that it was impossible to find a nice guy in this hugely competitive city, she'd already found a lovely one, her own age, who'd liked her so much he hadn't even played games after they'd had sex, but had come round the next day, only to be crushed when she'd turned him down.

I look stunning, she told herself firmly, doing a slow turn on her heels in front of the mirror. Any man would be lucky to have me.

But she couldn't help seeing herself through Jacob Dupleix's eyes.

'Great shoes,' Emily sighed, handing her a Michael Kors black leather crop jacket. 'Here, this'll look great. You don't have to do it up,' she added kindly. 'Just let it hang open.'

Style fashion cupboard, Coco thought ironically, slipping on the jacket, which didn't quite meet over her chest. The only place a size 6 feels like a size 16.

'I'm dying to know who you're going out with,' Emily said hopefully, but Coco just favoured her with an enigmatic smile.

'You know I don't want to talk about it,' she said. 'I don't want to jinx it.'

Emily nodded vigorously; dating was a high-risk, high-stake

sport in Manhattan, and no one could blame a girl for playing her cards close to her chest.

'I was actually going to ask you,' she started even more hopefully, 'that since you've sort of kicked X to the kerb, as they say over here . . . would you mind if I had a go at him? I mean, I think he was always into you, frankly, but now you've given him the thumbs-down, I might sneak in there and try to cheer him up – you know, catch him on the rebound. Things are winding down with Sean, we've sort of burned out.'

Sean was the go-go dancer, whose time had clearly come to an end. Behind Emily, Lucy rolled her eyes, but Coco couldn't help smiling: Emily was unstoppable.

'No, go for it,' Coco said, thinking that this was a great solution. If Xavier and Emily got together, that would get her off the hook very neatly. They could still hang out; he couldn't possibly be resentful, or still have a crush on her, if he were dating one of her best friends.

Briefly, she felt a wash of regret for Xavier, his strong young body, his sweet dark eyes. And then she thought of his apartment, with its crumbling paintwork, its stinky stairs – it had looked much more rundown by daylight – and she shook her head. *I'm being awful and snobby. I'm trying to jump up the ladder in one go, not climb it slowly. But I'm in a hurry, and Xavier can't get me to where I want to be, while Jacob can.*

'Emily?' A thought hit Coco, as she remembered, couldn't help remembering, the instant physical attraction that had flared between her and Xavier as soon as they had touched. 'Just go back to his if anything happens, okay? It would be really weird to bump into him in the loo in the middle of the night.'

'Oh, *absolutely*,' Emily said enthusiastically, already starry-eyed at picturing herself overnight in Xavier's apartment.

Coco couldn't put it off any longer. She checked her phone – past seven. Time to go. Especially as she was walking slower than usual in the Kandee heels.

'Wish me luck,' she said to Emily and Lucy, surprising herself with the words.

I don't sound like someone going on a first date, she realised. I sound like I'm embarking on a life-changing experience.

And she could see, from Emily and Lucy's wide-eyed expressions as they chimed in: 'Good luck!' that they were just as taken aback as she was.

The Lipstick Building's doorman, seeing Coco emerge from the elevator, called over: 'Miss? Your limo's outside.'

'Oh!'

Coco had thought she was making her way to the restaurant under her own steam; she hadn't known he'd be sending a limo for her. Anticipation rising in her with almost unbearable pressure, she crossed the lobby as fast as she could, leaving via the revolving doors. There were always limos waiting outside the Lipstick Building, and tonight there were several, but the driver of hers had clearly been briefed, because he pushed off from the side of the limousine, gesturing to her as soon as he saw her come out of the building.

Swallowing hard, she wove across the crowded sidewalk and slid into the limo. Where she received her second surprise of the evening.

'Hello, Coco,' Jacob Dupleix smiled from the far corner of the seat.

Coco nearly jumped out of her skin.

'Oh!' she exclaimed, stammering in shock. 'I d-didn't expect – I didn't realise—'

'Champagne?' Jacob asked, but it wasn't really a question; he had a glass already waiting for her on the bar.

'Thank you.' Coco drank some, feeling ridiculous for being so gauche. After all, she'd been expecting to meet him in half an hour or so, in the restaurant he'd chosen for their date: this was just a little earlier than planned. But he had taken her by surprise, changed the rules. The tinted windows meant she could barely see outside; it emphasised the isolation in which they were travelling.

It's as if he's ambushed me.

Mentally, she gave herself a slap round the face. *The reason he liked you in the first place was that you talked back to him. It wasn't your devastating beauty or your blinding dress sense. So pull yourself together and use your wits!*

She twisted around as the limo pulled away, wedging her back into the corner of the seat, placing as much distance as possible between herself and Jacob, crossing her legs as a symbolic barrier; even the champagne glass, which she held in front of her chest, was an obstacle separating their bodies.

'How's the new job?' Jacob asked, still smiling. 'Are you happy to be out of the fashion cupboard?'

'I'm happier that Victoria's new assistant's working out,' Coco said dryly, managing to find her voice. 'That's a huge relief. It means I'm only doing one job now, not two.'

'Victoria misses you terribly,' Jacob said, amusement in his voice. 'Did you realise? She told me the other day that you were the best assistant she had ever had.'

Coco, always susceptible to praise, couldn't help blushing at the compliment. 'Really?' she blurted out. 'That's brilliant!'

Jacob nodded. 'But of course, the really talented girls don't stay long as assistants,' he purred, leaning forward to clink his glass with Coco's. 'They find themselves noticed and promoted very fast. Even – if they're really talented – being taken out to dinner by the boss.'

Coco's breath caught in her throat as Jacob moved closer to her along the leather seat; when he pulled back after touching his glass to hers, she felt less relieved than disappointed.

'By the way,' Jacob added, sipping more champagne, 'I imagine you haven't mentioned that you're having dinner with me this evening to any of your colleagues at work?'

'I haven't told anyone at all!' Coco exclaimed, horrified that he would even ask the question. It would be incredibly indiscreet of her to breathe a word, to boast that Jacob Dupleix thought her worthy of a dinner invitation.

And then, looking over at Jacob, who was nodding in approval, she understood that he had never thought she had said anything to anyone. It had simply been a test to see her reaction, to judge whether she would brush the idea aside lightly, or take it as seriously as she had done.

Jacob does like to test people.

Confused, she turned her head away from him, staring as best she could out of the window. They were driving through Central Park; she could tell from the embankment that rose on either side of 79th Street, the unmistakable steep stone walls with foliage above. For a moment, she shivered; it intensified the sense of being utterly alone, almost claustrophobically so, with Jacob, in this small space.

And then she felt his hand on her thigh, just below the sequinned hem of her dress, his wide, spatulate fingers so warm they almost scalded her through her chiffon-sheer, 7-denier Wolford hold-up stockings. Normally, she would have jumped, or started, even a little, at this intimate touch from a man with whom she was sitting in close proximity. But there was something extraordinary about the feeling of his hand on her leg. He wasn't stroking her, or caressing her in any way; he simply rested his hand on her, its weight surprisingly heavy. It was calming, reassuring. As if he were quieting down an animal.

It's another test, Coco thought, fighting to get some clarity, her senses drugged, her body swimming with heightened sensation. Do I let him leave it there? Do I say something, to acknowledge this? Do I put my hand on his?

The solidity of his hand, the heat of his skin, made her picture, all too vividly, what it would be like to have the entire weight of his body on hers. And once she had that image in her mind, she couldn't, for the life of her, think of anything else. She felt as if she were blushing from head to toe. The limo swung in a curve, emerging from the park, turning downtown on Central Park West, but Jacob's hand remained on her thigh, unmoving. It excited and unnerved Coco so much that she could barely breathe without her diaphragm going into spasm. Her quadriceps muscles were stiffening up, keeping her legs crossed, trying not to move at all; she didn't want to dislodge Jacob's hand. Even when the limo slowed, coming to a halt on Columbus Avenue, she stayed frozen in place, and Jacob's hand didn't move either, not until the limo door swung open. Only then did he lift it, awarding Coco two deliberate pats of approval before gesturing that she should precede him out of the car.

Balancing awkwardly in her ridiculously high heels, she clambered over the carpeted divider, taking the driver's extended hand to help her out; hired drivers in the city were very used to supporting female passengers whose stratospheric shoes meant they could barely walk on their own. Coco had never heard the term 'limo shoes' before she moved to New York. Now she understood exactly what it meant: shoes that were designed to impress rich men. The deal for dates in Manhattan was that the men paid for the cabs, the theatre tickets, the dinner and drinks, every expense incurred on the date itself. The women put their money into their maintenance, the hairdo, the waxes, the mani-pedi, the clothes, the shoes, the perfume, all of which could easily add up to a four-figure investment in snagging a husband who would finance them in the future.

The restaurant was all glass and pale blue walls, elegant and minimal, their corner booth discreet and secluded. But if you had made Coco put her hands over her eyes and describe her surroundings during dinner, she would barely have been able to do it. All she could think about, all she could see and feel, was Jacob Dupleix, sitting next to her in the booth, the exquisitely soft fabric of his shorn-wool and silk suit trousers pressing lightly against her thigh, his left hand resting once again on her leg, hardly ever moving. He drank, used his chopsticks, raised a napkin to dab his lips with his right hand; the left remained there almost through the whole meal, a constant intensely physical reminder of what this dinner was all about.

He ordered them saketinis as soon as they sat down, and it was only the strong alcohol, garnished with a perfect swirl of cucumber peel, the palest green from a hint of cucumber infusion, that kept Coco's lips moving, kept up her side of the conversation, as she felt his hand placed possessively on her thigh.

'I've ordered us the omakase menu,' Jacob said, smiling as he held up his martini glass, waiting for her to mirror him, to clink their glasses together in a toast. 'Do you like sashimi?'

'I never had any before I came to New York,' Coco confessed. 'I'm still getting used to it. That's the one without the rice, isn't it?'

Jacob burst out laughing at this naïve description. *He's always smiling, or laughing,* Coco thought, her excitement rising. *I hope this is me – being with me. I hope he isn't always like this. I hope it's something about me that entertains him so much . . .*

He wasn't being cruel. That she knew for sure. There was nothing mocking about his laughter, just genuine amusement; his eyes sparkling, his teeth flashing.

'All right, laugh at me,' she said, pretending to be cross, her confidence growing. 'I always love it when I'm unintentionally hilarious.'

'There's never a dull moment with you, Coco,' Jacob said, sitting back in the booth and observing her with frank interest, a smile still curving his wide lips. 'Why don't I take out English girls to dinner more often? You're so much more intelligent than the indigenous species in this country.'

'No, we're not,' Coco said pertly, drinking some more martini. 'We just seem like it to Americans because of our accent.' The sake and vodka giving her Dutch courage, she added: 'I could sit here and just say bum, poo, fart for two hours in an English accent and you'd think I was brainier than Einstein.'

As soon as the words had left her lips, she bit her tongue. *Oh Jesus, did I actually just say bum, poo and fart to Jacob Dupleix? What was I thinking?*

But then to her great relief, she realised that Jacob had had to set down his drink, he was laughing so hard.

'Coco,' he said fondly, when he had caught his breath, 'you make me feel young.'

'In a good way, I hope?' Coco said quickly. *I don't want him to think of me as some immature twenty-something, a toy he can pick up and put down. I want to be his equal – in brains, if nothing else.*

But then his hand closed for a moment around her thigh, a brief squeeze, a surge of heat so paralysingly charged that the thoughts switched themselves off as she focused, completely, on not showing how Jacob's touch affected her, how much she wanted that big hand to slide up under the hem of her dress, touch her in increasingly intimate places . . .

'Tell me something,' he said, and she leaned towards him, her lips parted, the word 'Anything' on the tip of her tongue.

'Your real name,' he said softly, obliging her to lean in still further. Coco could smell his aftershave, the subtle scents of leather and tobacco. Her crash course learning from Victoria had taught her to be much more discerning than she had ever been before joining *Style*; she could tell immediately that the aftershave was extremely, dizzyingly, expensive.

'My . . . my . . .' she stammered.

'Your real name,' Jacob repeated. 'It isn't Coco, is it?'

'Oh!' She was so distracted by him, so dazzled by his interest in her, that she had actually forgotten for a moment that Victoria had renamed her. She had been Coco for over a year now, at work at least, and work had been her entire life ever since she'd been hired at *Style*; it was second nature to her to answer to Coco now.

Embarrassed, she ducked her head. Jacob reached out, and again, as on that first time she had met him, she felt his fingers, gentle on the soft underside of her chin, lifting it, inexorably, until her eyes met his.

'There's nothing to be ashamed of,' he said. 'Tell me.'

'It's Jodie,' she said, half under her breath. 'Victoria thought it was too common for someone who worked on *Style*.'

Colour flooded her face, but by a huge force of will, she managed to keep her eyes on his. Velvety-dark, full of comprehension and sympathy, they seemed to take in her whole essence, understand who she was, where she came from.

'I think Jodie's a very pretty name,' he said soothingly. 'Very pretty indeed.'

'Thank you,' she mumbled.

He raised his eyebrows, and she knew, instinctively, what he meant, what he wanted.

'Thank you, Jacob,' she said, and shivered from the sheer pleasure of saying his name.

'*Hamachi-kama*,' came a soft voice, and Coco jerked away from Jacob as the waiter slid an ebony trencher onto the table. 'And *ankimo*. Enjoy.'

'Excellent,' Jacob said, reaching for his napkin and chopsticks, unabashed at having been interrupted while engaged in actively seducing his date. He rubbed his hands together in anticipation. 'This is one of my favourite Japanese appetizers, *hamachi-kama*. Do you know what it is?'

Coco shook her head.

'It's the jaw of a yellowtail,' Jacob informed her, turning the piece of fish on the trencher to show her the V-shaped jawbone. 'Very tender. Grilled. No oil at all, just a little lemon juice. All lean protein, practically zero calories. Here.'

He used his chopsticks expertly to flake the fish from the bone, selecting a piece and picking it up, lifting it to Coco's mouth.

'Open,' he said, and she parted her lips obediently, the tips of his chopsticks sliding into her mouth; she closed her lips over them, pulling the fish off, chewing it, and as Jacob withdrew the chopsticks, his smile was complacent.

'It's delicious,' she said, just grateful that it wasn't raw. She still wasn't comfortable eating raw fish, though she knew how good it was for you, how low-calorie; for a Luton girl, who, before she moved to London, had never eaten fish before that wasn't battered and fried; sushi and sashimi were a huge culture shock.

'Excellent, isn't it?' Jacob said, as Coco eagerly tucked into more *hamachi-kama*.

I'll fill up on this, she thought. *That way I won't have to eat too much raw fish*.

'And now, the *ankimo*,' Jacob said, picking up a small round slice of what looked like meat from the second plate. Pale pinkish-brown, garnished with fine curls of daikon and green onions, it was also, unequivocally, cooked: Coco was even more relieved.

'It's monkfish liver,' he announced, his smile deepening. 'Steamed, very lightly.'

Coco's eyes stretched as wide as they could go, the whites showing all round the irises as she looked in horror at what was approaching her mouth.

'*Fish liver*?' she mumbled in disgust.

'It's delicious,' Jacob said happily. 'You'll love it.'

She recoiled against the booth as the chopsticks came closer. 'I don't think I can,' she said hopelessly.

Jacob's hand on her thigh slid an inch higher up, easing fractionally under the hem of her skirt. He leaned in, his breath warm on the side of her face.

'Oh, I think you can,' he said softly. 'You do trust me, don't you?'

'I—' Coco began, and the next thing she knew, the smooth, rounded tips of the chopsticks were pushing gently at her lips, and she was taking the disc of liver into her mouth. *If only he hadn't told me what it was!* she thought desperately, chewing and swallowing as fast as she could.

The monkfish liver was rich, tasty, the twist of daikon radish Jacob had picked up with it a refreshing crunchy contrast. But the knowledge that she was eating fish liver almost made her gag; as soon as it was down, she reached out for her martini glass and took a long, cleansing gulp.

'Have some daikon,' Jacob suggested, watching her closely. 'It freshens the mouth after strong-tasting food. The Japanese know exactly what they're doing. Like the Italians. Parsley and radish to freshen the breath and help the digestion.'

He was right; the daikon *did* help. And to her huge relief, Jacob didn't insist that she have more liver; he ate it himself with great enthusiasm, trailing the pieces through the ponzu sauce, licking his lips after each one.

'Ah!' he said happily, as the waiter slid the empty trenchers away and placed in the centre of the table a long, elaborately-carved, shallow wooden boat, on which, beautifully arranged on flakes of ice, lay various perfectly sliced pieces of raw fish. Coco recognised bright pink tuna and equally bright orange salmon with relief: those she could manage.

The others, however, she wasn't so sure about.

'Lobster,' Jacob said, indicating different pieces with his chopsticks. 'Fluke ceviche, chopped crunchy eel . . . mmn, fatty tuna . . .'

'Brilliant,' Coco said faintly. 'Fluke. My favourite.'

Jacob glanced at her and laughed. 'Your face!' he said. 'Don't worry, you'll love it all. And it's raw fish – you can eat as much as you want. Here.' He dolloped a chopstick-full of ginger on her plate. 'Ginger helps. Shall we start with the lobster? *Everyone* likes lobster.'

'I've never had lobster in my life,' Coco admitted bravely.

Jacob's hand squeezed her leg, and kept the pressure on, a warm, tight caress that melted Coco, sent an electric charge up her inner thigh all the way to her groin, a pulse of excitement and anticipation. She longed for his fingers to slide up further, between her legs . . .

'Only you would admit that,' he said with great appreciation. 'All the other girls I've taken out would pretend they ate it all the time, to impress me.' He leaned over and dropped a kiss on her ear. 'You're different, Coco,' he whispered. 'And you know something?'

'What?' Coco was barely able to speak.

'I love the way you say "Brilliant",' he said intimately. 'Every time you do, it cracks me up. Keep saying it, won't you? For me?'

Coco turned to look at him. His face so close, his golden tan skin crinkled so appealingly around his eyes and mouth, laughter-lines that seemed to speak of age and wisdom; she wanted to learn from him, to soak up everything he had to teach her. To be mentored by him, to become as sophisticated as Victoria and Mireille, as successful as them. And if that meant playing his games, passing his tests, she'd do it – she'd do anything he wanted her to do.

His hand slid another inch up her leg, and she shuddered from head to toe, picturing, once more, having the whole weight of his body on her . . .

'Yes, Jacob,' she whispered back.

By the time they finished dinner, Coco was in a trance. Jacob had fed her a dizzying array of sushi, and allowed her a few spoonfuls of sorbet afterwards, watching her lick the sugary ice off her spoon with great appreciation; she had drunk strong green tea, which had sobered her up a little, but she knew that she was more intoxicated by Jacob's presence than by the alcohol she had consumed. Jacob ushered her out into the waiting limo, and as it pulled away, he took both her hands in his, pulling her towards him.

It was dark inside, only the faint under-lighting illuminating their faces, too faintly to read his expression.

Oh, God! Coco thought, panicking. He's going to tell me that I'm too young, too naïve, too inexperienced – that I'm not ready for him. He's turning me down. If he wanted to have sex with me, he'd be kissing me, not holding my hands . . .

'Coco,' Jacob said softly, his voice as rich as brandy. 'Lovely young Coco. You make me feel so very alive.' He raised her hands to his mouth, kissing each in turn. 'I want to ask you to come back home with me, but . . .'

Her heart sank to the soles of her shoes. No! she thought frantically. No 'buts'. I have to seduce him somehow – to convince him to have sex with me. After all this build-up I'll explode if we don't have sex tonight.

For an awful moment it occurred to her that she could always text Xavier, go round to his for a booty call. And then she felt horribly guilty. *I can't use him like that. I know he has feelings for me.*

'But,' Jacob continued, a smile in his voice, 'if you do, I warn you, I'll be unable to keep my hands off you. Will you trust me, Coco, if I tell you something?'

She nodded, heady with relief, heat building at the pit of her stomach.

'I know how things work in New York between a man and a woman,' he said, bending his head closer to her. 'Women think if they have sex on a first date, the man will think they're easy. He'll never ring them again. And most of the time, I must admit, that's true. But not with me and you. I promise you that. I want to take you to my home and make love to you tonight, and it won't end tomorrow morning.'

She felt his breath on her face, fragranced with nutty, smoky green tea. He dropped a kiss on her lips, briefly, the same promise in it as there had been in his words.

'So if you come back with me, you know what's going to happen,' he said against her mouth. 'I'm fascinated by you. Utterly fascinated. I want to know you, all of you. Your brain, your body, your heart.' His voice dropped to a bare whisper.

'I want to hear the sounds you make when you come. I want to come inside you. I want to feel what it's like to come inside you, how you feel there, how you taste . . .'

Coco's hands were squeezing his now, as tight as she could, holding onto him as if she would drown if she let go of him. She cleared her throat, moistening her lips, which were dry with tension.

'Brilliant,' she managed, and was rewarded with a soft laugh of approval.

She didn't even remember walking into his building, the chequerboard tiled floor of the lobby, the Art Deco lighting and the doorman jumping to hold the door for them. She didn't remember the elevator, the way it opened miraculously into his apartment, or the rich glowing interior of his living room, the manly colours in which it was decorated, the oxblood leather chesterfield sofas, the cherrywood humidors, the deep red and indigo silk rug, warm and inviting. All she remembered was his arm around her, guiding her through, down a hallway, into the room beyond.

Into his bedroom.

The bed loomed up, the huge carved mahogany headboard dominating the room, two great knotted poles of wood at the bottom corners, a fantastic Gothic work of art, piled high with velvet cushions on the deep blue brocade coverlet. It was impossible to look at that bed and not think of sex, and as Jacob's arms wrapped around Coco's waist from behind, as his lips started kissing her neck, finding each sensitive spot in turn, working her slowly and expertly into a state of excitement that she had never experienced before, she stared at the bed, imagining Jacob on top of her as she lay on the high mattress, already desperate for it to happen. He could have pulled up her skirt then and there, bent her over the edge, pushed himself into her, and she would have screamed in pleasure, already wet and ready for him.

But Jacob was no Xavier. He had decades of experience that

Xavier did not have, decades of practising to make perfect in drawing out the anticipation and building tension. She felt his hands at her shoulderblades, drawing down the zipper of her dress, easing it off her shoulders; it fell to the floor with a shush of silk and sequins collapsing into each other. A second later, her bra was unfastened, falling to the floor in its turn, and she felt Jacob's hands close over her breasts, so hot she cried out in pleasure, his square-tipped sculptor's fingers pinching her nipples, pulling them gently, twisting them, playing with them on the boundary between pleasure and pain. She winced and moaned and arched her back, her head slumping forward so he could kiss her neck, completely pliant in his arms.

And then he spun her round, so she was facing him, her naked breasts pressed into his shirtfront; he had taken off his jacket as they entered the apartment, discarded it on one of the sofas. Jacob lowered his head and kissed her, his tongue driving into her mouth, his hands hard on her bottom, lifting her towards him, pressing her into his crotch. She writhed against him, wanting it to happen now, now, to feel his cock inside her . . .

'Do you want me to fuck you?' he said.

'Yes!' she panted. 'Yes, please, Jacob. Please fuck me.'

'Then take off your panties,' he said.

She stared up at him.

'Do it,' he said, his eyes boring into hers. 'Take off your panties.'

Hooking her thumbs into the lace border, she wriggled them down her thighs, kicking them away as they fell to one ankle.

'Now lie on the bed,' he said. 'Face down.'

Coco was beyond questions or protest. Eagerly, naked, she climbed onto the bed and lay down obediently, arms at her side. She heard Jacob's shoes being pulled off, a drawer opening, felt the mattress shift and yield as he climbed onto it, beside her, and turned her head to catch a glimpse of him; the next thing she knew, his hand closed round her skull, stroking her hair, sliding under her forehead, lifting it as his other hand slid a pillow underneath it so her face was turned back downwards again, raised enough with her forehead propped on the velvet pillow so she could breathe.

And then she gasped, because something was trailing down her vertebrae; feathers, it felt like, tickling her deliciously, up and down her spine, circling her buttocks, teasing her, toying with her, each individual one flicking and caressing her delicate nerve-endings, making her sigh and squirm against the coverlet. The feathers were at the very base of her spine, tracing the split between the cheeks of her bottom, parting them gently, so that she splayed her legs a little, then a little more, wanting more and more, wanting to feel the feathers between her legs . . .

And then they stopped stroking her, lifted away. Coco moaned in frustration, her legs in a V on the coverlet, desperately hoping to feel Jacob's hands on her hips, lifting her, his cock inside her . . .

'Oh!' she gasped. 'Oh God!'

Instead of the feathers, his palm had slid between her legs, his fingers where she wanted his cock, dampening in her moist warmth, his wide thumb now on her clitoris, playing with her as if he were plucking a guitar string, thumbing her slowly and surely to orgasm, her body weight on his hand, her hips driving into him as he made her come as he had promised her he would. She was whimpering in release, her mouth open, making a ring of wetness on the coverlet as she came, and as she did, as the spasms began to hit her, her whole body jerked in shock.

Because Jacob's other palm had come down on her buttocks in a brisk, open-handed slap that brought the blood surging to the surface.

'Aah!' she protested, but then his thumb circling her, his fingers driving inside her, made her come again, and he spanked her again as she did, pleasure and pain, pain and pleasure, until she could no longer tell the difference. Until she was arching up to feel his palm coming down on her bottom, waiting for the next spank, relishing the fizz and shock of the impact, feeling her bottom growing hot and red, grinding into his palm below her to find her next orgasm, sandwiched between his hands, thrashing with excitement.

When he stopped at last, when his hand slid out from beneath her, she knew what was about to happen, and eagerly she pushed herself back, buttocks in the air, more than ready for him. The next thing she knew, he was shoving a pillow under her hips, pushing her back down onto it, climbing up the bed beside her, wrapping something round one of her wrists, and then the other.

'You trust me, don't you?' he said, as he tied the velvet ropes around her wrists. 'Say it. Say you trust me.'

'I trust you, Jacob,' she whispered, caught between sudden fear and deep, equally frightening excitement. She pulled on the ropes, but they held firm. She heard him undressing, his belt being unbuckled, his trousers unzipped, heard the clothes being discarded, the crinkle of a condom wrapper being ripped open.

And then he was on top of her, as she had dreamed of him being, heavy and finally naked. She felt his hairy chest against her back, the thick hairs at his groin and the base of his penis as he adjusted her hips, pulled her back onto his cock, and began to fuck her. His cock wasn't long, but it was thick, like his body, and its entrance drew a cry from her, wet as she was. Each pound of his hips made her feel the coarse hair of his groin, his balls smacking against her.

'Anything I do,' he said, his voice hoarse now, 'anything I do when you're tied up, if you want me to stop – say your name. Your real name. Say that, and I'll stop at once.'

With every thrust, the velvet ropes tightened and loosened, throwing Coco back and forward; she worked to get the right angle, her fingers closing round the velvet, pulling on the cords, as she tilted her bottom into the pillow below, lifting it for Jacob, feeling his whole cock inside her, slamming against her bottom, fractionally wider at the base, each thrust followed by a groan of his as he finally reached climax. The strokes became faster, juddering, as he lost the steady rhythm, felt his orgasm building, his fingers digging into her hipbones, forcing her to be still as he throbbed his release deep inside her, not letting her move an iota until he had spilled every drop, until his cock finally stopped shuddering inside her.

It felt like forever until he unclamped his hips and let her go; she slumped to the coverlet, still feeling the imprint of his fingers hard on her skin, his body following her, collapsing on top of her, as heavy as she had wanted, hairy and solid, hot as an oven. She could barely breathe under his weight, and she turned her head to the side, not wanting him to know, wanting him to stay there, pressing her down, anchoring her, utterly relaxed in the aftermath . . .

She sighed in disappointment as he lifted, slid out of her, pulled off the condom and padded off the bed to discard it and wash himself. She had forgotten that she was tied up; it was a surprise when he circled the bed, undoing the knots around her wrists, chafing them carefully with his hands to make sure her circulation hadn't been cut off.

'I have a toothbrush for you,' he said in her ear, kissing her cheek. 'And nightdresses. All new. Everything you need to get ready for bed.'

'I just want to sleep,' Coco mumbled, but he was pulling her arm, guiding her off the bed, helping her stumble down a few steps, onto a tiled floor, to a black granite sink; he stood beside her as she fumbled toothpaste onto a brush, washed her face, dabbed on some Crème de la Mer from a jar he handed her, pulled on a silk nightdress, soft as a cloud, and, her eyes almost closed with exhaustion, climbed the steps again and fell onto the bed.

It was unbelievably comfortable, the most comfortable bed

in the world, huge and luxurious, the 400 thread-count sheets as silky as her nightdress, the pillows downy and yielding. The last thing she remembered was Jacob beside her, his arm thrown over her possessively, big and rough with dark hair, his hairy legs tangled around hers, silk boxers covering his tumescent penis.

Stroking back her hair from her forehead, he kissed it. And, lips against her ear, reaching back to turn out the last light, he whispered to her, 'Good girl,' as she fell asleep.

Mireille

So. It's definitely happening.

Mireille traced a perfect semicircle on the parquet floor of her studio with the tip of her ballet shoe, a neat, warming-up, *rond de jambe*.

Jacob took Coco out to dinner last night. And I know exactly what that means. She sank into a deep *plié*, her turnout impeccable, her knees exactly in line with her feet. *I wonder if Victoria knows? I doubt it. She's somewhat distracted at the moment.*

Mireille's lips curved as she rose into a *demi-plié*, and then onto the balls of her feet, a *relevé* that stretched her hamstrings, long and lean.

What with being pregnant, and having sex with our new cover model, Victoria had enough on her plate without noticing that Jacob had selected a new protégée to *mentor* – among other verbs Mireille could use in this context.

Mireille lowered her heels and drew her feet into first position. As she ran through the five basic positions, performing *elevés* in each one, she congratulated herself on her excellent network of eyes and ears, which had let her know as soon as Jacob's secretary had obtained Coco's internal Dupleix extension for him, when the dinner booking had been made at Gari, that his driver had, last night, dropped off Jacob and Coco at Jacob's Washington Square apartment . . .

If Victoria had only bothered to cultivate an equally alert group of allies and satellites, she would have the same information that I do. But unfortunately, Mireille reflected complacently, *she's much too abrasive to inspire loyalty in her employees.*

The mirror opposite the barre on which Mireille's hands were placed showed her elegant figure, dressed in a pale grey leotard over matching tights, her hair drawn back into her signature bun, its white streak running dramatically from her forehead to her crown, twisting through the bun. There wasn't a scrap of make-up on her face, but with her customary bravery and poise, she faced the merciless early morning light, streaming through the north-facing windows of the small studio she had had constructed when she moved into this Riverside Drive apartment, decades ago.

The studio's walls were mirrored, so that Mireille could observe herself from every angle, judging her body and her alignment with the same merciless green gaze that picked out and eliminated every potential flaw in her fashion spreads. The leotard and tights were the same size, the same brand, that she had worn since she was a *corps-de-ballet* member at the Paris Opéra. Any infinitesimal bulge on the stomach or the hips, any tiny gain in weight, would be immediately obvious in the harsh white light.

How will Victoria feel when she finds out that Jacob is . . . mentoring Coco? Mireille asked herself as she turned to the right, resting her left hand on the barre, elbow relaxed, and took up fifth position, preparing for her series of *battements. Because this is serious. Gari, and back to his apartment the first night. His favourite restaurant, and an instant decision to take her to his place. That is no light choice for Jacob. I know exactly what it means, and Victoria should too: this is no casual fling. Coco is his new protégée.*

I don't imagine Victoria will be very happy about this new development. Mireille slid her right leg out in front of her, straight as a steel bar, the toe pointed. *Victoria considers* Coco *very much her protégée – she found her, re-named her, brought her to New York . . .*

And now that Jacob has taken Coco *under his wing, as it were,* Coco *is no longer Victoria's eager little apprentice. In fact, it means she'll soon be a rival to Victoria. Younger, fresher – even keener, if that's possible. Victoria probably expected Jacob to have a little fling with* Coco *– a couple of blow-jobs in his limo in return for a nice present from* Chanel, *a scarf from* Hermès *– but this is now on a much more elevated scale.*

Mireille's leg flashed out to the side, to the back, *grands battements* now, beautiful sweeping movements, up and down, like a knife slicing through the air, precise and perfect.

No, Victoria will not be happy at all.

She was smiling now, the crow's-feet at the corners of her eyes creasing. Mireille did not want Victoria's job: her primary desire was to be left alone to fulfil her own role at *Style* with the skill and taste that she had refined to perfection over many years. She had seen editors come and go; the recently-sacked Jennifer Lane Davis had actually been one of Mireille's favourites. Jennifer had respected Mireille's vision, realised that the Frenchwoman brought elegance and sophistication to the magazine; had refrained from tampering with her layouts and concepts.

Switching to her left, resting her right hand on the barre now, Mireille allowed herself a tiny little shrug, a pursed *moue* of her mouth, before she began the series of *battements* on the other side. Unlike Jennifer, Victoria was incapable of leaving anyone alone; that was her great defect. She was terrible at delegating.

Because she does not trust people, Mireille observed. And that is a weakness. One that can be used against her. One should be wary, but one should trust in the measure to which it is deserved.

Mireille was becoming increasingly tired of Victoria's insistence on supervising, double-checking and second-guessing every decision she made. I am the fashion director, the creative heart of the magazine, she thought, her irritation rising. If my editor tells me she wants all the girls to jump and run in the photographs, I do it, even though in my opinion it is vulgar. But I do what she asks, I provide her with superb, graceful photographs, and in return, does she give me what I ask for?

No, she interferes. I cannot shoot a cover without her flying to the location to make sure I'm doing it exactly the way she wants. Of course, Victoria had had an extra motive for coming to St Louis. She had wanted to see Lykke again, after their torrid encounter in the Lipstick Building's studio.

She is such a fool! Mireille thought, her irritation fading. To have sex with a model, in our own studios, in a hotel suite with all of us staying in the same hotel. That little assistant editor Emily saw Lykke coming out of Victoria's suite, and now she's telling everyone. Such a shame. I wanted that information all for myself, to use when I saw fit. That bloody Ludovic – he can't keep his hands off the young women, and he kicks them out as soon as he's finished. Such bad luck for me that Emily happened to be in the same corridor when Lykke was leaving Victoria's suite . . .

Mireille knew all about that, of course. She knew everything, certainly about Ludovic's unpleasant tendencies when alone with his latest victim. That was one aspect of fashion that would never change: older men preying on women barely out of their teens, the latter so keen to succeed in this cut-throat world that they would never complain about the indignities the men visited on them in private.

It is inevitable. Mireille shrugged. Jacob and Coco, Ludovic and every model or assistant he can get his dirty hands on. But he is a wonderful photographer, and the girls are two a penny. What can one do? *Rien du tout*. Nothing at all.

She sighed at the frustration of not having the gossip about

Lykke and Victoria all to herself. But you couldn't bolt the stable door after the horse had fled, and it had most definitely fled by now. Rumours had already spread beyond the *Style* offices. It wouldn't be long before everyone in the fashion industry knew.

And Victoria had made plenty of enemies. Someone, somewhere, was bound to tell her husband.

Mireille herself would never have dreamed of doing anything so vengeful, so crude. It was by no means her style. However, the more distracted Victoria is, she thought, the less time she has to bother me, to interfere with my art.

Mireille's leg swept up, to a ninety-degree angle in front of her, slightly turned-out; she drew it in a straight line, all the way round to the back of her body, a faultless *rond de jambe en dehors*. She winced; her hips were not what they had been, and the strain on the hip flexors of keeping the turnout, the leg parallel to the floor, was more noticeable as the years went by.

It was a shame, sometimes, that Mireille had no equal to confide in. Because as soon as she had met Coco, she had wagered with herself that Jacob's wandering eye would alight upon this new girl. Coco was everything Jacob appreciated in a protégée: dedicated, talented, very bright, very focused, a star in the making, a girl who did every job she was given better than any of her predecessors. Attractive, yes, but not a great beauty; like Mireille and Victoria before her, Coco was in need of Jacob's help to truly make her blossom.

Jacob will make her over. Style her, buy her a new wardrobe, slim her down, polish her like a jeweller with a precious stone until she shines from every facet. Make sure she's promoted, as fast as I was, as fast as Victoria was.

Until she's a worthy rival to Victoria.

And the more Coco was promoted, the thinner she grew, the better she dressed, the more stylish she looked, the more nervous Victoria would become. The more concerned that Jacob was grooming Coco to, one day, supersede Victoria. Take her job.

And the more Victoria will leave me alone to do mine.

Mireille had made her decision. Carefully, discreetly, she would encourage Coco, give her extra help to speed her journey up the career ladder. It would unquestionably annoy Victoria, be a thorn in her side. Victoria herself, having elbowed Jennifer Lane Davis out of the way two years early to take her job, knew better than anyone how an ambitious young woman could work on and influence the boss of a company to get what she wanted from him.

Decided. I'll set Coco against Victoria – working in the shadows, of course, so that Victoria can't see my hand in it. No matter who eventually comes out on top, it'll be a win-win situation for me, as the Americans say. If Victoria stays as editor, she'll be wounded, vulnerable, less secure, more willing to trust me and give me my head. And if Coco wins, she'll be so grateful to me that she'll let me do whatever I want.

And really, all I want is to keep shooting some of the most beautiful fashion spreads in the world.

Mireille was so content with this conclusion that she did something she rarely tried any more: she spun away from the barre, rising *en pointe* and executing five *fouettés en tournant*, the viciously difficult 'whipped' pirouettes that were the hardest turns to execute in the entire ballet repertoire. Once, long ago, Mireille had been able to cover the whole length of a stage, performing the thirty-two *fouettés* that were the famously challenging centrepiece for the lead ballerina in *Swan Lake*.

While now I can barely manage five, she thought ruefully, lowering her heels to the floor again. *My pictures are my art now.*

And I'll do what I must, in order to keep them perfect.

Victoria

The dress was too tight. Seam-strainingly, eye-wateringly tight. Victoria gritted her teeth, sucked in everything she could, and snapped at Alyssa: 'Try it again.'

'I'm scared of zipping your skin,' Alyssa wailed.

'Just do it!' Victoria ordered. 'Push me in with one hand and zip with the other.'

'I sort of need both hands to pull the sides together,' Alyssa said helplessly. Gritting her teeth, she took hold of the soft red silk chiffon, dragged it together as tightly as she could, and started to inch the zip up once more. It reached a certain point, the widest part of Victoria's hips. And then, it stopped.

'Erm . . . I think you might need another pair of Spanx, Victoria,' Alyssa mumbled, the words almost inaudible because of her fear of how her boss might react.

'Fuck!' Victoria yelled. 'Fuck, fuck, fuck! This stupid, bloody, *shitty* pregnancy!'

Spinning around, the ankle-length skirt of the dress sweeping around her legs dramatically, she put both hands on her hips, staring at herself furiously in the full-length mirror. Alyssa, kneeling beside her, had to shuffle frantically out of the way to avoid being stepped on.

'I'm going to wear this dress,' Victoria said furiously. 'I don't care if I can't drink a glass of water, I don't care if I can't *breathe*, I'm going to wear this dress tonight!'

'It *is* gorgeous,' Alyssa agreed sycophantically.

Vintage Valentino, in lipstick-bright red, the evening dress had a dramatic halter neckline, fastening just at the base of Victoria's delicate collarbones with an elaborate diamanté circle through which two wide pleated bands of red chiffon were drawn, tying behind the neck and falling dramatically down her narrow, bared back. Valentino knew exactly how to dress underweight women; the halter style concealed her frighteningly-slatted upper ribcage, but bared the shoulders and arms, showing off how slim they were. In the early 1980s, when the dress had been made, the woman wearing it would not have been lean and toned from Pilates press-ups; now, she was expected not just to be thin, but to look as if she had completed a triathlon the day before.

Reaching down, Victoria hauled up the skirt and held it around her waist. 'Get me another pair of Spanx,' she commanded grimly.

It was incredibly difficult to get the third pair over the two which Victoria was already wearing. Tugging, grunting with the effort, Victoria hopping from foot to foot, holding up the dress as Alyssa hauled the thick, elasticated high waistband of the control pants up and up to its final resting place, inches above the waist, midway up Victoria's ribcage.

'Great,' Victoria gasped. 'I can hardly breathe. Try it now.'

She dropped the skirts before Alyssa had let go of the last Spanx; awkwardly, Alyssa struggled to extricate her hands from its waistband.

'Come on! I haven't got all day,' Victoria said, clicking her fingers.

Sweat beaded at the base of Alyssa's Afro as she tugged the open sides of the dress together once again, underneath Victoria's raised left arm, and started to pull up the zipper tag.

'I think this is it,' she panted, praying with everything she had that she could get the dress closed this time. 'I think we've got you in . . . *yes*!'

Triumphantly, she snibbed the tag up the last few teeth. The dress had already been hooked closed at the top; the metal hook and eye were digging into the sensitive skin on the underside of Victoria's left breast, leaving red marks. Much as Alyssa resented Victoria for making her perform intimate menial tasks, she was reluctantly impressed by her boss's grit and high pain tolerance. Victoria would wear the Valentino all evening, smiling and making conversation and whirling elegantly from one group to another, never showing the pain she was in. Because when she took it off, she'd have weals on her body from the hook and the boning of the dress.

But you won't ever know that from the expression on her face, Alyssa thought, racing to get the slingback Louboutins Victoria had picked out to wear tonight, kneeling in front of her boss as she lifted one foot, then the other, sliding them in.

'Shit! I swear my sodding feet are bigger too,' Victoria snarled. 'I'm retaining water for bloody Kate Middleton!'

'Oh, those are going to be such amazing photos,' Alyssa sighed devoutly, rising to her feet. 'I can't wait to see them.'

'No talking about that!' Victoria rounded on her assistant, the translucent red silk chiffon layers swishing beautifully as she moved, each finished with the finest, hand-sewn strip of red satin ribbon. 'No talking about my pregnancy, no talking about the Kate Middleton shoot, you understand? Zip it and keep it shut!'

'I haven't said a word, Victoria.' Alyssa trembled from head to toe. 'I promise.'

'And don't stand next to me,' Victoria continued, staring viciously at Alyssa's reflection in the mirror until the girl obediently jumped out of the line of sight. 'Not until I've had the damn baby and I'm back to size zero again! The last thing I need as I get bigger is some six-foot tall, hundred-pound, twenty-something, thin-as-a-rake black girl making me look like a beached white whale by contrast.'

'I'm so sorry, Victoria!' All the elation Alyssa had felt about getting her boss into the dress she was hell-bent on wearing tonight ebbed away; she sounded on the verge of tears as she backed towards the door. It opened just as she reached it, hitting her a glancing blow on the back.

'Oh, gosh! I'm terribly sorry,' Jeremy blurted out. 'Are you all right?'

Heaving a bubbling, gasping sob, Alyssa shot past him and out into the main office.

'You are awfully hard on your assistants, darling,' Jeremy said, glancing after her. 'That one looks as if she's going to cry her heart out.'

'*Her*!' Victoria said crossly. 'I miss Coco. Coco never bloody cried. *Coco*,' she added unfairly, 'would have got me into this dress with only *two* pairs of Spanx on.'

'With *what*?' Jeremy said blankly.

'Corsets, basically,' Victoria said. 'I can barely sit down. And don't worry.' She smiled at her husband. 'They won't hurt the baby. I got Alyssa to check with the gynaecologist.'

'Oh, well done, darling.' Jeremy bustled across the office to kiss her. 'You knew I'd worry, didn't you?' He pulled back to look at her. 'Oh,' he cooed, 'you look so lovely! Like a princess.'

Victoria rolled her eyes. 'Darling,' she drawled, 'I dress *much* better than the average princess. My God, have you seen some of those European ones? Oh, and you haven't even had the whole effect yet! Alyssa!' she called. 'Send in the Van Cleef & Arpels man, will you?'

Moments later, a heavyset man in a grey suit that strained over his shoulders came lumbering into the office. From his inside jacket pocket, he produced a velvet-covered jewellery box, which he snapped open to reveal a pair of ruby and diamond earrings, mounted in platinum. Crimson light flashed from the huge rectangular rubies, their deep scarlet set off and framed by the brilliant-cut white diamonds, a larger square diamond topping each setting, concealing the hook behind. Victoria slid them into her ears and pivoted to look in the mirror for the full effect.

'One point eight carats each,' she said smugly. 'Stunning, aren't they? And look at the colour match! I sent the dress over so they could pick out rubies as close to the shade of red as possible.'

'I wish I could buy them for you,' Jeremy sighed. 'But God knows what the bonuses are going to be like this year, with the crisis in Europe—'

'Shh, silly.'

To his great surprise, his wife leaned forward and kissed him on the cheek.

'I don't need to buy jewellery,' she said cheerfully. 'I can borrow anything I want, any time I want. That's one of the best parts of this job.' She looked him up and down. 'Very smart,' she said approvingly. 'Nothing like an Ozwald Boateng suit on an Englishman. Two-button. Perfect for you.'

Jeremy smoothed down his grey silk tie. 'I just wear what you put out for me,' he said self-deprecatingly.

'It's such a relief that you have your own dressing-room now,' Victoria said. 'It makes life so much easier. How did things go with the interior designer today?'

'Oh, the nursery's coming along great guns,' Jeremy beamed.

'Fantastic!' Victoria picked up her silver snakeskin clutch and took a last look at herself in the mirror. Her signature blonde chignon was the ideal hairstyle for the dress; she'd had it pulled back more severely than usual, the hair absolutely smooth to her scalp, to show off the magnificent earrings. Her YSL lipstick was cerise, a little brighter than the crimson dress, to avoid an overly-matched look, and Hervé himself, one of the best make-up artists in the world, visiting from LA, had spent an hour giving her the ultimate barely-there make-up.

The shades and contours were so expertly done that in pictures she would look flawless, but as if she had barely tried, just slicked on some lipstick, pulled on a wonderful vintage Valentino and headed out for the evening's cocktail party and exhibit opening.

'Where is it tonight?' Jeremy asked as they headed out of her office, the Van Cleef & Arpels-employed bodyguard following on their heels, his job to shadow Victoria all evening to make sure no one tried to steal the earrings.

'Darling.' Victoria tapped him playfully with her clutch. 'You know – look what I'm wearing. I've been talking about this for weeks! It's the Valentino Very Red show. Oh, thank you,' she said to Alyssa, who was waiting by the door with her sheared-mink capelet.

Alyssa looked visibly taken aback. Victoria swept past her and through the *Style* reception, draping the capelet carefully over her shoulders. She smiled warmly as she saw Coco, waiting for the elevators.

'Coco,' she said, 'I've been meaning to tell you how fabulous your polka-dot shoot was. I just saw the stills. So vibrant and witty. And *young*,' she added fervently. '*So* young. I loved it.'

Coco flushed with pleasure. 'Thank you,' she said, her voice heartfelt.

'You're getting positively skinny,' Victoria commented, looking her ex-assistant up and down with approval. In a tight Vanessa Bruno black snakeskin-print sheath and olive suede bootees, her hair pulled back to the nape of her neck in a short, clubbed ponytail, her make-up discreet, Coco looked like the archetypal Manhattan girl-about-town.

'Your eyelashes are the best they've ever looked,' Victoria said with a little nod of professional approval. 'And is that a Hermès Picotin?' She leaned forward for a look at Coco's dark brown leather bag, a deceptively simple, open bucket shape, with a hanging silver lock and two short, wide straps.

'Goodness!' Her eyebrows shot up. '*Someone* has a rich admirer.'

Coco went even redder. She tried to say something, but no words would come out.

One of the lifts in the bank pinged, a green light coming on over the doors as they slid open, and the handful of people waiting scurried back, wanting to make it clear that they wouldn't try to share a car with the editor of *Style* and her entourage.

'Join us,' Victoria said to Coco benevolently as she stepped inside.

Envious stares watched the doors close behind Coco, unaware that she would infinitely have rather not been trapped into an elevator ride with Victoria.

'I hope he's nice,' Victoria said to her favourite protégée. 'Rich is important, of course, but you're a very talented girl, Coco. You shouldn't marry money and then give up work, like so many of the *Style* girls. Pick someone who doesn't expect you to turn into his housekeeper as soon as he gets his ring on your finger.'

She flicked the Hermès bag lightly with her finger. 'Still, a two-thousand dollar bag,' she added. 'He must be in love! Are you going to meet him now?'

Coco was blushing so hard now that she would have fitted in perfectly to the Valentino Very Red show. She nodded fast.

Coco doesn't realise that I know she's fucking Jacob, Victoria realised, very amused. *For goodness' sake! First he wanders into my office asking me where to find her, and then he's made a point telling me that I need to make sure she's promoted fast – how would I* not *be aware that Jacob's taken a shine to her? And she's doing very nicely out of it. A Hermès bag, her hair restyled very chicly, and clearly, Jacob's been making sure she loses more weight. She's a very lucky girl.*

And Victoria had given her fair warning: 'Don't get ahead of yourself,' she had said a few weeks ago, when she was sure of the nature of Jacob's interest in Coco, 'and don't forget it was me who gave you your first break.' *Coco's a smart girl, she knows which side her bread is buttered*. Jacob would play with her for a while, a new toy. He would make sure she did well out of it, and Victoria would play along too, move his protégée up the career ladder, but ensure that Coco was grateful and loyal to her.

Really, if Jacob had to pick someone on Style *to fuck for a while, he couldn't have done better: I'm happy to promote* Coco. This way, Victoria wasn't forced to elevate a protégée of Mireille's – she'd briefly wondered if Jacob had taken a shine to Mireille's assistant, Zarina – but one of her own. *Much better this way*.

Clever girl, Coco. Get as much out of Jacob as you can.

Victoria didn't think for a moment that Coco would be anything but a fling for Jacob. In Victoria's opinion, Coco simply wasn't refined enough for him.

Yes, she's clever and talented, but really, look at Mireille and myself – if there's one thing we have in common, it's that we're well-bred, naturally elegant. Whereas Coco – well, I can't see Jacob taking seriously someone who wanted to work in fashion but didn't have the nous to change her name from Jodie, *of all things!*

This observation amused Victoria so much that she gave Coco a particularly warm smile as the lift reached the ground floor.

'Have a lovely evening,' she said kindly, sweeping out of the lift, the scarlet skirts of her dress moving wonderfully in the breeze coming through the open door of the lobby; she looked like a fashion illustration come to life as she passed the tall pink granite, steel-banded pillars.

'Darling,' Jeremy said, as she tucked her arm through his, 'do you realise how nice you're being lately?'

'What?' Victoria, a scion of the upper classes, would never have dreamed of saying 'Pardon,' or even 'Excuse me,' if she thought she had misheard something.

'Nice,' Jeremy said happily, as they ensconced themselves in the Town Car, the bodyguard taking his seat discreetly next to the driver. 'You're really being very nice to everyone. You said thank you to your assistant, you were lovely to Coco – even the nanny I settled on said she wasn't as scared of you as she thought she was going to be.'

'Hooray for me,' Victoria said dryly, sitting up even straighter than usual because it was so hard to bend at the waist in the three pairs of Spanx.

Jeremy took her hand, lacing his fingers through hers. 'It's the baby,' he said, his voice deeply contented. 'All the hormones. They're making you a nicer person.'

Victoria stared straight ahead of her, at the shiny black Perspex screen between the passengers and the driver, in which she could make out her pale face, crowned with its blonde chignon, her long straight nose and bright red lipstick.

It isn't the baby, she knew, her stomach shifting under all the layers of elastic wrapping that was flattening it down. It's Lykke. If anything's making me a nicer person, it's her.

Victoria had not seen Lykke since St Louis, a fortnight ago. She had pored avidly over the results of the shoot, which had been truly spectacular; she, Dietrich and Clemence had oohed and aahed and clutched their chests dramatically and rolled their eyes at each other in excitement even more than usual. Victoria had even sneaked a couple of Polaroids for herself, keeping them in a zipped pocket in her handbag, bringing them out in absolute secret to obsess over, with the door very securely locked . . .

But a couple of Polaroids just weren't enough.

She longed to feel Lykke in her arms again, to have that smooth silky skin against hers, that long, extraordinary hair trailing over her face, Lykke's cool lips on hers. She had never felt anything like this before, certainly not for poor sweet Jeremy. She felt consumed, eaten up by her desire for Lykke. It was like a drug; she had hoped that seeing Lykke in St Louis would appease her craving, and it had, temporarily; but the trouble was, it had left her wanting more. She had woken up the next morning and rung Alyssa, instructing her to put her on an earlier plane back to New York, not wanting to travel with the rest of the *Style* team. She had scrambled to the airport and fled back home, knowing that she would not be able to see Lykke in a group of people and disguise the feelings she had for her.

She could be anywhere right now, Victoria thought jealously. On a Caribbean island, in London for some arty indie magazine, visiting Milan to meet Armani. God, Lykke would be perfect for Armani . . .

Victoria heaved a deep sigh. She couldn't bear it if she didn't see Lykke again . . . Come on, Victoria, call a spade a spade, she told herself in her crisp tones. What you mean is, if you don't fuck Lykke again.

And then a wave of guilt hit her, as if she were standing on board a boat, holding onto the rail, and the bows had hit a swell and sent a spray of seawater into her face, cold and salty, a slap of reality.

Don't lie, she berated herself. Victoria was famous for her biting honesty; it was only fair that she turn that blinding white light on herself when necessary. *It wasn't just a fuck. You and Lykke made love.*

She bit her lip, hard, and to her great surprise, felt something jump in her stomach. No, not her stomach. Lower down.

I can't be feeling the baby yet! she thought. It's barely been three months. That's much too early, surely?

With perfect clarity, she remembered Lykke telling her that she wanted to see her breasts in a month's time, her stomach . . . saying that pregnant women were supposed to have even better orgasms.

Even through the three layers of Spanx, swaddling her crotch as thickly as if it had been mummified, Victoria felt herself twitch and throb, that involuntary electric stab of excitement that was impossible to fake.

Oh God, I have it so bad.

She saw Lykke's face floating in front of hers, the beautiful, serene features framed by the cloud of silvery hair. For the first time in her hyper-controlled, super-ambitious, perfectly-organised life, Victoria understood what passion was: why it made sensible, intelligent, rational people throw caution to the winds and steer their trains spectacularly off the rails into headlong collisions with disaster.

I have an excellent marriage, she told herself, and a baby on the way. Jeremy's everything any woman could want in a husband: sweet, supportive, with a good job. He puts my interests before his own, he lets me make all the big decisions, he'll take time off work so my job isn't disrupted by having a baby. We have one of the strongest marriages in fashion . . . I'd be lying if I didn't say that Jeremy's a big part of my power base.

Victoria had never subscribed to the ridiculous idea, so assiduously peddled by certain tabloid newspapers and every single recent Hollywood romantic comedy, that it was hard for a successful, ambitious straight woman to find a man to marry her. That was nonsense: she knew plenty of high-powered women with very strong marriages.

But still, Jeremy was unquestionably a gem. Victoria knew how much she was envied – had always, frankly, been very smug about it. She looked at him and met his eyes, soft and blue behind the lenses of his glasses, full of love and admiration.

So am I going to put all this in jeopardy just for some model I'm obsessed with? My God, it's like the worst cliché in the book. If a man were behaving like this, he'd be a laughing-stock.

'Oh, thank God!' she exclaimed as the car came to a halt behind a long line of identical black Town Cars on West 27th Street, hugely relieved to have a distraction from this uncomfortable speculation. 'Here we are. Oh my *God*, look at the dresses!'

The party, at the Museum at Fashion Institute of Technology, was as small and exclusive as the museum itself. A-list, Oscar-winning actresses, fashion insiders, professional beauties of both genders, were the only attendees; no padding, no non-entity plus-ones. It was being thrown to publicise an equally small and perfectly-curated exhibition: just twenty-five of Valentino's most beautiful and celebrated evening dresses, all in the signature bright red for which he was famous.

'Darling Vicky!' Dietrich ran up to her as soon as she set foot on the red carpet, his cape trailing behind him, his eyebrows plucked and tattooed into winged arches. '*Such* a party! Inge's pruned the guest-list to within an inch of its life. Have you seen Halle? And Nicole?'

'Not yet,' Victoria said. 'I'm dying to see what Halle's wearing. Are there cut-outs? She pulls those off like nobody else. Not much of an actress, but *such* a clothes-horse.'

'Cover! Cover cover cover!' Dietrich clapped his suede-gloved hands. 'I can't wait.'

'I'm steering away from Jennifer's celebrity covers, Dietrich,' Victoria said as she gathered her skirts, making sure the layers hung perfectly before she turned to face the waiting photographers. 'She was so vulgar! Any little TV-show actress, she'd put on the cover for a quick thrill. And look at Anna at *Vogue* – Oprah on the cover, for God's sake! How is that fashion? I'm going back to the professionals. And some actresses – but only really famous ones – those who've modelled and actually know how to sell a dress . . .'

Further down the red carpet, Anna Wintour's heavy signature bob swung in their direction as Victoria's penetrating tones carried to where she was standing, talking to Nicole Kidman and Kanye West.

'I can't believe *he's* here,' Dietrich muttered. 'After his disastrous débâcle of a show in Paris last year.'

Victoria felt Anna Wintour's eyes boring into the side of her head, and very deliberately didn't turn to meet them; she smiled, however – a small satisfied smile that said *Oh yes. You may have had it all your own way in New York for a while, but I'm here now. Get used to it.* Swivelling towards the bank of photographers, her arm wrapped through her husband's, Dietrich on her other side, his cape tossed artfully back over his shoulders, she flashed her best, most photogenic smile as the cameras clicked and whirred.

'Victoria? It's Gina from E. Love your dress! It's Valentino, of course, isn't it?' chirped a reporter, pushing a microphone in Victoria's face.

'What else?' Victoria said lightly, and saw the reporter's eyes widen in excitement at a new arrival on the carpet, behind Victoria.

'Darling!' said Kate Moss, kissing the air in front of each of Victoria's cheeks. 'You look sensational.'

'Oh, you too,' Victoria cooed as the cameras went wild.

What a fabulous party, she thought with great pleasure as she descended the steps that led down to the museum space; the staircase had been covered for the occasion in Valentino-red carpet. Deferential flunkies were circulating with trays of champagne glasses filled with a bright red cocktail.

'Goji berry bellini?' one flunky murmured, proffering the tray.

'Ooh, lovely!' Dietrich said, taking one and cruising the waiter in a single, efficient movement.

Victoria waved the drinks away; not only was she completely off alcohol now – she felt horribly guilty about how much she had drunk in St Louis – but she couldn't allow any liquid to pass her lips; not when going to the toilet would entail the painstaking removal and replacing of three pairs of Spanx. The small foyer, with its central pillar, had been impeccably decorated for the exhibition: videos were set into recesses in the white walls, showing iconic catwalks from Valentino's most famous shows, models swaying down narrow white runways, elegant spindly girls with necks like giraffes, dressed in streaming silk ribbons and swirls of scarlet and crimson and cherry-red.

Across the room, standing next to the pillar in the centre, she saw Inge Kavanaugh, the editor of *Dialogue* magazine, who had curated and organised this exquisite little show. Short and stocky, built like a fire hydrant, with pocked cheeks and a no-nonsense attitude, Inge dressed to suit her figure, in square-cut, double-breasted men's suits, silk pocket handkerchiefs, and, occasionally, trilbies. Her dark, slightly greasy hair was cut short and tucked back behind her ears, her hands usually shoved mannishly into her pockets.

Frankly, she's the stereotype of the old-school lesbian, Victoria thought, feeling horribly homophobic.

The irony of fashion editors' professions, of course, was that while they spent their working lives telling their readers what to wear, what the current trends were and what they would evolve into – that this winter was all hearts, stars and neon-brights, while spring would be floaty lace and ankle boots – they were very unlikely to be seen dressed in anything that featured on the pages of the most recent edition of their magazine. The most famous icons and muses were always fashion-forward, creating new trends, pushing boundaries. And the editors found their own style and stuck to it firmly. Anna Wintour's bob and Prada dresses, Victoria Glossop's chignon and mini-skirts were instant signatures; they knew what suited them and adapted the fashions of the day to their own ends.

Like Inge. She always looks striking, in an eccentric-British kind of way.

But if I start seeing women, Victoria thought, if I say I'm bisexual, won't people associate me with that kind of lesbian? Won't they make jokes about who's the 'man' and who's the 'woman'? I know I shouldn't be thinking like this – my God, there are tons of gays and lesbians in the fashion industry, right up to the very top! I couldn't be in a better place to realise that I like having sex with women – love having sex with women. Well, one woman . . .

And then, as Inge raised a hand to wave at Halle Berry,

stunning in a red and gold Valentino mini-dress, Victoria saw who Inge had been talking to. From behind the pillar, swaying in what must be five-inch heels, emerged Lykke, wearing the white jumpsuit she had had on the first time Victoria met her, her hair crimped into a white frizz around her face that added an extra few inches to her height. She had added false lashes to her own, darkened with brown mascara, and painted her lips palest pink; the effect was a Twiggy-like, 1960s style that made her eyes look enormous. But, as usual, their expression was grave, considering, giving her an air of serenity that was at odds with the controlled mayhem around her.

'Ooh – our new cover girl. Love the look. Very happening!' Dietrich cooed, pointing at Lykke.

As if I hadn't seen her already, Victoria thought, her heart leaping. As if I could look anywhere else . . .

'Is she with Inge?' Dietrich asked, always avid for gossip. 'I must say, good for Inge if she is! That Lykke's definitely got it going on. I'd do her in a heartbeat.'

'Who are we talking about?' Jeremy asked, drinking some goji berry Bellini.

'Lykke!' Dietrich carolled, waving enthusiastically at her. 'Isn't she fabulous?'

'God, she's quite something, isn't she?' Jeremy said appreciatively. 'Scandinavian, I imagine.'

'Finnish,' Dietrich said.

Victoria couldn't move, couldn't speak. Lykke's eyes met Victoria's, their expression changing, becoming challenging. Between them, some of the most famous actresses in the world, spectacularly dressed and made up, laughed and chatted with the most influential people in the fashion industry. The air was heavy with perfume, and everyone was raising their voices to be heard over each other; through the propped-open double doors to the exhibition space were a dizzying array of bright scarlet dresses on white mannequins.

'He's here!' hissed someone close to the steps, and the next moment Valentino Garavani himself, perma-tanned to a deep, rich shade of mandarin, his skin the same texture as Coco's new Hermès Picotin bucket bag, dressed in an impeccably tailored pale grey silk suit, came into view round the corner of the stairs. He paused for a moment, looking down at the gathering, and his handsome face creased into a smile as everyone, seeing him, broke into tumultuous applause.

There was a mass surge to the bottom of the steps, drawn as if to a magnet, everyone wanting to congratulate Valentino, to press his hand and kiss his cheek. Officially retired for several years, it had been a coup for Inge that he had agreed to attend this show, and she was right in the forefront, greeting him and Giancarlo Giammetti, his partner, with the familiarity of years of friendship.

Victoria slipped back, however, surreptitiously easing against the flow of partygoers, looking for the distinctive, white-clad shape of the woman with whom she was obsessed.

'Lykke,' she said in a whisper, as she crossed the room. It was almost a plea.

It was the first time Victoria had said Lykke's name to her since they met. Pronouncing it casually to others – Mireille, Dietrich, Clemence – had given her a secret thrill, the buzz that came from summoning, as it were, your lover in a business environment, when no one knew of the bond between the two of you, the instant, flaring attraction. She had been curt when she said it before, simply asking Lykke where she came from. Now she sounded vulnerable, and utterly unlike herself. Victoria never whispered, never lowered her voice. Ever.

Lykke was standing at the far side of the room, half-hidden by the pillar. Next to her a video screen was looping through its endless catwalk sequences, and with a start, Victoria saw Lykke on the screen, her amazing hair dressed in elaborate ringlets tumbling around her face, high-stepping, like a show pony, the classic model's walk in high heels and long skirts. She wore a red satin dress, cut on the bias, like a slip but infinitely more subtle, flowing like water around her long thin frame.

'That was the only dress I could wear,' Lykke said, a flicker of amusement in her voice as she saw where Victoria was looking. 'I don't really have enough breasts for Valentino.' She looked down at her almost-flat chest in her tight white jumpsuit. 'I can't do Dolce, or Versace. They never book me.'

Victoria nodded. Dolce, Versace, both wanted girls who, though thin, had a naturally hourglass shape, while Lykke was what they called in America a 'tall drink of water', straight up and down; if she'd been curvier, the white jumpsuit would have looked vulgar, rather than elegant.

'I was just thinking you'd be perfect for Armani,' Victoria observed.

'I've walked for Armani,' Lykke said. 'I love him.' She took in Victoria's dress. 'You look very beautiful,' she said simply.

Victoria felt the blood rise to her cheeks. 'Thank you,' she said softly.

Lykke, on screen, had turned, was walking away, disappearing, with a last swirl of red satin, behind the white screen. And Victoria returned her gaze to Lykke in flesh and blood.

She had wanted so much to be here, standing next to her. To anyone in the room who wasn't clustered eagerly around Valentino, who was now being led through into the exhibition space by Inge, Victoria and Lykke's tête-à-tête would seem completely innocent; an editor making conversation with the model who was about to feature on her December issue cover.

But Victoria, who was never at a loss for words, suddenly realised that she had no idea what to say.

'I came to you once,' Lykke said solemnly, gazing into Victoria's grey eyes. 'Maybe twice, if we count when I first came to your office. But I won't do it again.'

Victoria's heart plummeted. Her lips parted, but all she could think of to say was a desperate 'No!' or 'Why?' and she couldn't trust her voice not to come out so high and panicked that it would draw unwanted attention. Already the Van Cleef & Arpels bodyguard was hovering by the pillar in case Lykke tried to rip off the rubies and make a run for it, his hands in the classic ball-covering clasp at his crotch.

'Now you must come to me,' Lykke continued, and Victoria's heart shot up again, dizzying her with the speed of its ascent, making her light-headed.

'What does that mean?' she asked.

Lykke shrugged, a small movement of her narrow, bony shoulders. 'I don't know,' she said quietly. 'But this is too strong. I can't be casual with something that is so strong.'

Her lips lifted into a haunting, sad smile. 'I should be more clever for my career,' she said. 'I should tell you that, yes, I will be with you whenever you want. Many models I know would do that with any editor, any photographer, so that they will be hired, be put on covers. But I cannot do that with you. Maybe it is stupid of me, but I feel too strongly about you.'

Her eyes fluttered, the fake lashes falling and rising, dark and spiky on her white cheeks. She regarded Victoria with the same beautiful, melancholy smile, and said directly, 'You must come to me now, if you want to see me. You must take a step towards me, as I did towards you.'

'And then what?' Victoria blurted out. 'What do we do then?'

She darted a glance over at Jeremy, half-hidden in the crowd, who was happily sipping his bellini and chatting to Mireille as they followed the crowd through into the exhibition room. Sensing his wife's eyes on him, he lifted a hand cheerfully as he was carried along by the press of people around him.

Mireille had not dressed in red for the occasion; it didn't suit her. Her Valentino trouser suit was black, but her clutch was red, clever accessorising to fit in with the theme of the evening while still not compromising her desire to look as good as possible. Her green eyes flashed with amusement as she put her hand on Jeremy's arm and made a comment that had him smiling and joking back.

'I'm married,' Victoria said hopelessly, looking at her unsuspecting husband. 'I have a baby on the way.'

One of Lykke's hands lifted, as if to reach out to Victoria, and then fell to her side again. 'I want to see what you look like now,' she said intently, gazing at Victoria. 'And when you get bigger. I want to see you, to taste you, to hold you . . .'

Victoria swallowed so hard that the back of her throat felt bruised. 'I can't do this,' she whispered.

Lykke nodded, tumbling her crimped fall of hair over her face so that Victoria couldn't see her expression. She turned towards the exhibition room.

'Are you with Inge?' Victoria asked, the words tumbling out of her mouth, jealousy spurring her on. 'Are you two together?'

'You cannot ask me that,' Lykke said sadly as she walked away.

It was too painful for Victoria to watch her go. Tears pricked at her eyes, and resolutely forcing them back, she stared blindly at the pillar in the centre of the room, where the screen next to the guard was playing the same catwalk show as before. Lykke emerged, began to walk down the runway towards Victoria, her blood-red dress eddying around her like viscous liquid. A surge of longing rose within Victoria, a passionate wish to be that dress, to wrap around Lykke that closely, embracing her, stroking her long slender white limbs . . .

'Darling, are you all right?'

Victoria jumped, and then gasped with pain as the boning and the hooks of the couture dress cut into her with the sudden movement, the dress so tight that the boning was working its way even through the layers of Spanx. She hadn't noticed Jeremy coming up to her, had been oblivious to anything but Lykke on the screen in front of her.

'Are you not feeling well?' Jeremy's forehead was creased

with concern. 'You don't look wonderful, I must say. Should I take you home?'

Victoria managed to shake her head. 'No,' she muttered. 'I'm OK.'

'Sweetie! Is it true?' Dietrich rushed over, cape fluttering, Clemence on his heels. 'Are you really pregnant?'

Victoria's eyes widened in shock. Her encounter with Lykke had stripped away all her well-established defences: she felt as vulnerable as a child.

'I . . .' she started, almost babbling. 'I . . .'

'You know what? We're almost into the second trimester. We can tell people,' Jeremy broke in, his face open and joyous. He pushed his glasses up to the bridge of his nose. 'We *are* pregnant!' He threw his arm around Victoria. 'Isn't it wonderful? We're over the moon!'

Victoria stiffened in his embrace. I wasn't ready! she thought furiously. I wasn't ready to tell everyone about the baby!

Whether she would ever have been ready was another issue. Victoria was fiercely private, refusing almost all interview requests. She considered it her business, as editor of *Style*, to look the part, to dress perfectly, be groomed at all times; but the idea of giving other people permission to comment on the changes in her body, to think they were somehow entitled to coo over her and ask intensely personal questions, was an idea from which she recoiled in horror.

Really, I'd just like to go through the next six months and have the baby and never have anyone say a single word about what's happening, she thought. And then her brain added: *Apart from Lykke. You wouldn't mind Lykke doing that. Stroking your stomach, your breasts . . . telling you how you tasted, licking your skin . . .*

Irresistibly, her eyes were drawn across the room, trying to spot Lykke's tall white figure, and failing.

I'll ring her. I have to. I'll get Alyssa to book her in for an appointment through Elite in the next couple of days. Okay, it'll be in my office, but we can talk at least, and then I'll sort out a hotel suite where we can meet – no, even better, the Dupleix penthouse at Columbus Circle! No one's there at the moment, we've moved out but I still have the keys. It's the perfect place for a rendezvous.

'A baby! Too exciting! What lovely news,' Clemence sighed in exactly the slushy, overdone tones that Victoria had been imagining. 'A *Style* baby – how fabulous. Think of all the lovely little outfits you can dress it up in.'

She tilted her head theatrically to one side and considered Victoria.

'You're hiding it very well,' she said approvingly. 'I didn't notice a thing. Though, now I look at you, your waist isn't quite as small, and your face is a little softer, don't you think, Dee?'

'Ooh, maybe.' Dietrich tilted his head too. 'Maybe a little under the chin, do you think? Oh, don't worry,' he hastened to reassure his boss, whose eyes were flashing in anger. 'Just a tiny dusting of bronzer under there, and it'll disappear completely.'

How dare they? Is this what it's going to be like for the next six months?

Victoria shuddered. Then: oh *God* – another thought hit her. *It won't just be six months – it'll be ages after that too. Because then they'll be commenting on how my breasts look, if I'm breast-feeding – if I'm losing the weight again, and how that looks . . . this is a nightmare!*

'How did you know I was pregnant?' Victoria demanded, her voice so sharp that both Dietrich and Clemence took a step back.

'Mireille told us,' Clemence said quickly, passing the buck.

'We thought you'd want to be congratulated straight away,' Dietrich chimed in nervously, clasping his hands together in front of his chest.

Face clenched like a fist, Victoria scanned the room furiously for Mireille. Failing to spot her, she stormed towards the exhibition room, Clemence and Dietrich falling back to let her pass, identical tiny wails of apology and regret trailing from their lips. The room was a stunning wall of red, the Valentino dresses on podiums behind sheets of glass, positioned in groups; the effect of their proximity was mesmerising, the rubies and crimsons and fire-engine reds like a fire licking up the glass. Despite herself, Victoria stopped in her tracks, the impact of the collection so breathtaking that it required a moment to absorb it.

'*Superbe, n'est-ce pas?*' Mireille murmured from behind Victoria.

Victoria swung around, the chiffon layers of the dress swirling, the boning cutting into her cruelly now.

'How dare—' she began, but Mireille, smiling widely, was leaning towards her, her right hand up, the emerald on her fourth finger gleaming as she laid her palm on Victoria's shoulder and dropped a kiss on her cheek.

'*Mes félicitations*!' she said, her voice full of warmth. 'It is such happy news. I am so pleased for you and Jeremy.'

Victoria pulled away with a jerk. 'How did you know?' she snapped, loud enough that people around them turned their heads in surprise to see Victoria Glossop raising her voice to her legendary fashion director, in public, at a Valentino party. 'And how *dare* you go around telling everyone my private news?'

'*Mais, ma chère Victoria* . . .' Mireille's hands opened wide, the palms upturned theatrically. Her eyes creased in bemusement, her full lips pursed in a *moue* of surprise. '*Je suis désolée*!' she exclaimed. 'I am so sorry! Of course, when I heard the happy news from the model, naturally I thought that it was common knowledge, *c'est tout*. I would not have dreamed of telling Dietrich and Clemence if I had realised that you—'

'Which model?' Victoria's teeth were gritted now.

'*Mais* Lykke, *bien sûr*! The Finnish girl who is on the St Louis shoot. I know you have only the most passing acquaintance with her, so when she told me just a moment ago that you were pregnant, I of course assumed that she had heard it from someone else on *Style*.' Mireille's green eyes were full of embarrassment now. 'I should have realised, when Dietrich and Clemence did not know either, that it was something more private. I can only apologise.'

Victoria was struck dumb. *How could Lykke do this? How could she betray my confidence, and not only that – to the biggest thorn in my side at* Style? *And how could she know to go straight to Mireille with news like this – to blindside me as a sort of revenge?*

'Victoria, my dear.' Mireille, her delicate skin now creased even more with concern, reached out tentatively to put a hand on Victoria's bare arm, but Victoria was already turning on her heel and stalking further into the exhibition room, looking for Lykke.

How dare she? And to think I was going to ring her, to do what she wanted, to be stupid enough to start an affair with someone who's just shown that she absolutely can't be trusted . . .

The huge glass walls that held the dresses winged out into the centre of the room from all four corners, like an X whose centre had been removed. The arrangement allowed viewers to look from dress to dress, gave them an opportunity to compare ones in all four cabinets, and to see both the front and the back very effectively. It also created little nooks where visitors could gather and gossip.

As Victoria rounded the side of one of the wings, she heard the tittered words: '. . . *totally* swings both ways. Apparently, she didn't come out of there till morning!'

'Oh my *God,*' another girl gasped. 'That's *beyond* juicy! I completely thought she was straight.'

'Then what was she up to with Lykke in her suite till dawn?' the first girl said triumphantly. 'They were Lykking!' She giggled. 'Oh my God, did you *hear* what I just did? That's hilarious! I'm going to Twitter it right now.'

'Lykking,' the second girl repeated. 'I could *die*, that's so funny. Are you, like, completely sure?'

'Yes! Gospel! Absolutely! You'll never *guess* who told me . . .'

If Victoria had been able to, she would have slammed to a halt and executed a swift reverse before the girls realised she was within earshot. But the force with which she was hunting Lykke down precipitated her forward, sent her fully round the side of the glass wing before she could stop; she was almost on top of the two gossiping girls before she knew it. They swung round, and it would have been comical, in another context, to see the horror on both of their pretty faces.

Oh God, they're *Vogue* girls, Victoria realised in an instant. That means this has already spread beyond *Style* . . . it's all over New York. And everyone will be Twittering and Facebooking. London, Milan, Paris, Moscow . . . everyone will know by now that Victoria Glossop spent the night with a model . . .

'Victoria!' breathed one of the girls, her eyes as wide as saucers. 'I – I didn't—'

'You'd both better work your arses off at Condé Nast,' Victoria bit out. 'Because you just lost any hope of being hired at Dupleix. Ever.'

Everyone's looking at me! she fumed as she stalked back through the flaming lines of red dresses, her own chiffon skirts swirling dramatically, the diamonds in her ears burning fire. Everyone's turning to look at me, laughing behind my back. *Victoria Glossop, stupid enough not only to fuck a model but get caught doing it.*

Victoria was so absorbed in her furious interior monologue that she didn't realise that there was a tiny step up from the exhibition room to the lobby. One of her slingback heels caught on it and snagged. If she'd paused for a moment, lifted it and continued smoothly on, disaster would have been averted. But Victoria was, literally, in a tearing hurry, and all her fury was vented in one sharp, vicious lash of her foot as she tore her shoe free of the impediment. Louboutins were beautifully made, but the fragile heel, wrenched with such pressure, couldn't help but give way.

Victoria, off balance, toppled sideways and had to catch at the door jamb to avoid falling. Her flailing attracted instant attention, and in a mere few seconds everyone at the launch was turning to look at Victoria Glossop, grabbing onto the door lintel, precariously propped on one heel, all her dignity gone as she struggled not to crash to the ground. Silence fell as everyone goggled at the sight: for a moment, the only noise in the lobby was the broken heel, with its distinctive red back, rolling away across the rake of the floor.

'Darling!' Jeremy exclaimed, running towards her. 'What happened? Are you all right?'

Tears were pricking at Victoria's eyes again, and it was all she could do to repress them.

'My heel . . .' she managed, and couldn't say any more, because she really thought she might burst into sobs if she uttered one more word.

'Lean on me,' Jeremy said, wrapping her arm through hers.

The crowds parted, still in silence. It was just too good a spectacle to miss: Victoria Glossop, walking like Quasimodo, hopping from the ball of one foot to the high heel on the other and back again, her skirts hoiked up so she didn't trip, hobbling awkwardly across the room and up the stairs.

'She *has* put on a little weight,' someone whispered. 'Don't you think? I'd say at least seven pounds.'

'She'd better watch it or heels will be snapping under her like driftwood,' someone else sniggered maliciously.

Seven pounds? How dare they? It's only five and a half, Victoria thought furiously, humiliation rising in her like bile in her throat. She held her head high, limping up the stairs, and as she and Jeremy disappeared from view, she heard a roar of voices as everyone started, with feverish haste, to gossip about her. Her weight gain. Her pregnancy. Her affair with Lykke.

At least she had got Jeremy away before someone had the

chance to drip the poison of her recent indiscretion in his ear.

But how long will it be before he finds out? she thought frantically. *Someone's bound to make it their business to tell him. How long do I have? Weeks? Days?*

Panic rushed through her. And, from the bottom of the staircase, laughter floated up as people started cracking witticisms about her, the high-pitched, gleeful cackle of the fashion pack sinking its teeth into a victim.

Coco

Jacob hadn't just given Coco a Hermès bag; he had loaded her down with presents. Coco wasn't stupid: she could see, very clearly, that the gifts were not simply an attempt by an older multi-millionaire to spoil his younger lover, sweep her off her feet with glamour and luxury, but were principally designed to improve her, make her over into a sleeker, more sophisticated version of herself.

And since that was exactly why she had been attracted to Jacob, she wasn't at all offended. In fact, she welcomed it with open arms.

Ever since she had woken up that first morning, lapped in the delicious softness of Jacob's enormous bed, wrapped in a tangle of soft-as-silk Egyptian cotton sheets, Coco had been unable to believe that her dream had come true. From the moment she had first met Jacob, and realised that she was intensely attracted to him, this had been the fantasy: to land in a world of absolute luxury, with someone who not only wanted to spoil, but to mentor her.

Sitting up, blinking in the sunshine streaming through the windows of the penthouse apartment, so high up that there were no other buildings to block any light, Coco pulled up pillows behind her, propping herself against the huge carved wooden headboard. Jacob, she sensed, was long gone. The other side of the bed was cool, and, with a blush, she remembered the oven-like heat of Jacob's body. If he had been here recently, the indentation in the mattress would still be warm.

Sliding her legs off the bed, dropping the long fall to the silk rug on the wooden floor, she felt the subtle warmth beneath the soles of her feet that indicated underfloor heating. But right beside the rug was a pair of fur-lined, backless velvet mules, and she slipped her feet into them gratefully, walking carefully down the black granite stairs to the bathroom area. It felt weird to use the toilet in such an exposed situation, beautiful though it was. The wide, panoramic terrace beyond the French doors wrapped around two sides of the bedroom and bathroom, and the maple trees in huge silver planters, the trellises trained with climbing jasmine and wisteria, made it impossible to tell if there was anyone out there. And this room itself was so big, there might be more doors that she didn't see, through which someone might come in at any time . . .

Coco went as quickly as she could, flushed the toilet and pulled her nightdress down again, relieved that she'd been able to relieve herself in privacy. Along the wide marble shelf that ran above the double granite sinks were set out moisturisers, cosmetics, separated out in polished silver trays. Mostly Chanel, Coco noticed, smiling at the coincidence between the brand and her adopted first name. This was a level of luxury that she had never experienced before. Of course, girls on the beauty desks of *UK* and *US Style* had passed on creams and lotions and make-up removers in the past, but it wasn't the same as standing in front of an entire line of products – cleansers, toners, exfoliators, moisturisers, eye creams – all new, all unopened, all especially for her. And across the room, on a dressing-table, she could see a row of Chanel perfumes and body lotions: Coco Mademoiselle, Chance, Cristalle Eau Verte.

All chosen for someone my age, she realised. Like the skin

creams. These are all for twenty-something girls. Walking over to the dressing-table, her eyes widening as she looked at the range of products Jacob had laid out for her, she saw a note on its cherrywood surface, crisp black ink on the most expensive vellum, written in the clear, legible handwriting of someone who had grown up before it became so commonplace to use computers that all people could manage was an illegible scrawl.

Good morning! Use anything and everything you want, Jacob had written. *Clothes in the dressing-room cupboard – I've left the door ajar. Amira will make you breakfast when you're ready. There's a car downstairs to take you to work. I'm off to LA for meetings for two days – dinner on Friday, when I'm back? Leave me your cell number and email.*

You were amazing, my dear.

He had signed it simply with a big, swooping *J.* Coco picked the letter up and pressed it against her chest – a silly, dramatic gesture of which she was instantly ashamed.

But he wants to see me again! He called me 'amazing'!

And there were 'clothes in the dressing-room cupboard' – what did that mean?

It took her a good five minutes to find the dressing-room, which really was a room, accessed from a door to the side of the enormous bed. Her jaw dropped as she stepped inside, its lights coming on as she did so, triggered by a motion sensor. No question that it was very clearly the lair of a bachelor: dark, custom-made mahogany, narrow racks of shelves holding cufflinks in velvet recesses, perfectly-rolled up merino socks, folded and ironed silk boxers, all with spotlights above each set of shelves that came on as soon as Coco slid them out to goggle in wonder at their perfect order. Superbly-polished Italian and British shoes, their leather gleaming as if it had been oiled, filled half of an entire wall. A quick look inside a closed cupboard revealed stacks of cashmere sweaters and cardigans in muted shades, the interior lined with cedar to protect against moths, smelling rich and woody.

By the time Coco investigated the cupboard whose door was ajar – she had been saving it for last, wanting to prolong the anticipation – she was prepared for anything. Even so, its contents took her breath away. On the rack hung a perfectly-curated range of clothes, black and grey and cream, silk T-shirts, pencil skirts, crepe dresses, leather and suede jackets. A row of shelves down one side held fine cotton T-shirts, silky beige knicker and bra sets, 10-denier tights in soft, natural tans and smoky greys; on the floor of the closet were three pairs of shoes, all the same, dark grey suede stack heeled, high-cut sandals in American sizes 5½, 6, and 6½, beautiful, elegant shoes that would work with any outfit Coco assembled from the wardrobe.

It could have been photographed for *Style* as an ideal example of a young working Manhattan girl's June capsule wardrobe; it would have fitted right into the *Make It Work!* section of the magazine, high style on a careful budget, a selection of a few quality pieces which would mix and match and take their wearer anywhere she needed to go. Who had assembled it, Coco couldn't imagine, but her mouth watered as she rifled through the rack. Only the time constraint – because she needed to be at work in forty minutes – limited her, otherwise she would have tried on every single piece.

And, in an orange Hermès box, tied with the classic brown grosgrain signature ribbon, was the *pièce de résistance*: a deep brown handbag in thick, textured leather, an open bucket shape, equally suitable for day or for night, with a decorative silver padlock hanging from the front. Coco's mouth dropped open as she lifted the lid of the box and saw the bag inside, nestled in orange tissue paper.

He's thought of everything, she noted. I can go straight to work, perfectly dressed. I won't even have to go to the office holding my clutch bag from last night as a walk-of-shame giveaway.

Twenty minutes later, wearing a cream and grey print Diane

von Furstenberg short-sleeved wrap dress over bare legs and the size 6 sandals, her face made up with a veil of exquisite Chanel cosmetics, her clutch bag and heels from the night before stowed in the Hermès handbag, Coco found her way through the living room and down the long corridor to the kitchen at the very far end. It was a surprisingly compact space, smaller than Jacob's dressing room; the architect who designed the place had been fully aware that anyone occupying this penthouse would be entertaining frequently but not doing any of the catering themselves. New Yorkers who lived at this financial level never, ever did their own cooking, entering their kitchen, at best, to pour themselves some water or, more likely, request it from the housekeeper. Though it was lavishly done out in marble and chrome, its counters lined with the latest appliances, its size was appropriate for a room which would be used by the staff, not the owner.

It was possible that Jacob had hired his housekeeper specifically because she was small enough to fit neatly into the kitchen. Amira, a tiny Middle Eastern woman with a charming smile, informed Coco that the clothes she had worn last night were being cleaned and would be returned to her later in the day, at her work. Swiftly, she prepared Coco a tray with a cafetière of black coffee, a glass of water, and a bowl of granola, berries and non-fat Greek yoghurt, which she carried out onto the terrace, placing the tray so that Coco would have her back to the morning sunshine, warming her, but not getting in her eyes.

He really has thought of everything, Coco sipped her coffee and stared in wonder at the panorama around her; the castellated grey buildings, with the tiny balconies and terraces at their tips, little puffs of green foliage indicating private gardens, like this one, thirty or forty storeys above the city. Below was Washington Square Park: she could just about make out the top of the marble arch. It was a typical blue-skied New York early-summer day. *Even my clothes – the Max Mara dress, I'd have had to get that dry-cleaned before I took it back to the fashion cupboard – God, I'm not even going to* think *about Amira coming in while I slept and picking up my bra and pants and stockings from the floor. I'm just not.*

He even told Amira what to give me for breakfast. Skimmed milk in my coffee, sweetener in a bowl, low-sugar fruit and granola. No fat. No bananas, no juice: barely any sugar at all.

After the light sushi dinner of the night before, followed by their sexual exertions, Coco was ravenous: she could have easily polished off a full English. Even after devouring everything on the tray, she was still hungry. But that was normal for her nowadays; she was used to an almost-perpetual feeling of hunger, and had trained herself, whenever she noticed the pangs, to immediately remind herself that it meant she was losing weight.

I know Jacob wants me to be thinner, she thought, standing up and slipping on the butter-soft black leather jacket with ruffles at the cuffs she had chosen from the dressing-room cupboard. It would be too hot to wear later in the day, in 80-degree, humid June in New York City, but up here on the terrace, early in the morning, she could put it on without breaking out in a sweat immediately – and honestly, she couldn't bear to leave it behind. It was so beautiful.

Her heart sank, though, as she noticed the label. *It's a medium. It fits me, and it's a medium. Jacob's right – I am too big. Look at Victoria and Mireille – they're XS, not even a small! They can wear anything. If I really want to be a fashion editor, I should be able to wear sample sizes, and I can't yet.*

Jacob's absolutely right. He's looking after me, thinking of what's best for me and my career.

Coco started to pick up the tray, to take it back to Amira in the kitchen, but she had only taken a few steps towards the French doors leading back into the dining room before Amira dashed out to meet her, horrified, gabbling, 'No, no, lady! I do! I do!' and grabbed the tray from her.

Embarrassed, Coco went through into the living room, pressing the button for the lift, still awed by the lavishness of having your own personal elevator whose doors opened directly into your own apartment. As she descended to the ground floor, she couldn't help contrasting this exit from a man's apartment – the luxury, the wardrobe of clothes, the delicious breakfast – to the occasion that she had stayed at Xavier's and sneaked out at dawn. His flat was the apartment of a twenty-something on a small salary in Manhattan, scruffy and budget-conscious, furnished from IKEA and the Salvation Army and pieces people left out on the street when moving apartment.

The lino tiles of the kitchen, on which her crumpled, sweaty clothes from the night before had been lying, had been stained, cracked and peeling. The smell she had noticed on coming through the front door the night before had been explained, the next morning, by the fact that a French restaurant, on the ground floor, had a wooden cupboard right next to the stairwell, with a sign on the door reading *CHEESE STORE. PLEASE KEEP LOCKED*. The odour of mature Roquefort was overwhelming enough in June: by August, it must be unbearable.

It isn't fair to compare Xavier and Jacob directly, Coco told herself. Xavier works hard – he didn't inherit a family company like Jacob. He's a great catch – he's at my level, after all.

But once you had been dazzled by Jacob Dupleix, by a wardrobe custom-filled just for you, by the deep attention and focus he had given her last night at dinner, when Coco had talked about her dreams, her ambitions, what she wanted to achieve in her career, it was hard to think of anyone else. And by how incredibly dominant he was in bed, she made herself add, trying not to blush, remembering how she had fantasised about Jacob's big hands on her, and how the reality had proved to be even more powerfully erotic than she could conceivably have imagined.

She'd never thought he'd tie her up. Or spank her. And if

that was what he'd done on the very first night, what on earth did he have in store for her on Friday?

She was blushing now; she could see herself in the mirrored walls of the lift. *Only two days till Friday! I'll be so careful with what I eat. I'll work out like a maniac; maybe I can lose another pound before then.*

But Coco had no idea how thorough Jacob had been in his plans for her self-improvement. That afternoon, when she was buzzed at her desk to say that there was a package for her in reception, she assumed that it was her underwear and the Max Mara dress, laundered and ready. She was unprepared for the sight of a delicate bouquet, deep pink roses and darker pink agapanthus nestling in pale green leaves, on top of a large white box.

'Someone's really into you,' the receptionist sighed in envy, as Coco carefully set aside the bouquet, unfolded the top panels of the glossy box and pulled out a vellum envelope lying on top of her folded clothes. She recognised the stationery immediately; it was the same as the note Jacob had left for her that morning. And the envelope bore a C on it, in the same bold black calligraphy which had handwritten her the note.

Inside, a matching piece of paper, the size of a compliments slip, was folded over two business cards.

For you, Jacob had written. *They're both waiting for you to call and set up appointments. I've taken care of everything. Let me know how things went when we have dinner on Friday.*

Again, he had signed it with a simple, sweeping *J.* Coco turned the business cards over in her hands, taking in what they meant. One was for a personal trainer, called Brad Lowry, who specialised, according to the lettering, in 'body sculpture'. And the other was for a lingerie shop in the Village, called La Petite Coquette, a shiny pink card.

The thought of presenting herself to Jacob, newly body-sculpted, in the kind of sexy underwear sold by a boutique called La Petite Coquette made Coco shiver from head to toe in sheer excitement. Tinged with the tiniest hint of fear.

'O-kay!' carolled Brad Lowry at seven a.m. the next morning. 'Let's see what we're working with!'

Coco had balked at the idea of working out so early, and her eyes were struggling to stay open, despite the coffee that she'd grabbed and done her best to drink on the subway ride from Fort Greene to his Chelsea studio.

To be honest, she was grateful that she could barely focus. Brad had specified that she had to come dressed in tight leggings and either a leotard or strappy cami. 'Nothing bulky,' he'd said on the phone, in a swift, clipped voice. 'I have to see exactly what's going on, okay? If you wear anything loose, girl, you're taking it off.'

Terrorised by the idea of a body sculptor forcing her to reveal her torso in just a sports bra, Coco had dashed to Paragon Sports, above Union Square, the night before, and bought a tight black cami-top. She'd pulled it on that morning, over equally tight black leggings, but hadn't dared to look at herself, just thrown a loose cardigan straight over both clinging pieces of clothing. If she'd really examined all her body flaws and bulges before leaving for her early-morning appointment, she'd never have got up the nerve to go.

And now, as Brad walked all around her, slowly, looking at her from every angle, hissing quietly to himself under his breath, she wanted, very badly, to cry. Her hair was pulled into a short ponytail, held back with a sweatband; the only make-up she was wearing was a tiny amount of cover-up and waterproof mascara. The studio was lined with mirrors, which were, when you were wearing skintight workout clothes, even more frightening than the equipment at the back: a fearsome array of weights, poles, huge rubber tubes with grip holes cut into them, medicine balls, Pilates balls, a suspension rack with gravity boots hanging from the top, and many other torture devices at whose purpose Coco could only guess.

Brad himself was in such good shape that he put the male models with whom Coco had worked to shame. Male models, like their female counterparts, needed to be slimline to fit into clothes, which meant keeping their muscles to a long, lean minimum. Whereas every single muscle Brad had on his body was worked out and sculpted to maximum effect; the ribbed ridges of his six-pack, clearly visible through his tight white vest, the split caps of solid muscle on his lightly-freckled shoulders, and his almost wasp-waist made him resemble a professional athlete in peak condition, a gymnast or a pentathlete. Nothing was overdone, everything was in proportion.

And next to him, I look like a podgy dumpling, she thought miserably.

'O-kay!' Brad had finished his circuit and was facing Coco again. He wasn't handsome, not really, but his body was so good, his posture so confident, that you overlooked his only-average face, with its Irish freckles and snub nose. 'Ready to hear the verdict?'

Coco nodded, horrified to realise that she was choking back tears. Beyond Brad, in the mirrors, she could see her stomach bulge, pooching out a little over the waistband of her tight leggings, no matter how much she tried to suck it in. All the way around, like a doughnut. It's so unfair! she thought. I've done Pilates twice a week, and I've lost so much weight. Below the tight ribbing of her sports bra, there was another, smaller, but distinct doughnut, which the cami was trying and failing to flatten. And her hips were a whole size too wide.

She pegged her chin in the air, preparing to face utter humiliation.

'Oh, girl, don't look like that.' Brad took her hands in his, squeezing them reassuringly. 'It's not so bad. You're no Miss Piggy. You just need some hard work and focus, that's all.'

This kindness was unexpected and overwhelming. Coco

gulped, and felt one stray, betraying tear trickle down her cheek. *I want so badly to look perfect for Jacob.*

'Go get some water,' Brad ordered, tactfully releasing her so she could wipe it away. 'But come straight back, okay?'

She dashed to the water fountain in the corner, filling a paper cup, and turned back to see that Brad was sitting on a big blue Pilates ball, his hand resting on its twin, a bright smile on his face.

'Sit down,' he said. 'I'm gonna lay this whole thing out for you. No!' he hollered immediately as she gingerly lowered herself onto the ball. 'Back straight! Straight! Thighs out at a ninety-degree angle, feet flat on the ground. Now you use your core to keep yourself there, o-kay?'

She nodded, eyes wide, sipping her water gratefully.

'First rule: when I say "o-kay", you always answer: "Yes, Brad!" O-kay?'

'Yes, Brad!' Coco repeated, her thighs already starting to burn from the effort of keeping the slippery ball relatively stationary.

'Here's the thing, honey.' Brad swept his own ball around in perfect, tight, tiny clockwise circles, his feet remaining flat on the floor, his control exemplary. 'You're a woman in New York City. The rules are different for women. It's not fair, but that's life, amiright? The guys can get away with way more than you can, especially if they're loaded. Let's put our cards on the table, o-kay?'

'Yes, Brad!' Coco said quickly, always keen to please a teacher, but he swept over her.

'Jacob sent you here, and told me to whip you into shape,' he continued. 'So I know *exactly* what that means. Lucky you!' He winked. 'You scored yourself one of the biggest sugar daddies in town. You must be a very clever girl. Did you know I train Jacob too?'

Coco shook her head.

'And now you're thinking,' Brad said, winking again, 'Jeez,

Brad's not that good at his job, is he? 'Cos Jacob's not exactly in this kind of shape.'

Swirling the ball now widdershins, Brad looked down complacently at his washboard stomach.

'But Jacob doesn't need to be in kickass shape,' he told her. 'You know what I'm saying, right? He's Jacob Dupleix! He can have anyone he wants! He's fit, he's pretty healthy, his cholesterol levels are great, he doesn't need to look like a gym bunny.'

Raising his sandy eyebrows, Brad looked at Coco pointedly.

'I know I need to lose some weight and tone up,' she said frankly.

Brad nodded. 'It's Manhattan, honey,' he said. 'Four girls for every single guy, or some shit like that. All of 'em fighting to be thinner and blonder and bigger-titted than the next one. It's not LA, but we're getting there, you know? Now you told me on the phone you've been doing Pilates and all. Where've you been taking those classes, by the way?'

'Core Pilates,' Coco said. 'On University.'

'Hey, Kim and Michelle!' Brad smiled. 'I know those girls. They're the best. But you're in for a shock with me. The best Pilates class in the world is no substitute for hardcore one-on-one training. I'm gonna tailor everything, personally, to your weak points. I'm gonna work you like you've never been worked before. In a month, you're gonna see a major, major change in your shape. We're gonna slim down those hips and work the hell outta those abs.'

He jumped off the ball in one lithe movement. 'Well, what are you waiting for, girl? Let's warm up with some jumping jacks!'

Coco did her best to spring off the ball as easily as Brad had done, tripped on the flanged heels of her sneakers and nearly went flying.

'I'll just throw this away,' she said quickly, dashing over to the bin by the water fountain, pretending she had meant to tumble off the ball, but pretty much sure that Brad knew the truth.

'Here's the thing,' Brad said, starting to do star jumps in the centre of the studio, his voice as light and even as if he were still sitting on the ball, rather than bouncing back and forth through the air, arms swinging open and closed. 'You know who works out the hardest of all?'

Coco, facing him, already finding it hard to keep up with the speedy pace he was setting, managed a panted 'No'.

'Gay men!' Brad said, as if it were the most obvious thing in the world. 'Who's the fussiest of all, most body-conscious? Gay men. We're really judgey! So, who's the best person to work you out? A gay man! Honey, I'm going to treat you like you were a little twink looking for a sugar daddy. No mercy! You're going to work harder than you ever did in your life. O-kay?'

'Yes, Brad!' Coco wheezed.

'Great. Now, catch this!' Brad raced over to the far side of the studio, grabbed a medicine ball, and threw it at Coco, who barely managed to catch it; the impact against her stomach half-winded her.

'Lie down, sit up, throw it to me, stand up, catch it, sit down again, lie down, sit up and throw it to me all over again. Twenty-five reps, off we go! We don't stop unless you break something, okay? O-kay?'

'Yes, Brad!' Coco gasped, just about managing to sit down while clasping the ball to her chest. That was hard enough. *Twenty-five times?* she thought in panic, trying to glance around for a clock, to see how long the rest of the session would last.

'There is no clock,' Brad barked happily. 'Don't even bother looking. *I'll* tell you when you're done. Now throw me that ball – and put some muscle into it!'

This is worth it, Coco told herself, gritting her teeth, throwing the ball so feebly that Brad had to take a step forward to catch it. *This is totally and completely worth it.* She clambered to her feet and grunted in pain as the medicine ball came flying back at her, so hard that she thought she'd break her fingers catching it. *Oww!* she wailed internally. But she set her jaw and knelt down again, plopping her bottom back on the mat, throwing the ball back to Brad once more.

I can do it. I have *to do it.* I *want Jacob to think I'm a fighter, that I'm strong, that I don't give up. I want him to be sure he's made the right choice in picking me. I want to be the editor of* Style.

And I'd walk over hot coals to get there.

Part Four
Manhattan: Now

Coco

'I don't understand,' Coco said, confused, staring at the woman who had just appeared on Jacob's terrace. 'What do you mean, Jacob called you? Why didn't he let me know you were coming too?'

'I can't imagine,' the woman said, smiling. 'It's very exciting. He told me to be sure to pour us both a glass of Cristal. There was a bottle in the kitchen, chilled and waiting in an ice-bucket.'

Taken aback, Coco accepted the champagne coupe that the woman was handing her.

'I didn't know that you and Jacob were . . .' she started, still bewildered, but not wanting to be rude. She trailed off, not knowing how to finish the sentence. *So close*, she meant. *Close enough for him to invite you round without even telling his fiancée you were coming. And to tell you to give me a drink, when this is practically my home now*.

'Oh, it's a professional connection,' the woman said, still smiling. 'I'm sure that's what he wants to talk to us both about. Something to do with Dupleix, don't you think?'

Of course, the woman was very familiar to Coco: it was seeing her in this context that seemed so odd. She nodded, still bemused.

'And we're celebrating,' the woman continued. 'Your engagement! Your job! You must be on top of the world.' She clinked her champagne coupe against Coco's.

'That's exactly what I was thinking,' Coco said, smiling back at this perfect echo of her thoughts. 'On top of the world.' She sipped some of the Cristal. 'Ooh, lovely. But I'd better go slowly with this,' she said wryly, looking at the glass in her hand.

'You're not pregnant?' the woman gasped. 'Oh, that would be . . .' She seemed to be searching for a superlative.

Coco laughed, taking another sip of champagne. 'That would be much too much,' she said. 'I'm only twenty-five. I don't want kids for quite a while.'

'Have you told Jacob that?' the woman asked, arching her eyebrows. 'I thought he was getting broody.'

'Broody? Really?'

It didn't occur to Coco at that moment to wonder how on earth the woman knew such a personal detail about her fiancé; she was more concerned with the idea that Jacob might be expecting her to pop out babies as soon as he put the wedding ring on her finger.

'I'm really not ready,' she said, furrowing her brow. 'I mean, I want children, but definitely not yet.'

The woman grimaced sympathetically. 'Jacob's a lot older than you, though,' she pointed out. 'Now he's finally made the decision to get married and settle down, he's probably in quite a hurry.'

'I'll have to explain things to him,' Coco said with certainty. 'I'm sure he'll understand I don't want to start right away. I've only just been made editor – I can't possibly take time off for at least two years.'

'Oh, that sounds very reasonable,' the woman agreed. 'After all, it was Jacob who gave you the editor's job. I'm sure he'll understand when you put it like that.'

Relieved to hear this, Coco drank some more champagne.

'Phew,' she said, giggling. 'You gave me a nasty start there.' She shivered. 'God, I'm cold. Shall we go in?'

'Just a moment. Look at the sunset,' the woman sighed, strolling over to the balustrade. 'Isn't it gorgeous?'

It truly was. The setting sun burned hot golden-red to their right, over the Jersey shoreline, behind the huge new buildings that lined the bottom edge of the West Side Highway, the new Frank Gehry office tower on 18th Street, and the three Richard Meier glass apartment blocks at Perry and Charles. Streaks of crimson, gold and pink traced across the mauve sky, reflecting, dizzyingly bright, in the mirrored windows of the skyscrapers, a whole series of miniature fires.

'It warms me just to look at that view,' the woman said, leaning her elbows on the wide stone rail. 'You're moving in here, aren't you?'

'For the moment,' Coco said, joining her at the balustrade, admiring the panorama. She sipped some more champagne, relishing the warmth as the bubbles trickled down her throat. 'But this won't be big enough for both of us in the long term.' She smiled at the woman. 'Especially when we do start thinking about a family. We'll be looking at a duplex, at least. Downtown, though,' she added. 'Jacob wants to stay here, and I don't want to go above Fourteenth Street.'

'It sounds perfect,' the woman said, sipping some Cristal. She glanced over. 'I thought you were going to take that slowly,' she said, amused, noticing that Coco's coupe was nearly empty.

'Oh dear.' Coco pulled a face. 'I have to be more careful nowadays, now that I've lost weight. It goes to my head much faster than it used to.' I'm below a hundred pounds! she wanted to say proudly, but knew that it would sound like boasting.

'You *have* lost a lot of weight,' the woman said, turning to look Coco up and down. 'Perhaps even a little too much? You look very thin, frankly.'

'That's what I wanted,' Coco said happily. 'To be thin! And now I am. I'm really, really thin. Oops.' She put her hand to her forehead. 'I knew I should have gone a bit slower. I feel rather tipsy now.'

She took a step back from the parapet, and staggered a little on her heels.

'Oops! Actually,' she said, surprised at how light-headed she was, 'I think I should go inside and sit down. I feel woozy all of a sudden.'

'Here.' The woman put an arm around her waist, steadying her. Coco realised that she was being turned, again, to face the sunset.

'I want to go inside,' she said, but was taken aback at the weakness in her voice.

'In a moment,' the woman said sweetly. 'I did want to ask you about how thin you are. You don't look healthy, Coco. Do you know that? You can't be eating anything.'

'No one eats anything on *Style*,' Coco said, her brain beginning to spin in slow, intoxicated circles. 'You know that.'

'Of course, but people should be healthy, shouldn't they? You must be eating like a bird.' The woman's arm tightened round her waist. 'You feel as light as a bird. As if you weigh nothing at all. As if you could fly.'

Coco liked that; she liked it very much. 'As light as a bird,' she repeated dizzily.

'Yes! Look out there.' With her free hand, the woman stretched out her long, elegant arm, pointing to the horizon, the tip of the island, directly in front of them, the high, irregular shard of the new tower at the World Trade Centre. 'Wouldn't it be lovely to fly over there? Like a bird? To soar over the buildings, ride the air currents over the rivers, to the sea . . . Wouldn't you like to be able to fly?'

Her arm was firm around Coco's narrow waist, supporting her now. Coco was feeling so weak, so overwhelmed with giddiness, that keeping her balance was becoming increasingly difficult. Her feet felt as if they wanted to turn under her, trip her up; she was swaying on her heels. The loss of control was scary – but very far away, like a tiny clear voice, the last remnant of sense in her brain was telling her to get a grip, to be afraid, that what was happening wasn't right.

But the wooziness flooding through her was like a whole bottle of champagne, fizzy and delightful, and the woman's arm was warm and steady round her. She was still speaking, her tone soft, dreamy, hypnotic.

'You can't weigh anything at all. You're so light, you could just float away, like a balloon, soar up into the air, over the city . . .'

Coco was entranced by her words, by the picture of herself, a light, beautiful bird in her black coat, spinning effortlessly, weightlessly, through the crisp evening air.

'I *would* like to fly,' Coco murmured, her head whirling.

And then she felt the hands close round her waist, lifting her up, tilting her over the edge of the balustrade.

Part Five
Paris: Then

Victoria

For the last couple of months – ever since Lykke's betrayal of her at the Valentino show – Victoria had been in the worst mood of her life. Gone was the happier, kinder, more sympathetic Victoria, who actually thanked underlings occasionally and refrained from humiliating them in public. Poor Alyssa had been crying regularly on Coco's shoulder; nothing she could do was right as far as Victoria was concerned. The daily de-linting sessions had become especially painful: Victoria had taken to examining herself at random intervals during the day with a magnifying mirror and screaming abuse at Alyssa if she spotted even the tiniest amount of fluff anywhere on her body.

It had been the worst possible timing for the organisers of London Fashion Week to beg Victoria for help. London was always the Cinderella in the two bi-annual Fashion Weeks, squashed perilously between New York, Milan and Paris, the schedules perpetually squabbled over by the Big Three, with London desperately trying to elbow enough space for itself in between the behemoths. New York, Milan and Paris had the big names, the labels that anyone would instantly recognise, with the diffusion lines, the perfumes, the sunglasses that made billions for their investors: Michael Kors, Donna Karan, Gucci, Armani, Chanel, Calvin Klein. London was fashion-forward, directional, up-and-coming designers and eccentric creatives: Hussein Chalayan, Giles Deacon, Christopher Kane, and Vivienne Westwood.

Fun as the London shows were, its week was by no means the big-money, well-oiled machine that the Big Three could provide, and wasn't the same draw: Stella McCartney and Alexander McQueen, much to the London Fashion Week organisers' distress, showed not in London, but in Paris.

'We're being deliberately sabotaged, Victoria,' one of the directors of the British Fashion Council had practically sobbed down the phone to her in July. 'I just heard that Gucci's insisting that all its runway models come to Milan four or five days before the shows, for some "pre-casting" nonsense! You know what that means – they'll all have to pull out of the shows they're booked to do for London Fashion Week, because Gucci trumps us. Temperley, Aquascutum, Burberry – everyone's having absolute meltdowns over here!'

She drew a long, bubbling breath. 'They've been doing this for the last two seasons! And when we complain, they just say it's New York and London's fault, because we're before them – you know, the time that Marc Jacobs show ran late so the models couldn't make the last flight to London and couldn't do the Friday LFW shows. As if that had anything to do with anything! Milan's already told us our fashion week should be shorter. They're trying to squeeze us out of existence!'

They probably are, Victoria thought. But what the hell do you want me to do about it? I'm an editor, not an activist.

'If you'd guarantee to come, Victoria, it would be such a PR boost for us,' the director pleaded. 'It's this whole third-week-in-September mess, you know? Everyone's fighting over it. Condé Nast have promised they'll do New York and London but skip Milan. If you'd definitely say you'd come to London, that would be huge. Please say you will! You know, without

British designers, there'd be no wit, no whimsy, no true creativity in fashion. We drive fashion, we're the seedbed for every new innovation—'

'Oh, please. Spare me the PR shtick,' Victoria sighed, bored now. 'Blah blah Erdem, blah blah Preen. I'll be six months' pregnant then, you know. I'm not lugging myself to London this year – I have to do Milan and Paris. I'll send you Mireille instead.'

The director actually wailed aloud.

'Oh, Victoria, Mireille always comes! And she's wonderful, but it's not the same for PR at all. We need *you*! It would be such a powerful statement – you know, back to your roots, in the States now but acknowledging that London's the fount of—'

'No,' Victoria snapped. 'You'll have to make do with Mireille and Coco.'

'Coco? You mean your *assistant*?' the director said, hugely offended. 'You're fobbing me off with an *assistant*?'

'She's an editor here now,' Victoria informed her. 'My new star. Fabulous editorial eye. I'm sending her everywhere. Suck up to her – she's going places.'

And, as was her wont when she had nothing else to say, Victoria hung up. The poor British Fashion Week director could not have known it, but she had never stood a chance of convincing Victoria to come to London, because Victoria was already well aware that Lykke had been booked solidly for the entirety of London Fashion Week. Her otherworldly looks made her perfect for London's avant-garde aesthetic. Victoria would not be able to avoid seeing her completely: Lykke was doing some New York shows, and, of course, Milan and Paris. But the thought of seeing her five times a day for five days in London – where the shows were smaller and the front row closer to the catwalk – knowing that she would be at every single after-party, too – was a torture that Victoria simply couldn't bear.

The pregnancy was a good excuse, of course. But sheer capriciousness would have worked just as well. Victoria had been so intolerable recently that nothing she did would have surprised her terrorised staff. Congratulations on her pregnancy had been met with such hostility from her that now everyone was pretending that it wasn't happening, that their editor's bump was invisible; it was one of two elephants in the room. Victoria could mention the pregnancy; no one else dared to.

Nor had Lykke's name been breathed in Victoria's presence by anyone on *Style*. It was the other elephant in the room. And since Victoria was determined that nothing would induce her to ever be alone with Lykke again, there were no clues for the *Style* staffers to follow. No secret rendezvous, no suspiciously regular repeat bookings of Lykke for *Style* shoots, no mysterious phone conversations that Alyssa might overhear: nothing. No contact at all. She was hoping desperately that the absolute lack of any contact between herself and Lykke would make people believe that the entire story had been a farrago of lies.

I can never be close to her again. Because I can't trust her. Telling Mireille about my pregnancy, of all people! And I'd be a fool to think that it wasn't Lykke who spread the story that she and I were having sex, too. My God, she's a fast worker. She walked away from me at the Valentino party, and within five minutes everyone knew both pieces of information. She's a vile, backstabbing bitch, and I'm better off without her.

Victoria heaved a long sigh, remembering the humiliation of that night at the Valentino show, the sheer horror of everyone staring at her, barely suppressing their amusement at her mortification, the laughter that had burst out after she had exited the room. It had been all she could do to go into work the next day as normal, acting as if nothing whatsoever, apart from the annoyance of a broken slingback, had happened the night before; she had managed it, of course, through sheer willpower, and her staff had fallen right into line. Even Clemence and Dietrich had refrained from a word of gossip in her earshot.

They know what's good for them, Victoria thought savagely. They're both brilliant at their jobs, but I'd have sacked them in an instant if they'd dared mention anything to me apart from sympathy for that bloody heel snapping.

She was staring out of the window of her customary suite in the George V Hotel in Paris, where she always stayed for Fashion Week: the seventh-floor Suite Anglaise, whose creams and yellows and chintzy, faux-English overstuffed sofas Victoria had always found very calming after the hustle and bustle of dashing from one show to the next. It looked out onto the grey marble courtyard at the centre of the building, one of the hidden, internal gardens for which Paris was famous, planted with miniature trees and topiary, huge carved stone urns rich with deep green foliage. Wrought-iron tables covered with white tablecloths were placed in the centre, the pink and mauve flower arrangements providing a perfectly-studied touch of colour among the delicate palette of green, grey and white.

The view of the courtyard had always, before, been a balm for any stress and strain caused by the previous weeks. Victoria always craved the peace and tranquillity of the George V after the manic rush of Milan. Much as she enjoyed the Four Seasons in Milan, there was something hugely special about the George V, and about Paris itself. Milan was all big business, constantly on the go, in perpetual rivalry with Rome, determined to show itself as better, more vibrant, more cosmopolitan than its southern rival. In Milan, Italian women with vast amounts of make-up and hairdye chattered at you constantly with snapping teeth like crocodiles: jewellery clattered on their skinny frames; both women and men overloaded their aftershaves and perfumes till you felt your nose perpetually itching. It had been unexpectedly overwhelming for Victoria this autumn, a sensory overload; the pregnancy was making her more sensitive to noise and scents and crowds.

And it's Lykke, too, she thought, staring down at a waiter laying out silver cutlery in perfectly symmetrical lines on the square white-covered tables in the courtyard. If she were here, with me . . . if I knew that I'd be seeing her in the evenings, that I could be alone with her, everything would be different. Nothing would bother me. I'd be calm. I'd be happy.

She bit her lip.

I'd be nice to people again.

Victoria knew that no one had said a word to Jeremy about her and Lykke: the gossip had clearly not spread to him, because there was absolutely no way that Jeremy would hear something like that and not instantly confront her. Honesty was integral to Jeremy: he believed you could get through anything successfully by telling the truth. Victoria thought that Jeremy was hopelessly naïve sometimes, but she knew, too, that his natural integrity and candour were a good foil for her.

He stops me from being a completely vicious cow, she knew. Right now, I'm only a partial one. But I'm also a cheating wife, and he doesn't know about that either.

And he never will. It would break his heart. What good would it do me to tell him? I cheated on him with a worthless slut who dangled me on a string, got a cover out of me, then screwed me over when she saw she'd gone too far and overplayed her hand.

Victoria closed her eyes, remembering Lykke's words to her at the Valentino exhibit. 'You must take a step towards me, as I did towards you.'

Victoria pressed her head against the cool glass of the window. 'Oh, Lykke,' she whispered, a deep, pang of yearning transfixing her.

How she longed to take that step towards Lykke! She remembered Lykke walking for Armani, just a few days ago, in a deep blue sequin sheath that clung as tightly to her long slim frame as Victoria longed to do, and the memory was almost unbearable. Her attraction to Lykke, she knew, wasn't just about sex. It was much more profound. Much more strong, as Lykke had put it. Mad as it seemed, she felt that somehow, in the brief time they had spent together, she and Lykke had started to fall in love.

In five minutes, the car will be picking me up for the Chanel show. I'll see Lykke again, walking in it. God, this is like Chinese water torture . . .

'Victoria?' Coco said from the doorway; she was standing in the dining room of the suite. 'The car's here already. I thought we might get a jump on getting to the Grand Palais.'

Oh great, Victoria thought bitterly, pulling back from the windowpane, opening her eyes. Exactly what I want, to get a jump on seeing my ex-lover walking down yet another catwalk, looking so beautiful it breaks my heart every single time.

She turned to face Coco, very grateful that it was her and not Alyssa who had come to summon her. Alyssa was so frightened of Victoria after the last couple of months of hell that even the excitement of visiting Milan and Paris hadn't balanced out the stress of catering for Victoria's every whim; Alyssa's eyes were permanently red-rimmed, and she had bitten her nails so obsessively that they were ragged as claws.

'Jesus, Coco, you look positively skeletal,' Victoria observed, taking in Coco's appearance.

Coco beamed happily. 'Thanks!' she said. 'I was freaking out about all the travelling, and eating food on the go, but my nutritionist worked out meal plans for me and gave me her special snack bars, and my trainer did a daily programme I could follow. Half an hour every morning. I've been doing it religiously.'

'My God, you've gone *so* New York,' Victoria said drily. She took in Coco's skinny arms and legs, exposed in her Chanel ruffled skirt and matching elbow-length fitted jacket, white trimmed with black, young and girlish, utterly suitable for Coco's age.

Finally she's managed to get into sample sizes, Victoria observed. *Good for her*. It was obligatory to wear clothes by the designer whose show you were attending, and if Coco hadn't been able to wear samples provided by Chanel, she would have been in trouble; there was no way she could have afforded them, not on her still-small salary.

She had a flash of envy at Coco's thinness; although Victoria had managed to only put on eleven pounds so far, was aiming for a maximum gain of fourteen with the pregnancy, the sight of her newly-skinny, size two ex-assistant, dressed head-to-toe in Chanel, while Victoria felt like a waddling duck by comparison, was by no means a welcome one.

'Goodness,' she added, noticing Coco's little Chanel clutch bag, quilted orange patent calfskin leather with a chain handle. 'Isn't that a Mini?'

'Yes,' Coco said, doing her best to tuck it under her arm.

'Same admirer as the Hermès?' Victoria inquired teasingly, watching Coco squirm with embarrassment.

Does she really think I don't know about her and Jacob? Still? After all, it's been going on for a few months now.

A little alarm bell rang in Victoria's head at this observation.

A few months? Really, has it been that long?

She looked at Coco again, more closely.

Wait – was that outfit sent to her by Chanel, or did Jacob buy it for her? That ruffled skirt, those cute little saddle shoes – is this Jacob dressing her? It's just how a fifty-something wants his little twenty-something piece to look – young, flirty, girlish. A man closer to her own age would want her to look more sophisticated.

Victoria frowned, biting her lip.

Is it possible that this could be more serious than I thought? I've been so distracted, trying so hard not to think about Lykke. Do I need to keep a closer eye on what's happening with Jacob and Coco?

'Victoria, I wanted to catch a word with you,' Coco said hesitantly. 'Is this a good time?'

It gives me a few minutes' respite from heading off to see Lykke, Victoria thought, and shrugged. It was all the encouragement Coco needed.

'It's Ludovic,' she said seriously. 'I don't think *Style* should book him any more.'

Victoria stared at her incredulously.

'Are you serious?' she exclaimed. 'Have you *seen* the pictures from St Louis? He did the most fabulous job! Totally modern!'

'But Victoria, he's a pig,' Coco said bravely. 'A rapey pig. Emily went back to his room after that shoot, and he was really awful, he wouldn't take no for an answer. She had a horrible time.'

Coco grimaced, thinking of the state in which Emily had returned from St Louis, bruised, scratched, her bright happy confident demeanour a thing of the past. Lucy and Coco had rallied round, wrapped her in cotton wool, helped with her work and got her into victim counselling. Emily was doing fairly well, all things considered, having been able, after Ludovic's assault, to come back to good friends who looked after her; she'd found a support group, too, which was apparently helping even more than the counsellor. The teenage models on shoots, flying all over the world, with no continuity in their lives from one day to the next, weren't so lucky. And from what Coco had found out since hearing from Emily what he had done to her, Ludovic made a regular practice of picking out a young girl and putting her through his own particular wringer, knowing that she wouldn't complain for fear of ruining her career.

'There are other photographers who don't do that to the girls,' Coco continued. 'Really good, talented ones.'

'You want me to blacklist Ludovic because he's a bit over-enthusiastic in the bedroom?' Victoria said incredulously. 'You *must* be joking.'

'No, I'm not.' Coco stood her ground. 'It's not acceptable,

what he does. It's *wrong*. He preys on women. And he won't stop, because no-one will ever press charges. But we can at least keep *Style* girls – and models on our shoots – safe from him.'

'Oh, *please.*' Victoria swept dismissively past Coco, out of the suite. 'This is fashion, and they'd better get used to it. Young women, older men, what do they think's going to happen? I don't want to hear any more of this nonsense. Ludovic's the talent, and Emily had better keep her mouth shut and learn her place in the pecking order, like the rest of the girls do.'

But what if it had been Lykke? her brain, very inconveniently, asked her. *What if Ludovic had managed to corner Lykke and groped her, or worse? How would you feel if that had happened to her?*

I'd want to castrate him with a pair of rusty pliers, Victoria answered savagely. The thought of Ludovic's hairy hands on Lykke's pale skin, his carefully-cultivated stubble rasping her breasts, made bile rise in Victoria's throat. She knew the rumours about Ludovic were true: he'd tried it on with her once, years ago, backed her into a cupboard on a shoot and started pulling up her skirt, and only a stiletto heel jabbed into his foot had made him let her go. It hadn't been the most pleasant of experiences.

She glanced back at Coco, following her down the wide, luxuriously-carpeted hallway, and read her expression: Coco looked positively disillusioned.

'I'll think about it,' Victoria said, surprising herself; it was even more of a surprise to her when she was positively gratified to see Coco's eyes light up in relief.

'Oh Victoria, that would be *wonderful* – thank you so much!' Coco blurted out.

'Don't get excited,' Victoria snapped. 'I haven't made any promises.'

Jesus, bloody Lykke! she thought crossly. *I just think of her and I get soft, damnit!*

Coco was dashing forward to press the button to call the lift, flashing her boss a smile of absolute gratitude. It occurred to Victoria, for a fleeting, lunatic moment, to ask Coco whether the story about her and Lykke was still going around. Whether Lykke was still talking about it; how many people actually believed it. Whether Coco had spent any time with Lykke at after-parties in New York or London or Milan; whether Lykke had ever actually had an affair with Inge Kavanaugh; if she were seeing anybody else. Whether Coco knew, at all, in any way, if Lykke still thought about Victoria, ever mentioned her name, seemed at all wistful when Victoria's name came up in conversation, as it inevitably must . . .

Jesus Christ, Victoria, pull yourself together! she commanded herself, as sharply and as briskly as she would have reprimanded one of her subordinates who was drifting off into sentimental insanity. You sound like a fifteen year old with a crush on a film star!

Taking a deep breath, she rested her hands on the swell of her stomach, visible under her custom-made Chanel shift dress. Now that there was no hiding it with three pairs of Spanx, Victoria had, ironically, become more resigned to having a convex belly: she almost found its curve satisfying, in a totally unexpected way. She stroked her palms over it to calm herself down.

This is what you need to focus on now, she told herself firmly. The baby. Jeremy. Put everything else behind you.

As your father would tell you: Victoria, pull yourself together, young lady, and get a bloody grip.

Judge Glossop's wise words lasted with Victoria through almost all of the Chanel show: it was dazzling enough to provide a perfect distraction. The location alone was breathtaking: the soaring glass nave of the Grand Palais, Paris's answer to London's Crystal Palace. Like the Eiffel Tower, the Crystal Palace had not been intended to last: both monuments were due to be torn down after the World Fairs for which they had been built, and only survived because of their popularity: but the Crystal Palace, originally in Hyde Park, had been moved away from the centre of the city.

The Grand Palais, however, had been built to last, sited on Cours-la-Reine, right next to the River Seine, which ran through the centre of Paris. It was a deliberate one-up gesture from the ancient rivalry between France and Britain, a determination to show that anything London could do, Paris could do better. Restored recently at great expense, Chanel had been showing its spring/summer and autumn/winter collections there for several years now: Karl Lagerfeld had famously adored the venue since being brought there as a child for its iconic car shows, and, later, to see Maurice Béjart ballets in its sumptuous surroundings.

Now, sitting in one of the prized front-row seats, the mini-amphitheatre, painted completely in white, rising behind them, Victoria told herself determinedly how lucky she was to be here, at the pinnacle of her career. In the coveted front row, she could see the UK, Russia, France, Italy editors of *Style*, along with their *Vogue* counterparts. Only the most important actresses and socialites were seated beside them: Catherine Deneuve, Uma Thurman, Diane Kruger, Claudia Schiffer, Vanessa Paradis.

None of the riffraff you get in London, Victoria thought, reminding herself how happy she was to have skipped it this autumn. There, they'll sit you next to some skinny-boy rocker, so strung out that he's forgotten to wash for days. Or pointless beings, like those awful, vulgar daughters of rock stars who haunt the London shows. Little nonentities who'll be completely forgotten in a few years' time because they have nothing but youth and loudness and a famous parent to recommend them.

A gigantic seashell, ten feet high, painted white shading to deeper and deeper shades of pink in its whorled folds, stood in the centre of the white, circular stage, and models were filing out of it, walking in two concentric circles around the borders of the stage, dressed in delicate, ombré-shaded hues of grey, white and pink. The pearls that Lagerfeld had used for his spring/summer collection last year were embroidered onto hems, twisted around the girls' necks, dotted into their plaited hair, less in evidence than in the year before, an echo back to its underwater theme. This collection was equally dreamy, but less aquatic; an invisible solo piano played a haunting, oddly familiar accompaniment.

And then a gasp came from the audience as, out of the centre of the enormous shell, rose none other than Lady Gaga, dripping in pale grey chiffon and pearls, an elaborate pearl tiara on her golden head, wearing much less make-up than usual and consequently looking infinitely more beautiful. As she began to sing, her clear soprano perfectly in tune, Victoria realised that the song was a deconstructed version of one of her biggest hits, done in a minor key.

Applause broke out, the swift patter of discreet clapping that was the fashion world's equivalent of a standing ovation. Victoria joined in: the *coup-de-théâtre* had been stunning, the music exquisite, Lady Gaga's appearance would be talked about for months, and the clothes were stunning.

I haven't thought about Lykke for fifteen minutes! she thought with great pleasure. I haven't even seen her, and everyone's out on stage now – no one else is coming out of the shell. Maybe I was misinformed and she's not walking for Chanel, after all.

Relief and disappointment, in equal measure, flooded through her. She sank back a little in the uncomfortable seat.

And then Lady Gaga's voice soared impossibly high, a pink glow began to suffuse the stage, and a final figure emerged from the opening in the seashell.

Further gasps greeted her. The last model out was the bride, the showstopper whose dress would, ideally, encapsulate the entire collection and provide a romantic, yet unsentimental, finale. This challenge set the bar very high, but the bridal dress seemingly effortlessly surmounted it. Palest blush-pink at its bodice, the ombré shading flowed down to the hem, darkening to a deep rose red in the train that trailed in a silky pool behind its wearer. It was strapless, the bodice designed to resemble overlapping petals, and might have been specifically designed for its model, whose snow-white skin showcased perfectly the delicate hues of the wedding dress.

Lykke looked like a marble statue come to life. Her colourless hair was braided close to her head, like that of the other models, but the pearls woven through her plaits were blush-pink, and there was just the faintest trace of rose on her lips and cheeks. The effect was breathtaking, and applause broke out once more, rising as Karl Lagerfeld himself stepped out of the shell, wearing a dove-grey suit, a pale pink silk bow at his neck, his signature fingerless gloves grey suede. He took Lykke's hand, leading her like a groom in a long circle round the stage, blowing kisses to Lady Gaga as he went. Lykke, swaying next to him like an orchid, managed her train with consummate professional skill, so it spread out behind her for the cameras. She made it look the easiest thing in the world to walk, with cameras all around her, on the arm of Karl Lagerfeld, while simultaneously manoeuvring a floor-length dress which finished in a pearl-hemmed, ten-foot length of silk.

She looks wonderful, Victoria thought, sadness diffusing through her like a block of ice melting around her heart. Sensing eyes on her, she glanced sideways, to the next curved block of seats, and saw Mireille, sitting next to Natalie Portman, dressed impeccably in a Chanel trouser suit, the house's signature camellia pinned onto the lapel of her jacket. Mireille was looking at Victoria, who sensed that her fashion director was watching her to gauge her reaction to Lykke's stunning appearance: the green eyes were intent, full of calculation.

Please, Victoria thought coldly. As if I can be caught out like that! As if I'd give anything away somewhere this public.

She smiled at Mireille, lifting one hand in a little gesture of acknowledgement that Mireille promptly returned, smiling back, the creases round her eyes deepening, the lift of her lips supremely knowing. It took all Victoria's self-control to look back at the stage, knowing that Mireille's eyes were on her, observing her, acutely perceptive. Across the width of the huge circular stage Victoria saw Coco, back in the fourth row as befitted her lower status, but clearly visible because of the raked seating: Coco was aglow with happiness, her face radiant with delight at attending her first Chanel show.

She, too, raised a hand in a tiny wave at Victoria, smiling shyly as if to thank her for this amazing opportunity, and Victoria deigned to nod back at her, a queenly gesture that acknowledged Coco's expression of gratitude. Beside Victoria, in his customary seat, Jacob Dupleix leaned close to her ear and said; 'Knocked it out of the park, I'd say.'

It took Victoria a split-second to realise that he meant the show: she was staring at Lykke, watching her, so poised, following Lagerfeld's cue to take the final bow.

'Oh, absolutely,' she agreed brightly. 'Very editorial.'

'That's our September cover model, isn't it?' Jacob nodded at Lykke.

'Yes,' Victoria said, her mouth suddenly dry.

'Quite something,' Jacob said appreciatively. 'If I weren't head over heels, I'd definitely be asking her to dinner.'

The thought of Jacob asking Lykke out was so paralysing that Victoria's entire face froze for a moment, the small smile she had plastered on it – to show how easy it was for her to see Lykke, how unimportant the sight of her was to Victoria – becoming a rictus that would have fit right in with the gargoyles on Notre Dame Cathedral, further down the banks of the Seine.

And then she took in the full sense of Jacob's words, and her eyebrows shot up almost to her hairline.

'You're head over heels?' she repeated.

Never before had Victoria heard Jacob use this expression about any of the models/actresses/whatevers he had amused himself with over the years. It was more than a decade since she and Jacob had parted company as lovers, and for the first few years Victoria had kept a beady eye on his conquests, afraid that a new protégée might upstage her, try to take her spot in line for the editorships of *UK* and *US Style*. But she had eventually relaxed, as it seemed that all Jacob was interested in doing was to dip his hand again and again in the huge sweetie jar that was the available pool of barely-twenty-something beauties who were more than happy to date a charismatic multi-millionaire head of a media conglomerate.

With amazement, Victoria saw Jacob's features dissolve into the goofy grin of a man who was unquestionably loved-up.

Well, at least I can stop worrying that he's getting a little too serious about Coco*!* she thought with a flash of relief. *That's one concern I can tick off the list – no way would Jacob ever be head over heels about a provincial little nobody like her*.

'You don't know?' he asked her, and though they were speaking sotto voce, under the last ringing notes of Lady Gaga's powerful soprano, his tone was as amazed as it was happy. 'I thought you'd know by now! Vicky, you're slipping. Well,' he added affectionately, 'you've got an excuse at the moment, I suppose.'

He patted her small bump affectionately.

'You've never looked more beautiful, by the way,' he said, his grin positively avuncular. 'Pregnancy suits you. You're blooming.'

It was all Victoria could do not to hit his hand away; she loathed it when people touched her bump, calling attention to a part of her body that she was quite unable to control.

'Why should I know who you're seeing this week?' she asked.

On stage, Karl Lagerfeld was waving a goodbye at his admiring audience as he led Lykke back into the shell once more. Her red train whisked behind her, and Victoria followed it with a gaze of longing.

'I'm not just seeing her, Vicky,' Jacob said, and Victoria realised that he was staring now across the whole circumference of the stage, a fond smile on his wide lips. Her eyes lifted, trying to see where he was looking.

'It's more than that,' he continued, almost dreamily. 'I have feelings for her. She's really something, you know? The whole package. Looks, brains, smarts. I think she might just be the one.'

Uma Thurman is the one? Victoria thought, because the beautiful blonde actress, now standing up to leave the show as the models filed back offstage once more, seemed to be directly in Jacob's eyeline. *Well, that would certainly make sense . . . she's closer to Jacob's age than his little girlies. A grown woman, absolutely stunning, high-status enough for Jacob to settle down with – but she has kids. How's that going to work? Jacob's never cared about kids at all.*

Wait! Since when was Jacob looking for 'the one'? I always thought he was going to be the George Clooney of the media world, the perpetual, debonair bachelor to whom having a girl stay the whole night was a big deal.

And then she saw that Jacob's head was tilted higher, too high for him to be looking at Uma Thurman, and, following his line of sight, Victoria noticed Coco, in her girlish outfit and her skinny new figure, returning his smile, lifting her hand in the same little gesture of acknowledgement that she had made to Victoria—

Jesus, it's Coco! He really is talking about Coco! I can't believe it!

Victoria stared at Jacob with absolute incredulity. He was

gazing up at Coco, who was on her feet now, wearing the short ruffled skirt and girlish jacket which he had doubtless bought her. His expression was as smitten as a boy who's in love for the first time, his eyes soft and dreamy. Slinging the chain of the Chanel Mini bag over her shoulder, filing out along the row of seats with the rest of the attendees, Coco glanced down at her lover and then over at Victoria, who had stood up too. Hands on her hips, Victoria glared at the girl whom she had deliberately selected to be her protégée, the girl she had mentored and promoted and groomed for big things, and was now, all of a sudden, the most dangerous rival Victoria had ever had.

Meeting her editor's eyes, Coco's own went wide with fear as she read, only too unmistakably, the expression in Victoria's steely glare.

You little traitor! it said, clearer than words. *Don't think you'll get away with stepping on my toes like this!*

Then Victoria felt Jacob courteously sliding his arm through one of hers, escorting her out of the show.

'I have a fantastic idea for Coco,' he said, brimming with enthusiasm. 'Something she can really sink her teeth into.'

It's more likely to be me sinking my teeth into her! I'm due to give birth in nearly three months, and even though I'm barely going to take any time off for maternity leave, this is the worst possible moment for me to be unable to give this crisis my full attention, Victoria thought viciously, turning her face away from Jacob so he couldn't read her expression.

In doing so, she found herself looking directly at Mireille, the tell-tale scowl still on her elegant features, her long nose crinkled up in fury. Before Victoria could recover, could paste on a neutral expression, she knew that Mireille had taken in her furious grimace. Mireille's eyes flickered from Victoria, to Jacob, looking tenderly up at Coco, who was descending the stairs from her fourth-row seat, and when Mireille's gaze returned to Victoria's, it was so full of comprehension and – worse – sympathy, that Victoria cringed beneath.

Oh, I've been where you are right now, my dear, Mireille's gaze said. *I've seen myself supplanted, eventually, by a new interest Jacob has taken up. I've watched as he promoted you, made you editor of* UK Style *and then brought you to New York to be my boss.*

My shoes are very tight, aren't they, Victoria?

Coco

Coco was cringing at the memory of the look Victoria had given her. Hours later, it was still seared into her memory so vividly she felt branded by it. Coco had, Cravenly, she had hidden from Victoria after the Chanel show, had buried herself in the thronging mass of lower-level fashion junior editors and PRs at the Givenchy and Dior catwalks, and had chosen the Chanel after-party to attend that evening specifically because she was sure that Victoria wouldn't be present.

She's barely been to any parties at all this time, Coco had calculated. Not in Milan, not in Paris. She's staying in, because of the pregnancy, and maybe because she doesn't want to bump into Lykke and have any gossip flare up again. And Lykke will definitely be here – which means that if Victoria goes to any parties at all, they'll be Givenchy or Dior.

Coco actually didn't know what to think about the Victoria and Lykke situation. She trusted Emily, and Emily had sworn blind that she'd seen Lykke come out of Victoria's suite in St Louis. But the more Coco thought about it, the more unlikely a scenario it seemed that Victoria and Lykke had actually been having sex.

Not only had there never been any lesbian rumours about

Victoria before, there hadn't been any at all about her cheating on Jeremy.

The world of fashion was insular and tightly knit: gossip spread like wildfire through a redwood forest, fast and furious. If Victoria was attracted to women as well as men, it seemed very implausible that no one had ever noticed or reported any sign of it before now; there hadn't been a single instance, even, of Victoria adjusting a model's clothes a touch too intimately, walking in on one while she was changing, repeatedly booking a favourite for lingerie shoots, all the little giveaway signs of an editor who was crushing on a model.

Besides, Victoria and Jacob were an item for a while, Coco thought. *And no one knows better than me that Jacob's as straight as they come – and very sexually demanding. I can't imagine a gay woman wanting to go through some of the things Jacob asks you to do . . .*

Coco was glad of the darkness surrounding her in the night-club; any thought, no matter how brief, of Jacob's sexual tastes made her go turkeycock red.

At the time, I'm so caught up I don't even think about what's happening. To be honest, he doesn't leave me any room to think at all. The intellectual part of my brain completely turns off. It's all feeling, reaction, emotions.

Coco had never said 'no' to anything Jacob did to her. He had given her a safe word, but it was her own name, and she'd have felt ridiculous calling out her real name: having no experience in the world of S&M, she didn't know that it was the submissive who chose the safe word, not the dominant.

I don't want to say 'no' to Jacob, anyway, she told herself firmly. *I want to go wherever he takes me.*

It was as if she had been looking for someone like Jacob for as long as she could remember. Coco had always known that she was different from the rest of her family, who were easy-going, unambitious, content with their lives, like trams happy to pootle back and forth on familiar rails. Her brother Craig had always assumed he would follow in his father's tracks, had taken a job in Baggage Services at Luton airport as soon as he had left school; her sister Tiff was more than happy working at Boots, so much so that she'd emailed Coco recently to say that she'd been offered a promotion which would entail moving to a London branch, but hadn't wanted to shift that far from home.

I can't imagine it, Coco thought. I can't imagine having the opportunity to get out of Luton and not taking it like a shot.

Coco had had no role models when she was growing up, no older figure to look up to and pattern herself on. Teachers at school had wanted Coco – Jodie, as she was then – to go on to university, and had been disappointed when she told them that she couldn't wait three years to get into the workplace and embark on the brilliant career of which she'd been dreaming, ever since she found out that editing a glossy fashion magazine was a real job. They'd told her that a media studies or journalism degree would be a passport into the magazine world, would help her into internships and give her useful contacts, but Coco had researched the careers of her idols – Victoria Glossop, Anna Wintour, Liz Tilberis – and discovered that none of them had taken that kind of conventional route to becoming editors of the best fashion magazines in the world.

Instead, she had taken a word-processing course, got herself on the books of temp agencies, hassled them incessantly to place her in media-related jobs, snagged a week's work on *Wow!* and parlayed that into copy-editing stints, freelance writing and eventually a staff job. With no family connections to help her out, no relatives already working in journalism or the media, unlike so many of the middle-class girls, Coco had had a long hard struggle; nothing had been beneath her. She'd freelanced for most of the cheap weekly magazines, exposed love rats, ghosted 'true-life confessions' of women who'd accidentally dated their long-lost brothers, had plastic surgery which had gone horribly wrong, or squandered their life savings to toyboy husbands met on holiday in Turkey or Ghana. She'd done pieces on cats with two heads, teenagers who had affairs with their boyfriend's fathers, women who hadn't known they were pregnant till a baby popped out of them on a RyanAir flight to Magaluf.

She'd even been asked once to write a bonkbuster novel that a D-list celebrity, with a boob job and an affair with a football manager as her claims to fame, would put her name on. Coco hadn't been shocked at the offer itself – none of the glamour girls in modelling or TV wrote their own novels, they could barely scrawl their own name in them when they did supermarket signings – but had turned it down because they'd proposed paying her much less per word than she could make writing for *Take A Break* or *Woman's World*.

And at least with those – mostly – she got her name on the article.

No one had helped her, no one had given her a leg-up: everything Coco had achieved had been done all on her own. That was why, when she had finally snagged the job at *Style*, she'd worked so hard to make a success of it, to ensure that she was the best assistant Victoria had ever had.

And it had made her uniquely susceptible – and attractive – to Jacob Dupleix. No wonder that Coco would do anything he wanted, pass any test he put her through, never think of letting the safe word pass her lips. Jacob was the mentor, the father figure, for whom she had been searching her whole life without even knowing it.

But suddenly, she couldn't help wishing that Emily or Lucy were here in Paris too. She missed hanging out with girls her own age. Being with Jacob was a whirlwind of luxury and glamour, and although the Dupleix travel department had booked her a room in a Paris hotel, she hadn't even checked in; she was staying in Jacob's suite at the Ritz. It was ridiculous: she had a marble bathroom to herself which was no doubt bigger than the entire room to which the travel department had assigned her.

I'm at one of the trendiest clubs in Paris, and I'd kill to have a couple of girlfriends to scream to about being freaked out that Victoria's hating me for being with Jacob, and then to hit the dancefloor with them, let our hair down, be silly for a change . . .

The memory of dancing with Xavier at Urge flashed into her brain, and she pushed it firmly away.

If I were with Xavier, I'd never even have got in here tonight. No one invites lowly junior editors to Chanel *after-parties at L'Arc.*

L'Arc's owners had named it after the Arc de Triomphe, which was only a few hundred metres away, down the Champs Elysées. From the outdoor terrace, where all the smokers congregated, the view of the arch by night was stupendous; lit up spectacularly, it glowed golden through the trees planted elegantly along the avenues which led to it like spokes of a wheel. Inside, L'Arc was as dark and sexy as the Parisian night: booths of black quilted leather, tables dominated by large silver ice-buckets, walls and bar illuminated by flashes of bright pink and cobalt and lime neon.

Coco was used by now to seeing A-list celebrities at play, but she had never, since these last few weeks of shows, seen so many all together, chattering away; it was still a breathtaking sight. She noticed one small, Oscar-nominated actress, a tiny, slender girl, join a group of fashion insiders, realise that she was next to skinny Lykke, over six foot tall in heels, and immediately, without even breaking step, move across the group so that she was standing next to André Leon Talley, *Vogue*'s editor-at-large, whose much larger frame was an infinitely more flattering contrast to hers.

'Darling!' Jacob, who had been circulating in the thick of the party, leaned over the side of Coco's booth. 'Why are you hiding away here? You should be in the thick of it.'

'I have been – really,' Coco said, tilting her head up to his. 'I'm just a bit . . .' Her voice tailed off.

'What?' Concern flashed across Jacob's face. 'You're young,' he said jocularly. 'You're supposed to be partying till dawn.' He slid into the booth beside her, familiarly close, his hand immediately finding its habitual position on her thigh. 'What is it?' he said, squeezing her gently.

'Oh, nothing,' Coco mumbled.

I'm so lucky to be here – this party is like the centre of the particular universe I've wanted to join ever since I was a teenager. Here I am, with my unbelievably influential, rich, successful boyfriend, and I'm complaining. How spoiled is that?

Jacob's hand tightened on her leg; now that she was so much slimmer, his big fingers covered her entire quadriceps, wrapping around the lower part of her thigh as well. For a second, his grip dug in more deeply, a reproof to her, and she added quickly, 'Sorry. I know you don't like it when I do the "nothing" thing.'

'Say what you mean, mean what you say, and stick by it,' Jacob said, lifting his hand to tap the tip of her nose playfully. 'Be like a man in business. What are the main rules?'

'No self-deprecating, no apologising,' Coco said, smiling at him. 'Attack, don't defend.'

'Exactly! Good girl.' Jacob's finger trailed to her lips, and she kissed it. 'So,' he continued, his voice deepening as he watched her kiss his finger, 'tell me clearly and simply what's on your mind, and we'll see what we can do to fix it.'

'It's just – *Victoria*,' Coco blurted out, cuddling up to him as his hand returned, heavy and warm, to her leg. 'The way she looked at me at the Chanel show today. I hate that she's angry with me. She's done so much for me – she gave me a job as her assistant when, honestly, I had probably the worst CV of anyone who interviewed for it.'

'And you worked your ass off for her,' Jacob reminded her. 'You earned that job. Victoria told me you were the best assistant she ever had.'

'She did?' Coco flushed with pleasure.

'Hey! No self-deprecating.' Jacob squeezed her leg again, hard.

About to say 'Sorry', Coco remembered one of the other main rules, caught herself, and shook her head instead.

'Okay,' she said obediently.

'Quick as a whip,' Jacob said appreciatively. 'I saw that straight away, the first time I met you.'

As always, Jacob's approval made Coco warm with pleasure.

'I've been talking to Vicky,' he started, but just then Coco jumped in surprise as, from the crowd jostling with their drinks in front of their table, she saw a familiar face turn towards her. Pink and green light fell on his smooth skin, his high flat cheekbones, his jet-black hair.

What's *he* doing here? she thought, confusion roiling through her at the sight of Xavier. She had seen him at some of the shows, and been grateful for the fact that he seemed just as keen to avoid her as she was to avoid him; they had traced paths deliberately parallel to each other's, never crossing, their eyes occasionally meeting and then sliding straight away again. Coco had never been any good at the kind of casual sex that meant you could fuck someone's brains out one night and then have a coffee with them the next day as if nothing had happened. That night with Xavier, for her, had changed their relationship permanently, and clearly it was the same for him too; neither of them was capable of managing a fuck-buddy situation. At least not with each other.

It had been a relief for Coco to assume that, in the evenings, she wouldn't bump into her one-night stand. The restaurants and parties to which Jacob took her were far above Xavier's pay grade. No way did a junior editor at *Men's Style* snag an invite to the Chanel after-party – and you couldn't blag your way into one of these dos; the bouncers were the toughest she'd ever seen. How on earth had he got in?

A woman's hand on his arm, slender and dark on his tight-fitting white shirt, caught her attention, and a second later

Coco recognised one of the models from the show, Haymanot – a stunning Ethiopian girl with dramatically-hollowed cheekbones and red-brown skin like rich earth. She was laughing up at Xavier, her hand wrapping around his forearm possessively.

He must be her plus-one, Coco thought. *Well, good for him.*

But she was oddly distracted by the sight of Xavier.

It's because I was thinking before about dancing, letting my hair down, being silly, acting my age, she told herself. And the last time I really went for it, he was there. That's why. It's just an automatic association.

She had been looking at him for this whole time, and Xavier couldn't fail to be aware of a gaze on him; turning, Haymanot still attached to his arm, he spotted Coco sitting in the booth and froze, looking back at her, his eyes widening fractionally.

'Friend of yours?' Jacob said casually. But Coco, who was an excellent observer, knew him well enough to be aware by now that the more casual Jacob sounded, the more focused he actually was.

'He works on *Men's Style*,' she said lightly. 'A group of us used to go out some evenings.'

'Xavier, right? Xavier Fan?'

Jacob was famous for his attention to detail at Dupleix. He raised one hand to summon Xavier over, smiling widely at him. The other hand, the one on Coco's thigh, slid up under the hem of her mini-skirt to the wide ribbed lace of her stocking tops. Coco's purchases at La Petite Coquette, the lingerie store to which Jacob had sent her in the Village, had been very much guided by the manageress, who, in the nicest and most tactful way possible, had made it clear that Coco was not the first young woman who had been sent there to make purchases on Jacob's account, and had discreetly steered Coco towards the ranges that she knew from experience would appeal most to her wealthy client. Nothing slutty, nothing remotely trashy; nothing black, nothing red. Coco had bought lace bras that lifted and presented her breasts like white velvet apples, basques that narrowed in her waist, silk knickers that tied with matching bows on each side, and a whole selection of garter belts, some retro and boned, some flimsy little straps.

Jacob's attention to detail was not just for work. He disliked tights, and Coco had duly given all hers away to Goodwill. Hold-up stockings were tolerated, if they were particularly attractive, but really, he preferred garter belts, and Coco's unlimited account at La Petite Coquette, and the Bloomingdale's charge card he had recently given her, made it possible for her to indulge his tastes as fully as he wanted.

Plus, I save on knickers, Coco thought ironically, as his fingers stretched up beyond the top of her stocking, twisting around the clip of her garter. Because Jacob prefers that I don't wear any when we're out together . . .

'Hey, Coco,' Xavier said, stepping over to their table. Haymanot, distracted by a comment Lykke had made to her, let go of his arm, turning away, and Xavier propped both his hands on the black glass tabletop. 'Mr Dupleix.' He nodded respectfully at Jacob.

'Oh, Jacob, please,' Jacob insisted, smiling even wider. And his fingers slid further up Coco's leg, pushing aside the fabric of the mini-skirt, tracing up the garter strap, brushing against the soft skin of her groin.

'Jacob, then,' Xavier said gamely. He barely glanced at Coco now, his dark eyes firmly fixed on his boss. 'Great shows today, didn't you think?'

Xavier's being pretty cool, Coco thought. This can't be easy for him – chatting to the big boss, trying to ignore the fact that he's had sex with the big boss's girlfriend . . .

She was desperately trying to concentrate on the conversation, and not Jacob's hand, which was turning now, swivelling on his wrist, his fingers between her legs flicking her seductively, teasing open her legs a little more.

In accordance with his wishes – and, to be fair, New York custom – Coco was entirely hairless now, almost as smooth as a baby's bottom. On a very regular basis she attended a European day spa on 44th Street where a middle-aged Russian woman called Lyubya – Russians were apparently the experts in this particular form of aesthetic torture – spread hot wax on her most intimate parts, stroked on a strip of fabric and whisked it away, applying an emollient cream afterwards so quickly that the pain was kept to a bare minimum. Coco had expected the process to hurt much more; to her surprise, much worse than the actual pain itself was the humiliation of having to lie on her back, naked from the waist down, legs spread wide, and then, even worse, to clamber onto all fours on the table, present her bottom to a bored Lyubya, and reach her own hands back, grabbing her buttocks, to spread them in turn, so that Lyubya could first wax the area around her arsehole, and then bleach it . . .

Jacob's index finger found her outer lips, tickling up and down between them, easing a passage through into her hot moist inner heat. It was all Coco could do not to give any outward sign of what he was doing to her; she grabbed her champagne glass from the table, clutching it with both hands, bringing it to her mouth, a visual distraction that would hopefully keep Xavier looking up, rather than down.

'Chanel was definitely my favourite,' Jacob said amicably to Xavier. 'Great cohesion, didn't you think?'

'Oh, definitely,' Xavier agreed.

Jacob's finger, damp to the knuckle now, slid out of Coco just far enough to flick her clitoris, moistening it with her own heat, drawing the faintest of moans from her. Despite herself, her hips ground fractionally into his hand, her buttocks twisting against the leather seat.

'Coco, honey?' Jacob turned to look at her, and for a second his big white teeth looked like a crocodile smile. 'Chanel your top pick too?'

Another test. A big one.

'No, actually,' she managed to say.

Agreement would look weak in the circumstances: she knew she'd chosen correctly when she saw Jacob's expression.

'I preferred the Dior,' she continued, forcing her voice to be stronger. It was exciting and directional – more elegant, less theatrical than when Galliano was in charge.'

Jacob's hand curved around her groin, cupping it, a gesture of possession and approval. Heat flooded through her; it was all she could do not to rock her pelvis against him, rub even tighter against his palm.

The only thing that stopped her was Xavier, so close, just a few feet away, only the width of the table dividing them. She was petrified that he might guess what Jacob was doing to her; the tabletop was smoked black glass, and she had no idea now opaque it was. Would it give Xavier a view of her widened legs, of Jacob's big hand wedged between them?

Coco darted a fleeting look directly at Xavier. He looked composed, interested in the conversation, but she thought she could detect a vein pumping at his temple, and when she looked down at his hands on the tabletop, she saw that the fingers were gripping the edge as tightly as if they were all that was stopping him tumbling from a clifftop. Jacob must have noticed the direction of her swift glance, because his fingers sank into her soft mound, deep enough to draw a stifled gasp from her lips, almost hard enough to bruise. His thumb slid inside her, short and wide and stubby, tracing circles inside her dampness so tantalisingly that she had to brace herself against the table to stop herself from moving against it.

'She's very smart, isn't she?' Jacob said to Xavier, still smiling.

I'm right here! Coco wanted to say. Don't talk about me as if I'm not! But Jacob's thumb was reaching further inside her, up to her G-spot, and she wouldn't have dared to utter a word, in case her voice came out in a squeak of excitement.

Xavier's jaw tightened. 'Coco has a lot of fantastic qualities,' he said, and for the first time, he deliberately turned his head to smile at her.

'Oh, *absolutely!*' Jacob's smile widened.

Crocodile smile, Coco thought. He looks as if he's about to eat Xavier alive.

'And I'm a very lucky man,' Jacob continued, speaking leisurely. 'I get to experience all those fantastic qualities on a daily basis. Don't I, honey?'

His hand twisted more at the wrist, allowing his thumb to penetrate Coco even further, its base now entering her, wide enough to rub directly against her clitoris. She sank her teeth into her lower lip so she didn't scream with pleasure. Jacob was juddering his hand back and forth steadily, a small rocking movement exactly where she needed it most; *he's done this before*, she knew, as she gave herself up, helplessly, to the rhythm he was imposing on her. *That's how he got so good at screwing me under a table, making me come – oh God, I know I'm going to come if he doesn't stop – without the slightest sign to anyone else that he's got his hand up inside me . . .*

Jacob's upper body had swivelled to face Coco, to allow his hand full access between her legs, but he had calculated the angle perfectly; he just looked like a fond boyfriend who wanted to look fully at his girlfriend while talking to her.

Or about her, Coco thought, her last coherent one before the orgasm began to flood through her lower body, one hot spasm after another, rendering her completely incapable of anything but holding onto the table and trying not to cry out. Her eyes widened, and she bit even harder into her lip, using that pain to focus her, remind her that she couldn't let go completely, no matter how intensely she was feeling the sensations between her legs. Jacob's thumb was pressing her G-spot, his hand curved like a sex toy designed to stimulate both her inner and outer zones, a C against which she was dying to rock herself back and forth, rub against those points like a cat butting against a stroking hand, come over and over again . . .

'My congratulations,' Xavier was saying, his voice clipped. 'She's a wonderful girl, and she deserves the best.'

Coco couldn't have moved, even if she had been prepared to humiliate herself by doing so. Jacob's fingers were still clamped hard on her mound, a vice that held her groin exactly where he wanted it, his control on her precise and expert: with one last twist of his wrist, he sent the fleshy base of his thumb powerfully against her now-swollen clitoris, forcing her into a last spasm of orgasm. Her eyes closed, her lips parted, a sigh flowing, involuntarily, from her mouth as her entire body tensed and then released fully onto Jacob's clever hand.

'Glad you agree, honey,' Jacob said fondly, interpreting her small exclamation for Xavier's benefit. 'Well, mustn't keep you.' He tilted his head in the direction of Haymanot, who was coming over to cling once more to Xavier's arm. 'I can see you have business of your own. Nice to touch base.'

And, withdrawing his hand from inside Coco, he flicked his fingers between her legs as he did so, emphasising, for his amusement, exactly how he had just been touching base.

It took Coco a few minutes to completely regain control of herself, to come back to normal after Jacob's manipulations of her. Her crotch felt, simultaneously, completely fulfilled, and sore with incipient bruises; she was sure that the tips of Jacob's fingers were imprinted in her mound of Venus. She flushed with embarrassment when she realised that below her, the leather of the seat was damp with her own moisture. Jacob was wiping his fingers on his handkerchief, smiling at her, nodding to Xavier, who was back at the bar, his shoulders very much turned to the booth, his arm now round Haymanot.

'Well, that young man won't come sniffing around you any more,' Jacob said with certainty. 'Tell me, did you ever fuck him?'

Coco jumped, shocked at the question. The words had been spoken lightly, but their content was serious, and she knew instinctively that if she answered in the affirmative, there might be consequences equally as serious.

Not for me, she knew. For Xavier. I don't think Jacob would

let him stay at Dupleix if he knew that he and I had ever hooked up.

'God, no!' she said, mirroring Jacob's tone. 'We all hung out from time to time, but that was it. Emily likes him, but I don't think anything ever came of it. You know me.' She smiled up at him. 'I prefer men with much more experience.'

It was the perfect line to end on. Jacob looked deeply complacent.

'Yes,' he said smugly, looking over at Xavier's back. 'He's a handsome young pup, but much too callow for you.'

He took Coco's hand, and she thought he was going to pat it in satisfaction, as he often did after she had said or done something he particularly liked: but instead, his eyes still on Xavier, Jacob slid their linked hands under the table, to his crotch now, closing her palm around his cock, which was lying sideways on his thigh, fully hard.

'My turn,' he said, his voice soft with anticipation.

Coco stared at him in shock. '*Here*?' she blurted out.

Jacob smiled at her, and started to slide out of the booth, pulling Coco with him.

'Top up my glass and bring it along,' he instructed her, and she scampered to fulfil his instructions while simultaneously following the insistent drag of his hand. He wove through the crowd, finding his way effortlessly to the black-tiled corridor off which doors led to the bathrooms; this, too, he had obviously done before, because he knew exactly where he was heading, turned the handle of the door and shouldered through, never letting go of Coco's hand, pulling her inside and locking the door behind him in a matter of moments. He stood with his back to the door, unbuckling the belt of his trousers; pulling it out through his trouser loops, he kissed her as he took both her arms, guided them gently behind her back, and wound the belt around her wrists, the tail coming through the whole binding, fastening it securely. A final thrust of his tongue into her mouth as he took the champagne glass from her hand; then she felt his fingers on her skull, guiding her down to her knees as he undid his trousers, shoving them down his legs, his silk boxers coming with them, his wide stubby cock springing free, its base a nest of thick dark curly hair.

Coco wriggled forward on her knees, taking his cock in her mouth, feeling it jump with excitement as her lips closed around it, the soft velvety skin of the head swelling with her touch. Jacob didn't like preliminaries; no licking, no caresses, no playful twists of her tongue around his shaft or flicks up and down the prominent vein on its underside. He just wanted her to suck him, hard and fast, though up till now she had never had to do that with her hands tied behind her back, nothing to steady her, on the cold hard tiles of a bathroom floor.

He'll come fast, she told herself as she fastened her lips on him as tightly as she could, wrapping them over her teeth, and began to work away, his width already filling her mouth. Above her, she was dimly conscious of him leaning against the black-painted bathroom door, his knees a little bent, sipping champagne, looking down at her head as she sucked his cock, her back curved with the effort of keeping upright, keeping her rhythm, his black leather belt snug around her wrists.

'If that boy could see you now,' he said with huge satisfaction. 'Looking at you like that, when you were sitting next to me, when he *knows* you're with me – cocky little fucker, I put him in his place . . .'

The thought excited him even more; his penis swelled, stretching Coco's mouth, and she knew he wasn't far away from climax. His hand came down, gripping the back of her head, forcing it further onto his cock, the black hairs at the base rubbing against her lips as its head jammed against the back of her mouth, again and again, ramming her hard, fucking her mouth mercilessly. Coco struggled to breathe, gasping breaths in through her nose, yielding completely to Jacob's cock as it drove as deep as it could within her mouth, his hand on her hair tilting her head back still more, making her deep-throat him. High above her she heard his groans rise in volume, grunting with each thrust, his hips jerking against her face with such force that, without the hand on her head, her own hands tied up, unable to balance her, she would have fallen to the floor.

It was overpowering, the transcendent sensation of being completely and utterly used by the man she loved. In this moment, Coco knew, she was just an object to Jacob, a symbol of his victory over Xavier, the territory he was marking so comprehensively. Her eyes were closed in concentration, her entire focus on her mouth and what it was doing to him. The next second, as his hand convulsed in her hair and his cock engorged even more, almost choking her, she felt him begin to pump his triumph into her, flooding her tongue with scalding hot sperm.

The hand on her skull relaxed enough for her to draw breath and swallow, again and again, taking it all, gulping it down, licking first her own lips and then, as his cock eventually with-drew from her mouth, licking it too, taking every last drop. Just as he wanted, as he had trained her to do. She sagged back on her heels, still gasping for breath, working her mouth to relax the muscles of her lips and jaw which were locked in rigour. She was dizzy, her head spinning from the intensity of the blow-job she had just given, and though her eyelids fluttered open, her vision was still clouded.

She felt his hand come under her armpit, helping her up; she staggered to her feet, felt him turning her round, undoing the belt around her wrists, sitting her down on the toilet seat, giving her his glass of champagne, which she sipped gratefully.

'Good girl,' Jacob said as he walked over to the sink and dabbed at his detumescing cock with a damp hand towel. He studied his face in the mirror, his features relaxed, his expres-sion one of utter satisfaction: carefully, he wetted his finger at the tap and smoothed down the silvering hair at his temples. 'You made me come like a geyser.' He smiled at her reflection. 'Like a man half my age. You make me feel very young, Coco, my dear.'

Coco finished the champagne and stood up, steadying herself with a hand on the tiled wall. The lighting in the toilets of L'Arc was appropriately dark and flattering, soft and dim, glowing pink candles against the black background.

'That's a gift,' Jacob said, turning to face her. 'A gift you give me. And I have something to give you in return. Something I know you want very badly.'

Coco had no idea what it could be. She was very careful not to express admiration for anything she saw while out with Jacob; she didn't want to look, ever, as if she were hinting for gifts. As well as the clothes and the bags, he had given her the one-carat diamond earrings that she was wearing, which she loved, and never took off. But the benefits that came from dating Jacob, the ones she truly craved, were not financial. His advice, his mentoring, the way he encouraged her ambition and her career aims – and yes, fast promotion, that would be amazing, she admitted – those were what she wanted him to know that she valued from him.

'An editorship,' Jacob said, very amused by the expression of amazement on her face. 'Created just for you, my dear. I've been looking at *Teen Vogue* for some time now and thinking that *Style* should really have its own, younger spin-off.' He smiled. 'I was waiting for the right candidate to come along. And here you are!' He stepped forward and took her hand, looking down at her with great admiration. 'My little Coco. Time for you to have your own magazine. When we get back to New York, your offices will be all ready for you.'

Raising her hand to his mouth, he kissed it.

'You're the first-ever editor of *Style Mademoiselle*,' he informed her. 'Like the title? It's done very well with focus groups, but if you have strong feelings, we can consider changing it.'

Coco's jaw had dropped. She stared at Jacob incredulously. This was her dream job, everything she had hoped to achieve at her age, the most amazing, exciting development she could have imagined.

But when she finally managed to speak, the words that came out weren't the thanks that she, and surely Jacob, had expected.

'I can't believe you told me this in the loo of a club,' she said in a small voice. 'After I just gave you a blow-job!'

It was Jacob's turn to look thunderstruck. 'Coco, I—' he began.

'It makes me feel like a prostitute!' she heard herself say. 'Like it's just – tricks for treats.'

'Tricks for treats?' Jacob repeated, dumbfounded.

'It's what my dad says to the dog,' Coco mumbled, tears coming to her eyes.

The breath whooshed out of her as Jacob enfolded her in an embrace.

'Baby!' he said, his lips warm against her hair. 'I'm so sorry. I never meant you to feel like that! I was going to tell you when we were sitting outside, in the bar – remember, I started to say that I'd been talking to Vicky? But then that boy was staring at you as if he wanted to eat you up, and I couldn't resist. It's a stupid male impulse, you know. When we love a woman, we get jealous. We want to show the world she's ours.'

Coco stiffened in his arms. Jacob, completely misunderstanding the reason, took hold of her shoulders, pulling back a little to look down in her face, his own a mask of concern.

'God, I'm like a teenager around you,' he said in despair. 'I just had to have you, there and then. I tell you, if I could have, I would've shoved you to your knees under the bar table and got you to suck me off there. It was totally primitive. You got my dick so hard—'

'No!' Coco finally exclaimed, laughing up at him though her eyes were wet, barely taking in this stream of words. 'It's not that. You said just now – you said you loved me!'

Jacob took a deep breath. 'I do love you,' he said, very serious. 'I'm madly, crazily in love with you.'

'Oh, Jacob.' Coco flung her arms around his neck. 'I love you too! I love you so much!'

His mouth closed over hers, his arms wrapped round her waist, sweeping her off her feet in a long passionate kiss. Coco returned it with equal passion; only the sound of banging on the door of the toilet broke up their clinch.

'Ahh, my back.' Jacob set her on the ground again, wincing. 'I'm not as young as I was, I should be more careful.' But his eyes were gleaming with pleasure as he opened the bathroom door to see a huge bouncer standing there.

'No drugs,' he said to the bouncer, slipping his hand into his trouser pocket, pulling out his slim leather Italian clip wallet and extracting a 50-euro note, which he pressed into the bouncer's enormous hand. 'Just some mutual affection. We'll be out in a moment, okay?'

The bouncer nodded and stepped back from the door. Coco smoothed her hair quickly as best she could in the mirror, re-fixing its clip. She was glowing, she saw. She had never looked so beautiful. It was the crazy sequence of events, the ups and downs of the day and night; incredible shows that day, her first Dior and Givenchy and Chanel, the fear of Victoria, the excitement of being at Jacob's side in this prestigious company, the encounter with Xavier, the highly-charged game of sex and dominance that Jacob had played with her—

He loves me! she thought with mile-high exhilaration. He loves me! I'm the one that Jacob Dupleix loves, and I'm going to be the editor of my own magazine!

Taking Jacob's outstretched hand obediently, she trotted out of the toilet behind him, flashing a brief smile of apology at the bouncer, who remained stone-faced. They were almost back at the bar when someone came round the corner, moving swiftly. Victoria was on them before they knew it.

She took in the two of them wordlessly, her gaze slicing up

and down their bodies; Jacob holding Coco's hand as they left the bathroom area, both of them flushed with sex and excitement. It was obvious what they had just been doing, and Victoria's glare made that very clear.

She's been where I am, Coco thought, bridling under the stare of disapproval. She's dated Jacob, been promoted as a result of being with him. She has no right to judge me.

'Well! Congratulations on your new job, Coco,' Victoria eventually said. 'Jacob told me earlier about *Style Mademoiselle*. I see you've wasted no time in starting the celebrations.'

And brushing past them, she dashed into the nearest toilet cubicle.

Victoria

That little bitch! Victoria thought furiously as she struggled to get her support pants down over her bump. She had reluctantly abandoned the Spanx for this even-more revolting garment, which was technically a maternity girdle, but was, effectively, the most enormous pair of control pants she had ever seen in her life. Victoria, whose underwear, pre-pregnancy, had consisted of the flimsiest, tiniest Chantelle thongs, now had an entire drawer in her dressing room stuffed with ghastly, gigantic white granny knickers.

The worst part was that she now couldn't live without them. A couple of months ago, she had been driven to her ob-gyn by persistent pain around her groin; the doctor had explained that her body, preparing for birth, was releasing a hormone called relaxin, which softened and stretched the joints in her pubis area.

'It can cause discomfort and pain quite often,' the ob-gyn had said sympathetically. 'And of course, I can't prescribe you anything. But a lot of my ladies do very well with maternity control pants. They seem to hold everything together so you don't feel the stretching out quite so badly.'

Of course, I can't prescribe you anything were the words

Victoria had focused most on at the time. The words that she was already utterly sick of hearing. If I'd known it would be like this, she thought savagely, finally wrestling off the pants and plopping down, with huge relief, on the toilet, well – let's just say no one ever mentions all the shitty parts of being pregnant. God, now I completely understand why so many film stars and singers use surrogates or adopt. I can't wait to get this baby out of me and go back to normal.

No decent prescription drugs, barely any wine by way of alternative self-medication, incipient stretch-marks, plus the fact that she needed to use the loo seemingly constantly. It was a total and utter nightmare. Jeremy had no idea what she was going through, none at all.

And perhaps the worst part of all was the sympathetic, tolerant, poor-you glances other women gave her. The men she didn't mind so much; either they were oblivious, didn't even notice that she was pregnant – it was amazing how imperceptive men could be – or their eyes slid right over her bump, pretending not to see it at all. The males in the fashion world were mostly gay, and they were inevitably the kind of gay man who preferred women to be as flat-chested and narrow-hipped as possible; to look, ideally, like pre-pubescent girls or slender teenage boys, on whom clothes could hang without interruption from any annoying curves or protuberances. Faced with the kind of protuberance that not only was far beyond their normal range of tolerance, but also brought with it vivid images of the kind of female mess and unpleasantness that they did their best never to think about, they simply ignored the entire situation.

But the women – it was as if their assessing glances and empathetic comments were intended to drag Victoria down to their level. She had always, to be brutally honest, thought she was better than other women; more intelligent, more beautiful, more ambitious, more well-bred. And now this pregnancy was reminding her that although she might have all those qualities, she was still subject to the basic laws of biology, which applied equally to all women, no matter whether they were a cleaning lady or the editor of *US Style*.

Emptying her bladder, on which the baby had been pressing insistently, Victoria thought jealously of the actress who was taking Prednisone to make her face swell up so that no one would know she wasn't carrying her own child, the model who'd had her own sister carry her baby, the singer who'd bought a baby from the mistress her husband had carelessly knocked up, avoiding both the scandal and the stretch-marks in one deft move . . .

Lucky bitches! she thought wistfully, standing up and beginning the process of easing the big knickers over her bump once again. And it's not even as if they had the problem of maternity leave. If I have a Caesarian, I'll have to take more time off, damnit. Now Jacob's given Coco her own magazine, I won't have to worry about her destabilising me while I'm away, but they always say it's better to have your enemies inside the tent pissing out, rather than outside the tent pissing in, don't they?

Now she's outside the tent. Or rather, on the next floor down. With her own magazine to build up, so she can prove herself as an editor, set herself up to make a play for my throne . . .

She's playing her cards perfectly.

Adjusting her velvet Chanel dress, smoothing it over her swollen stomach, Victoria took a deep breath, set her chin high in the air, and opened the cubicle door. Sailing back into the bar, she accepted the respectful smiles and nods of acknowledgement as a tribute to her power and influence. In the corner of her eye, she was looking out for Lykke, so that she could steer clear of her.

At least I had the good sense to have a fling with someone who is so noticeable it's easy not to bump into her at parties, Victoria thought with grim humour. After Jacob's revelation at the Chanel show, not only that he was head over heels for Coco, but planning to create a whole magazine for her – why not just bloody buy her some Barbies to play with? She's barely out of the nursery! – Victoria had decided that it was time for her to bite the bullet and stop avoiding situations where she might encounter Lykke.

I need to shore up every single contact and point of influence I have before the baby comes, now that I have a fully-fledged rival in Jacob's bed, ready to jump into my shoes as soon as she can . . .

'Victoria! I did not expect to see you here.'

Mireille glided up to her, holding a glass of champagne. She was wearing the Chanel suit she had had on earlier, at the runway show, but she had removed the silk blouse and now had nothing on under the jacket but a forest-green bra whose lacy trim was just visible below the lapels. A multi-stranded glass pearl and strass sea-horse necklace, the characteristic Chanel overlapping Cs executed wittily as a black Plexiglass is and enamel pendant hanging from its centre, cleverly filled in much of her exposed skin and concealed any crepey folds at her neck. On an American woman in her fifties, the outfit would have looked irredeemably vulgar, but Mireille's dancer's poise and innate Parisian style made it seem supremely elegant.

Mireille air-kissed Victoria on each cheek, then stepped back politely. 'So,' she said, her eyes gleaming with anticipation. 'You have seen Jacob and Coco together?'

'Oh yes,' Victoria said grimly. 'Love's young dream.'

'There is no fool like an old man with a young woman,' Mireille sighed.

'*So* bloody true,' Victoria said, looking across the room at where Coco and Jacob were standing, his arm wrapped around her waist, his other hand gesturing expressively, his face beaming with happiness. 'He's setting up a whole new magazine to give her a toy to play with. Can you believe it? He didn't do that for me, damnit!'

'Nor me,' Mireille said economically.

Victoria stared at Mireille, at her high dancer's bun, the white streak at her temple woven through it as perfectly as always. For the first time ever, Victoria imagined Mireille as she must have been when Jacob met her: young, fresh, her face unlined, her body smooth. Jacob's age, his first protégée, a Parisian ballerina whose talent for fashion styling he had spotted and nurtured into full flowering.

'He did everything he could for me, and then he moved on,' Mireille said, reading Victoria's mind with her customary effortless ease. 'It is the same for you, *n'est-ce pas*? There is nothing more that you need from Jacob. *Comme moi*, you have the job you have always desired. We have achieved our dreams, we have no more need of him. And Jacob must be needed by someone. It is of profound importance to him to be needed, to be able to give gifts. To be the Svengali figure – you know, of course, the novel by du Maurier – *Trilby*?'

Victoria nodded, even though she didn't: she had no wish to show Mireille that she was ignorant of a book that Mireille spoke of as if everyone should be acquainted with it.

'You reach your dream,' Mireille continued, 'you become the editor of *Style* in America. And Jacob sees you happy, and gradually, he begins to look around. Slowly. He does not rush with his protégées, he does not make a mistake. He chooses wisely. We must both agree, little Coco makes an excellent candidate for his attentions.'

Victoria remembered Jacob's attentions all too vividly. It had been fun, most of the time; she had been young and wild, happy to experiment, to play Jacob's games. The most important thing to Victoria had been winning, and she had approached all of the tests he had set her in that light. But there was a crucial difference between her and Coco when it came to Jacob, and, looking at Coco's face, upturned to her mentor's, mesmerised by him, she knew exactly how to define it.

'I was never in love with Jacob,' she said. 'Coco is.'

'*Oui*,' Mireille said, and it was obvious that she was agreeing to both statements.

Which makes Coco much more dangerous, Victoria thought. Much more dangerous than I ever was to you, Mireille.

And she could see, from Mireille's little confirming nod, that Mireille had once again read her mind and was agreeing with this statement too.

'Jacob always made it clear that you were sacrosanct,' Victoria said slowly. 'Untouchable.'

Give something to get something. Show Mireille that we need to bond together against the threat that Coco poses.

'*Ah oui?*' Mireille did not, however, seem surprised by this. 'Jacob is very loyal.'

'Not,' Victoria hastened to add, 'that I ever thought about – I mean, you do your job superbly. You're the best creative director anyone could have. I'm sure publishers are trying to poach you constantly.'

Mireille's lips curved up at the corners. '*Plutôt souvent,*' she admitted. 'But I am content where I am. It is perfect for me. I do not like to move, to have change, at my age. I just prefer,' she met Victoria's eyes straight on, 'to not have too much interference. I have my style, and it works very well. Besides, it is good to have some variety in the magazine, *non*? To have all the pictures where girls run and leap and throw themselves, it is exhausting. Sometimes the reader require images that are more serene, more posed, *n'est-ce pas*?'

Victoria took a deep breath. *Give something to get something,* she repeated to herself.

'Absolutely,' she agreed. 'You must do things as you see best.'

'*Très bien,*' Mireille said with great contentment. She patted Victoria's arm lightly. 'And as for *la petite Coco*, she is still very young. She looks up to you, she sees you as her role model. You must continue to dominate, as it were. To make her seek your approval. *C'est tout.*'

She smiled ironically. 'With that one, the need for approval is very strong,' she said. 'It is her weakness.'

Mireille is absolutely right, Victoria realised. She sees everything; she's the power behind the throne. Instead of fighting her, I need to embrace her, make her an ally. If Mireille and I are a team, we can withstand any attempts Jacob may make to replace us with Coco. He can't face down both of us. I know he can't.

With ever-increasing respect, Victoria inclined her head regally towards Mireille.

'I completely agree with you,' she said, words that rarely, if ever, had passed her lips before.

Mireille knew immediately what a concession Victoria had made. A flash of perfect mutual understanding passed between the two women, so complete that not a single further word needed to be said.

'Mireille, darling! *Love* the necklace!'

André Leon Talley bustled over to talk to her, and Victoria turned away, surveying the room. Her heart jumped as she spotted Lykke's unmistakable white hair, piled on the crown of her head in an artfully messy pile, giving her another couple of inches of height; she towered over almost all the other models. Lykke was moving towards the doors to the terrace of the bar, but she sensed Victoria's gaze on her. For a moment, her pale blue eyes met Victoria's, just long enough to acknowledge that she had seen her former lover, but Lykke never stopped in her tracks; her head turned away and she flowed outside, disappearing from sight.

Victoria watched her go with the same longing that she had felt ever since she had first seen Lykke. It had never diminished, not by one iota. She was as obsessed with Lykke as she had always been. Will this ever go? she thought hopelessly. Or will I always feel this constant, terrible craving for her?

'Victoria?' came a voice next to her, and it was with huge relief that Victoria welcomed the interruption.

Her eyebrows shot up, however, when she realised it was Coco. She's come over specifically to talk to me, she thought. Interesting.

'Can I get you something to drink?' Coco asked, seeing that

Victoria's hands were empty. 'Non-alcoholic, of course,' she added quickly.

'No, thanks,' Victoria said shortly, looking down her long nose at her former assistant. I'm having to pee all the time as it is, she thought. I'm not having another drop to drink till I get back to the suite.

'Victoria, I just wanted to say . . .' Coco began awkwardly. 'I felt I should come and talk to you, about – you know, officially leaving *Style*. I didn't want just to go without talking to you. You've been such an amazing role model for me, I've learned so much from you—'

'You're scarcely going very far, though,' Victoria cut in. 'Just down one floor. At the helm of your own magazine.' Her smile was icy. 'A start-up, too. You're certainly running almost before you can walk.'

'I'm terrified,' Coco said frankly. 'It's such a huge deal, to start up a magazine.' She looked imploringly at Victoria. 'I'd really like to feel that I could use you as a sounding-board sometimes. You have so much experience. If I could run some ideas past you, get you to look at a few mock-ups – that would really help. I know you'll tell me exactly what you think, and that's what I'll need more than anything.'

She sees you as her role model. Mireille's recent words rang in Victoria's ears. *You must continue to dominate, as it were*.

'I'll see what I can do,' she said crisply.

'Oh, thank you,' Coco gushed. She knew Victoria well enough to be aware that if her former boss had meant to say 'No', she would have done. 'That means so much to me.'

Much as Victoria wanted to turn on Coco, to rend her from limb from limb, to call her a disloyal little slut who hadn't had the decency to tell Victoria herself that she was fucking the boss – Victoria's former lover! – to get her own magazine, she knew that the momentary satisfaction would not, in any way, be worth it. To make an enemy of Coco would be a very bad move, one which Mireille had just warned her against making.

Coco had Jacob's ear now, could pour all sorts of sweetly-spoken negativity about Victoria into it as they lay in bed at night – *after he's untied her, of course,* Victoria thought sardonically. *And made her brush her teeth*.

So much better if Coco was telling Jacob that Victoria was being hugely helpful and supportive, doing everything she could to ensure that *Style Mademoiselle – ugh, terrible title* – was a raging success.

'I don't like the title,' Coco was saying. 'I thought *Mini Style* would be better. We'll do it in a small format, like *Teen Vogue*. Teenage girls like minis of everything. They love tiny products. Charm bracelets, little mini-clutch bags, mini-skirts, mini-lip-glosses – I want to get a special mini-lip-gloss giveaway for the first issue. What do you think?' She had pitched the title idea confidently, but there was anxiety in her expression as she looked at Victoria.

'Chanel Mini,' Victoria said, nodding at the orange quilted patent bag hung over Coco's shoulder.

Coco flushed. 'That's where I got the idea,' she admitted.

'It's very good,' Victoria conceded. 'I'll back you up with Jacob about changing it. *Mini Style* it is. Fuck the focus groups. I make a point of not listening to a word they say if I don't agree with it. Tell Sales and Marketing to piss off if they try to push their surveys on you.'

'Thank you!' Coco looked transported with pleasure.

'And now I think we ought to be circulating,' Victoria said, the standard line with which she moved on from one cocktail-party conversation to the next.

'I just wanted to say something else. About Lykke,' Coco blurted out.

Victoria wasn't moving as fast as she had done, pre-pregnancy: she swung back to face Coco again more with a lumber than an elegant swivel of the high heels she was still determinedly wearing. Her expression was a mix of fury and incredulity; she couldn't believe that Coco had dared to mention the name that, in Victoria's hearing, was utterly taboo.

'I've spent some time with her recently,' Coco said, not daring to look into Victoria's eyes, which were grey shards of steel now. 'Working on that sweater shoot she did with Mireille. She's never even mentioned your name.'

'I don't know why you would remotely think that information would interest me,' Victoria heard herself say, her lips as stiff as if they were carved from wood.

'Well, I've heard some silly rumours going round,' Coco continued bravely, 'and I'm pretty sure you have too. I just wanted to tell you that I really don't think Lykke had anything to do with it. She's incredibly discreet.'

Victoria stared at Coco, dumbstruck that the elephant in the room was being named so openly.

'I actually like her,' Coco went on, 'and I can't believe she'd say a word about anything she'd been up to. She never joins in with any of the usual chitchat and gossiping. Honestly, I'm sure that even if something really *had* happened, she'd never breathe a word about it.'

She cleared her throat. It was so unlike Victoria to be silent that delivering this information was unnerving Coco even more than she'd anticipated.

'And of course, no one believes anything happened anyway,' she finished up. 'It was a total storm in a teacup. I mean, you're pregnant, and you've never . . . anyway, I just wanted to let you know that no one's said anything about it for ages. Everyone realised how silly it was when they sort of took a breath and thought about it for a moment.'

Victoria's entire face now felt as stiff as her lips, hardened and calcified. She remembered, suddenly, the myth of Medusa, how a look from her turned men to stone, petrified them. And she understood for the first time the double meaning of that word: she was frozen in place with terror, afraid that if she moved, emotion would gush forth so unstoppably that she would be utterly unable to control it.

'Anyway,' Coco repeated quickly, 'I wanted to let you know—'

'You've done that bit,' Victoria managed to snap.

'Yes! Um, okay. Well, great. I'll just . . .' Coco couldn't finish the sentence; she emptied her champagne in one long gulp and dashed away instead.

Victoria didn't see where Coco went, didn't care one iota, had actually forgotten that Coco existed the moment she disappeared into the teeming crowd. Her face, as immobile as a mask, swivelled in the direction of the French doors that led out onto the terrace. Only her eyes were alive, bright with speculation.

I want so much to believe what Coco's saying, I'm scared it could be some sort of trap to make me give myself away.

But that isn't Coco's style. Not at all. If it came from someone else – Mireille, Clemence, Dietrich – then I'd be very wary. I wouldn't believe a word until I had had it corroborated by someone I could trust.

But despite how angry I am with her right now, one of the people I do trust to keep a secret of mine is Coco. If she says someone's discreet, she should know; in all the time she worked for me, she didn't breathe a word about anything she organised for me. Not even the smallest, most minor detail.

So maybe, just maybe, she's telling the truth. And maybe, Mireille was lying at the Valentino exhibit when she said that Lykke had told her about my being pregnant . . .

Victoria was moving towards the terrace. She couldn't help it. Her feet were doing it for her, had made their own decision. People tried to stop her as she wove through the crowd, smiled to catch her attention, called her name, wanting to talk to her, but she just kept going, pretending she didn't notice, ignoring even a hand laid on her arm by Jacob himself.

The fresh night air of a Parisian September evening, soft and velvety, was deliciously refreshing after the closely-packed atmosphere inside L'Arc, even though it was more than tinged with smoke – no gathering of fashionistas was complete without large groups of skinny people dragging incessantly on their cigarettes to dull their hunger pangs. The terrace was a prow, pushing out on a promontory overlooking the Arc de Triomphe, whose elaborately-carved marble pediment, illuminated pale gold against the black night, was visible over the high silvered walls. Brilliant green uplighters flooded dramatically up the sides, around the chrome outdoor bar, casting eerie pools of neon light and – very importantly – providing areas of darkness where habitués could lurk in relative privacy.

Victoria kept to the shadows, ensuring that her very recognisable face was never lit up by one of the jade-green spotlights. Slipping between tables, she worked her way over to where she could see Lykke, leaning against the square tip of the prow, a glass in her hand, half-concealed by one of the ball-topped topiary trees that softened the sharp edges of the terrace. It was only when Victoria was almost beside her that she realised with excitement that Lykke was all alone.

And then, the opportunity that Victoria had craved was suddenly overwhelming. Lykke was so close, close enough to touch, if she reached out her arm; she was by herself, utterly unusual at a fashion party, where a model would normally be surrounded by admirers. It was so perfect that Victoria stopped in her tracks, paralysed with anticipation.

Lykke's head turned, like a white chrysanthemum on a stem. Her eyes widened as she took in the sight of Victoria, who had so stringently avoided her for months, now deliberately seeking her out.

Victoria was tongue-tied. Lykke's proximity was dazzling, the play of light and shadow on her face from the pale green lighting flickering through the leaves of the tree like a series of fashion photographs, haunting and beautiful. Lykke regarded Victoria with her customary gravity, her pupils dilated; only the swift rise and fall of her narrow ribcage, visible through her clinging silk blouse, betrayed that she was agitated by Victoria's presence.

'I wanted to talk to you,' Victoria managed to say eventually.

'You are not worried by what people will say?' Lykke asked seriously.

Instinctively, Victoria stepped towards her, bringing most of her body into the shelter of the tree, rendering her almost invisible to the other guests on the terrace.

'I am,' she confessed honestly. 'But I wanted to talk to you anyway.'

'So,' Lykke said. She had moved backwards a little, making space for Victoria in the little niche formed by the angle of the tree and the terrace wall. But it was also, Victoria knew, because Lykke didn't want to be that close to Victoria: not yet. Not until she had heard what Victoria had to say.

'I thought it was you who told everyone I was pregnant,' Victoria blurted out. 'And that you and I were together in St Louis. That's why I've been avoiding you. I thought I couldn't trust you.'

Lykke's eyes dilated still further. Even in this dim light, Victoria knew their colouring so well that she could see, perfectly, the dark ring around the light-blue irises deepen in shock.

'No!' Lykke breathed. 'No, I promise you, it is not true. Never – I would never speak about you, not at all. I have not said a word!'

'I believe you.' Victoria moved closer, till their bodies were separated by barely a few inches. 'I should have known you wouldn't say anything.'

'Why would you even *think*—'

'It was Mireille.' Victoria was keeping her voice down, but now she lowered it to a whisper. 'At the Valentino party in New York, just after you and I talked.' Her body felt suffused with heat at the memory of Lykke's words to her at FIT. 'She told me you'd come up to her and said I was pregnant – and then I heard some *Vogue* girls talking about me and you in St Louis, so I assumed that had come from you as well.'

She reached out for Lykke's hand. 'I'm so sorry,' she said, her voice choked. 'I should have known you wouldn't do anything like that.'

For a brief, intoxicating moment, Lykke's long fingers wound through hers, and Victoria's bones began to melt with excitement. And then, with a swift pull, Lykke withdrew her hand again; Victoria gasped at the feeling of rejection.

'I can't . . .' Lykke drew in a long, shuddering breath. 'I must confess to you. I must tell you something first.'

'Oh God!' Victoria actually trembled from head to toe, fearing some awful revelation. Mad speculations tumbled through her brain: Lykke's in a relationship with Inge Kavanaugh – no, worse, they're engaged. And I don't care! she thought frantically. No matter how bad it is, I don't care! As long as Lykke's forgiven me, as long as she still wants to be with me, I don't care what she's about to tell me.

'My coming to see you, at *Style*,' Lykke was saying quietly. 'It was not chance. It was planned. Did you not think it was strange? When does a model come like that for a go-see with the editor of the magazine? Never.'

'But you were supposed to see Mireille, and she was delayed, and there was some mess-up with Clemence and Dietrich, so . . .' Victoria's voice tailed off as she took in the import of what Lykke was telling her.

Lykke nodded. 'It was Mireille,' she admitted. 'She told me, "Victoria will like you. You must meet her, alone in her office, you must show her your book." So she arranged it. I think perhaps she arranged it with your assistant, but I am not sure.'

Victoria's mouth had fallen open; she was gaping like a fish, completely gobsmacked. 'She said that I'd like you?' she repeated, amazed. 'How would she know that?'

'I don't know.' Lykke's shoulders rose and fell, signifying equal bafflement. 'But she knew that *I* liked *you*. That I found you very attractive,' she corrected herself.

'How would she know that?'

Lykke hung her head in embarrassment. 'I have said it, before,' she confessed. 'At a fashion party, last year. We were in a group, talking, and someone said your name, and I said, "Oh, she is such a beautiful woman." You know,' she added in parenthesis, 'it is not a secret that I am a lesbian. I said: "She is just the kind of woman I find most attractive, that I would like to be with." I had maybe had a few glasses of champagne,' she acknowledged. 'But I did not say it disrespectfully – just that I found you very beautiful. And then, much later, this year, Mireille calls me in to see her, and she says, "Lykke, I know you would like to be on the cover of the magazine, very much, and I think too that Victoria Glossop would like to put you on the cover. And I think she will like you." So I am surprised, because I never hear that you are the same as me, that you like women. But I am very excited to meet you – and not just to meet you, to be alone with you, if Mireille will organise that. So I take the opportunity.'

She reached out for Victoria's hand, and Victoria did not draw hers away.

'Please forgive me?' Lykke asked in a soft murmur. 'You know that what we do together is because I want to do it, because I want you. Not because I want the cover. You know that it's real. I was scared to tell you, because you might think it wasn't real. But I can't pretend like that. For me, sex is very important. I can't pretend with sex, I can't do what I don't want to do. And,' her hand tightened around Victoria's, 'I have never felt like this before. I promise. *Never*.'

'I haven't either,' Victoria whispered, her fingers now clinging to Lykke's. 'But how could Mireille know? I was never with a woman before . . . how could she know?'

'She's like a witch,' Lykke said, her shoulders lifting and falling again. 'She sees things about people – things sometimes they don't know themselves.'

Victoria nodded. *It's as if Mireille reads my mind sometimes.*

'But I'm glad,' Lykke said. 'Even if she told you a lie, that I said you were pregnant—'

'I don't believe it.' Victoria's voice was heartfelt; the two women were moving closer and closer, almost breast to breast now.

'– I'm still glad, because she brought us together.' Lykke's breath was warm on Victoria's lips now. 'Even if you never want to be with me again, I'm grateful for that. It was the most beautiful thing that has ever happened to me.'

Victoria parted her lips to say, 'For me too,' but as they opened, Lykke's mouth was on hers, Lykke's tongue tracing the contours of her soft, damp skin, and all thoughts of speaking swept from her mind. Eagerly, she threw her arms around Lykke's neck, dragged her body close, frustrated only by her bump, which meant that not every inch of them could touch. But Lykke's hands slid down, cradling the sides of Victoria's swollen stomach, stroking her with such tenderness that Victoria felt as if an extra flood of relaxin had been released into her lower body, inundating her.

'It's been so long!' she moaned into Lykke's mouth. 'I've missed you so much!'

'Too long.' Lykke showered her mouth with tiny kisses. 'I've thought of you every day – thought of you growing, feeling the baby, wanting to touch you, to see how your body's changing, your breasts, your taste.'

Victoria was sure her entire body was suffused with red now. 'Lykke,' she protested feebly, clinging to her lover.

'But I want to taste you!' Lykke said fiercely. 'You want it too! To lick you, to see how you taste now, to kiss your breasts.' She hugged Victoria as tightly as she could, with the bump between them. 'To look after you, protect you and the baby. To have you be mine. I would do anything for you, Victoria. I would make sure no one could hurt you. I would always defend you, stand by you. If people tell lies about us, even Mireille, though she made us meet, I would stop her. I would never let anyone damage or hurt you. Victoria, I love you—'

'Victoria? My God!'

The voice from behind her wasn't loud: it was a stunned exclamation, not a shout. But it cut through Victoria's delirious haze of excitement like a cold bucketful of water tipped over her head. Wrenching herself away from Lykke, she swung round to see her husband, standing not two feet away from them.

'*Jeremy!*' she exclaimed in horror. 'What are you doing here?'

Green light picked out her husband's curly hair, flashed on his glasses as he stared disbelievingly at his wife, caught in the embrace of another woman.

'I came over to surprise you,' he said, his voice a thin thread. 'You've just got one more day of shows, so I thought we could grab some time together in Paris – have a romantic night out before the baby comes.'

Victoria's head swam. She actually thought for a moment that she might faint. Reaching out for support, she found Lykke's hand, and she clung to it like a life-raft.

'I've been looking everywhere at the party for you,' Jeremy was babbling, 'and then someone said they saw you going out to the terrace. I couldn't find you, I thought you'd gone home, but then I heard a voice that sounded like yours, and I thought it couldn't be – what would you be doing, hiding right at the back here?'

Jeremy's voice was thick with what sounded like imminent tears.

'Vicky, what are you doing?' he finished hopelessly. 'What on earth is going on?' He looked at Lykke. 'And who the hell is *this*?'

Mireille

Le Cirque restaurant was a New York legend. It had opened in the mid-seventies on 65th Street at the Mayfair Hotel: Frank Sinatra, Sophia Loren and Luciano Pavarotti, the Kennedy clan and Ronald Reagan had all been regulars. Elizabeth Taylor had come there to squabble with Richard Burton; Nixon and Kissinger had famously lunched there to bury the hatchet. Le Cirque's move to Madison and 51st, as Le Cirque 2000, had been considered a mis-step, but it was now triumphantly ensconced in a custom-built space in the Bloomberg Tower, a glowing glass ceiling rising like the circus tent after which the restaurant was named over the dining space below. Sirio Maccioni, its voluble, charming Italian owner, liked to say that the history of Le Cirque was the history of the last forty years of New York itself, and certainly politicians and agents still flocked to the third Le Cirque to broker deals. Donald Trump and Ivana Trump were often to be seen there – though not together; Woody Allen, Joans Rivers and Collins, past and present mayors of New York City.

But the film stars were aging, and thinner on the ground. East 58th Street was no longer fashionable; it incarnated money now, not trendiness. The young hip movie actors and musicians went to Da Silvano, Il Cantinori, Periyali, Pastis, downtown restaurants where the food was indifferent and the prices sky-high. But since none of them actually ate a bite, preferring to push their food around desultorily in between nipping to the toilet for a line of coke or the sidewalk for a cigarette, the quality of the cooking was unimportant: the important thing was to see and be seen.

Whereas at Le Cirque, the food was never less than spectacularly good. And once Jacob had given his loyalty to a place – or a person – he never withdrew it. He had been lunching with Mireille at Le Cirque for nearly thirty years, and in late autumn, he always, without exception, ordered the risotto that was the seasonal speciality of the restaurant, made with white truffles flown over from Alba in Italy. He was emitting moans of appreciation as he forked up the buttery, Parmesan-coated grains of Arborio rice topped with paper-thin slices of truffle.

Mireille, naturally, wouldn't have dreamed of ordering anything that fattening: she had chosen a starter of sliced, marinated tuna with a tomato gelée and rocket sorbet. Le Cirque had been home to many chefs who had made their reputations in its kitchen, but Sirio Maccioni had always known that the key to keeping its distinguished clientele was to instruct his cooks to provide rich food for the gentlemen, and equally light dishes for the ladies who barely lunched.

Mireille glanced with amusement at Jacob's visible enjoyment of his risotto, which the sommelier had paired with a glass of crisp white Gavi dei Gavi.

'Ah, Jacob,' she said, cutting off a small piece of almost-raw tuna and scooping the calorie-free tomato gelée onto it. 'Do you know what I am thinking, *mon cher*? That if your women ate the same food that you allow yourself, they would not remain your women for very long.'

Putting the tuna into her mouth, she chewed it with slow, deliberate motions, making each bite last as long as possible. It was a trick dancers used, to eat only a little but cheat yourself into feeling that you had had more; Jacob had seen her do it, decades ago, and been impressed.

I'm sure he's taught it to all the girls who came after me, she thought wryly.

Jacob looked up, his fork, loaded with truffle risotto, momentarily suspended halfway to his mouth, his face a comic caricature of disbelief.

'It's fine,' Mireille said with even more amusement. 'Continue, please.' She sipped some fizzy water. 'I merely observe that the double standard is alive and well at this table.'

'I work out with Brad three times a week,' Jacob protested. 'Plus I play tennis every Saturday. My yearly work-up with Dr Kreizner was great this year – my bloodwork's in tip-top shape.'

'I am very glad to hear it,' Mireille said; she was holding her water glass, and she raised it to him in a mock toast. 'Long may that last.'

'You love to break my balls,' Jacob grumbled cheerfully, undeterred by her mockery, forking up more risotto. 'For thirty years, you've been breaking my balls.'

'Moh.' Mireille shrugged elegantly. 'Everyone must have a hobby, *n'est-ce pas*?'

Jacob grinned at her and she smiled back at him; it was a mutual look of perfect and absolute understanding.

'I didn't have any bread,' he said virtuously, finishing off his risotto. 'Did you notice? I'm cutting back.'

'*Très bien*,' Mireille said with teasing approval.

Jacob reached for his wine glass. 'It's Coco, really,' he said. 'I don't have bread on the table any more. It's her weakness. She says she finds it a hell of a lot easier if she doesn't see me eating it.'

Mireille's plucked eyebrows shot up. 'Most thoughtful of you,' she observed.

'She's trying real hard,' Jacob continued, his expression softening into a mush of sentiment, as it always did when he talked about Coco. 'I'm very proud of her. Brad's putting her through hell, and she never complains. He says she's the pluckiest girl he's ever trained.'

'Coco is certainly determined when she wants something,' Mireille commented, pushing her half-finished starter away to indicate to the deferentially-hovering waiter that she had finished.

'You're not going to eat the rest of that?' Jacob asked.

Mireille rolled her eyes expressively. 'You know it is a rule with me never to finish a plate of food,' she said. 'No matter what it is.'

'It looks so good, though! Hey, hang on a minute.' Jacob reached over and speared a piece of tuna, dipping it into the melting rocket sorbet. 'Mmn, excellent!' he said. 'Melts in your mouth. I wish you could teach Coco never to finish her food,' he added wistfully. 'I told her you do that, and she nearly bit my head off. Okay, you're good to go,' he added in a friendly tone to the waiter, who promptly whipped the plate away.

'Coco is hungry all the time,' Mireille said, sitting back in the circular booth that ran around the entire arc of the dining room. 'I can assure you of that. You are lucky she did not truly bite your head off and try to eat it.'

Jacob laughed, sitting back too as their plates were cleared. A wine waiter bustled over, removing his empty white wine glass, replacing it with the larger red wine glass: Brunello, to accompany his entrée.

'She's looking so good, though,' he said happily. 'So beautiful! I think she's only got five pounds to go till she's perfect. I got her this amazing Chanel dress in Paris – couture, of course. Made to her ideal measurements. I told her, "When you get into that, you'll have your first couture piece. First of many".'

'Jacob,' Mireille said cautiously, 'Coco is already extremely thin. You are aware of that, *n'est-ce pas*? You know, some girls are not meant through nature to be a size zero. They are built differently. Their bones are not tiny. They may starve themselves, but they will never be really small.' She looked a little sad. 'I have seen many talented dancers realise that their frames will not allow them to be prima ballerinas. They leave for modern dance, which is more . . . accommodating.'

But Jacob, clearly, was not listening to her.

'I'm over the moon, Mireille,' he said, beaming happily. 'She's such a bright girl! You know, she talks back to me. She doesn't let me have it all my own way.'

Then why is she starving herself to please you? Mireille thought, but did not say. There was no point. I tried, she told herself. I have made an effort, and now my conscience is clear.

'And she's making such a success of *Mini Style*,' he continued, his smile even wider. 'She fought me on the name, you know? Said I hired her because she was in touch with the younger generation, so I had to trust her on what to call the magazine. And guess what, she was right! We're killing *Teen Vogue* already at the newsstands, and subscriptions are already really healthy, considering we've only put out two issues.'

Mireille nodded. 'It is indeed a great success so far,' she agreed.

'She's a pistol,' Jacob said contentedly, his eyes misting at the thought of Coco. Companionably, he put his arm over Mireille's shoulders. No one observing them would have thought that the charismatic, fifty-something man was confiding in the elegant, fifty-something woman about his pride in his twenty-something girlfriend.

'You know, I thought it would be Zarina that you would choose,' Mireille said consideringly. 'I saw you notice her; I thought she had sparked your interest.'

'Zarina?' Jacob looked blank. 'There are so many girls,' he confessed, a little shamefaced. 'And they're all so pretty.'

'My assistant! With the long dark hair and excellent eyebrows,' Mireille reproved him. 'Zarina de Ruiter. If I am not mistaken, you took her out to dinner at least once.'

'Oh, yes.' Jacob's brow cleared as he remembered the girl in question. 'Very pretty – and very smart,' he added appreciatively. 'We hit it off. But . . .' he hesitated. 'She was already so polished, do you see? She knows everyone there is to know in New York already. A Vassar girl, right?'

'She comes from a very good family,' Mireille agreed. 'The de Ruiters were among the first Dutch settlers – part of Mrs Astor's Four Hundred.'

'My point exactly!' Jacob spread his hands wide. 'She didn't need me. She had everything already. Now Coco – I can give her a real cultural and social education. I'm taking her to the Met, to the ballet at Lincoln Centre, to private views. Venice for Carnival in January, Wagner in Bayreuth. Skiing in Verbier and Aspen – did you know she's never even skied before?' He pantomimed shock and horror.

'That poor deprived child,' Mireille said dryly. 'How has she survived all these years?' Poor child, indeed, she thought more genuinely. At her age she should be dancing in downtown clubs, jumping in swimming pools on the top of LA hotels, not being dragged to the Ring Cycle in Bayreuth with a bunch of opera-goers old enough to be her grandparents.

But, one must remember, the girl has gained her own magazine out of her association with Jacob. And she will be travelling the world in five-star luxury. A few years, and Jacob will have tired of her. She will be free to see someone her own age, and he will spend some years working his way through the latest crop of young models, eventually choosing another young woman to mentor.

'This time it's different,' Jacob was saying, his eyes agleam. 'Mireille, I have something very important to tell you.'

Two waiters arrived at the table, each bearing a plate which they presented and then laid in front of Mireille and Jacob with the veneration of priests placing holy items before devout worshippers.

'You are certainly celebrating,' Mireille said. 'Tournedos Rossini, no less.'

'Tenderloin with foie gras for the *signore*,' Jacob's waiter murmured reverentially. 'With a *millefeuille* of carrots, honey and pepper.'

'And for the *signora*, turbot with ginger and herbs, accompanied by Swiss chard, tomato and Japanese mushrooms,' Mireille's waiter chimed in. 'The citrus vinaigrette is on the side, *signora*, as you requested.'

'*Grazie*,' Mireille said, as the waiters faded away from the table with deferential nods.

'I'm going to marry her!' Jacob announced, raising his glass of Brunello. He looked at Mireille's glass of water and shook his head, clicking his fingers to summon back one of the waiters. 'You can't toast with water. Champagne for the lady!' he said. 'Krug, I think.'

'*Signor*, we do not serve Krug by the glass,' a wine waiter said apologetically, materialising instantly by the table.

'Then bring us a bottle!' Jacob bellowed cheerfully. 'And two glasses!'

He had managed the extremely rare feat of silencing Mireille: she sat there, lips parted in sheer disbelief, until the champagne arrived, was ceremoniously opened and poured. Jacob turned to look at her, and saw her expression: he picked up the glasses and gave one to her.

Its warmth, its reassurance, brought Mireille out of the shock into which she had sunk. She took the glass and lifted it to his, clinking in a toast.

'Jacob—' she began, after she had taken a long pull at the glass.

But he interrupted her swiftly, his hand still on her thigh. 'Nothing will change between us,' he reassured her, his eyes serious. 'I promise you that. We'll still have our lunches together. You'll still be my confidante, my oldest friend – my dear, dear Mireille. *Je te promets, mon amour. Toujours*.'

Mireille was mortified to realise that she was blinking back tears. She tilted her head fractionally, placing her hand on top of Jacob's.

'Your French accent is execrable, *mon cher*,' she said, managing to smile. 'It never improves. Well.' She drank some more Krug. 'I must congratulate you. I must admit, I never thought this would happen. Not in a million years.'

'Me neither.' Jacob was grinning boyishly. 'But that's not all – you'll never believe this. I want to have kids!'

Mireille almost dropped her glass. She couldn't help herself; she burst out laughing. She wasn't amused, not in the slightest: it was sheer amazement.

'I know, right.' Jacob was positively gleeful. 'I swore up and down I wouldn't ever have kids! But hey, you get older, you start to think about the legacy you're going to leave . . .'

His hand left Mireille's thigh; he picked up his steak knife and started to slice into his tournedos with gusto.

'Coco's young, she's healthy, she's bright as a whip. She's a career woman,' he said. 'That's really important to me. I don't want one of these stay-at-home wives, with their charity lunches – they're all drunks and Valium addicts. What kind of role model would that be if we have daughters?' His expression went mushy again. 'A little girl. How cool would that be?'

'But, Jacob . . .' Mireille was beginning to feel dizzy, as if this man, whom she had known for more than thirty years, had been taken over by aliens. 'Does Coco *want* to have children? She's only twenty-four.'

'Twenty-five in a week,' Jacob said through a mouthful of steak and foie gras.

'Still, that's so young nowadays for a career girl. They wait until their thirties to have children, usually. I assume you're going to leave it for a while?'

'No way. I want to get started now!' Jacob said happily. 'I thought a June wedding – five months to organise, that's tons of time if I throw money at any problems that pop up – and then we can start making babies straight away. I know Coco won't want to be pregnant at her wedding,' he added.

No, you don't want Coco to be pregnant at the wedding

because you want a thin-as-a-stick bride, Mireille thought cynically.

'And that's another reason for her to get her weight down now,' he said ingenuously, as he forked up the tender, fatty tenderloin, the plump, rich foie gras. 'So it'll be easier for her to stay slim even when she's pregnant. Look at how well Victoria's doing.'

'Jacob, Coco is not a doll,' Mireille protested. 'I'm sorry, but it must be said! You are taking a clever girl, a career girl, one who is not a natural size zero, and trying to make her into something she is not. Are you sure she even *wants* children? Have you asked her?'

She looked down at her turbot with something near disgust; she couldn't have eaten a mouthful. The hovering waiter refilled her champagne flute, and very unusually for her, she let him.

'Oh, she's not like you, Mireille,' Jacob said. 'I know you never wanted kids. Your art was your children – isn't that what you always liked to say? But she's really tight with her family. Nice group of people, by all accounts. She's a family girl. She's definitely going to want kids.'

Mireille paused until she had regained full control of herself: it was a heroic effort. Drawing in a deep breath, she tried one more time.

'Jacob,' she began, 'you want to marry, to have children . . .' She couldn't quite believe the words she was saying, but she pressed on anyway. '*Très bien*! So marry! Have children! But pick a girl who wants to be a trophy wife – a gallery assistant, a PR girl, a model with brains. Not this one. She's truly ambitious. To her, a career is the most important thing in her life right now. Not something that she does while she is waiting for a rich man to propose.'

'I love that she's ambitious,' Jacob beamed. 'I don't want some gallery girl, I want someone who's going to make a success in her own right. Like you,' he said fondly. 'Like Victoria. My girls. My strong, successful girls.'

He set down his cutlery and looked at her, full in the face.

'I'm ready, Mireille,' he said simply. 'You know? I'm finally ready to settle down. Get a townhouse, or a big condo on Central Park West. Leave Fifth Avenue. I'm ready,' he repeated.

Mireille smiled wistfully. 'Women worry so much,' she said softly, 'about whether a man will marry them or not. What they do not understand is that a man will decide that he is ready to settle down, and then the next girl he meets will become the one he proposes to. If women could realise that, they would stress themselves so much less. So often, it is a simple matter of time and of fate.'

Jacob heaved a deep sigh, leaned forward, and kissed her on the cheek.

'Thank you, honey. Thank you for understanding. I've got lawyers on it already,' he said. 'Sorting out all the paperwork. No pre-nup, believe it or not. They're screaming, but I'm an old romantic. I'm in this for life. And hell . . .' He shungged. 'I'll be gone long before she is.'

He stroked Mireille's cheek where he had kissed her.

'I'll always be here for you,' he said gently. 'You'll never have to worry about a thing. The apartment's in your name. And I'm settling a lump sum on you as well.'

'Jacob!' she exclaimed. 'That really isn't necessary.'

He shook his head: 'I insist.' He looked at Mireille, and for the first time, he seemed anxious. 'She's a good girl,' he said. 'A really good girl. You like her, don't you, Mireille? It's so important to me that you like her.'

Mireille hesitated for a moment. *How important is my approval, truly? If I say I don't really like Coco, don't trust her, will that put a spanner in the works?* She thought of Coco, pictured her walking down the aisle to meet Jacob in the silk, bias-cut Vera Wang dress that all New York upper-crust trophy wives favoured, to show off the slim figures which had caught them a rich older husband. But Coco would be, not slim, but gaunt as a fever victim, letting a man older than her own father slide a ring on her bony finger . . .

The temptation to lie was huge, the image before her eyes more than distressing. She looked at Jacob, who was beginning to frown now with concern at what her answer would be.

Speculations, calculations, raced through her clever brain. But eventually, Mireille decided: *I will keep it simple. I will tell the truth*.

'I do, Jacob,' she assured him, slowly. 'I like her very much indeed.'

Coco

'So *this* is what you do all day, Jodie!'

Tiff stared around at the scene in front of her: three skinny teenage models, in pleated skirts, ankle boots and tiny striped sweaters, jumping on mini-trampolines set up in the lobby of the Brooklands Hotel. The Art Deco design was breathtaking; a huge twisted silver sculpture hung from the ceiling, between two equally huge light fixtures that were perfect Deco tortoiseshell discs. Daylight flooded in from the double-height glass entrance wall. The photographer was up a long ladder, shooting the girls through the sculpture as they jumped, their limbs thrown wide, but artfully fixing into dramatically elegant compositions, their expressions lively, excited, youthful.

'Tanisha! More fizz with the arms!' the photographer yelled across at the girl on the central trampoline.

'It's fun,' Tiff said, impressed.

Coco laughed. 'It *looks* fun,' she corrected. 'Did you see the shots we got earlier? The girls racing the vintage cars? Or them with Concorde?'

Brooklands, in Surrey, was the first purpose-built motor-racing circuit in the world, and the glass-fronted hotel had been set, dramatically, right next to the original track. Its wings reached out for ideal viewing, from its balconies, of the vintage car rallies and motorsport festivals hosted by the Brooklands Museum. A Concorde airplane in the museum had provided an excellent backdrop for shots earlier that day. By contrast, Mercedes-Benz World, at right-angles to the hotel, was a showcase for the very latest cars on the market. Jacob, together with Coco and Tiff's father and brother, was out there right now, roaring up and down the speed track and sliding round a wet-skid circuit with great enthusiasm.

'Nah, I was in the spa,' Tiff said. 'See my face?' She shoved her head forward at her sister. 'Like a baby's bum! I went and sat in the Jacuzzi, did you see that? It's like this big wooden barrel, outside on that big balcony at the top of the hotel. You can see all the cars on the track, and there's this whole off-road hill thing over the side as well, where all these twats are going round in jeeps, getting stuck in tiny little water puddles – I laughed my head off, watching them fuck up! Practically boiled myself like a lobster. But it's really nice up there, Coco. You should go. All cold outside and the water's really hot. It's like being in one of them hot springs in Iceland.'

'I won't get a chance today,' Coco started, but Tiff was unstoppable.

'And then I had a facial. Get this – they're all designed by Jo Malone's sister! You know, the one that does those really posh oils and things? The sister's, like, this famous facialist. Fancy or what? Skin plumping, the girl said it was. Feel my cheek – go on, feel it.'

Coco stroked Tiff's cheek, which did feel incredibly soft and plump.

'Lovely. Where's Mum?' Coco asked, biting nervously at the cold sore she was sure was developing on her inner lip.

She felt consumed with stress. On paper, it had seemed like a perfect scenario: she had flown over to the UK to do a shoot for *Mini Style* at this extraordinary location conveniently close to London. The PR that Dupleix worked with, Katharine Walsh, the beautiful blonde, rake-thin, By Malene Birger-wearing reigning queen of London's publicity girls, also represented a small group of luxury, boutique hotels. Katharine had taken Coco to Brooklands while she'd been in London in September for Fashion Week, and Coco had immediately spotted how perfect the location would be, with its fabulous Deco furnishings, its cars and its Concorde, for a youthful, fast-moving photo spread. She'd learned so much from Victoria. This shoot would be called *Need For Speed*, the photos fashionably blurred with motion.

But then Jacob, hearing that she was off to London, had decided to come along, saying that this would be the perfect opportunity for him to meet the whole Raeburn family.

And that would have been manageable, Coco thought, if he hadn't heard that we were shooting right next to a racetrack, and got his assistant to check out Mercedes-Benz World and the hotel, and insisted on inviting everyone to stay overnight in the best suites, as his guests, and booked Dad and Craig in for driving experiences and Mum and Tiff for spa treatments . . .

And now it's like everyone's talking to me at once, and I can't focus on anything properly. My head feels as if it's going to explode, I'm starving hungry and I'm not due another energy bar for two hours.

Tiff was chattering away, but Coco didn't hear a word.

'Tiff, could you just pop to the bar and get me a double diet tonic?' she asked, cutting in. Sugar was out, of course, but she was allowed the next best thing, and she needed a hit of sweetener really badly. 'It's just through there. Put it on the magazine's tab.'

She indicated the bar, just off the hotel lobby, floored in rich dark wood, anchored by a long, double-sided leather booth in matching dark brown leather, five spectacular, gleaming silver propellers rising from the centre. It was stunning, a triumph of interior design. Coco would have loved to photograph in there, but it was *Mini Style* she was shooting for, and there was no way she could set a shoot for a teen magazine in a bar, even if the bar itself didn't appear. American advertisers were unbelievably strict.

'And Tiff – I'm Coco now,' she added. 'I didn't choose it, but it's what everyone calls me now, and actually, I quite like it.'

Tiff pulled a face. 'It's weird,' she complained. 'And it freaks Mum and Dad out.'

'Well, they'll have to suck it up,' Coco heard herself snap. 'There's nothing I can do about it, and they're being put up in a stunning hotel, all expenses paid, treated like royalty – if all they have to do is call me Coco instead of Jodie, it's not much to ask in return, is it?'

Coco's voice had risen much higher than she'd meant it to: the last thing she'd intended was to have a public squabble with her sister while supervising a shoot for her magazine. Out of the corner of her eye, she could see heads turning – not just the people on the *Mini Style* shoot, but the reception staff as well were staring.

Tiff looked stunned. 'Well! There's no need to get shirty,' she said huffily. 'I'll go and get your tonic.'

'*Diet* tonic,' Coco corrected swiftly. *Oh my God*, she thought in horror, as Tiff stalked away to the bar. *I sounded just like Victoria then*.

'Coco? Want to take a look at these last ones?' the photographer called, descending the stepladder, which was being held for her by a couple of minions. 'I think we've got it. Fantastic stuff. And the light's almost gone, anyway,' she added hopefully.

This was the last set-up of the day: Coco felt a wave of exhaustion sweep over her. They had been working since first thing that morning, and she had been run ragged supervising every detail of the shoot, while simultaneously keeping Jacob happy, welcoming her family to the hotel and making sure they checked into their suites and were introduced to Jacob—

Oh God. My boyfriend, meeting my parents. That was one of the most uncomfortable moments of my life. Worse even than my first interview with Victoria. The Raeburn family had been assembled in the lobby, waiting to meet their host before the men departed for their slot at Mercedes-Benz World and the women their appointments at the spa. Coco was keeping one eye on her BlackBerry and one on the huge glass doors, waiting to see Jacob's limo pull up outside; but she hadn't realised that he wasn't coming from London by car. The helicopter had circled dramatically in a loop past the hotel, over the historic old Brooklands racetrack, drawing oohs of appreciation from Mr Raeburn and Craig, who had stood up to get a better view.

'Not every day you see a helicopter landing almost next to you, is it?' Coco's father had said appreciatively, as the feather-light, bright blue Twin Squirrel set down on the Mercedes-Benz World airstrip. 'Must be some real bigwig coming in.'

Oh no, Coco had thought hopelessly, dreading what was to come; *as if the contrast wasn't going to be bad enough* . . .

Despite its being only a few minutes' walk, a car had been laid on to drive Jacob from the airstrip to the hotel. He was in and out in thirty seconds, smoothing down his hair as he stepped out of the limo, a gofer following him, pulling his suit-cases out of the boot and loading them onto a cart. He had flown in overnight from New York to London, gone straight to the office for meetings, and then, obviously, charted a helicop-ter to pop to Surrey for an afternoon of driving and dinner, but he looked fresh as a daisy; first-class travel and accommodation were infinitely more relaxing than the economy versions. He was wearing the international businessman's off-duty uniform of chinos, a cashmere sweater, and Gucci loafers: casual, comfortable and clearly extremely expensive.

'Ooh!' Mrs Raeburn had commented, her eyes lighting up as Jacob strode into the hotel. 'Now that's a man who's ageing well. He reminds me a bit of George Clooney. Nice. Why don't you take care of yourself like that, Brian?'

'Mum! Gross,' Tiff complained, as Coco writhed, realising that the penny hadn't dropped. She had told her family that Jacob was older, the head of the company, but she hadn't had the nerve to give his exact age. Clearly, her mother, eyeing up Jacob with open enthusiasm, had no idea that she was actually talking about her daughter's boyfriend.

'Honey!' Jacob caught sight of Coco, and opened his arms wide. 'Here you are, all ready and waiting!'

She couldn't run into his arms, not in front of her family; not when they were all turning to gawk at her, four faces all with exactly the same dumbfounded, uncomprehending expression. She compromised by walking swiftly towards him and giving him a hug. Jacob insisted on kissing her, though, and on keeping one arm around her as he extended the other hand to the Raeburns in welcome. They were to come to him; he was the Master of the Universe, after all.

'It's so great to meet Coco's family,' Jacob beamed. His outstretched hand, nails buffed to a dull gleam, ten-thousand dollar Rolex dangling from its wrist, hovered in the air for a long, awkward moment before Craig elbowed his father frantically and Mr Raeburn, jolted into action, stepped forward to shake Jacob's hand.

'Very nice to meet you, I'm sure,' he said, barely able to meet Jacob's eyes. Like Jacob, Mr Raeburn was dressed in his best casual clothes – a check shirt belted into beige trousers, and a dark blue jacket – as advised by Coco, who had said to bring a suit for dinner. And as he and Jacob greeted each other, Coco firmly encircled in Jacob's embrace, the contrast between the two men could not have been more apparent. Jacob practically reeked affluence; Mr Raeburn's Sunday best from Debenhams did not. Jacob's aftershave was subtle and expensive; Mr Raeburn had dabbed a bit of Brut on his neck, at his wife's insistence. Mr Raeburn's shoes . . . but, recalling Victoria's comment on hers, Coco didn't dare to glance down at the contrast between Jacob's polished Guccis and her father's cheap leather high-street lace-ups.

The worst part, of course, was that the two men were almost the same age. Like most working-class couples, Brian and Sue Raeburn had started their family early; Craig was twenty-seven now, and the Raeburns were barely into their fifties.

Jacob's actually older than Dad, Coco realised for the first time, her heart sinking. But he looks – well, not younger, exactly, but so much more privileged. Close up, doing his best to smile at Jacob, her father's skin was windburned, prematurely aged from all the years of working outside, loading and unloading suitcases off airplanes and onto cargo belts, his hands chapped, his cuticles torn. Now that his job as supervisor meant less physical work, he had put on weight, and his belly hung over the waistband of his trousers.

Coco had always been proud of her father, his confidence in his work and at home, his role as the man of the house, the main provider. But next to Jacob Dupleix, head of an entire corporation, international business tycoon, multi-millionaire, one of the Masters of the Universe, it was inevitable that a baggage handling supervisor for Luton airport would look somewhat diminished by contrast.

'Lovely to meet you too, Mr Raeburn,' Jacob was saying with unabashed warmth. 'And you, Mrs Raeburn.'

Coco's mother, pink in the face, smoothing down the layered linen dress that she had run out to buy from Phase 8 for this occasion, came forward to be greeted by Jacob in her turn.

'It's a pleasure,' she said bravely.

'Coco talks so much about all of you,' Jacob said, smiling benevolently at all of them. 'Tiffany, Craig . . .'

Craig was pumping Jacob's hand now, using both hands, determined to make a good impression on behalf of the Raeburn men.

'Great entrance, mate,' he said. 'Landing in that helicopter. Nice one.'

Jacob was grinning now. 'Should be about time for us to get out on that racetrack, eh?' he said.

'Yeah! Can't wait to give it some welly!' Craig said enthusiastically.

'Craig means he likes to drive fast,' Coco said to Jacob, whose smooth brow – he Botoxed, but only very carefully – was trying to furrow in confusion.

'Cool! Know what, Craig? Me too! We should bring you along to translate, honey,' Jacob said, kissing the top of her head. 'Coco's so sharp, isn't she?' he said fondly to her parents. 'You raised a real live wire here.'

'Thank you,' Mrs Raeburn said, looking from her daughter to her daughter's boyfriend, her stare still bemused, as she slowly took in the reality of the situation, that Jacob, older than her husband, was complimenting her daughter as a boss would an employee, a teacher would a pupil.

Tiff, pushing forward to receive a kiss on the cheek from Jacob, was equally pink, equally dazed, but still as game as ever.

'Lovely to meet you,' she giggled. 'You're not at all what we were expecting, I can tell you. Mum thinks you look like a film star.'

'Tiff!' her mother snapped at her, outraged, going even redder.

'Thanks so much for having us here and everything,' Tiff went on, undaunted. 'It's well posh.'

Now it was Coco's turn to cringe, but Jacob had eaten this admiration up with a spoon.

'Is that good, honey?' he said, looking down at Coco. '*Well posh*? I sure hope so!'

His attempt at Tiff's accent was funny without being in the least offensive; like all Americans, he loved to imitate a British accent and could do either an exaggerated version of *Downton Abbey*, or 'Dick Van Dyke Cockney'. The second one, which he went for now, was so comical that all the Raeburns fell about laughing at his willingness to make a clown of himself, and the ice was finally broken.

The men disappeared back out for the driving session, the

women up to the spa, and Coco had had a few hours to get on with the job she was actually here for – hard as it was to concentrate, after the embarrassment and confusion that Jacob's meeting of the Raeburns had engendered. It was everything mixed into one; the powerful differences of class and of money, the even-more-powerful similarities of age, and, above all, the sheer gulf that had so obviously opened up between her life a year and a half ago, a struggling, underpaid assistant to a magazine editor, and her life now, editor of her very own magazine.

It was the gulf between Jodie and Coco.

Tiff never told me how Mum was getting on at the spa, Coco realised now, drawing in a long deep breath. I hope that went all right. Mum's not used to anything so posh – facials created by Jo Malone's sister, for goodness' sake! She'll have needed a lot of hand-holding and reassurance.

'Coco?' The photographer was standing by the stepladder, looking at her, holding out the digital camera. Everyone, in fact, was looking at her, their expressions identical: anticipation, carefully-veiled but nonetheless present.

They all want to go home, Coco knew. Back to London. They're all hoping I'll check out these ones and say that we're done for the day. She glanced at the Cartier watch Jacob had bought her for Christmas. Five already! Shit! Oh God, I so hope we're finished. We've been going at it since eight this morning . . .

'Here you go, madam,' her sister snapped, handing her a glass of diet tonic water. 'Hope it's to your satisfaction.'

She stumped off crossly, back to the bar; *off to start drinking,* Coco thought ruefully. *Great – by dinnertime she'll be plastered*.

The glass of water was brimming, and slopped on the toes of her boots as she hurried over to the waiting photographer. *Oh no, they're suede – my new Vuittons – damnit!*

Coco was close to tears, overwhelmed by the combination

of hugely-pressured work, everything riding on her shoulders, with the always-stressful situation of her boyfriend meeting her family.

Dinner tonight's going to be a total nightmare, Coco thought miserably, staring down at the damp patches on her boots. *Oh God, why did I ever let Jacob talk me into this?*

But a couple of hours later, over cocktails in the bar, Coco's mood had improved considerably. She had managed to visit the spa, and though their appointments schedule was booked solid, they turned out to have what they called a 'meditation room'. The sympathetic receptionist had taken one look at Coco's white, stressed face, its skin drawn much too tight over the bones, and led her there. Coco, dreading a yoga studio with mats and Pilates balls, had been hugely relieved to find instead a softly-lit room with glowing, deep-red walls, hypnotic, trance-like music playing, and three wide, deep beds, two of which were already occupied by people who seemed to be slumbering in perfect contentment. When she took her boots off and lay down on the third bed, she realised why: not only were they waterbeds, the water was heated to blood temperature.

She sank into the mattress, its warmth enveloping her through the sheets with which it was made up, the pillows equally soft below her head. The receptionist placed a pillow under her knees so that her legs could relax completely, covered her with a blanket and tiptoed from the room. The lights dipped from red to an equally-comforting purple, the music rose and fell: Coco closed her eyes in bliss and went out like a light. She would have been there still if Jacob, back in their suite, hadn't rung the spa to track down his girlfriend, and the receptionist hadn't slipped back in to gently shake Coco's shoulder and rouse her once more to the world of the wakeful.

God, that was lovely, Coco thought dreamily, sipping her

VLT. I wish I had a room like that in my apartment. Maybe one day . . .

'Those skids were brilliant!' Craig, her brother, was saying animatedly.

An afternoon spent tearing around the racetrack, shooting down a straight section at high speed while water fountained over both track and car from sprays positioned on each side, and sliding with great screeches of tyres around the equally wet skid pan, had successfully dissolved most of Craig's inhibitions around his sister's extremely sophisticated and wealthy older boyfriend. And the couple of pints he'd sunk already were helping with the final stages.

'Dad, did you see me?' he said to his father. 'I thought I was going to spin right off the sodding pan!'

'Yes, mate, I saw you,' Mr Raeburn said, rolling his eyes and smiling at Jacob in a 'boys will be boys' way. Coco's father seemed to have decided to cope with the fact that his daughter was dating a man probably five years older than his own fifty-one by treating him as a peer, rather than Coco's boyfriend.

'Honestly,' he said indulgently, still to Jacob, 'it's as if he's still seven years old, not twenty-seven. When he was a lad, he couldn't swing from the bars in the playground without yelling to make sure we were watching.'

Jacob beamed back. 'It must be great to have a son,' he said. 'Shoot hoops with him, throw a ball in the park.'

'Do you have any children, Mr Dupleix?' Coco's mother asked politely.

'Jacob, please!' he said, giving her his best, most charming smile. 'And no, I haven't been that fortunate. So far,' he added, squeezing Coco's leg where his hand, as usual, lay.

Mrs Raeburn followed his gesture with her eyes, and then looked up, taking in her daughter's face. The waterbed had helped, but Coco was still exhausted, her skin still taut over her bones, and a mother's eye couldn't fail to miss the weariness in Coco's expression.

'Are you all right, Jod— Coco?' she corrected herself, after a quick jerk in the ribs from her husband. 'Sorry, dear,' she apologised. 'I keep forgetting. It's just hard to call you something else, after all these years.'

'Oh, that's all right, Mum,' Coco said quickly, smiling at her mother. 'I know it'll take a while.'

Next to her, Tiff sniffed and muttered, 'Oh, so it's all right when *Mum* does it,' but Coco ignored her, continuing: 'And yes, I'm fine. Just a bit tired. You know, jet-lag – we only flew over yesterday, and I've had a whole shoot to coordinate today.'

Her mother sucked in a long, disapproving breath. Plump and pink-faced, like her husband and two other children, she looked well-fed and well-rested, her skin lovely and shiny from her afternoon facial and massage.

'Honestly, the way they work you in your job,' she tutted. 'I'm sure I'm sorry, Mr – Jacob – but ever since she went to London, we've barely seen her. And I miss her, I really do.' She leaned across the bar table to touch her daughter's hand affectionately. 'She's my baby, you know? We had all three of them very close together.' She giggled. 'Once we started, we couldn't stop! But though I love them all equally, I do miss my baby.'

'It's me working myself hard, Mum, not Jacob,' Coco said swiftly. 'And now I'm editing *Mini Style*' she blushed with pleasure, still not used to the thrill of announcing, casually, that she was the editor of a magazine, 'I'm going to be even busier for the next couple of years.'

'Oh no,' her mother said in distress. 'Really? I was hoping that now you're doing so well, we'd see a bit more of you. You weren't back for your birthday, or for Christmas.'

'Sue, give it a rest, love,' her husband said, elbowing her again. 'Coco doesn't want to hear you giving her a hard time, does she? Remember what I said – if you go on at her like this, she isn't going to fancy coming back any time soon, is she? Sorry, love,' he mouthed apologetically at his daughter.

'Well, why don't we host you all for Christmas next year?' Jacob offered expansively. 'I have a great chalet in Aspen. I'd love to fly you all over there for the holidays.'

'Cool,' Craig said happily.

'Where's Aspen?' Tiff asked.

'I'm sure that's very kind of you, Mr – Jacob,' Mrs Raeburn started, 'but really, I don't think—'

'Another round?' The handsome Italian waiter leaned over their table, smiling flirtatiously at Tiff, who lit up immediately, sitting up straighter and waggling her bosom at him; the cocktail she had just finished had been her third of the evening. 'Or would you like to go to your table, *signori*? It is all ready for you in the brasserie.'

'We're still waiting for my wife,' Craig said to him, lifting his glass. 'She's driving over after work – couldn't get away earlier. But I'll have another Peroni when you get a chance, mate.'

'I'd love another Italian Job,' Tiff said, giggling. 'Mum, you'll have another as well, won't you? Yummy! And that's not the only thing that's yummy round here.' She licked her lips at the waiter, who grinned back at her. 'What is it again?'

'Frangelico and Amaretto, *signorina*,' he said.

'Ooh, I'm not sure if I should have another one,' her mother said nervously. 'They're a bit strong. And Jacob's treating us, very kindly, but I don't want us to take advantage. Brian and I were thinking we should be getting dinner, really, all things considered.'

'Absolutely not! No way.' Jacob shook his head vehemently. 'I won't hear of it. You're all my guests here.'

'Jacob, I agree with Sue,' Brian Raeburn said bravely. 'You're being very kind, but I don't think it's right for us to let our daughter's boyfriend treat us like this. Dinner's going to be my shout.'

'Aw, Dad,' Craig said, rolling his eyes just like his father. 'Let the man pay if he wants. He's got tons of dosh!'

Mr and Mrs Raeburn looked absolutely horrified, but Jacob, to his credit, burst out laughing.

'You know what?' he said, looking at the assembled Raeburn family. 'I do have, uh, "tons of dosh". Hope I said that right!' He smiled at Craig. 'And Brian, I get how you're feeling. Believe me, I really do. But there's something you haven't heard yet.' He took Coco's hand in his, lifting it above the tabletop. 'I'm not just your daughter's boyfriend. I'm madly in love with her, head over heels, and if Coco does me the honour to accept my hand . . .'

'Oh my God!' Tiff squealed. 'He's only fucking *proposing*!'

'I'll be your son-in-law!' Jacob finished, taking Coco's other hand and pressing them together in his larger ones. 'How about it, honey? You know I love you to death. Say you'll make me the happiest man in the world! Oh, hang on . . .' He fumbled in his pocket and brought out a pale blue box.

'Aaah! *Tiffany*!' Tiff yelled, as Mrs Raeburn cooed, 'Ooh, that's lovely . . . isn't that lovely, Bri? Did you hear what he said?'

'Of course I heard it, Sue! I'm right here!'

'What's going on?' Craig's wife, Kelly, had arrived by now, and, spotting her husband and in-laws in a cluster over a bar table, had rushed over, not wanting to miss out on anything. 'Oh my God, will you look at the *size* of that thing!' she screamed, as Jacob clicked the box open with his thumb, revealing a gigantic princess-cut diamond. 'Is it *real*?'

'Course it's real, Kell. He's fucking loaded,' Craig scoffed at her. 'What d'you think, he's going to give her cubic zirconia?'

'Well, Coco, honey? What do you say?'

Jacob smiled at her, his dark eyes lit up with love, his teeth flashing white. There was no hint of concern on his face, not the faintest fear that his proposal might be turned down. Coco felt a wave of panic rush through her, a panic immediately followed by dizziness. The world seemed to be pressing in on her; everyone was staring at her, leaning towards her, their eyes wide, their teeth bared. They were caught between smiles and shock, not aggressive but still overpowering, a level of attention that bore down on her like a force field.

It was Mrs Raeburn who saw her daughter start to sway, who said quickly: 'Love? Are you all right?'

'I just need . . .' Coco managed to get to her feet, to take her mother's outstretched arm, leaning on her for support. 'I need to get to the loo for a moment.'

'Wouldn't fresh air be better?' Mrs Raeburn said, as she bustled her daughter away from the ring of staring faces.

'No – please, the loo . . .'

Coco did want fresh air, but the whole front of the hotel was glass; she couldn't collapse, as she was desperate to do, without being observed by multiple sets of eyes. The toilets were closer and safer. She made it into the handicapped one and sank onto the seat, her mother gently pushing her head down between her knees so that she hung over, doubled up, her breathing slowing down to something resembling normal.

'That's night, get some blood to your head, love. You looked like you were about to faint,' Sue Raeburn said, going over to the sink and dampening some paper towels. 'Here.' She put one on the back of Coco's neck; it felt wonderful.

'Thanks, Mum,' Coco muttered.

'Ssh, now. Just keep taking long deep breaths. Oh dear, look how thin you are! I can see every bone in your back through your top! This just isn't healthy, love. You're as skinny as those nice little girls who were jumping on those trampolines for your photos.'

All Coco heard from this was: *You're as thin as the models*.

'When's the last time you ate solid food?' her mother was fussing. 'That Jacob seems nice enough, but he's so old, dear. Old enough to be your father. I'm sorry, but I can't help saying it. I pictured you with a nice boy your own age, not a grown man who's got no business, really, with a young girl like you. And why isn't he saying anything to you about eating proper meals? Is he not even noticing how thin you've got?'

Oh, Mum . . .

Coco raised her head slowly, putting one hand to the paper towel on the back of her neck, so it didn't slide down.

'Here,' her mother said efficiently, taking it from her and replacing it with a freshly-dampened one, deliciously cool. 'When you can, get up and run your wrists under the cold tap. That always helps when you've had a bit of a turn.'

'It all just got too much,' Coco heard herself say.

'Well, of course, it did.' Her mother patted her shoulder sympathetically. 'What a time and place for him to choose! Men just don't think about the way we feel, do they? Anyone with an eye in their head can see that you're exhausted, poor lamb. You're worked off your feet, aren't you? And girls like a romantic proposal – not being ambushed in front of their whole family when they've just finished a hard day's work.'

Coco drew a long breath, standing up again, going over to the sink. Mrs Raeburn was quite right – cold water on the wrists was a great pick-me-up. She dabbed some on her temples, too, careful not to smudge her foundation.

'Jo— *Coco*! What's happening? Are you all right? You're not pregnant, are you?' Tiff bounded into the handicapped loo, hyped up on rum cocktails, tactless as always.

Coco stared at her in the mirror, horrified.

'No,' she said firmly. That, at least, she was sure of. 'Do you *mind*, Tiff?'

'Well, it wouldn't exactly be a disaster if you were,' Tiff said, quite unabashed. 'Oh, Coco, he asked Dad for your hand in marriage this afternoon – isn't that lovely? He said he wanted to do the proper thing.'

'He never! Ooh, I can't believe that Brian never breathed a word to me about it,' Mrs Raeburn said indignantly. 'Honestly, men!'

'He's well hot,' Tiff said, ignoring her mother. 'Silver fox or what?' She nudged her sister in the ribs. 'Nice going, Coco! I didn't see you as the sugar daddy type, but if that's what you fancy, you couldn't do better. Jacob's stinking rich!'

'Tiffany Raeburn!' her mother hissed, in such a terrible tone of voice that her errant daughter's stream of words crashed to a halt like waves breaking against a sea wall. It was one thing for her to criticise Jacob, alone with Coco, quite another for Tiffany to break in and start a flood of vulgarity about his financial status. 'How dare you talk that disrespectfully about Mr— *Jacob*? He's being more than generous to us, and he's clearly very much in love with your sister!'

'Sorry,' Tiff muttered, abashed.

Coco smoothed down her hair and turned away from the mirror. 'I need to get back outside,' she said. 'Jacob will be getting really worried.'

'What are you going to do?' Tiff asked, agog. 'What are you going to say? Because—'

'*Tiffany*!' Her mother grabbed her arm, holding her back to let Coco pass. 'Give the poor girl a moment of peace, can't you? She's got enough on her plate without you badgering her.'

Coco stepped back into the bar. The buzz and bustle of a busy room calmed her, surprisingly enough; she felt like a part of something bigger than herself. No one turned to look at her; the smartly-dressed clientele were all deep into their own conversations, the waiter, hurrying past her carrying a tray with two wooden trenchers on it, each bearing two stuffed, fried courgette flowers, tipped artfully to lean against each other like little teepees, was balancing his prettily-arranged load much too carefully to bother about her.

I can do this, she told herself. And when she rounded the long leather bar in the centre of the room, rejoined her table, the light in Jacob's face as he saw her was hugely reassuring. He didn't look angry that she had humiliated him by running out on him, making her look foolish in front of her family.

He jumped up, arms open wide, saying, 'Baby! I'm so sorry I sprang it on you like this. Believe me, I wasn't planning to. I was just telling Brian – and Craig and Kelly,' he smiled charmingly round the Raeburns still seated at the table, 'I had this all planned out. I was going to do it over dessert, get some champagne, make a speech, build up to it, make it special.'

Jacob embraced Coco, his big arms wrapping right around her slender frame.

'Baby, forgive me,' he said against her hair. 'I was way too enthusiastic – I know that's not how a girl wants a proposal. I'm so sorry. Can you forgive me? Say you will. Say yes!'

He pulled back a little, taking hold of her shoulders, looking down at her earnestly.

Aren't I too young? Coco thought. Am I really ready to get married? I've got my career to forge out, a new magazine to pour all my energy into.

'I didn't expect this,' she tried to explain to him. 'I wasn't ready. I still don't know if I am.'

'But we love each other,' Jacob said, perplexed. 'I want us to get married and be together forever.'

'Aww!' both Tiff and Kelly sighed romantically.

'Give us a moment,' Jacob said to the Raeburns, putting his arm round Coco's waist, leading her out of the bar, through the lobby, out of the glass doors and into the cold winter night air outside. He slipped off his jacket and put it round her shoulders, taking her hands.

'Look, honey, I know it's sudden, and I know I didn't do it right, okay?' He kissed her hands. 'But you make me feel so young, you know? Like a crazy kid. I just love you so much, I can't keep it to myself. I want to tell the world!'

He smiled at her. 'Listen, you and me – we'd be New York media's top power couple if we get married. Think of the dinners we'd have, the parties we'd throw! Anyone and everyone'll be killing their best friends to get an invitation. New York's the media capital of the world, baby, and you could be the ruling queen! I know how ambitious you are – doesn't that tempt you? Think it over.'

Coco drew in a deep breath of icy air. Her head was spinning again; out here in the cold, Jacob was so warm, his physical presence so compelling, that she just wanted to cling to him, to press herself against his heat, bury her head in his chest. Her body had given in to Jacob completely, a long time ago. Her brain was the holdout, and even her brain wasn't used to saying 'No' to him.

'Coco, you're really hurting me,' he said, when she still couldn't manage to give him an answer. He withdrew his hands from hers and shoved them in his pockets, turning away, staring across the dark racetrack towards the glowing, lit-up glass building that was Mercedes-Benz World: some kind of concert was going on inside, a party, music bubbling out, applause rising and falling.

'I'm so disappointed,' he said sadly. 'It was such a great day – I had real fun with your dad and brother. I thought we were all bonding so well.'

Jacob's disappointed in me? Coco felt the panic rising again. By now, his approval was the most important thing in her life. *If he withdraws his attention – turns away from me – I honestly don't know what I would do*.

Neediness, desperation, began to flood through her. She felt her heart pounding, faster and faster. The idea of being the queen of New York, of ruling the most elite of media circles, was terrifying but also – she couldn't deny it – immensely seductive. But even more important was to hold on to Jacob, to make him turn back towards her . . .

'Can I have some time?' she asked, her voice thin and frightened. 'Please, Jacob. Don't be angry! We've only been together for a few months, it's so much to take in. I never saw myself getting married this young. I've got the magazine now, too – I need to make a success of that first.'

'You can do all that and get married,' Jacob said over his

shoulder, still not turning round. 'You'll move in with me, everything will be taken care of. I don't want a wife to do the damn housekeeping. You won't have to worry about a thing.'

The cold was seeping through the jacket now; its light wool and silk blend was not enough to keep it out, not when she was standing still. Cold was rising through the thin leather soles of her shoes as well. Coco shivered from head to toe, her teeth beginning to chatter.

'Just a few months more?' she pleaded. 'You know I love you. You know I want to be with you. I just need to get my feet under me at the magazine, catch my breath—'

'You don't love me enough,' he said bleakly, swinging back to face her. Under the lights from the parking lot she saw his expression; his features were set so grimly that she was frightened to her core. He looked as if he had already decided that it was all over.

'You can keep your job,' he said slowly. 'I'm not a vindictive man, Coco. You're a great girl and a really talented editor.'

'Jacob!' she screamed. She rushed towards him, stumbling in her haste. 'Don't *say* that! I want to be with you – I love you! All I'm asking is—'

He disengaged her clutching hands, holding her at arm's length.

'I'm ready *now*,' he said. 'I love you, Coco. God only knows how much. But I want this now. It's just an engagement! I'm not forcing you to get married next week.' He heaved a deep sigh. 'I'm an all-or-nothing kind of guy. I made this decision. I want to marry you. And you have to be in or out. If you can't say right now, this moment, that you love me and want to marry me too . . . then I can't be with you any more. I'll have to walk away.'

Coco was crying, tears pouring silently down her face, hot on her cold cheeks.

'Jacob,' she sobbed, 'please don't make me choose like this. It's so soon, everything's just going so fast.'

The thought of losing him – her rock, her mentor – was utterly unbearable. She had never felt alone before she met Jacob; now the mere idea of being without him made her feel terrifyingly bereft. She looked up at him, trying to blink the tears away, and every instinct in her body told her that he was immovable. What he had said was how it was going to be. There were only two options, and she had to choose one and bear the consequences.

Coco felt as if she was being ripped apart.

'All right, I'll marry you,' she sobbed. 'I will – I'll do it. I can't bear to lose you!'

Her reward came instantly; he dragged her towards him, enfolding her in a bearhug, hot and all-encompassing, his mouth closing on hers in a deep passionate kiss that left her dizzy and still sobbing, now with relief. Dazedly, she felt him wiping her face with a handkerchief, kissing her again, tenderly now, telling her that she was a good girl, that he would make her happier than she had ever been in her life.

Reaching into the pocket of the jacket draped over her shoulders, he pulled out the Tiffany box, snapping it open. Taking her left hand, he slid the ring onto her finger.

'Two and a half carats,' he said.

It was so heavy it actually weighed down her hand. Coco turned her wrist back and forth, marvelling at it, watching the colours spark from the centre of the diamond, flashes of bright red and blue. She had never seen anything like it before, never remotely possessed anything this valuable. It was extraordinary.

'I'm going to shower you with diamonds,' Jacob said, smiling at her stunned reaction to the enormous stone. 'It's just the first of many.'

'Jacob, you don't have to.' She sniffed, and took the handkerchief from him to blow her nose. 'It's not about what you give me – I love you for *you*!'

'I know that. It's why *I* love *you*!' He hugged her again, so tightly she could hardly breathe. 'We're going to get married and you're going to make me the happiest man in the world!'

Tears were springing to her eyes once more. It's because I'm so happy! she told herself, clinging to Jacob, putting her hands up and trying to work them between their bodies just enough to make a tiny bit more breathing room. I'm so happy I could cry my eyes out with happiness!

She shivered again. *I just didn't think it would be quite like this when I got engaged. In the cold, sobbing, terrified that he'd leave me if I said I wasn't quite ready.*

No. This is not how I pictured it at all.

Victoria

It felt as if everything in Victoria's perfectly-organised, perfectly-constructed life was falling to pieces.

Of course she had known that a caesarian was an operation. Of course she'd realised that having a simultaneous tummy tuck was going to exhaust her still more; after all, there was a reason that the combined surgical procedure wasn't advertised, wasn't openly discussed, that the names of doctors who would do it were passed around by an underground network of women who could afford the extremely high prices and wanted near-total discretion. A caesarian scar was the perfect concealment for a tummy tuck; one incision, rather than two, was always preferable. Victoria had been assured that hers was minimal by the usual standards, would fade very successfully with the regular application of Vitamin E oil. She'd managed to keep her weight gain down to 12 pounds; apparently there had been very little stomach excess for the surgeon to remove.

Still, it had been much worse than she'd anticipated. The anaesthetic might prevent pain, but she'd felt everything, nonetheless; the slice of the scalpel, cutting her open, the reach in to pull her baby out of her. And then, worst of all, because she had the tummy tuck scheduled as well, she couldn't hold her baby straight away, had only the swiftest glimpse of a tiny, squawling mite, covered in blood, the cord dangling from its stomach, held up above the screen that prevented her from seeing her gaping, open abdomen, before they told her it was a girl and whisked her away so that they could concentrate on removing the excess fat from her tummy.

Victoria had lain there, sobbing, feeling utterly bereft. Utterly empty. Her little baby girl was a bloody, gunky mess, covered in fluids and her own poo, and all Victoria had wanted was to have that gunky, messy, pooey baby laid on her chest, so that she could look at her, hold her, take in, awed, what she and Jeremy had created between them. The operation had seemed to go on forever, and it was the single worst experience that Victoria had ever had in her life, that sensation of loss and misery, waiting endlessly to finally hold her baby. Her lips had moved, but she was dazed from the drugs they'd given her and couldn't get a word out; she had wanted to beg them, plead with the surgeon, to stop the tummy tuck there and then. *I don't care about having a flat tummy*, she had thought desperately, something that would previously have been heresy to her. *I just want to hold my baby – give me my baby!*

Jeremy had been wonderful. Baby Sasha – the name they had chosen, whether the baby turned out to be a boy or a girl – had been cleaned up, checked out and handed to him, and he had insisted that Victoria see Sasha as soon as the incision in her stomach was sewn up and the operating room no longer needed to be sterile. Overriding the medical staff's protests that Victoria needed to rest a little, he had demanded to bring Sasha to her, pointing out that Victoria – visible through the glass viewing window – had tears pouring down her face.

She had cried even harder when Jeremy had bent down and touched Sasha's tiny little hand to hers where they lay, temporarily paralysed, folded on her chest by the nurses; Victoria could just feel the baby's fingers, and she could see the miniature, magical half-moons of her nails. A fierce, protective surge of love had flooded her, stronger than the anaesthetic, stronger than anything she had felt before.

She'd managed to move her numbed lips to whisper possessively, triumphantly, 'She's perfect.'

Jeremy was beaming with pride, his eyes wet with emotion, Sasha cradled in his arms. Her face was bright red; there was still a little green gunk in the corners of each of her piggy little eyes; her nose was squished flat. If she had been anyone else's baby, Victoria would have turned her head away, utterly revolted by so unaesthetic a sight.

Instead: 'So beautiful,' she added, her mouth curving into a smile, achieving some movement in her fingers, enough to curl them around Sasha's tiny ones.

'She's a wonder,' Jeremy said devoutly. 'A total wonder.'

And then the doors banged open, metal whacking against metal as if someone were wheeling in a trolley, and a stream of high-pitched, screeching voices rose over the clamour.

It wasn't a trolley. It was a clothes rail, heavy with padded hangers from which a whole rack of clothes hung, each in transparent zipped-up cases. It was wheeled in by Alyssa, followed immediately by Clemence and Dietrich, both of them talking nineteen to the dozen, dressed up like peacocks crossed with parakeets, Clemence actually having to duck as she came in because the plumes in her Philip Treacy hat would have brushed against the top of the doorway. The couple would have been extraordinary in any setting – Alyssa was over six foot and Dietrich's mohawk was always a show-stopper – but here, in the operating room, they looked like alien gods. Behind them, the protesting nurses in their green scrubs, trying to impede the triumphal progress of the clothes rail, were small, squat peasants.

'Darling!' Clemence announced. 'Congratulations! I have brought your post-maternity wardrobe. Dietrich and I have spent weeks working on practically nothing else. A special surprise for you! *Voilà*!'

Alyssa pulled the rack right along Victoria's bed, nearly bumping into Jeremy and Sasha.

'It's to *die* for,' Dietrich sighed eagerly. 'Wait till you see it, Victoria. It will make you feel so much better after all this doom and gloom. Ugh, hospitals are so *depressing*!'

'It smells of bleach in here,' Clemence complained, sniffing. 'Revolting.'

'Where shall we start?' Dietrich scampered to the rail and started flicking through the hangers. 'Hmm, I think the Lanvin—

'Fuck off, all of you!' Jeremy shouted. Sasha, in his arms, had started crying at all the sudden noise and commotion. Jeremy's face was bright red, his eyes flashing madly behind the lenses of his glasses: with one step, he placed himself between Victoria and the clothes rail, his shoulders squared. His voice was so loud that Clemence and Dietrich fell silent, goggling at him like exotic fish in a tank.

'Get the fuck out of here!' he yelled. 'My wife has just had a *baby*, for fuck's sake! Our baby's crying, and I just swore in front of her, which I promised myself I would never, ever do!' Jeremy's curly hair was sticking up in rage; he seemed to swell before Victoria's dazed eyes. Head throbbing, tears forming yet again in her eyes, she was deeply impressed by her husband's titanic defence of his family's privacy. It was like watching the transformation of Bruce Banner to the Incredible Hulk.

'Out! *Now*!' Jeremy hissed. With Sasha held protectively in his arms, he couldn't gesture, but he jerked his chin towards the doors. 'Or Victoria will sack you all!'

It was the only threat that would have worked. Squeaking in fear, no longer exotic gods but frightened mice, Clemence and Dietrich fell over each other in a scuttle to the door. Clemence made it there first; Dietrich's knee-high black wedge boots, and the tight leather trousers over which he was wearing them, prevented him from moving at any kind of speed. They both abandoned Alyssa completely; it was the furious nurses who had to hold open the doors to allow her to roll the clothes rail out as quickly as possible, babbling apologies to Victoria as she went.

'That's it!' Jeremy told his wife with great severity as the rail disappeared. 'Fashion's all very well, Victoria, but there are *limits*!'

And Victoria, collapsed on the mattress, every nerve in her body feeling ripped to pieces, desperate only to fall asleep with her baby in her arms, her cheeks wet with tears, could only manage the words: 'Thank you,' more devoutly and lovingly than she'd ever spoken to Jeremy in her life.

Three weeks later, Victoria was still completely shattered. *The actresses and models who schedule the abdominoplasty caesarian take off weeks for complete rest after the operation,* she thought. *I was back to work after ten days, damnit.* She was being driven home from the office, rather than attending the three evening parties to which she had been invited; she simply didn't have the energy to manage anything after work hours. Her breasts were sore and aching: she'd have to express, or feed, as soon as she got back, and either option would take forever.

All I want to do is pass out. But I can't. Not only do I have to feed Sasha, I have to strategise about the god-awful news I got this afternoon . . .

Her BlackBerry rang: exhaustion momentarily forgotten, Victoria reached into her bag eagerly. *Please, she thought, please let it be her, let it be her . . .*

Her heart leaped in happiness when she saw the name on the display.

'Darling!' she sighed blissfully into the phone.

'Darling,' Lykke echoed just as ecstatically. 'I miss you so much.'

'I miss you too – so much! How was the flight?'

'Oh, very bumpy,' Lykke said as serenely as ever. 'There was a storm. Some people threw up. But I never mind turbulence. I am lucky.'

'What time is it there?'

'Eight-thirty in the morning,' Lykke said. 'I am very excited. I have not been to Japan before, you know, and already I can see that it is so beautiful.'

'I wish I were there with you,' Victoria said wistfully. 'We could visit the temples in Kyoto and Osaka and soak in those lovely baths at the ryokans.'

'I wish you were here too,' Lykke said softly. 'It would be so romantic.'

Victoria heaved a deep sigh.

'How are you?' Lykke asked.

'Hungry all the time!' Victoria complained.

'Victoria – you must eat more. Please tell me you are not doing the five-finger diet any more – that is mad!'

'Five-*hand* diet,' Victoria corrected.

It was the latest way of structuring a minuscule amount of food consumption: five 'handfuls' of protein a day i.e. no more than would fit into a woman's palm. The protein itself, of course, was the highest quality: Victoria was allowed smoked salmon, prawns, fillet steak, yellow-fin tuna sushi and scrambled eggs. No salt, no sugar, as many green vegetables as she wanted. She was drinking gallons of water, to fill her up, and snacking on goji berries and nuts. It was three weeks after Sasha's birth; in another week she would start gentle exercise, a specially-tailored Pilates regimen specifically for new mothers who had had the combined caesarean and abdominoplasty. And after that, she'd be allowed to start having algae wraps; the Pilates trainer had said their effects could be miraculous.

'It is not enough food for you, yet alone for Sasha,' Lykke said fondly. 'Please, Victoria, promise me – eat some brown rice as well, yes?'

'I still feel podgy,' Victoria whined.

'Victoria, you are always in a rush! You must not be so much in a rush! It is more important that you are not hungry all the time and your baby is not hungry. I diet, of course I do – before the important shows I do not eat solid food for days sometimes, just fat-free protein shakes – but I am not a mother, okay? You must be strong to make good milk for Sasha.'

Victoria sighed again. 'All right,' she said reluctantly. 'I've got some Japanese rice crackers at home. I'll have some and think of you.'

'Eat them, and think afterwards of eating me,' Lykke said, laughing. 'Will you do that?'

'*Lykke!*' Victoria said, torn between excitement and embarrassment, as she always was when Lykke talked about sex. Victoria automatically looked up to check that the partition between her and the driver was closed, the intercom was off.

'I can't wait to see you again,' Lykke said softly.

'When do you come back?' Victoria asked. 'How long are you in Japan?'

'Three days. You know, it is for a catalogue, they have a lot of pages. And then to Hong Kong, for a trunk show. Wait, let me check my organiser . . . it's ten days, I think. I come back in ten days.'

'Too long,' Victoria objected. 'Much too long.'

Although she missed Lykke, it was a delicious luxury for Victoria to love and be loved so much, to indulge in the kind of sweet, babyish talk that she had never, ever done before. Lykke and Sasha, she thought wonderingly. I never knew what love was before, and I didn't miss it. And then, in the space of a few months, I fall in love for the first time and have a baby, and fall in love with my baby, too, as soon as I hold her in my arms.

I always thought love weakened you. And I was right. It's terrifying – I feel vulnerable now, constantly. And I never felt vulnerable before.

Victoria shivered.

'Oh God, Lykke,' she said, suddenly remembering the awful news she'd had that afternoon. 'Something ghastly's happened – you'll never believe this. Jacob has proposed to Coco!'

Lykke was very fast: she barely took a moment to assimilate what this meant for her lover.

'Oh no!' she exclaimed. 'That's terrible.'

'I know. I never thought this would happen. He's a perpetual bachelor – plenty of girlfriends but never any commitment. You should see his apartment – it's the ultimate single man's pad.'

Victoria's voice was rising; she was still incredulous, hardly able to take in the news.

'She went to London for a shoot, and he followed her, met her family and bloody proposed! And her damn spin-off magazine's doing really, really well, Lykke. I'm shattered, my boobs are killing me, I can't take painkillers because I'm breastfeeding, I miss Sasha all the time I'm at work, I'm in love with a woman, my husband hates me, I'm so distracted at work it's not true, and that little bitch has not only jumped into bed with the boss, she's somehow managed to get him to ask her to marry him. Devious little horror! If it goes on like this, she'll be asking for my job as a wedding present – and he'll give it to her!'

'Really?' Lykke sounded incredulous. 'Surely not.'

'You should have seen him today,' Victoria said grimly. 'He was like a schoolboy with a major crush. He came into my office and sat on the edge of my desk and blurted it all out with the biggest smile on his face. I mean, I'd heard the rumours, but I didn't quite believe it. They're telling me her ring's a diamond the size of a goose egg.'

'Aaah,' Lykke said seriously. 'This is not good. Not good at all.'

'You know what? He bloody told *Mireille* he was going to propose – can you believe it!' Victoria was getting crosser and crosser. 'Didn't bother to warn me, but he told *her*! I confronted her as soon as he waltzed out all hearts and flowers, and she did one of her shrugs and said she'd hoped it wouldn't happen and didn't want to trouble me until it was definite. So I couldn't even get angry with her. She's so good at that – it drives me crazy!'

'Wait . . .' Lykke's voice was faint; it sounded as if she were talking to someone else. 'Darling, I have to go,' she said regretfully. 'They are calling me. I try to ring you tomorrow at this time, okay?'

'Oh no, don't go! Lykke, darling—'

'I have to – I have delayed already. I am so sorry.' Lykke drew in a deep breath. 'Victoria, remember what I said in Paris? I am for you, completely. On your side, always. I will do anything to protect you, and now Sasha. To make sure you are safe, and happy. That no one conspires against you.'

'Oh, Lykke . . .'

'I love you, Victoria. Completely. To me, that is everything,' Lykke said with utter conviction. '*Everything*.'

The line clicked off. Victoria made a little moaning noise into the mouthpiece, frustrated at losing contact with her lover. Snapping the BlackBerry closed, she saw that they were parked outside of their house on Riverside Drive. The driver had been too scared to interrupt her conversation.

He did the right thing, Victoria thought wryly, looking out of her tinted window to see him hovering outside her door. I'd have bitten off his head if he'd disturbed me when I was talking to Lykke. She tapped on the window and he instantly bent over to open it.

'Thanks,' she said. 'Sorry to keep you out in the cold.'

Ruefully, she noticed his surprise. I'm working on being nicer, she thought. Even before Sasha came, meeting Lykke was making me nicer. And now I'm really making an effort. I don't want my daughter to copy me, to be a bitch like me.

It was icy outside. She unlocked the front door, her hand shaking with the cold, and dashed inside the warm house with relief. Jeremy and the decorator had done a wonderful job of making it both stylish and cosy; the tongue and groove panelling of the long hallway was painted soft cream, hung with framed silk textiles, and its floor was polished wood, gleaming around the runner whose blues and greens echoed the wall hangings.

Victoria slipped off her coat, hung it in the built-in cupboard – oh, the bliss of American built-in cupboards! – and walked down the corridor, towards the kitchen. Delicious smells greeted her as she entered, wide white pillar candles clustered in the centre of the table, burning softly.

Jeremy and the decorator had gone for an American Colonial look for the kitchen, mixed with the Austerity Britain, 1940s vibe that was so fashionable in the little homeware boutiques in Hoxton and Shoreditch; the tongue and groove walls were painted light green above the cream patterned tiles, the fridge and most of the electrical items were pale sage, that retro colour that looked simple and inexpensive but actually cost a fortune to source. The big wooden kitchen table was Italian pine, the countertops tiled in the same pattern as the splash-backs. Jeremy had longed for an Aga, and the designer had had a terrible job talking him out of it, pointing out how hard it would be to get oil deliveries in central Manhattan; Victoria had consoled him by assuring him that when they got their country house, in Connecticut or the Hamptons, that the first thing he could do was buy a top-of-the-range Aga.

Though I doubt we can afford a country house, the way things are going, she thought bleakly, pausing in the doorway. With that scheming little bitch Coco out to take my job! I'm at the top now – Anna's never going to leave *Vogue* – the only way for me is down. Everyone will pretend to be sympathetic if Jacob kicks me out so his wife can edit Style, but really, they'll laugh their heads off behind my back.

Should I start considering my options? Try to jump before I'm pushed?

Jeremy was standing with his back to her, stirring something at the stove, singing to Sasha, who was in a sling on his back, rocking gently with his rhythmic movements. Ever since her birth, Jeremy had held Sasha close to him as much as he could and swaddled her in a specially-designed blanket like a papoose when she slept. He'd read up on swaddling and been very struck by the theories that it made babies feel secure and happy. Certainly, Sasha couldn't have been a happier baby; Victoria stood for a moment, watching her daughter bob lightly back and forth with her father's movements, her eyes closed, her feathery eyelashes fluttering on her plump pink cheeks. A Mozart flute quartet played from the Bose stereo, exquisitely soothing.

He's a wonderful father. A perfect father. How can I ever take her away from him? But how can I bear to live away from her? I can't! This is what I want to come home to every night – Jeremy, taking care of our child, doing the best job imaginable of looking after her.

They were barely using the nanny whom Jeremy had taken such pains to select after a long and gruelling process of interviews: he wanted to take care of Sasha himself, was blissfully happy doing it. He had already asked his employers if he could extend his paternity leave, and they'd agreed. Victoria had a strong feeling that he would be going part-time from now on, if he worked at all outside the home. For at least the first years of her life, Sasha would be raised by her father, an ideal solution.

But if I leave Jeremy to be with Lykke, Victoria reflected unhappily, *he might fight me to get custody of Sasha, and he could win. He's doing all the work of looking after her: I'm out all day, he's the primary caregiver. Jeremy might even want to move back to London, take her away from me, to punish me for cheating on him.*

And what if I fought him for custody and won? How cruel it would be to try to take her away from him, when he's already living for her, his little princess? And if I won, how could I watch my daughter being raised by nannies, instead of the father who adores her?

We could try for joint custody, but how much would I really see her? Realistically, Victoria knew that the answer would be 'barely at all'. She would slip back all too easily into her world of parties and openings, early-morning exercise sessions, work dinners. Sasha would spend more and more time with Jeremy, and Victoria would miss out on watching her grow up.

No, this is what I want – to come home to my baby and her father, this lovely, warm domestic scene.

But I want Lykke, too. And not just for sex. I want to be with her, to have her in my arms, to sleep with her every night.

I have the perfect husband, the perfect father for my child, the perfect lover.

Oh God – why can't they be the same person?

She shifted involuntarily, the heels of her boots scraping on the terracotta tiles. Jeremy, who hadn't heard the front door over the music, broke off his lullaby, turning his head to look over his shoulder at his wife.

'You're back early,' he said flatly. 'Was your mistress not available for a quickie?'

Victoria bit her lip. 'She's in Japan,' she informed him.

'So Sasha and I get the pleasure of your company,' Jeremy said, turning back to the stove, the lenses of his glasses misting in the steam from the soup. He took them off and wiped them on his apron. 'Aren't we lucky to be second-best!'

'*Jeremy—*'

'I've made pumpkin and sweet potato soup,' he said. 'You're allowed those, aren't you? I looked at the list the nutritionist left. They're under "occasional carbs".'

Victoria was immediately anxious.

'Yes, but did you put any—'

'There's no normal potato in the soup,' Jeremy said, rolling his eyes. 'And no butter, just a tiny bit of olive oil. Which you need,' he added firmly. 'Though since there's only a teaspoon in the whole pot, it's scarcely even there.'

He put the spoon down in the ceramic holder on the

countertop, turned down the soup to simmer, and began to carefully unwind the elaborate wrappings of the papoose in which Sasha was held. Jeremy, always thorough, had practised the various ways to wrap the baby sling with a doll before Sasha was born so that now, already, he was an expert; he had her untied and gently swung round into his arms in a bare minute.

'My boobs are really sore,' Victoria said. She looked down at her silk sweater, grateful at least to see that the milk hadn't leaked through. Easing it away from her bra, she winced: the pads inside the cups were damp. 'I need to feed her or express soon.'

'Have some soup first,' Jeremy said, laying Sasha down in the small wooden rocker crib in the corner of the kitchen. 'She'll wake up in about half an hour or so, if she's on schedule. You can feed her then. Eat something – that way you can relax when you're sitting feeding her.'

He started to ladle the soup into bowls. Victoria poured herself a glass of water and sat down at the kitchen table.

'This is so nice,' she said, but she could hear that her tone of voice was sugary and artificial. I'm so tired, she thought. I don't want Jeremy to give me a hard time tonight . . .

'How long is this going to go on?' Jeremy asked, putting down a beige leather placemat in front of his wife, setting a brimming bowl of soup on it, pulling spoons and blue-and-green striped fabric napkins from drawers set into the table.

Victoria wasn't a coward; she didn't pretend not to know what Jeremy was talking about.

'I don't know,' she said honestly.

Jeremy was slicing a poilane loaf from Le Pain Quotidien which he had been warming in the oven; the scent of hot doughy bread made Victoria's mouth water. He buttered two slices with thick sweeps of yellow, farm-churned butter, drizzled pesto from a jar onto the surface of his soup bowl, and took his seat at the table, opposite his wife. In her rocker crib,

Sasha shifted a little, began to make the small, murmuring, exploratory sounds that were the precursor to beginning to wake up.

About twenty minutes, and she'll be opening her eyes and wanting some milk, Victoria thought, starting to spoon up her soup. Jeremy's bang on time with her schedule.

'Mmn, this is delicious,' she said. She'd have loved the bread that Jeremy was biting into, the pesto that smelled fragrant as it warmed up and melted into the soup. But bread was a forbidden carb, pesto a forbidden fat; she couldn't even allow herself to think about them.

'I wish this were enough for you,' Jeremy said sadly. 'Our life, our baby.' He looked around the lovely kitchen, lit by hidden soft spots and candlelight, the faint creaks as Sasha stirred in her crib.

'Most women would think they were incredibly lucky to have a set-up like this,' he continued. 'And you're throwing it all away for some model! It's such a cliché, Vicky, don't you see that? It's like the female equivalent of a mid-life crisis.'

'I don't want to throw it all away,' Victoria protested. She met his eyes across the table, holding his stare, seeing, unhappily, how very sad his expression was. 'I don't want anything to change, Jeremy.'

As soon as the words left her lips, she knew how ridiculous they sounded.

'Vicky, I caught you kissing that woman in Paris. You're having an affair with her! You're the one who's changed our whole life, and now you're saying you don't want change?'

Jeremy's spoon clattered into his bowl.

'Well, you can sort that out very easily,' he went on. 'Can't you? You can tell that woman you're never going to see her again. Stop having sex with her every chance you get!'

To her horror, Victoria saw tears begin to form in his blue eyes. He took off his glasses and put them on the table.

'I know I was never—' he said, 'I was never really what you

wanted in bed. I know you were just keeping me happy when we had sex. But I thought it was enough for you. I thought all you really wanted was yourself.'

'My God, Jeremy,' Victoria whispered, putting down her own spoon. She felt awful. He wasn't saying this to be cruel: he really meant it. Which made it so much worse.

'You know what I mean!' His voice rose. 'I thought you were a narcissist, that you couldn't really love me because you couldn't love anyone – or maybe you were so in love with your precious career that there wasn't room for anyone else! But I loved you! I still love you! And I want things back the way they were. That was enough for me, what we had. Why couldn't it be enough for you?'

He was crying now, the tears flooding down his cheeks.

'I thought you couldn't love anyone, not the way I wanted you to love me. And that was okay – until I realised that you *could* love someone. My God, the way you were looking at that woman! The way you kissed her! You've never kissed me like that.'

Baby Sasha, hearing her father's voice high with distress, started to cry in her crib, as if in sympathy.

'I'll feed her,' Victoria said, pushing back her chair and standing up.

'You've barely eaten anything,' Jeremy said, crying all out now, at that point of misery when every small slight becomes magnified to become part of the central grievance. 'I made that soup especially so you'd eat something filling and healthy after a hard day's work.'

'I'll have some later,' Victoria said desperately. 'I promise.'

She was picking up Sasha, taking her over to the rocking chair in the corner. It was designed especially for baby feeding, and Jeremy had ordered three for different rooms of the house. Sasha's face was red and wrinkled up, her tiny button nose sniffing the air like a mole's, smelling the milk that had leaked on her mother's bra: as soon as Victoria pulled up her sweater, unhooked the catch about the bra cup and let that down, Sasha was latching eagerly onto her mother's swollen nipple.

'Here,' Jeremy said, dabbing at his wet face with a napkin, coming over to pick up the big V-shaped bolster that lay beside the chair, putting it around her waist so that it could take most of Sasha's weight.

'Thanks,' Victoria said gratefully, settling Sasha against the bolster. It was early days; she wasn't yet into an easy feeding routine, had actually forgotten that the bolster existed.

'You're welcome,' he said, sniffing, still patting at his face. Looking down at his wife, their baby in her arms, snuffling happily at her breast, his expression softened into yearning.

'You look so beautiful, both of you,' he said, torn between happiness and misery. 'Why can't it be like this, Vicky? Why can't Sasha and I be enough for you?'

He knelt down by the chair, stroking the back of Sasha's head with one gentle finger.

'Tell me that this woman's just a crazy fling,' he pleaded. 'Pregnancy hormones, some sort of life crisis. Tell me it'll burn itself out, now you have Sasha.'

He was crying again, and Victoria felt her own tears start to well up.

I'm not the cold, hard bitch without feelings that everyone thinks I am. I'm making my husband unhappy, I'm breaking his heart, and it's unbearable. I hate to see Jeremy like this! He's done nothing wrong, nothing at all. I'm the one behaving badly, I'm the one who should be crying and pleading for him to take me back.

And instead, he's sobbing because he thinks I might leave him.

But what can I do? I'm in love for the first time in my life – with someone who loves me in return, cares about my baby. This isn't just a fling. I can't lie to Jeremy. What I feel for Lykke is real, and I can't believe it won't last.

How can I turn my back on that?

Miserably, she met her husband's eyes over their baby's head.

'I can't tell you that, Jeremy,' she whispered. 'I'm so sorry.'

He buried his head in his hands.

'What's going to happen to us?' he asked, his voice muffled. 'What's going to happen to our family? I want more kids, Vicky. I want to fill the house with them.'

Two, and that's my limit, Victoria thought, but had the sense not to say so aloud.

'And I want yours!' he sobbed. 'I don't want another woman, I don't want to start again – I've only ever wanted you!'

Victoria was crying now too. Tears fell down her face, off her cheeks, would have dripped onto her feeding baby if she hadn't turned her face away, managed to free one arm from holding Sasha to wipe her eyes on the arm of her sweater.

It should have been one of the happiest times of their life; husband and wife, their first child happy and healthy, watching her breastfeed, sitting in the lovely kitchen of their luxurious townhouse, surrounded by ease and affluence. The perfect family: the perfect life.

And I'm tearing it apart, Victoria knew, the pain of guilt a constant dull ache in her stomach as she cried onto her crooked elbow. I'm tearing it apart, and it's all my fault.

She and Jeremy had been sleeping in separate beds ever since they had come back from Paris: he hadn't discussed it, had simply come home and moved all his stuff from his bedside table to his dressing room, where he was ensconced on the large wooden daybed.

Sasha's room was on the other side of the dressing room, so Jeremy could get up when she woke in the night, and either feed her with expressed milk or bring her through to Victoria. As an arrangement, looked at from a brutally practical perspective, it worked . . . well, perfectly.

How does he think we'll manage more children if we aren't even sleeping together any more? Victoria thought desperately. She couldn't have sex with Jeremy again; she knew she couldn't. Not now. Not when she knew how wonderful it could be with the right person. How it was supposed to be, all along.

I can't ever have sex with a man again.

Her mind drifted back, before Jeremy, to Jacob. Jacob and his games, his tests. His big hairy body, his stocky torso, the weight of him on her. She grimaced in repulsion at the memory. Jacob had been fair: he'd made sure she had enjoyed herself too. She'd had plenty of orgasms. But any comparison of Lykke with Jacob was laughable, ridiculous. Lykke's smooth white body, her silky hair – *Hyperion to a satyr*, she thought, remembering a quote from Hamlet.

And then from Jacob she returned, once again, to Coco, and her face hardened.

What am I going to do about her? Even if she isn't after my job, Jacob will insist on giving it to her! I know him – he won't be able to resist the temptation of being a New York power couple. After a few years at the most, he'll be itching to push her up the ladder. And he won't have his wife working under anyone. She's an editor of her own magazine now, making a big success of that.

Next step would be editor of a magazine for grown women, not teen girls. And Jacob won't want her moving to London to edit *Style* there, though that'd be the next logical step. He'll never live in London – he's always complaining about the weather and the lack of world-class sushi.

So he'll maybe even skip over that step. For her. For his little baby-toy wife. Put her straight into the top job in New York, and leave me out on the street. I'll have to take some job styling a label, like Jennifer Lane Davis.

God, I'd hate that! I'd be the one sucking up to editors, hoping they like our latest collection. Right now, I have the power. How can I give that up? And, if Jeremy and I somehow manage to work things out, could we afford for him to be a stay-at-home husband if I take a job like hers? The *Style* editor's job comes with so many perks – not just the salary, but the car and driver, the zero-interest loan for our mortgage . . .

My God, we could lose this house if Jacob sacks me!

Bloody, bloody Coco! Victoria thought savagely. All the drama of her situation, the huge mess she'd made of her love life, subsumed into a slow-growing fury towards the girl who had once been her lowly assistant and had risen with stratospheric speed to be a rival far more deadly than any she had ever known.

If Coco weren't around . . . If Coco were out of the picture . . . if she fell under a bus, or off a cliff – then everything with Jacob would go back to normal. I could catch my breath, not be panicking all the time at work. I could work out a way to manage, somehow, to have Lykke and not lose my family.

To have it all.

And, in Victoria's mind, this thought swelled up to monstrous proportions.

If Coco fell off a cliff, everything would start to be all right.

If Coco fell . . .

Part Six
Manhattan: Now

Coco

'You can't weigh anything at all,' the woman was crooning to Coco, her voice gentle, hypnotic. 'You're so light! You could just float away, like a balloon, soar up into the air, over the city . . .'

'I *would* like to fly,' Coco murmured, her head whirling.

And then she felt the hands close round her waist, lifting her up, tilting her over the edge of the balustrade. She was so dizzy, so confused, that it took her what seemed like aeons to connect with the realisation that the woman was trying to kill her.

Her head was hanging over the wide stone shelf, her hands loose by her sides, knocking against the poles that supported the waist-high balcony. Her knuckles grazed against them, scraping her skin, and that pain helped to bring her out of the weird trance she was in; she pushed her hands against the rough stone, scraping them more, hurting herself in a desperate attempt to jolt herself into full consciousness.

Wetness ran down her hands. She was bleeding. The winter air was cold on her face: forty storeys below her, traffic flowed down 10th Street, yellow cabs, black limousines, the tiny wasp-like buzzing of motorbikes. The view swam beneath her, so far away, so close if she fell, and the thought of plummeting down to the concrete below was a jolt of pure white fear, a lightning bolt that hit her in the chest and galvanised her to action.

Her feet were still off the ground. Scrabbling frantically, she caught one against the stone, bracing herself, pushing the other foot back in a disoriented donkey kick that connected with the thin body behind her. The woman pushing her had hands like steel, her grip frighteningly strong, but Coco was young, and strong after her months of training with Brad, and the kick sent the woman off-balance, staggering back. Coco's attacker didn't let go in time; her hands stayed clamped to the girl she was trying to kill, and Coco fell back with her, away from the edge of the balustrade.

Away from immediate danger.

The crushing grip on her waist finally released as the woman struggled to find her balance. Coco flailed and bumped into one of the wrought-iron chairs that were grouped around the coffee table, grabbing onto its back, managing to steady herself. Incredulously, gasping for breath, she stared at the woman, keeping the chair between them. The woman's elegant features were distorted, her lips drawn back from her teeth in a grimace of sheer, feral aggression and frustration. Her hair had been disarranged in the struggle, dark locks falling out from her habitual bun, tumbling over her shoulders.

It was the first time Coco had ever seen Mireille looking anything less than perfect.

'Mireille,' she choked out. 'What are you doing? I don't understand. Is this some kind of awful joke?'

'He's *mine.*' The French woman's green eyes were wide, her teeth still bared. 'Jacob is *mine!*'

'He's *what*?' Coco had thought her eyes couldn't widen any more, but at this extraordinary exclamation, she felt the skin stretch back from her eye-sockets as she goggled at Mireille.

'He's mine!' Mireille screamed now, her hair whipped

around her face by the growing wind. 'He has been mine for more than thirty years!'

Mireille's hands were hooked into claws. She made no effort to raise them and put her hair back into place, which, for some reason, frightened Coco more than anything that had come before. If Mireille, always perfectly groomed, perfectly composed Mireille, was shrieking insanely, her hair flying behind her, then anything was possible, anything at all; the laws of the universe had been upended.

Mireille was crying now, the tears falling down her pale cheeks, melting her black eye make-up, which was beginning to streak the paper-thin skin beneath.

'I loved him from the first moment I met him,' Mireille sobbed. 'I still love him with all my heart! Gradually, I began to realise what Jacob was. *Who* he was. He was too young to be tied to one woman, and I understood that. I let him go, but he was always still with me. He took care of me, and I was loyal to him.'

Coco stared at Mireille, struggling to take all of this in. There was something in the champagne, she realised. Something to knock me out, to make me woozy. Great waves of exhaustion were sweeping over her, one after the other, battering her consciousness, trying to roll her under.

I have to stay awake! If I don't, she'll come for me again – throw me over the edge. She shuddered, forcing her eyes to stay open, fixed on the woman who had just revealed herself as her rival.

Mireille's hands were clasped below her heart, the fingers twisted together so tightly that the knuckles were white. Black sooty tears were splattering down her face and onto her hands; she seemed oblivious to them.

'Victoria was like me, he said,' she continued. 'Ambitious, a career woman. He would make her a success, as he had made me one. I was angry – I did not like that he had a new protégée. But as soon as I met Victoria, I knew that she was not a danger.

She would never want to marry him – she would take everything she could get, play his games, use him in return. Victoria was safe. But *you* . . .'

Mireille took a step towards Coco, who whimpered in fear, swivelling to keep the chair between them.

'*You*! You and your pathetic father complex! You looked at him as if he was God, you stupid little fool! You were so vulnerable, so needy – he could see it in you, smell it on you. You little *petite bourgeoise*, so common, so socially insecure – you did whatever he told you. He could make you into what he wanted. Not like Victoria! *She* at least has some backbone. She was capable of saying no to him. But she is an aristo, and you – you are nothing!'

Coco opened her mouth to protest, but the truth of Mireille's words hit her like a series of slaps across the face.

I have done whatever he wanted. Things I didn't want to do, things that were utterly humiliating. I am needy and vulnerable. That's why Jacob wants me. I've given him control, I've turned into someone I wouldn't recognise as myself. Yes, I've been pathetic.

Everything she's saying is true.

'That is why he wants to marry you! Because you are weak, he can make you into a doll to play with, that he can control and boast about. He told me he was going to propose to you well before he did it, *tu sais*!'

Mireille beat her chest with her hands. The white lock of hair had come loose, the pins that had secured it into her bun hanging from it. She looked insane, like an evil witch from a fairy-tale, her eyes glittering through the wet black make-up smeared over her face.

'I am still first with him!' she screamed. 'I, not you! He tells me everything! He is only marrying you because now – now, after all these years, now that he is old – *now* he wants children!' She was panting in fury. 'He never let me have children, he said it would ruin my figure. He made me have a sterilisation, booked the appointment and marched me to the doctor. He said that if I loved him, I would do it. *Salaud!* And then he told himself the fantasy that it is *I, I* who do not want them, to make himself feel better for depriving me. He is a liar, *un menteur*! And now he thinks he can marry a girl, a pathetic little *petite bourgeoise* who is now the age that I was when he met me, and start again, make a family with her! *Non! Jamais!*'

Mireille took another step forward: she was between Coco and the French doors. Coco darted a frantic gaze sideways, to see if she could escape between the big bay trees in their terracotta pots, try to run to the next set of doors instead: but they were all locked from the inside, she realised, her panic rising still further, making it hard for her even to breathe. *I could try to smash the glass, reach through and unlock them, but Mireille would catch me well before I managed that*.

She looked round and screamed her head off. Mireille had glided forward, was facing her with only the chair between them. Her face was grotesque, a mask of black and tears, her hair dangling in rat's tails, her teeth bared still.

'He only wants babies with you because there's all this plastic surgery now,' Mireille hissed vindictively. 'He is terrible about women's bodies; when they are no longer perfect he discards them like rotten fruit. But now he sees Victoria – she is so stupid, she thinks no one knows she has had an operation with the caesarian to flatten her stomach, *imbécile*! He thinks, Oh, I can get Coco pregnant, and then I can pay the doctors to cut her afterwards, make her back into the doll I bought with a huge diamond ring!'

She shoved her face towards Coco; the girl recoiled in absolute terror.

'Or, he'll decide he wants to take out your eggs and have someone else carry your baby so you don't change at all. You wait! He will do that, *j'en suis sûre!*'

'Oh no,' Coco managed through frozen lips. 'I wouldn't like that. I want to have my own baby.' Are you mad? she thought in panic. Why did you say that? For God's sake, Jacob made her get sterilised! Of all the things to come out of your mouth – that'll drive her crazy!

But whatever medication Mireille had given her was growing stronger by the minute, not only weakening her but making her confused, so that the words that spilled out were the ones more designed to infuriate an already-incensed Mireille. Reaching out, the Frenchwoman took hold of the chair on which Coco was leaning and, with one powerful movement, ripped it from her grasp. The chair spun away, crashing into the bay trees. Coco staggered, and the next thing she knew, Mireille's hands were on her shoulders, pushing her back. Her heels buckled under her, one snapping off, destabilising her still further; she tried to bring up her hands, to fight Mireille off, but she had no strength. She was as weak as a kitten.

'Marrying *you*?' Mireille spat, shoving Coco against the balustrade again, the lean muscles of her trained dancer's body like steel rods holding Coco in place. 'You little nothing! He is mad if he thinks I will agree to this. Oh, I smile and nod and say I understand, but Jacob is mine! He thinks I will come to your wedding, watch him marry you, you who are so stupid that you drink the champagne I give you and believe the ridiculous story I tell you, drink it up without a question as you drink three sleeping pills as well – *ah oui, ma petite*, that is why, if I let go of you now, you would fall to the ground. You have nothing left to fight me with.'

Propping Coco against the balustrade with one hand on her narrow chest, Mireille bent down and, with an expert twist of her back, reached the other arm under Coco's legs, scooping them up. Coco could barely even manage to kick out. Waves of unconsciousness were rolling over her, turning her under, like a surfer swept into the undertow, board whipped away.

Submerged. Drowning.

Her kicks were so feeble they didn't slow Mireille down a fraction. Mireille's hands were clamped around Coco's calves, digging in, bruising her as they lifted them up, pivoting Coco's thin, fragile body onto the wide balcony, rolling her to the very edge, to the drop-off, the point of no return . . .

'What the *fuck*? What the hell is going on? Mireille, what are you *doing*?'

It was a woman's voice, not Jacob's. High, piercing, generations of command in it, certainly enough to make Mireille jump and turn to look at the new arrival. Victoria, swathed in a white fur cape coat, swept across the terrace towards their tableau, her red-lipsticked mouth opened into a dramatic O of shock. The phone started to ring inside the apartment, but everyone ignored it.

'Put her down!' she ordered, and Mireille, completely taken aback, actually let go of Coco's legs. Coco felt them fall, and managed, with her last iota of strength, to swing them enough so that she tumbled over the balustrade back to solid ground again. Her feet touched the stone flags below, her hipbones digging into the side of the rail. Though she was wearing her coat, she was so thin now that the contact was painful.

'Mireille, what the bloody hell? Have you taken leave of your senses?' Victoria demanded, gloved hands on her hips. 'What on earth is wrong with Coco? She looks like she's fainted! And *Jesus*,' she took in Mireille's black-stained face, 'have you seen yourself? Talk about a make-up emergency!'

'What are you doing here?' Mireille snapped back. 'This is not your apartment. How did you get in?'

'Oh please. As if any doorman could stop me if I wanted to come in. And I'm not exactly a stranger here, am I?' Victoria scowled. 'Jacob's been dodging me for days, and I have to speak to him! I'm going to insist that he puts a new clause in my contract. I want it in writing, signed and sealed, to say that he can't sack me and then install his wife. And if he doesn't do it, I'm going to threaten to walk. He can't replace me right now, I'm doing a bloody good job – and he certainly can't make *her* editor for a few years.' Victoria threw out a hand, pointing at

Coco's comatose body. 'She absolutely isn't ready for a job this important. But I need to protect myself for a decade. That's my bottom line.'

She stared more closely at Coco.

'Look, Mireille, what the fuck is all this? What were you doing when I walked in – were you fighting? And why the hell is Coco practically passed out?'

'Because she has drunk a glass of champagne with three Zopiclone in it,' Mireille said, bending to pick up Coco's legs again. 'She is about to fall, because she has leaned too far over the balcony. It will be a tragic accident. We will both see it, you and me, Victoria. We will both say how sad it is. We ran to try to catch her, but we were too late.'

'What? My God, that's what it looked like, but I couldn't believe . . .' Victoria stared at Mireille incredulously. 'But *why*? Why are you doing this?'

'It is in your best interests to have Coco out of the picture,' Mireille said, her tone efficient now. '*N'est-ce pas*? Look how angry you are at the situation that Jacob has created with this absurd marriage. She is a danger to you, a big threat! If she is not here any longer, you do not need to worry about your job any more.'

She made an effort to drop her voice, make it persuasive, encouraging.

'Think about it. I have done all the work, I have given her the pills – all you need to do is help me tip her over and agree that we will tell the same story.'

'You must be mad,' Victoria said, dumbstruck. 'You've gone absolutely barking, Mireille.'

'*Tais-toi*!' Mireille spat at her. 'You fucked him too! You whored yourself like a cheap *putaine* with him to get what you wanted – you, who were always so obviously a lesbian!'

Victoria's jaw was hanging open.

'*Ah oui!* To me, it was always very clear that you did not like men,' Mireille sneered. 'You should thank me on your knees for what I did for you. I see everything, *tu crois*. I saw the way you looked at some models, some photographs. I worked out your type and I sent you Lykke, like a present, all wrapped up for you.'

'You did that to fuck with me!' Victoria hissed back. 'To destabilise me! Lykke's told me everything. You weren't being kind to me – you wanted to mess with me, that's all.'

'*Eh alors?*' Mireille shrugged. 'And why should you care why I did it? You have your lover, you are very content. You should still thank me. When you fucked her in your office just last week, when you bent her over the desk and pulled up her skirt and licked her like an ice cream, you looked very content, *ma chère*, as did she! *Ah oui*, I know all about you and Lykke fucking in your office – not once, but many times! I have put a camera in there hidden inside a book on one of the shelves. It is so easy nowadays to spy, did you know? I have all of it recorded. For the editor of *Style* to fuck a model who has worked for her in her office, that is a big scandal.'

She smiled triumphantly. 'But more, it is harassment. You fuck this young woman that you have put on the cover of the magazine – it looks as if you have given her a favour in return for her body. In America this is very bad.' She rolled her eyes. 'In France, nothing would happen; it is normal. *Mon Dieu, la-bàs* you could fuck hundreds of models every day. But here, it is a lawsuit.'

'Lykke would never—' Victoria began furiously, but Mireille burst out laughing.

'And still you do not understand! No, Lykke would not sue you – she would lose her career. No one would ever work with her again if she denounced a famous editor in public! But Jacob – *Jacob* could use it as an excuse to sack you, whenever he is ready to put his fiancée in as editor of *Style* instead. This clause you are demanding, it is meaningless if you bring the company into disrepute. Any contract is invalid if that happens, *tu sais bien*.'

Victoria stood stock-still as the weight of Mireille's loaded words sank in.

And Mireille, her smile wide, her green eyes bright, lifted Coco's legs to the balcony edge again.

'Come, help me,' she panted. 'It will be easier with two. I do not want her to use her hands to grab the side. They look for that, I have seen it on the television shows. It must not seem as if she tried to hold on, to stop herself from falling.'

Slowly, Victoria walked forward. Coco felt a second pair of hands close around her legs. And with every scrap of energy she had left, in a desperate, futile plea for a rescue that wouldn't come, Coco opened her mouth and screamed.

The next thing she knew, she was being picked up and thrown violently through the air. Her eyes clamped shut, her scream tailed off into a moan.

The last thing I'll see is Mireille's mad face, she thought. The last thing I'll hear is my own helpless wail . . .

She landed, with a thump that knocked the breath out of her, on a lounger; it was a nasty fall, as the lounger was wrought-iron, its cushions taken in for the winter. The impact whacked her funnybone, pain shooting up from her elbow, and bruised her coccyx.

But I'm alive, The pain means I'm alive. I'm not plummeting over the edge to fall forty storeys down . . .

She dragged herself up, leaning against the back of the chair. Mireille was shrieking like a banshee, struggling with Victoria, who hauled back and slapped her across the face, an open-handed blow which landed like a whipcrack.

'Get hold of yourself, for God's sake!' Victoria yelled at her.

'What the *hell* is going on here!' bellowed Jacob from the doorway. 'Have you all taken leave of your senses?'

Striding across the terrace, he interposed his body, bulky in his black cashmere overcoat, between Mireille and Victoria. He was wearing his Russian black fur hat, which gave him extra inches of height; he loomed over the fighting women like a colossus.

'How dare you hit her!' he growled at Victoria, protectively setting Mireille behind him. 'What the *fuck*, Vicky? You leave me a string of increasingly psycho messages, you say you've got an ultimatum for me, my doorman rings me to say you've barged your way in here, and I have to rush away from a very important meeting to come and find out what the hell you're playing at. And when I turn up, I find you smacking Mireille in the face! You've gone out of your mind!'

'She was trying to kill your fiancée, Jacob!' Victoria screamed back at him, not a whit abashed by his rage. She set her hands on her hips again, her jaw jutted forward. 'I saved her bloody life! That mad French bitch has stuffed her full of sleeping pills and she's trying to shove her over the edge of the fucking balcony. You should be thanking me, and yelling at *her*!'

Jacob opened his mouth as if to deny it. For a long moment he stood there, a huge black-clad figure, completely silent, staring at Victoria, the winged sleeves of her white fur cape coat lifting and falling in the wind.

And then, very slowly, his big body turned around till he was facing Mireille instead.

'Mireille?' he said in a whisper. 'What did you do?'

Gazing up at him as if he were the only person on that terrace, the only person in the world, rat-tails of black hair hanging over her destroyed face, Mireille whispered back, 'What did *you* do, Jacob?'

There was a long pause. Jacob drew a deep breath.

'No,' he said. 'No, Mireille. Is Victoria telling me the truth? Did you try to hurt Coco?'

'No,' Mireille said, causing Victoria to exclaim in anger and take a couple of steps forward, about to contradict her. Without looking at her, Mireille held up a hand to stop her, and such was her power in that moment, the perfection of her gesture, that Victoria actually stopped in her tracks.

'I did not try to hurt Coco,' Mireille corrected him, still speaking quietly. 'I tried to kill her.'

Jacob groaned, a genuine cry of anguish. But Victoria, watching intently, heard no denial in his exclamation, no disbelief.

'Mireille!' He covered his face momentarily with his hands. 'Why?' he moaned. 'Why did you *do* this – ruin everything?'

'Because,' Mireille began, her eyes gleaming terrifyingly through the strands of hair, 'because, Jacob, you were going to marry her. And because, Jacob,' her voice was rising now to a banshee scream, 'because you already have a wife! Not her! *I* am your wife!'

Victoria gasped in shock at this revelation. 'You and Jacob?' she exclaimed. 'You're *married*?'

'Yes.' The white lock of hair blowing over her face, Mireille turned to stare with ghastly triumph at Victoria. 'Me and Jacob! *Toujours, Jacob et moi*! All the time that you were having sex with him so that he would promote you, he was my husband. All the time, he was married to me!'

'Thirty years?' Victoria echoed incredulously. 'But—'

'In Paris! Just Jacob and me, at the *mairie*. Two witnesses, the next couple waiting. It was like an elopement.'

Coco had collapsed back onto the lounger when she realised she was out of danger. But she had managed to prop her arms on the side, to watch what was happening, as thunderstruck as Victoria by the secret that Mireille had just exposed. To Coco's horror, she saw tears forming in Mireille's eyes.

'It was so romantic,' she wailed, her hands rising to clasp together. 'We wanted to keep it secret – at first, it was for my sake, he said. Jacob was going to make me a famous editor, and he didn't want me to be compromised by people knowing I was his wife. He said they would not take me as seriously, and I agreed. As long as you work for Dupleix, he said, people should not know. And I loved him. I would have done anything he wanted.'

She whipped her head back to glare at Jacob, her hands rising to pound on her breast with emphasis.

'Because,' she screamed, as loudly as if she were trying, after all these decades, to finally tell the world, 'I am your *wife*! I thought I would always be your wife! That was the one thing I possessed, the one thing that none of your other girls could ever have, because we were married already. Oh, I know some of those little sluts schemed all they could, thought they could get you to propose to them, but you always came back to me. Always! And then – then you tell me you are going to marry that *petite espèce de*—'

'Mireille!' Jacob interrupted, cutting short her insult to Coco.

'You don't control me any more, Jacob,' she shrieked, tears once more falling down her face. 'I have not signed the papers your lawyer sent me yet, and I never will! I will never divorce you!'

'Jesus Christ,' Victoria said incredulously. 'Jacob, you proposed to Coco without having got divorced from Mireille. Are you completely insane?'

Jacob's face was white as paper. 'I didn't think . . . after all these years, I thought it was just a formality,' he muttered. 'I didn't know she would react like this.'

'*Men*!' Victoria said contemptuously. 'You haven't even bothered to see how Coco is.'

She shot out an arm, the white fur winged sleeve falling from it dramatically, pointing with a matching white suede-gloved finger at Coco, half-sitting, half-lying on the lounger. Obediently, Jacob crossed the terrace to the lounger, kneeling down beside it on the icy stone flags, taking Coco's hands, which were nearly as cold as the stone by now.

'It's true,' Coco said faintly, dazed by the scene that was unfolding before her. 'Mireille tried to kill me. She said she was your wife – she gave me pills, in a drink. Victoria saved my life.'

Chafing Coco's hands, Jacob swivelled clumsily round to look at Mireille.

'I know you were upset,' he said to his wife. 'I didn't handle it right. Okay, I get that now. But to try to *kill* her? Mireille, she's just a girl! How could you do something like this?'

Mireille's hands were twined in her hair, her fingers blackened by the wet make-up on her cheeks. The great emerald ring she wore, the ring Jacob had given her for their engagement, decades ago, which she had moved to the fourth finger of her right hand when they had agreed to keep their marriage a secret, flashed in the last rays of the setting sun.

'How could *you* do this!' she raved. 'After all these years, how could you betray me like this? You said you would never divorce me, never. You said another woman would never take my place. You lied! You are a filthy, disgusting liar! *Dégueulasse! Tout à fait dégueulasse!* You took my chance of having a baby, you stole that from me with your lies, and now you are trading me in, like the filthy disgusting vulgar American that you are, for that little piece of pathetic nothing! You promised! Over and over again you promised that you would never divorce me, that I would always be your wife. I could endure anything, if I knew I was your wife. And then you take me to lunch and you say that you want to marry *that* –' she stabbed an arm at Coco in a furious gesture – 'and expect me to be happy for you, to drink champagne with you! You are not even brave enough to say the word "divorce", you dirty coward! *Salaud!*'

Jacob hung his head as her words sunk in. 'Mireille,' he said slowly. 'Oh God, *Mireille*.'

Heaving himself to his feet without a backwards glance at Coco, holding out his hands, he walked towards his wife imploringly.

'I'm sorry,' he said. '*Je suis desolé, mon amour*. I'm so sorry for what I have done to you.'

Mireille hesitated for a moment, staring at him, her eyes huge and wild, her hair whipping across her face.

'It's too late, Jacob,' she said, her voice low now, sounding sane once more. 'You want a divorce? *Bien*.'

She smiled sadly, a smile of immense, heartbreaking beauty that, even through the smears of make-up, transformed her face. For a moment, she was the young woman with whom Jacob had fallen in love, on the stage of the Paris Opéra, all those years ago.

'I will never sign the papers,' she said. 'I will never divorce you. But as always, Jacob, I will give you what you want. *Au 'voir, mon amour*.'

Turning away, she ran with a quick, graceful step towards the edge of the balcony, jumping up onto the balustrade as if she were still the prima ballerina she had once been. The skirts of her black coat billowed around her in the wind.

'No!' Jacob roared, lunging for her, arms outstretched to grab her and pull her back.

But as she had already told him, it was too late. Mireille did not jump: she let herself be taken by the wind, falling back into the open air behind her, her coat flapping like dark wings. Her eyes were on Jacob until gravity, pulling her down, took him from her sight; and then she closed them, so that the grief-ravaged face of her errant husband would be the last thing she would ever see.

Part Seven
Two months later . . .

Victoria

Victoria was standing with her back to the conference room, staring out of the window at the falling snow that was softly blanketing Manhattan. It was late for snow, nearly the end of winter, but the vagaries of climate change were confounding all the meteorologists' expectations, and just as March was coming round the corner, the first buds of daffodils pushing up in Washington Square Park, a freak cold front had closed in over the Eastern Seaboard. New Yorkers had not yet changed their wardrobes over for the spring/summer season, put their furs in climate-controlled storage lockers, but the unexpected snowstorm had sent everyone scurrying to pull out the salt-stained boots and ankle-length shearlings that had migrated to the back of their closets.

The figures Victoria could see on Third Avenue, below, looked like Russians. Few New Yorkers carried umbrellas in the snow; the winds that whipped from one side of the island to the other, down the canyons between the skyscrapers, could turn an umbrella inside out in a flash. Instead, Manhattanites crammed on big fur hats that wouldn't blow off, and zipped up equally bulky padded coats against the icy gusts.

Alyssa was waiting downstairs with Victoria's white

Arctic fox hat, a present from Jacob, brought back from Kazakhstan years ago, and her Prada belted coat. But Victoria had one more meeting of the day before she could go home. In American vernacular, this meeting was simply to touch base. But in some ways, it would be the most difficult of the entire day.

The double doors of the conference room swung open and closed again with a soft snick.

'Hi, Victoria.'

Victoria turned around to see Coco at the far end of the room, facing her over the long shiny conference table.

'Come up.' Victoria gestured for Coco to join her at the head of the table, where a pretty tea set was all ready for them on a silver tray. 'I know this room isn't exactly cosy, but I've been having meetings all day here, with tons of different people, and it was just easier to stay on in here. I hope you don't mind.'

Coco's eyebrows rose; Victoria was being positively conciliating, which was definitely unlike her.

'No, that's fine,' Coco said politely, walking around the curve of the table. She was wearing a knitted Mark Fast minidress, belted at the waist, over knee-high Marc Jacobs boots; she looked pretty, age-appropriate and fresh.

No Chanel, Victoria noted with irony. Coco's wearing hip young designers now – Mark Fast, Alexander Wang, Yigal Azrouël, Prabal Gurung. She doesn't look like Jacob's little designer doll any more: she looks like a chic young woman about town.

'You've put on some weight,' Victoria said frankly, surveying the younger woman. 'I hope you don't mind my saying it. But it suits you.'

'I know,' Coco admitted. 'I felt tired all the time. And hungry.' She smiled. 'I'm even eating bread sometimes now.'

'*Bread?*' Victoria said in an instant, shocked response. 'My God! Don't make a habit of it.'

Coco nodded. 'I won't. I'm still being careful. I'm just not chasing a size zero any longer.'

'Glad to hear it,' Victoria said, sitting down in one of the two big swivel chairs at the top of the table. 'It didn't suit you. Would you like some Earl Grey?'

'I think I would,' Coco said. 'Thank you.'

'It's very civilised, Earl Grey,' Victoria said, pouring a stream of fragrant, bergamot-scented tea into two small, white and pink Minton cups, sitting on matched fluted saucers. 'Perfect for the afternoons.'

She slid one of the cups towards Coco.

'I won't keep you too long,' she said. 'It's five already, and you probably want to be off home to beat the worst of the snow. I have a car waiting too.'

Coco watched the steam rising from the hot teacup.

'I'm not actually going home,' she said demurely. 'My sister's in town, visiting. I'm going out with her and . . . a friend.'

It was Victoria's turn to raise her eyebrows.

'Are you?' she said approvingly. 'Good. I'm glad to hear it. You're young. You should be out having fun.'

'I've been lying low for a while,' Coco said. 'Working, keeping my head down. I think I'm ready to socialise a little now.'

Victoria nodded, lifting her teacup and sipping her Earl Grey.

'Look, I wanted to let you know the current state of play with Jacob,' she said. 'I don't know how much he's been in touch with you.'

Coco winced. 'Not at all,' she said. 'Not since . . . we were all at his apartment.' She raised her bare left hand. 'I left the ring there,' she said. 'I just took it off and left it on the living-room table. That was it. I haven't heard a word from him since.'

She looked directly at Victoria. 'And I didn't want to,' she said.

'I don't blame you,' Victoria said, sighing. 'It was an absolutely horrendous scene. I don't think I'll ever forget . . .' Her voice tailed off. Even Victoria, tough, handbitten Victoria, couldn't bear to say the words: but she didn't have to. They both knew exactly what she meant: the sight of Mireille tumbling over that balcony to her death.

There had been scaffolding on the lower floors of the building, as there so often was in Manhattan; work being done on the façade. Mireille had hit it, bounced off, and, mercifully for any passers-by, landed not on the sidewalk but in the flatbed of the workmen's lorry, full of tools and equipment. The body had apparently been horribly mangled, according to the *New York Post*, which had eaten up this juicy scandal, reporting it with its usual salacious, staccato prose.

'Thank God at least Jacob managed to keep the fact that Mireille was his wife out of the papers,' Victoria said, shuddering. 'Can you imagine how awful it would have been if the press got hold of that?'

Coco shook her head, not in disagreement, but in rejection of the scenario Victoria had just named, the idea of all of them being doorstepped by the press. As it was, the Dupleix public relations division had spun Mireille's death as a horrendous accident; the official version was that she had been demonstrating poses for a projected fashion shoot, had climbed up onto the balcony to show one off, despite the protests of Jacob, Coco and Victoria, and tragically slipped to her death. The story might not have the ring of plausibility, but in lieu of any other theory, or any reason why Mireille might have wanted to kill herself, or the three others present might have conspired to kill her, it had been accepted.

It didn't hurt, of course, that Jacob was one of the most powerful media magnates in the US, and that those men had an unspoken compact to protect each other; newspaper and magazine owners did not gossip about each other in their periodicals. Other people's lives were fair game: theirs were not.

So no nosy tabloid journalist had dug too deeply into the story. No one had found Jacob and Mireille's marriage certificate in the records of the mayor's office in Paris. Mireille had died intestate, and all her belongings, the deeds to her apartment, had gone to a distant French cousin. Whether Jacob had had to pay off the New York authorities to bury any evidence of his marriage, or whether it had simply never arisen, neither Victoria nor Coco ever knew.

As soon as Mireille's death was officially declared a suicide, Jacob had left the country. Coco had heard, through the Dupleix gossip grapevine, that he had moved out of his apartment the very night of Mireille's death. It was common knowledge that he had put it on the market shortly after; the *Post* had enjoyed itself tremendously with coverage of the 'Death Plunge Penthouse', itemising every single detail of its luxurious interiors from the realtor's particulars.

'Unfair on you,' Victoria observed to Coco. 'The press making it seem as if Jacob dumped you, rather than the other way around.'

Coco smiled wryly, sipping her tea. 'No one could believe that I'd break off an engagement to my multi-millionaire boss,' she commented. 'They had to tell it that way. I know the PRs here were pushing that version. If they said I'd dumped him, it would have been so suspicious that some journalist might actually have started investigating why.'

Victoria nodded in approval. 'Very true,' she said. 'And very smart. I admire you, Coco. It's a rare woman who can put pragmatism over her pride.'

'Thank you,' Coco said politely.

Victoria set down her cup. 'You know Jacob went to India, afterwards,' she said, swivelling in her chair a little to fully face Coco. 'Just got on a plane and pissed off, leaving us all to clear up his mess.'

'I knew he was in India,' Coco said.

'Doing a retreat. Getting his head together. Taking some time to find himself.' Victoria tilted her head, looking down her long nose in contempt of this string of clichés. 'Working through his mid-life crisis. Hopefully,' she added coldly, 'finally working out why he treated poor Mireille so appallingly. I mean, she let him do it – and I'm not minimising what she tried to do to you – but *really*, I should have slapped *him*, not her. He actually needed it more.'

'I agree.' Coco's stomach churned as Victoria's words brought back more memories of that awful day.

'Sorry,' Victoria added. 'You've gone a bit pale. Would you rather not discuss it?'

'No, it's a relief,' Coco said, letting out a long breath. 'I haven't been able to talk about it with anyone. At least there's someone else who knows what happened.'

Victoria nodded in understanding. 'I haven't told anyone either,' she said. 'It's just too big a secret. It simply wouldn't be fair to burden someone else with it.'

The two women looked at each other, reliving the terrible events that had happened on the terrace of the penthouse.

'Thank you for saving my life,' Coco said quietly.

'Oh, please.' Victoria waved her away brusquely, with the awkwardness of an upper-class Englishwoman being openly praised for moral virtue. 'Anyone would have done the same. Honestly. Let's say no more about it. More tea?'

She refilled both their cups.

'So the latest news from Jacob, and the reason I asked you to come in for a meeting,' she said, her tone crisp now, 'is that he's taking a year of absence. He wants to go on with this hippy-dippy retreat and then walk the Himalayan Trail on a voyage of personal discovery with a native guide.'

Victoria flicked contemptuous apostrophes in the air with her long, elegant fingers.

'No fool like an old fool,' she commented. 'If he's not marrying a woman thirty years younger than himself, he's falling into the hands of some hippy quacks. They'll fleece him for millions, and he'll deserve it. I bet he'll come back with his hair down to his shoulders, stinking of patchouli oil and chanting mantras, or whatever it is that they do.'

Coco blinked at this vivid image.

'He's appointed me acting CEO of Dupleix,' Victoria said. 'Together with Barney.' Barney Cohen was the CFO of the company. 'It'll be a lot of work, damnit, especially with Mireille gone.' She sighed. 'Ironic, isn't it? I'd have put her in to helm *Style* for me on a temporary basis if she'd still been here. She'd have been perfect – she'd have done a great job, and she never wanted mine.'

She looked narrowly at Coco. 'Don't get any ideas,' she said firmly. 'I'm not asking you to do it. You're much too young and ambitious. Are you happy at *Mini Style*?'

'Yes.' Coco nodded vehemently. 'Truly I am. It's the perfect place for me. Look, I know I was really young to be put in charge of a start-up, and I know I got it because I was with Jacob. I'm not going to deny it. But I'm doing really well. The stats are great, I have brilliant ideas for the next few issues, lots of storyboards all ready to show you . . .'

'Stop!' Victoria held up a hand in the imperious gesture that was all too familiar to Coco. 'I'm not sacking you, for God's sake. I think you're doing an excellent job, though I have some notes for you we can talk over next week, let's say. I want you to stay exactly where you are. Keep doing what you're doing. Keep increasing circulation. Keep kicking *Teen Vogue*'s arse, as they say over here.'

She grinned a little wolfishly. 'And keep your eyes off my job, okay? Do all those things and your future at Dupleix is very bright, as far as I'm concerned.'

'Thank you!' Coco breathed, hugely relieved.

'Not at all. Oh, and you can stay on in your apartment on the Bowery. Dupleix will keep paying the rent as a perk of your job – or give you an interest-free loan if you want to take out a mortgage in future, as long as you stay with the company. It's the least we can do, under the circumstances.'

'*Thank* you!' Coco was breathless with gratitude at this news. She loved the Halston apartment, and even on an editor's salary, she couldn't have afforded to keep it. Magazine publishing wasn't a lucrative job; its salaries couldn't compete with equivalent jobs in advertising or PR.

Victoria flapped her hand to signal that Coco should say nothing more.

'Now—' Victoria pushed back her chair and stood up, 'I'll let you get off to meet your friends. I should be shooting back too. I've got to feed Sasha in half an hour or so.'

Coco stood up. The two women hesitated for a moment, looking at each other. Then, tentatively, they leaned in, and slowly, unsurely, because they had never done this before, kissed each other on both cheeks. Meeting, finally, as equals.

'Honeys, I'm home!' Victoria carolled as she walked through the front door.

Delicious smells emanated from the kitchen, soft music pouring down the hallway. Lykke came out of the living room, in a grey marl sweater over skinny jeans, her hair pulled off her unmade-up face, looking ridiculously beautiful. Ducking down, she helped Victoria out of her snow- and salt-stained boots, putting them on a wrought-iron rack to dry.

'It's so nice that you're home so early,' Lykke said happily, hugging Victoria, unzipping her coat.

'Well, don't get used to it,' Victoria said, kissing her girlfriend. 'I'll do what I can, but with Jacob off in India finding himself, you're looking at the new CEO of Dupleix. Lots of meetings, lots of dinners.'

'Oh my God? It's definite?' Lykke asked excitedly.

'Signed and sealed,' Victoria said, her eyes sparkling. 'You know, I'm terribly excited. It's a new challenge. I *love* new challenges. I have all these amazing multi-platform ideas just flooding in, twenty-four seven.'

'New power,' Lykke said, her smile full of amusement. 'You love new power.'

Victoria giggled. 'Well, yes,' she admitted. 'I do love new

power. I'm taking to this role like a duck to water. Barney's awfully impressed with my grasp of everything, if I do say so myself. Jacob had better watch out – I may not want to give him back the reins when he returns. *If* he returns,' she added. 'He's saying a year now, but who knows how long he'll be away? He's never taken time off before – he's always been so driven. Maybe he'll decide to buy a houseboat in Kerala or a mansion in Goa and never come back. Wouldn't that be fabulous?'

She wrapped her arm around Lykke's waist, kissing her neck. Together, the two women walked down the hallway towards the kitchen.

'Grilled salmon steaks and wilted spinach for dinner,' Jeremy announced as they came in. 'With risotto for me.' He pulled a face. 'And maybe one spoonful for you, Vicky? You have to have some carbs. Lykke agrees with me.'

'I do,' Lykke said firmly. 'A big spoonful for her.'

'You're both ganging up on me,' Victoria complained, but her smile belied her tone of voice.

I still can't believe how happy I am, she thought, looking from her girlfriend to her husband. Honestly, I don't deserve this. And I know everyone thinks we're crazy for trying this, for moving my girlfriend in to live with Jeremy and Sasha. But so far, it really does seem to be working . . .

Jeremy was flipping the salmon, Lykke setting the table, sticking out one long leg to rock a sleeping Sasha gently in her crib. It was a perfect – if unorthodox – domestic scene.

The main impetus to make it work was that all the alternatives would have been so much worse, Victoria knew as she went to the fridge and poured herself a glass of diet tonic. *I couldn't bear to break up my family, and I couldn't bear to live without Lykke.*

And the miracle is that Lykke and Jeremy felt the same. Neither of them wanted to break up the family either.

In fact, they both want me to have another baby.

She grimaced at the thought of another pregnancy. *I'll do it in a year. Everyone says the best way is to get it over with quickly.*

Victoria was, of course, no longer having sex with Jeremy: she would get pregnant by the turkey-baster method the next time around. Jeremy was permanently ensconced in the dressing room, while Lykke had moved into the master bedroom with Victoria. The deal, negotiated with much tactful manoeuvrings between the three of them, was as unorthodox as everything else in Victoria's private life. Jeremy would be allowed to crack the door open on occasion when Lykke and Victoria were having sex, enough to watch what they were doing. Victoria was so used to having Jeremy watch her while she satisfied her needs that to her this was not in any way a big deal. Lykke, although not entirely happy with the situation, was aware that she needed to compromise to some degree, and her direct, Scandinavian approach to sex meant that she was not inhibited in any way by knowing that there was a silent, but very appreciative spectator to what she and Victoria did together.

Fortunately, Jeremy's natural jealousy was alleviated by the fact that Lykke's job meant that she travelled a great deal. She might be sharing Victoria's bed, but she wouldn't actually be in it for more than a third of the year; while Jeremy would be here every day, every night, spending time with his wife, raising their daughter, being the heart and centre of their home.

'I'm so happy,' Victoria said, sitting down at the table, looking from Jeremy, who was dishing up dinner, to Lykke, who was watching him spoon out the portion of risotto he was giving Victoria, giving an approving nod at its quantity. 'I'm just so happy.'

'To your new job!' Jeremy uncorked a bottle of Chablis. 'We're all so proud of you. Even Baby Sasha's proud of Mummy! Here.' He poured a small trickle of white wine into a glass and handed it to his wife. 'This way Baby Sasha can join in the celebrations too.'

'Just a bit later than the rest of us,' Victoria said, taking the glass. 'Oh God, how I miss wine!'

Lykke had lit the candelabra at the centre of the kitchen table, and now she dimmed the overhead lights, since Jeremy no longer needed them to cook by. The candle flames flickered, warm and relaxing, and the Bach concerto playing in the background provided the final touch of calm perfection.

'To us,' Victoria said, raising her glass. 'To all of us. To making it work.' She reached out and touched Jeremy's arm. 'Thank you so much for dinner, darling,' she said appreciatively.

Jeremy went pink with happiness.

He knows that Lykke's making me so much nicer, Victoria thought. That's one of the reasons he's accepted her so well. Better to have half of me, being nice, than all of me being appalling.

'To us,' Lykke said softly, raising her glass in turn. 'Thank you so much, Jeremy, for letting me be part of this family.'

'To us,' Jeremy said, raising his own glass, clinking it with Victoria's and then Lykke's. He smiled at both the women. 'To making it work.'

He cleared his throat. 'Now sit down and eat,' he said gruffly. 'I didn't cook a lovely dinner to have you let it go cold. And Victoria, you make sure you eat up every scrap of that risotto. Lykke and I both have our eyes on you . . .'

Coco

'Is this place okay?' Xavier asked, as he came back with a drink in each hand, placing them carefully on the table before sinking down into the capacious sofa next to Coco. 'It's the latest Lower East Side hangout – it just opened last week. It'd be packed, usually, but with the weather, most people'll just have gone home. It's only locals here, really. So that's why it looks a bit empty . . .'

He caught himself. 'Sorry, I'm babbling, aren't I?' he said apologetically. 'It's just—'

'Just what?' Coco could hardly read his expression; the bar was as fashionably dark as all the hipster hangouts on the LES.

'Here.' Xavier handed Coco her cocktail glass. 'Your Earl Grey martini.'

'I had Earl Grey with Victoria this afternoon,' Coco said. 'I thought I'd continue the theme.' She clinked her glass with his, carefully, because they were both brimming. 'What did you get?' she asked.

'It's like a classy rum punch, as far as I could make out,' he said. 'Want to try some?'

'No, I'm fine, thanks,' Coco said, sipping hers. 'Mmn, yummy.'

'It has egg white in it,' Xavier said. 'Whipped up, to make it frothy.'

'It's really good,' she said.

'I'm glad.'

They both put their drinks back on the table. Cocktail conversation had been made, the social politenesses had been observed, and now there was nothing to talk about but the elephant in the room.

'What were you going to say – before?' Coco asked, squishing round on the sofa to try to get a look at Xavier's face.

'Oh.' He shrugged, ducking his head. 'I just thought, Jacob must have taken you to all the best places in the city. I can't compete with that. But I can take you to the hippest ones.' He was mumbling now. 'It's stupid of me, I suppose.'

'No, it isn't.' Coco wriggled round more, until she was almost in a ball, her knees pulled up in front of her, her back propped against the arm of the sofa. 'It isn't at all.' She drew a deep breath. 'If I'm being brutally honest, I suppose part of Jacob's attraction was that he did take me to the poshest places, showed me the high life. He dazzled me. He swept me off my feet.'

'You didn't owe me anything,' Xavier said fairly. 'You didn't make any promises to me or anything like that. When we hooked up, I thought it was going to be something more.' He reached for his drink. 'Okay, I *wanted* it to be something more,' he mumbled round his straw, taking a pull of rum punch. 'But I know how the game's played. I mean, we never said we were going to be exclusive – you had a total right to see other people. And then you decided you liked someone else better. You had a total right to do that too.'

'I don't want to play a game,' Coco said. 'Any games.'

She shivered, thinking of Jacob.

I never want to see him again, she thought. Thank God he's staying away for a year. I look back on the things I did with him and I feel really creeped out. He was old enough to be my father – God, older than my father! And he never asked me what I wanted to do, never. It was always his way.

It would always have been his way.

I starved myself down to skin and bone for him, and it was still never enough. I had an incredibly lucky escape.

'I rang you,' she said, 'not just because I wanted to apologise—'

'You don't have anything to apologise for,' Xavier insisted, but his shoulders were still stiff, and he had not yet turned to look at her.

'But I wanted to explain,' she said, realising that his pride wouldn't let him hear her tell him that she was sorry; he didn't want to see himself as injured, or as a victim. 'Because you and I,' she felt herself blushing, 'we had an amazing night. Really amazing.'

Xavier's shoulders softened a little. 'It was pretty good,' he muttered.

'I got carpet burns,' Coco said, pressing on.

'Oh, jeez, did you?' He turned to face her. 'I'm so sorry!'

'No, God! I really enjoyed it.' She was definitely blushing now, grateful for the darkness. And she thought, yet again, how different Xavier was from Jacob; her ex-fiancé would never have apologised for leaving marks on her.

In the last few weeks, Coco had been reading up on S&M practices on the internet. She had learned that Jacob had violated every canon of safe practice; he had not let her choose her own safe word, he had never asked her what she liked and what she feared, had never made sure she was consenting, had gagged her and never given her a gesture that would substitute for the safe word she couldn't utter with her mouth blocked. He had taken over completely, ignoring her wishes in a way that no reputable S&M dominant would ever do.

'I got some, um, abrasions on my palms,' Xavier admitted, embarrassed. 'I guess we were going at it pretty good.'

Coco giggled, equally embarrassed: but her memories of

that night with X were all lovely, she knew. *Okay, embarrassing, but lovely. Sexy, wild, lovely*. Her body was reacting to them; her nipples were hardening, and she felt that little twitch between her legs that was equally impossible to fake, that instant response of arousal that sent heat diffusing up through her lower body.

'It was fantastic,' she said frankly. '*You* were fantastic.'

He coughed. 'So were you,' he said, his voice soft now, becoming intimate. 'Coco . . .' He swivelled round to face her now. Their knees touched, and the contact sent a rush of excitement through her, an electric current switching on. Xavier waited for a moment, to see if she would pull away; and when she didn't, he pressed his knees more firmly against hers.

'I'm really glad we got this time by ourselves,' he said. 'Before the girls all storm in and start shrieking about what they bought today.'

Tiffany had arrived in New York the day before, and Emily and Lucy had taken her out shopping that afternoon: they were both employed now on *Mini Style*, one of the perks of being an editor being that you could delegate your friends-slash-employees to entertain your sister while you were hard at work. One of the other perks, of course, was that you could choose which photographers your editors would book for shoots. As soon as *Mini Style* had been set up, Coco had sent round a memo, not only telling everyone on the staff that Ludovic was permanently blacklisted from ever working for her magazine, but asking them to start compiling a list of other photographers whose behaviour had warranted a similar ban. It was growing fast. Victoria had, to Coco's astonishment, had also banned Ludovic from working for *Style* in the future, which had made Emily, in particular, very happy.

In another push to change fashion magazines for the better, Coco was focusing on getting what were called plus-sized models – a UK 12 or 14 – into the magazine, and featuring boutiques in *Mini Style*'s pull-out shopping guides to major cities that carried sizes beyond a US 8. Emily and Lucy had been researching the New York scene, and come up with an entire list of places where they could take Tiffany shopping and find a range of clothes she could fit into.

'Tiff's been texting me,' Coco said, smiling happily. 'It sounds like they're having a brilliant time.'

'Good,' Xavier said. 'I'm glad. But they're not here now. And I'm wondering why you called me and asked me to join you all.' He looked at her seriously. 'Don't get me wrong, I was really glad to hear from you, to come out with the girls. Like old times. But . . .'

He tailed off, prompting Coco to respond. She took a deep breath, knowing that it was her cue.

'I've been thinking about you, a lot,' she admitted.

Contrasting you with Jacob. Realising that all my memories of sex with Jacob make me cringe, and my memories of sex with you are really, really great.

'And I wanted to see you again. To see if . . .'

He didn't say anything; he wasn't going to help her out.

Which is fair, Coco thought. I cut things off, cold, when he wanted to keep going. I should have to do the work now.

'To see if we could sort of pick up where we left off,' she concluded, her voice small, sheepish.

'I don't want to be used, Coco,' Xavier said very intently. 'I don't want to be just your fuck buddy or booty call, the guy you pick up and put down when you've got an itch you want to scratch. Or a Band-Aid. You know – to stick on a wound. I have feelings for you.'

'I have feelings for you too,' she told him. 'I've been thinking about you so much. Ever since I broke it off with Jacob.'

Xavier's eyebrows shot up. '*You* broke it off with Jacob?' he said, his voice full of surprise.

'Yes, I bloody did,' Coco said indignantly. 'Honestly, is it so hard to believe? *I* broke up with *him!*'

Well, I left the ring behind, she thought. I did do that. But

Jacob never got in touch, never contacted me once, not even to see how I was. After the wife he hadn't bothered to tell me about tried to kill me, he couldn't even get in touch to apologise for not telling me he was married to Mireille, to see how I was doing.

I starved myself down to size zero for him, and he never even took the time to ring me and ask me if I was okay after Mireille tried to push me off his balcony.

'And believe me,' she said defiantly, 'I don't regret it – not one bit. I was an idiot to date him in the first place.'

'Oh, you weren't an idiot. I get it,' Xavier said sympathetically. 'Emily and Lucy did too. I mean, Jacob was so rich and powerful. It's a huge deal. They pretty much told me what you said just now – that he swept you off your feet and you couldn't think straight.'

'I *couldn't* think straight,' Coco said, passionate in her need to convince him. 'More than that – I lost my mind! I really did. I spent ages trying to be someone I wasn't. Trying to be some*thing* I wasn't – starving myself, working out two hours a day, to get into a size zero. And I was so happy when I got there! I must have been insane. I was skin and bone, I was hungry all the time. And cold.' She shivered. 'I lost my mind,' she repeated quietly.

'You looked God-awful,' Xavier said frankly. 'You really did. You were like a skeleton.'

'I know,' Coco admitted, grateful for his honesty – and not only that. Here was a man who positively didn't want her to be a size zero. 'Like I said, I was trying to be someone else.' She took another deep breath. 'I was trying to be Victoria.'

Xavier nodded. 'Everyone on *Style*'s trying to be Victoria,' he observed. 'I remember you girls telling me about all the bangles and the make-up and the heels.'

'Well, I'm not on *Style* any more,' Coco said. 'I'm making my own world on *Mini Style*. I'm *not* Victoria, and I never will be! I'm—' She stopped dead as the force of a revelation hit her squarely between the eyes.

'What?' Xavier said.

She burst out laughing. 'You know what? I was going to say I'm Coco. But actually, I'm *not* Coco, I'm Jodie. That's my real name, and I'm going to use it from now on. Who cares if it isn't fashion-y or posh enough? I'm the editor of a successful magazine now, not someone's assistant! I can call myself whatever the fuck I want!'

Xavier was laughing too. 'What's wrong with Jodie?' he asked. 'It sounds pretty cool to me.'

'That's because you're not British,' Jodie said, laughing even harder. 'Over there it's what glamour models are called – girls who get off with footballers and sell their stories.'

'But you're not in Britain now,' Xavier said, taking both her hands. 'You're in the States, and over here, we're going to think Jodie's a really cool, unusual name. Welcome to New York, Jodie. It's great to meet you.'

He bent over her, pulling her closer, hovering, waiting for a moment, to be sure, before he kissed her. As before, the attraction was instant, flaming, Jodie kissing him back with equal passion. For a moment, the strongest emotion which flooded through her was relief – utter, total relief. *This feels so right*! she thought with great happiness. They were both young, both eager, both, frankly, horny; *all we want to do is tear each other's clothes off and fuck like rabbits. No weird games, no mind control. Nothing but happy, healthy, crazy sex*.

She pulled back, gasping for breath. It was so dark that she couldn't see Xavier's features at all, with his head bent over her; a tiny speck of candlelight flickered behind him. She put up her hand and touched his mouth, tracing its contours, feeling his smile. He bit at her finger, and she gasped again with excitement.

'I want to have fun,' she said passionately. 'I'm only twenty-five! I want to go out dancing and stay up all night. I want to go out with Tiff and Emily and Lucy and drink silly cocktails and gossip about work. I want to go back to that gay club and see all your friends again – Jamie and Marco and Travis, right? And hang out with them. They seemed really cool.'

'They are,' he said, laughing.

She drew a deep breath. 'And I want to fuck my brains out on a regular basis. I want to have fun, I want to be silly and crazy and party hard, and I want a partner in crime. I want to do all of that with you.'

What I'm trying to tell him, she knew, is that I'm not ready for anything completely serious, not for a while yet. I've just come out of an insane relationship and an engagement that was a huge mistake. I was about to marry a man thirty years older than me and live a completely different life from the one I should be having at my age.

So right now, I just want to have fun. I want to be a normal twenty-five year old, living it up in New York. With a great job, and hopefully, a really hot lover . . .

'Oh, Jodie.' Xavier's arms tightened around her. 'I want to do that too. All of it. But most of all, right now, I want to fuck your brains out.'

She reached a hand down, feeling between his legs; he was like a rock already. Remembering what his cock had felt like inside her, in her mouth, she felt her lips go dry with sheer desire.

'Hold that thought, okay?' she managed to say, moistening her lips with her tongue. 'The girls will be here any second.'

'You'll come back to mine tonight,' he said, still holding her close. 'No excuses. I want you in my bed all night.'

'In your bed?' she said. 'Don't you mean on your kitchen counter?'

'Ah, hell, woman.' He kissed her briefly, a hard promise of things to come, and pulled back from her with obvious reluctance. 'Let me calm myself down before the girls come flooding in. Jesus, I'm in actual physical pain here . . .'

'Coco! Here you are, love!' Tiffany screeched across the length of the bar, causing every patron's head to turn as she tumbled down it, her padded coat rustling as she moved. 'It's fucking freezing out there! My tits are like bloody icicles! Ooh-err, what's all this then?'

Xavier and Jodie had pulled apart, but not quickly enough to fool Tiff.

'You were snogging!' she yelled happily. 'I saw you.' She came to a halt next to the table, unzipping her coat, her voluptuous bosoms, swathed in black jersey, emerging dramatically as she did so. 'Look at my new dress – fab, eh? And my bra! Finally I got to go to Victoria's Secret.' She tweaked a strap out from her neckline. 'Ooh, and look at you,' she added as she took in Xavier. 'Fit or what! Nice going, Coco! And this one'll keep it up all night, eh? Not like Old Mr Moneybags, I bet.'

Xavier, boggling under this onslaught of Luton frank-talking, stared at Tiff in dumbstruck silence.

Jodie said weakly, 'Did you not get anything else, Tiff? Just the dress and, er, underwear?'

'Are you joking? I got fucking *tons!*' Tiff plopped down next to her, making the padded seat whoosh as it took her weight. 'Didn't I, Em?'

Emily and Lucy, following more decorously behind Tiff, nodded in unison.

'She pretty much bought out Intermix,' Lucy said. 'We dropped it all off at the office so we didn't have to carry it around.'

'They got me brilliant discounts,' Tiff shrilled happily. 'I love New York! And look at my hair.' She tossed her head from side to side to show off her glossy, straight blow-dry. 'They call it a blowout here,' she said, giggling. 'Are you fucking joking? Sounds like what you'll be getting from her later on, if you play your cards right!'

She elbowed Xavier hard in the ribs, visibly winding him. Jodie resolutely avoided meeting his eyes as a vivid memory of doing exactly what Tiff was mentioning flooded back to her.

'So look, I'm starving now,' Tiff went on. 'Shopping always

makes me hungry. And Lucy and Em say there's a brilliant diner round the corner.'

'Tourists always love diners,' Lucy said apologetically to Jodie. 'But they do salads too, and you can get burgers in lettuce instead of a bun.'

'Nah,' Jodie said firmly. 'I'm having a cheeseburger. With a bun. And lots of fries.'

'And onion rings,' Xavier contributed, getting into the spirit of things.

'And mayonnaise,' Jodie said. 'God, my mouth's watering just thinking about it!'

'Aww, that's my girl.' Her sister enfolded her in a warm, bosom-bouncing hug. 'That's more like it. About time you started eating again!'

'And everyone,' Jodie went on, looking from face to face, all of them full of friendship and, in Xavier's case, even more than that, 'I've got an announcement. I'm changing my name back to what it was originally. From now on, I'm not Coco any more. This is official – we'll change it on the masthead and everything.' She took a deep breath. 'My real name's Jodie. Please call me that in future.'

'Oh, I say. How brave!' Emily exclaimed.

'Yay!' Lucy said supportively. 'Good for you!'

'Hello, Jodie,' Xavier said, and leaned over to drop a kiss on her lips, formally announcing their dating status to everyone. All the girls cooed happily. Lucy even went so far as to applaud.

'*Finally*,' she commented in heartfelt tones. 'You kept us waiting long enough.'

'Thank fucking God,' Tiff said. 'Mum'll be over the moon. You've dropped that Coco nonsense, you've got a boyfriend your own age, you're eating again – oh my God, she's going to go *mental* when I tell her!'

Jodie was writhing with embarrassment, but Xavier's hand slid into hers, squeezing it tight when Tiff used the word 'boyfriend'.

'Your sister's awesome,' he whispered in her ear.

'That's one word for it,' Jodie muttered dryly, but she couldn't help but feel warm with pleasure that Xavier liked Tiff.

'Right, what are we doing here?' Tiff jumped up and started shrugging herself into her padded coat again. 'Let's go off and stuff our faces to celebrate.'

Face bright with excitement, she reached down and grabbed her sister, pulling her to her feet.

'Come on, Jodie,' she said, wrapping her arm around her sister's shoulders. 'Let's go and eat a burger.'